THE PARETO PRINCIPLE

Mark Payne

PublishAmerica
Baltimore

First printing

All characters in this book are fictitious, and any resemblance to real persons, living or dead, is coincidental.

PublishAmerica has allowed this work to remain exactly as the author intended, verbatim, without editorial input.

Hardcover 9781462666799
PUBLISHED BY PUBLISHAMERICA, LLLP
www.publishamerica.com
Baltimore

Printed in the United States of America

To my beautiful wife Alyson who has been my unwavering source of strength.

My eternal gratitude to all those people I worked with in Information Technology around the world over the last thirty-five years, across almost every business sector, that have given me the vast wealth of experiences from which I was able to draw on for the plot and story line for *The Pareto Principle*.

AIR MAIL

'South African Airways is pleased to announce the departure of flight 843 to London Heathrow,' the confident female voice interrupted the background noise, her mild Afrikaans accent just discernible to those paying attention. 'Would passengers for this flight please ensure they have their passports and boarding cards ready, and make their way to departure gate six in the international departure lounge.'

Tom Brady glanced at his documents for a final visual check as he rose from his seat. He'd been waiting some considerable time for the flight, and had been watching the almost endless stream of passengers milling through the concourse.

It was 17:35; and as August was mid winter in Johannesburg, it would be dark soon enough. The last embers of the day were already fading and a purple hue could be seen on the horizon as he watched another jet hurtle down the runway, its lights flashing in their strange predetermined sequence.

Fixing his gaze on the aircraft, he witnessed its nose lifting in the distance; and he was sufficiently distracted that he hardly noticed the flight for JFK being called at gate five.

Another throng of passengers began amassing: only a matter of feet from where Tom was standing, sparking in him more than a vague interest—as he could see only one pair of shared exit doors for the two gates.

The entire wall before him had been constructed from glass—letting in the maximum amount of light; and because of its immense panoramic view, it created a pleasing distraction from the boredom for those passengers not suffering from interminable patience.

Immediately outside, two Boeing 747s were standing side by side: the one to the left was Tom's flight, and the one to the right was bound for New York. The apron was large enough to accommodate six of these huge aircraft, so Tom wondered why these two had been parked so closely together. His curiosity was only heightened as he watched those passengers that had been checked in and now approved for boarding, departing through the same pair of doors, but then heading left or right depending on their destination, with nothing preventing passengers from either flight embarking on the wrong one.

Nobody was shepherding the weary travellers to the correct planes; and it was only the attentiveness of one of the stewards that saved further potential confusion.

He watched as one passenger stepped across from the line for New York to the one for London. It was a man in his late forties. Being that Tom was still in his twenties; in his eyes it was an old man. Although dressed for business, his appearance let slip the fact that he'd had a long day; and at that point—just like many other commercial travellers—he didn't have enough hands to hold his briefcase, duty free and airline paperwork simultaneously.

Having watched him switch queue, the steward approached and asked to see his boarding card. As if to prove Tom's theories about passengers having too few hands and too many things to carry, the man passed his duty free bag to the surprised looking steward who reluctantly took it; and then he placed his briefcase between his calves, suspended above the floor, as though he was afraid of it making contact with the ground for some odd reason. It gradually tilted forward as he checked each of his numerous inside jacket pockets for the obscure article.

Before long, one end of the briefcase dropped to the tiled surface. After bending down, the man slid it out from between his legs and flipped it on its back, while he crouched to expose its contents.

The ensuing avalanche of paperwork prompted him to curse softly, and he quickly clamped the case to an almost closed position by the pressure of his hands alone. Then turning it over, he exercised more care as he opened it again; but faced with the precarious debris before him, he had no choice other than to delve through—all be it with caution.

After a few more moments—during which the queue behind him had gradually moved forward: and by mere luck had skirted around him rather than trampled him—he began waving one arm in triumphant success, having pulled out the elusive item; and trying his best not to fall over, he began to stand whilst attempting to close the case.

Oblivious to everyone else, he almost managed this feat flawlessly. But his sudden ascension to full height distracted the lady standing immediately behind; who in turn had been continuously struggling with an overweight trolley that appeared to have a will greater than hers.

The steward was talking into his radio hand set for those few critical moments. But from the corner of his eye, he saw the impending collision and he managed to reach out in time, and was able to steady the female passenger, during the process of which he almost assaulted her with the other traveller's duty free bag.

The queue jumper turned to her and after thanking the steward, he apologised profusely in what sounded to Tom like a well educated Oxford accent, all the while looking suitably and genuinely embarrassed, and then as if to hide his face briefly, or perhaps merely for an appearance of nonchalance, he swept his left hand back through his shock of slightly greying—but once clearly golden—hair.

The steward swapped the duty free bag for the boarding card, and scanning it swiftly, he then nodded at the passenger as he returned it to him, apparently confirming that he was indeed in the correct place.

Alone once again, the flustered traveller began stroking his grey and gold beard as he squinted out to the runway through his thin silver-rimmed glasses. He checked his watch and raised an eyebrow before clasping his briefcase and duty free with both hands in front of him; and then as the queue permitted he began shuffling forward.

Tom's attention meandered back to his own immediate world. It wasn't long before he'd progressed to the front of his line and the hostess smiled as he handed her his documents. She quickly and expertly opened the passport, turned it through ninety degrees and without moving her head she shot her eyes back to him to confirm the face in photograph was indeed his. In another instant, she passed the boarding card through a machine that tore it down to a fraction of its original size, leaving only the seat and flight number.

Smiling, she returned the items to Tom; and catching his eye she confirmed his seat number, '23 K, business section on the plane to your left sir.'

He'd booked a window seat, but being an overnight flight he realised that what was going to be visible after take-off was perhaps very little. However, there was one distinct advantage of the seat's location. It lowered the chances of him being jarred by wandering nocturnal passengers, which itself seemed to be almost a sport for some travellers.

He found his way to the steps and began ascending, making a semi-conscious attempt to stoop at the entrance—as he had more than once knocked his head on the outer door frame on other airlines.

'Good evening sir,' the smiling face greeted him. He read her badge bearing the name 'Sonnette'. 'May I?' she said, flashing her eyes at him, still smiling as she reached towards him for his boarding card. Tom turned it towards her. She noted the seat number and gestured to the aisle furthest from the door, 'row 23, window seat,' she added, still smiling pleasantly and making eye contact again.

Tom had wondered why the same information was passed to passengers many times over, but no matter how often people were told, some of them just didn't get it.

'Thank you,' he replied and threw her a brief smile as he started to make his way across. It seemed his luck was in, because most of the other passengers already aboard appeared to be congested in the first aisle.

As he counted back the rows, he noticed they jumped from 12 to 14. The observance to the laws of superstition aroused his interest, especially regarding how many hours of meetings it may have taken at the airline's offices to arrive at such a deliberate choice. He found it mildly amusing that somehow passengers in row 13 might feel less safe than those in 14 or 12; and that also somehow, by renaming the 13th row to 14 it was seen as a contribution to either in-flight safety or a reduction in passenger stress.

He counted the seats across from the far side. They started with those marked A and B; then in the middle were seats D,E,F,G and H; and finally J and K by the windows on his side. The aisles seemed to occupy the slots for missing seat positions C and I; and although the casual observer might have believed the aircraft had eleven seats from one side to the other from a cursory check, in reality it had been trimmed to nine.

The overhead locker was larger than he expected and still empty. Tom tossed his passport in the briefcase, which he then placed in the locker, closing the lid afterwards. He still held the crumpled and much diminished boarding card in his hand and slid it into his upper outside jacket pocket. Then having removed the jacket, he placed it on the hook in front of him, sat down and played the customary game of passenger watching.

For the first time he noticed the background music; he hadn't registered when he'd first heard it, but it was definitely playing at that stage; and as he relaxed so his senses began to ease in.

He'd become aware of new smells; aircraft fuel was the dominant odour but strangely, he also noticed the fresh outside evening air as it wafted by. As well as the music, other less noticeable sounds had become apparent too; a hum from a generator, or the electrics on board; and a slight sound of air flow from above—through the passenger air vents where one had been left open.

He scanned the cabin briefly. With the flight due to leave within 25 minutes—if it were to leave on time—more than half the seats were still empty and he hadn't particularly rushed to queue at the boarding gate, so he began to wonder where the missing passengers were.

His thoughts were interrupted by the captain's voice on the aircraft's PA system. 'Welcome aboard this Boeing 747 flight to London, ladies and gentlemen. I'd like to remind those passengers bound for New York JFK that they are on the wrong aircraft and should disembark now with their luggage and board the plane to our left. This is the London Heathrow flight.'

Tom watched an older man the approximate size of a buffalo board the aircraft, struggling with three bags, each of which easily exceeded the maximum allowable size. He squeezed up the generous aisles encumbered by his luggage; and although Tom couldn't know it, it did seem likely to him that the man had brought all of his luggage as carry on—perhaps to save time later.

Enthralled by this bizarre spectacle, Tom watched for nearly five minutes as the man opened one overhead locker after another searching for space. One of the lockers contained cabin crew equipment of some form, but he didn't notice this until his attempts at forcing his bag inside met with absolute unmoving resistance. Soon he was beginning to attract a bigger audience than just Tom, and it was no coincidence that moments later a hostess appeared and helped him stow his belongings. She searched swiftly for other available lockers, nimbly pulling the doors open and expertly flicking them closed again.

As the man lowered his huge bulk into one of the seats she asked him if he was bound for London and he nodded, but it was the kind of nod that someone makes when they're just trying to be polite and didn't really hear what the other person had said.

Listening to the music once more and just gazing around the cabin, Tom noticed the queue jumper had boarded and was walking down the other aisle to row 26 or 27, behind which was the separator for economy class, the galley and one set of toilets. This struck him as odd as the queue jumper had been ahead of him, yet was only now finding his seat. He began trying to work out how that had been possible but gave up only moments later due to tiredness and rapidly decreasing interest.

Boarding confusion had heightened to such a point that the airhostesses were walking along both aisles and asking to see everyone's boarding card in turn, to confirm whether or not they were on the correct flight.

The captain spoke again over the aircraft's PA system confirming the flight as being for London.

The hostess checked the boarding card of the buffalo sized passenger and spoke to him quietly, to which he exclaimed, 'London!' and standing up, he further added, 'you mean this plane's not going to New York?'

'I'm afraid not sir,' came the polite reply. The man added something extra in frustration. Tom smiled and shook his head. The hostess called over for some help from her male colleagues to search the lockers and find the man's luggage. By now Tom was gazing outside, but he could still see these intrusive events in the window's reflection. The man was holding his boarding card and then making large and wild arm movements clearly asking why no one had noticed earlier that he was on the wrong plane. The air hostess and her male colleagues gave no argument, but politely helped the man towards the door against the flow of passengers entering, many of whom were simply not moving.

Meanwhile the queue jumper was folding his raincoat and then meticulously fed it into the overhead locker next to his briefcase and over his duty free. He took off his jacket and neatly placed it on top. Closing the locker he took his seat and unravelled the seat belts to try and marry the correct seat belt plug with the correct socket, finding as most people do that he was sat on not just one, but both of the correct straps.

Once settled, a few moments passed and he tutted to himself, undid the straps, stood up and reaching for the locker he opened it. He carefully attempted to open his briefcase whilst the jacket remained on top, and pulling out a copy of the Times he placed it under his chin. But this meant keeping his head angled downwards, which stopped him from seeing properly, so he placed it between his teeth instead. Cautiously using his left hand to rummage in his pocket, he pulled out his boarding card and was about to place both it and his passport in his briefcase, just as the hostess stopped to ask him if she could check it.

She noted that he was on the correct flight, so he put the card and his passport into his case and then pressed it closed, engaging the spring loaded clips. Sitting down briefly, he then repeated part of the exercise to retrieve a large white envelope and a pen from what appeared to be the disorderly debris within—yet he managed it—mainly by feel alone. Finally, he was able to sit down and fight with the seat belts a second time.

'May I see your boarding card sir?' it was Sonnette, smiling at Tom once more. He felt in his top outside jacket pocket to retrieve it and showed it to her.

'Where are you bound for sir?' she asked, to be doubly certain.

'London. I hope.' Tom was now looking worried and as if to confirm his fears he qualified his answer twice by adding, 'England. Heathrow.'

'That's fine sir. In that case you're on the right plane,' she replied passing back the boarding pass.

'When are we due to take off?' he asked.

'About another ten minutes and we'll be taxiing sir.'

'But what about all of these empty seats?' Tom added, noticing that the queue had dispersed and no one else seemed to be boarding now.

'That's okay sir. The airline is run that way because we always take off on time, so if passengers are late they'll miss the flight. In addition we never double book or over book the flights and lots of people book and pay but never arrive. So you may find yourself with two seats tonight.'

As it was going to be a 15-hour flight, the thought of more space was refreshingly welcome.

Tom leaned forward slightly and reached for the crumpled in-flight magazine. Being that it was so early in the month, it was already very well thumbed, so he quickly checked its date to confirm it was the current edition. Written in small letters along its spine were the words 'August 2008'. The headline told of new routes being introduced by the airline. Inside, the leader article addressed how the airline had already selected the new Airbus A380 as its workhorse in preference over the Boeing 787 Dreamliner, and how it was going to respond to the new challenges of twenty additional destinations in Europe alone.

The captain's voice came over the PA system again. 'Welcome aboard this South African Airways flight to London Heathrow. My name is Andrew de Jongh and in the co-pilot's seat is Ben Church. We'll be flying this Boeing 747 for the first half of the journey. During the second half, in approximately eight hours, our second crew will take over and introduce themselves to you. We'll begin to taxi in just a few moments. Right now we're awaiting final approval of our takeoff slot from the tower and so we should be on our way soon. When we get under way, we'll fly west to the Atlantic and then north, following the coastline. After that we'll fly around the Sahara and then past Spain, through the Bay of Biscay, onto England and Heathrow, landing at 08:00 local time. I'll be updating you during the flight, so from myself and the crew may I wish you a pleasant trip; and if you need any assistance then please press the red button overhead and Diane or one of her colleagues will be happy to help you.'

The steps rolled away from the aircraft and two of the hostesses closed the door, giggling as they did so. 'Cabin crew, doors to automatic,' came the perfunctory instruction from the captain.

The hostesses then walked down both aisles, simultaneously passing out steaming white scented face flannels, using tongs to hand them to the passengers. Tom took one and covered his face, drowning in the fragrance momentarily. His mind drifted as the heat gently dissipated. Then letting it peel away from his skin he neatly folded the flannel and waited for it to be collected.

The same hostess walked by with an open bin liner and Tom gently dropped it in. A few steps behind, another hostess followed, carrying a tray with equal numbers of glasses of wine and orange juice. Knowing that he had to drive once he arrived at Heathrow, Tom took an orange juice, thanking her in the process.

It wasn't long before the glasses too had been collected. The rituals extended to the safety instructions and this took place in concert with the engines being started and the aircraft itself being jerked backwards from the apron by the guiding tractor.

Having been fully reversed, then, under its own power, it taxied away from the terminal to take its place in a queue for the main runway behind two others.

The darkness had crept in further by this stage and the sky was strangely black as viewed through the windows on one side of the plane and still blue—all be it a dark blue—on the other.

Tom checked his watch. It was exactly 18:00 as the plane turned and faced the length of the runway. He felt the brakes being applied, gently halting the aircraft. Then in a matter of seconds—as the throttle was opened fully—the noise and pitch of the engines began to drown all other sounds. The gentle vibrations through the floor and seat quickly changed to shaking and juddering through the entire plane. The noise levels rose still further and Tom looked out to the wing. Even in the half-light he could see it quivering; its power being held back until the right moment. Then, without warning, the brakes were released and the plane began to thunder along the runway.

Timing the take off, he could see the tarmac being eaten up by this huge metal beast. One minute and nine seconds passed by before the nose lifted off and then a further seven seconds later the rear undercarriage followed. Ten seconds after that the gear was up and locked as confirmed by the familiar clunk from underneath, but by this time they were not only airborne but were climbing steeply and banking.

Looking out of the window, there was little to be seen, even though they were heading west towards the setting sun.

Tom relaxed and taking out the menu card and in-flight magazine, he began dreaming up ways to kill 15 hours.

The meal came and went, as did the film, and setting his watch back an hour to align with BST, he noted that it was 21:15 in England.

Drinks were flowing well. Passengers were wandering about the plane. It seemed that some just couldn't stay in their seats for long. Various trips to the toilets interrupted the boredom for many of them.

By midnight, things were much quieter and many passengers were wearing eye covers and had been issued with pillows and blankets. Tom had placed his on the vacant seat next to him.

Noticing that the lights had been turned low, he decided to try and fall asleep, when out of the window, looking far to the east, he began to see distant flashes. At first he thought it was the lights from other aircraft, but watching closely for a few minutes he could see that it was an electric storm. He realised that from its position and magnitude it must have stretched for hundreds of miles and by his calculations of time and their probable location, he guessed that it was over the Sahara. He was mesmerized by its naked beauty, fluorescing randomly in nature's spellbinding performance, illuminating one area and then another in a spectacular yet enigmatic choreography.

He watched for a full thirty minutes until he began to notice that he'd become thirsty, so briefly forgetting the extravagant light show, he pressed the overhead attention button.

It took a few minutes; but when the hostess arrived, he asked her for a few cans of a soft drink to keep him stocked up and to stop him from needlessly interrupting her again.

As she returned, he lowered the tray on his absent neighbour's seat and she placed the cans on it precariously, largely because she had them all in one hand. This was an intriguing and yet unnecessary skill, Tom concluded. But he soon noticed why she'd done it. In her other hand she was holding an envelope; and passing it to him she explained, 'I've been asked to give this to you sir.'

'Thank you,' he said, somewhat bemused by the unexpected delivery and what it might have been, as he briefly scanned it to check that it was indeed for him. There was no address on it. He wasn't expecting to see a postal address, but the envelope had no outer markings, not his name, nor even his seat and row number. It was just a large white envelope. But before he could ask her who had sent it, she'd walked out of earshot. He momentarily thought of following her to ask, but that would have proved difficult due to the position of the tray on the neighbouring seat. Raising his voice wouldn't have worked either, because the continual drone of the engines created such an invasive background noise that conversation would have been quite difficult, unless the other person had been adjacent, which by that time she no longer was.

He assumed that he must have been picked out as a candidate for a survey by the airline, so he opened the envelope and took out its contents.

In all there were three sheets of A4 paper. The first contained the heading 'Classification Secret' and the words 'Codeword Elektra'. Printed underneath were details about himself:

Tom Brady; age 28; current employer Exterra Systems; wife Madeleine; home address, telephone number and other details, including bank account number, credit card numbers, car registration, passport, driving licence and national insurance numbers.

On the second sheet were what appeared to be scanned press cuttings. The cuttings referred to the deaths of three of his colleagues from Exterra. This was the first time he'd heard this news and so he was immediately filled with a sense of both alarm and disbelief too: disbelief to the point that he stared at the cuttings for some considerable time before he had any thoughts of assimilating the information. He read the text from beginning to end more than once, each time thinking he'd been mistaken or that he'd misread it. It was as though he was subconsciously looking for the mistake so that he could relax. All this time though he was consumed by its contents, and hadn't begun to consider the less obvious but more immediate ramifications of what he was reading.

Finally he glanced out of the window again and started thinking a little deeper, in an attempt to coalesce his thoughts.

Was it reasonable to assume that such news would not have found its way to him from his own company, he thought to himself; and if not, then why not? He wondered whether it was merely a sick joke. But he was both shocked and sceptical at the same time.

He read the articles in the cuttings again and noticed the dates were all within the previous fortnight. During that time he'd been in South Africa on behalf of the company, and had been in touch with his office many times, but hadn't been told of any deaths. As the company had only 25 personnel in all—or perhaps now just 22 if the information in his possession were to be true—it seemed bizarre that he would only hear of the news at that stage, and by such extraordinary means. Why would this news have been kept from him?

Finally he looked at the third sheet of paper; and that one contained a series of scanned photographs of himself in Heathrow on his outbound journey, at his home and lastly one of his wife.

He was beginning to feel both helpless and angry. He was angry at the thought that someone valued his life so little that they would casually and without warning imply that he and his wife were easy targets, to the point where she could have been in peril—and in fact still might have been.

There were no other pieces of paper. No hint of who had sent them. Tom turned over the last page trying to see if he had missed anything, and on the reverse side was written the message, 'If you want to make sure you're not number four, then meet me upstairs.'

He sat there momentarily watching the last sporadic flashes from the thunderstorm; and then looking first at the front sheet, and then the pictures of himself and lastly the photograph of his wife, he wondered whether this was a hoax. But if it was, then someone had gone to a lot of trouble. Even to the point of getting on a plane with him just to speak to him.

Ten minutes passed by whilst he weighed up his options. He thought of ignoring it, but he had worked for the MoD in the past and had security clearance himself and was familiar with security classifications and the style in which they were stamped or printed on information sheets. These looked authentic enough. The one thing that was too intrusive was the photograph of his wife getting into her car with shopping bags in her hands, outside their local supermarket.

Someone had composed the picture very carefully to catch Madeleine's face so that it was unmistakeably her. In addition, the car registration plate could be seen; and strangely, even though it was daylight in the photograph, the moon was showing and it was unnaturally large, indicating to Tom that the photograph had been taken from some distance away, with a zoom lens.

He realised that instead of a camera, it could just as easily have been a rifle that had been pointed at Madeleine. Then, looking at the second sheet of paper once again, he read the articles about his colleagues, one of which had died with his family, in what was described as a freak boating accident. His entire family had been wiped out. Not just Tom's friend, but his friend's wife and children too.

From his own standpoint Tom found the deaths very difficult to accept as murder. He didn't know how he should feel about it. Horror was the best description. He had previously known people who had died and even one who had been severely injured in a car accident, but he didn't know anyone who had been deliberately killed. Could it be that the deaths had just been accidents? Yet if so then surely he wouldn't have been approached? He didn't have anything that would be of any use to anyone, so he thought, and in which case then why approach him at all?

Was there really someone out there with enough incentive to want him dead, and so desperate to kill him that killing Madeleine was incidental to his or her cause. His heart sank as he then realised that no matter what happened he was about to be engaged in something beyond his control, and he had no idea how much of his life would be taken up trying to get out of this particular predicament. He wanted to find the people behind the deaths and let them know that he and Madeleine posed no threat.

The thought suddenly struck him that he didn't even know how much life he had left, whether it could have been days, hours, or merely minutes or seconds. This brought into sharp focus his attention on a matter he wasn't equipped to handle. But unfortunately he felt sickeningly sure that everything was about to change, and the quicker he accepted any new circumstances thrust at him the better it would be, regardless of the fact that he wanted nothing to do with it. His instinct was to get away from it, but he didn't know how; and to get away, he had to find out exactly what or whom he was getting away from. So he felt compelled to find out more just to assess the danger. But his compulsion was tempered with caution and a more than insignificant element of fear.

His thoughts began to dwell on Madeleine. He wasn't going to risk her life. Looking at the photograph of her once again, he saw in the background that there was a large sign in the window of the supermarket that boldly displayed the words, 'Only 3 days left of midsummer madness. Half price barbecue accessories 3rd to 9th August.'

The photograph had been taken on the sixth—his last full day away on the African assignment—as it was now the early hours of the eighth.

His heart missed a beat. Whilst he'd been away, someone had been close: too close. He began to look around the cabin, but no one seemed to even know he was there, let alone be taking an interest in him or his activities. He placed the papers back in the envelope and moved the drinks off the tray of the seat next to him. Returning the tray to the upright position, he clambered out and then reaching back across he took his jacket.

He made his way towards the nose of the aircraft and as he drew level with the airhostess that had given him the envelope he spoke to her. 'Upstairs?' he said quizzically.

'Me?' she responded pointing at herself with some bemusement and surprise.

'No,' said Tom partly smiling and shaking his head. He qualified his earlier statement. 'Is there an upstairs on the plane?'

'Oh yes,' she replied, pointing again, but this time forwards. 'There's a bar for business and first class passengers. You'll find the stairs just beyond the curtain sir,' she smiled at him again, 'but, if you wish to have a drink, I can bring you whatever you'd like.'

'Thank you,' Tom answered, now gently trying to get away, 'I'll try the bar if that's okay.'

'Certainly sir,' the hostess replied and continued strolling down the aisle.

Tom found the curtain in question, pulled it aside and on seeing the spiral staircase he began to ascend. It felt strange to him going upstairs on a plane, but his thoughts were soon refocused as he had only climbed a few steps when his eyes were at floor level. Feeling like he was sticking his head above the parapets with a hostile force waiting for him to appear, he slowed slightly and looked around as he emerged.

The bar did appear empty at first. But once he'd surfaced completely, he could see that the only other occupant—sitting on the far side—was the queue jumper from the airport departure lounge. Tom hadn't noticed him move out of his seat from the lower deck, but then he'd been enthralled and distracted by the storm for some time.

The man remained impassive, apparently reading his folded newspaper that lay on the seat next to him. He didn't even make eye contact with Tom nor did he make any signs that he was aware of Tom's arrival.

Tom was sidetracked briefly as he noticed something strange about that part of the aircraft. It was a second or two before he realised what it was. It might have been that it had better sound insulation than the cabin below, but the engine noise had all but abated.

He didn't know what to expect. But as he hadn't been approached, he surmised that perhaps the intent was merely to get him out of his seat. He decided not to approach the queue jumper: reasoning that as he'd been the only person on board who had earlier that evening got in the wrong queue, that someone so unaware of where to stand couldn't possibly be the person who'd sent the envelope; especially one with such detailed contents and information.

At the moment Tom turned to go back to the lower cabin, he heard a voice.

'Come in number four. Your time is up.'

Tom turned again and this time their eyes met. He recognised the voice from earlier. It was the queue jumper and although his look was serious it also had an amiable quality to it. Tom's look was more cautious, but he tried to give the impression of relaxed scepticism. The lateness of the hour was impacting his ability to control his facial expressions though and he was beginning not to care too much. His interest was more with his opponent—and wondering whether it was deliberate that he had been approached when so weary and whilst his guard was lowered through mild exhaustion.

He walked slowly across, stopping a few feet from the stranger, with his jacket over one arm, his hands clasped and the envelope just poking out from underneath. He waited with some uncertainty.

'Please sit down,' the stranger said to Tom, gesturing to the seat near to him. He was sat on a curved bench and Tom took the position at the opposite end, leaving a gap between them large enough for another person to sit, where in fact the man's newspaper was resting.

As if on cue, an airhostess appeared from below and asked if the two men would like anything to drink. Tom chose a coffee this time, as did the queue jumper.

The hostess walked behind the bar and started preparing the drinks.

The man began speaking to Tom, not quite in whispered tones but quietly enough to be beyond the earshot of the hostess. With less background noise Tom had no problem hearing him.

'Imagine that you have to meet a complete stranger and tell him that his life is in peril, but you don't have much time. How would you do it?'

'I have no idea,' replied Tom, 'it's beyond my field of experience.'

'It's not an easy thing to get right,' continued the queue jumper. 'Let's suppose you've never met him before and you have 48 hours at most—and you must keep him alive at all costs.'

Tom scrutinised him but waited before commenting. He wanted to say something cynical but decided to let the conversation unfold and not give away his scepticism.

'I understand the problem,' he said. 'Rush in too quickly and you scare him into believing that you're...well, that you're insane: some kind of nut. Too slowly and you run out of time.'

'What might get you to take that man seriously?' the stranger asked him.

Tom thought again before answering, taking the time to scrutinise the face of the man before him, attempting to weigh up what was going through his mind; looking for a clue in any mannerism, but there was no discernable movement beyond gentle breathing and the occasional relaxed blink.

'A cool approach, coupled with independently verifiable facts and proven ability to gain information about me,' he finally replied.

The airhostess returned with the drinks and placed them on the table in front of the two men, smiling as she did so. She turned to the bar and placed a saucer of chocolates and another of mints to the side of the coffees.

The man leant forward. 'Thank you,' he said to the hostess looking up to catch her gaze. Tom smiled at her, nodded and mouthed the word, 'thanks.'

Reaching for a sachet of brown sugar the queue jumper opened it and emptied it into his coffee cup, then, breaking open a milk carton he added it and gently stirred the drink.

'You've seen the photographs, but it's the news articles I'm most interested in. Are the deaths of your colleagues news to you?'

'Yes,' replied Tom, now adding milk to his own coffee and taking one of the chocolates.

'Then,' continued the man, nodding and thinking about the impact of Tom's answer, 'I'm afraid I have no idea whether that's going to help my cause. But you'll be able to verify the information when you get back home and then you can consider why your company has kept the information from you.'

'What do you want?' Tom asked, now believing the man to be more credible and even if he was only slightly more credible, he certainly had enough of Tom's attention to keep him there for the moment.

'You wouldn't believe me if I told you I wanted to save your life would you?'

Tom didn't rush with an answer. He kept looking the man in the eyes whilst he thought about what the man had said, only speaking when he was finally ready.

'No,' he replied almost cynically and without emotion, 'That's what I want. That's the carrot you're going to use to get me to do what you want.'

The man smiled at Tom's remark.

'It's not that sinister. Believe it or not I'm actually on your side. My name is Bob Selway and I work for Her Majesty's government: the treasury actually. My department's been following your company closely and in particular your boss Geoff Abbot.'

Tom remained silent, knowing that Selway may have been trying to elicit information from him. Because it was so late, each passing moment fed his tiredness, which ironically helped him suppress his emotions.

Selway took out his identity pass. 'I know this may not impress you, but then again it may add some credibility. You'll no doubt recognise it.'

On the pass were markings that Tom did recognise. It depicted Selway and had the requisite symbols to permit him access to multiple MoD sites. In Tom's eyes, this man's credibility had just increased but he let on nothing, handing it back impassively.

Selway continued, 'Your company—Exterra—was commissioned by the government two years ago to write half of the software for high speed trains, specifically the guidance and propulsion monitoring systems. The software is called Elektra: a poor name in my opinion—but that's not important. A French company called Vitesse Acquise is writing the other half of the software.

Neither company has access to the software of the other, and so neither can sell the complete package. But in a deal between the French and British governments the software will be touted to eastern European countries, to make follow-on sales that would be very rewarding to both nations. None of this—I am sure—is new information for you.

Our problem, is that we believe that Exterra, in particular Geoff Abbot, has acquired a copy of the French software and is preparing to sell both parts as a complete package.'

Tom looked on bemused, 'so send in the federation against software theft. It sounds like a job for them.'

'No teeth I'm afraid,' Selway added, 'You see the sales will be in Europe, we believe, and the federation only works in the UK. We can contact the similar authorities in the other countries, but that won't help the government. There are only so many sales for this stuff, and understandably as the two governments have invested heavily in it, then they're determined to have sole rights.'

Selway took a sip from his coffee whilst all this sank in with Tom.

Tom wanted to ask him why he made all the commotion at the departure gate, and whether it was deliberate or just foolishness. But the answer would have been meaningless, so he brought his thoughts back to the immediacy of the present matter.

'Where do I fit in, and why the deaths? You're obviously implying that these people were murdered.'

'Yes,' said Selway, replacing the cup in the saucer. 'I can't stress the seriousness of the situation. Each person who died worked as a development programmer on the project. The only people left with any knowledge of the software are Abbot and you.'

Tom said nothing. Selway was right, but Tom wasn't prepared to give anything away. But he did wonder whether even his lack of denial to Selway at this stage was a mistake.

'We can't be sure and that's why we need your help, but we believe Abbot is somehow behind this. His personal expenditure exceeds his income by a large factor. We've checked. His debts are spiralling out of control. His mistress has expensive tastes and he pays for her entire upkeep including her own flat— which they treat as a love nest. He drinks heavily and frankly is a liability.'

'What if I knew nothing about the software?' Tom asked.

Selway's face took on a more serious look. 'Even if that were true, then whoever is carrying out these killings is very well informed. So if you're bluffing, then you may convince me, but it's the killer's knowledge that you have to consider.'

Tom saw the sense of the argument and the futility of saying that he didn't know anything about it. He had worked on the project in its early days when the team were trying to hit deadlines and they had been short staffed. His expertise had been crucial.

'So what do you want from me?'

'Wait to be contacted once you get back home. When are you due back in work?' Selway inquired.

'Just over three weeks. I'm on leave as from now really.'

'We'll contact you before then.'

'Can you tell me anything else?' Tom asked, now concerned that there must have been something he should have asked.

Selway momentarily said nothing. His eyes visibly lost focus as he stared at a point over Tom's left shoulder. Then blinking and shifting his attention to Tom for a few seconds with an almost indiscernible squint, before gazing into the distance once again, he answered. 'There is one other thing actually.'

Tom waited, now looking more relaxed. Selway's eyes met his once more.

'There's something quirky about the details I handed you. I apologise for that now, but in the circumstances I was short of time. So I hope you'll forgive me,' he confessed.

'Quirky?' Tom asked, with a look of curiosity.

'You'll work it out I'm sure,' Selway continued, 'you're obviously intelligent and when you do work it out—it's no big deal—please understand that it was because I was short of time. In spite of that, don't dwell on irrelevancies. Remember that the important thing is the information about the deaths of your colleagues; and you can check the authenticity of those reports when you get home.'

Tom was too tired to pursue the issue. He extended his arm towards Selway with the envelope in his hand. Selway reached for it but Tom didn't release it. He wasn't sure whether to keep it or not.

Selway shrugged his shoulders and released his grip. 'It's up to you. Keep it if you wish.'

Musing over this for a few seconds, Tom shook his head. 'I don't need it,' he remarked almost in resignation and let Selway take it from him.

He stood and walked away without saying another word as his mind began working on weighing up all the things he'd been told. He wondered what might eventually be exposed as quirky. But it was too much information to process; and by that time it was 1:15 in the morning; and he needed to get some sleep before the plane landed.

CHASING CLOUDS

Although the aircraft landed on time at Heathrow, a full hour had passed by the time that Tom had retrieved his car from the long stay car park. Having paid for his ticket he drove out; and within a few minutes he was on the motorway, driving west.

The offices for Exterra were in Basingstoke. He toyed with the idea of making the necessary detour to visit, as it was a Friday. But as he thought more about it, he realised that it might be very foolish to turn up and present an easy opportunity to the murderer—if there was one.

He was disturbed by the fact that no one at the company had told him about the deaths. This made him uneasy about trusting anyone there. Although he realised that the information may have been untrue, someone had gone to a lot of trouble to make sure he'd been spoken to on the plane the previous night.

As he mulled over these thoughts, he factored in the additional elements that he was officially on leave and that he had no desire to delay being with Madeleine. There was nothing further to consider. Tom drove past the motorway junction without any inclination of getting off.

The trip home would take him an hour and a half, and he was driving in the opposite direction to most of the traffic, so it was relatively clear.

There was a blue sky and although clouds loitered in the distant west, it was going to be a warm, perhaps even a hot day.

During the last six hours of the plane flight, Tom had been able to get some sleep, which in the circumstances was exceptional as he often slept badly, if he managed to sleep at all on planes.

Because of the uncharacteristically large period of sleep, he didn't feel tired. In fact, he was both relaxed and alert.

He couldn't somehow believe the things that he'd been told by Selway and he wondered what proof he would need to satisfy his belief in these events—although that would be the easy part: just believing the events had taken place. The hard part would be trying to work out the motives behind them.

Even if he could take the matter to the police, time wasn't on his side. He began to conclude that he might have only managed to stay alive because he had been out of the country, and now that he was back, perhaps he was in more danger than he knew or even realised.

He felt that couldn't afford to make any mistakes. But he'd never been trained for this. He was intelligent and a quick learner, but against professionals—if that's who he was up against—he was completely at their mercy—whoever they were.

He'd already begun to armour himself with caution at the same time as tempering it to avoid paranoia. But instinctively he also sensed that moving quickly—along with any unpredictability on his part—would be of great benefit to him. He somehow knew that his best chance of success lay in not following someone else's rules, and not being sucked in to normal patterns of behaviour, particularly when reacting to new situations. Thinking on his feet was something he was good at: but now his life depended on it. He found himself in a sinister way almost enjoying the intellectual challenge; angry that someone would even think of dispensing with him in such a patronisingly arrogant and offhand fashion.

Being in the dark over the apparent motiveless deaths of his colleagues, he had no way to know how to defend himself, nor even what to defend against. Logically therefore, he would need the help of someone either with more resources than he had or at very least more information. Failing that he would need to go into hiding, but again he didn't know who or what he would need to hide from and for how long. He was also concerned that deep inside he was beginning to notice a thrill to the situation and he wondered whether this was normal; but it was counterbalancing his fear and so he allowed it to develop.

Regardless of his own well being, he knew that Madeleine's safety was paramount. He cared a lot less about what happened to him, as long as she was safe. But should he tell her?

Indeed, would she believe him, or merely think he was losing his mind, or perhaps even making it up? The deaths of his colleagues would be the key. She may have already known about it, but living so far from Basingstoke and the deaths occurring in three different ways, there was nothing sufficiently newsworthy to make the national headlines.

Tom's inability to reach any distinct conclusions, made his thoughts on the subject evaporate. The journey passed by quickly, and it didn't seem to be long before he approached the outskirts of Bath and soon afterwards the village where he and Madeleine had lived since they'd got married three years earlier.

Pulling into the drive, he noticed that he'd made reasonable time as the car's clock tripped over to 10:40 just as he switched off the engine.

He heaved out his luggage; and on reaching the front door he was about to place the key in the lock, when to his surprise it moved back, without him even touching it.

Standing in the doorway was Madeleine: a picture of beauty— even though she was wearing gardening gloves, a headscarf and large owl type glasses. She also had a kind of country and western style blouse tucked into a faded pair of blue jeans. Around her waist she was wearing a tool belt, in which she had a small garden hand trowel.

She was blonde and three years younger than Tom. The fact that he'd not seen her for two weeks meant that in his eyes she was a vision of perfection. He dropped his cases and fumbling to put his key back in his pocket he managed it just as she stepped outside. She grabbed hold of him and with a mischievous look in her eyes held his gaze. He smiled and they kissed.

Eventually pulling back from each other, he frowned slightly and after a moment he spoke. 'You taste of…,' he paused again '…chocolate?'

'Hmm,' she said, nodding like a naughty schoolgirl and then giggling. She pulled off first one glove and then the other. 'I thought I might need to keep up my energy levels now that you're back.'

'Of course you do,' came the disbelieving reply.

Madeleine stuffed her gloves into the holster on her tool belt.

Tom got his car keys out and pointed them at the vehicle, squeezing the fob to confirm it was locked and alarmed. The indicators flashed twice.

Picking up his luggage, he walked inside. Madeleine held the door open wide to stop him from being hit by it. As she closed it behind him, he turned to look at her and caught sight of the birthmark on the back of her right ear. It was more of a discolouration really. A strip that was about a two centimetres long and half a centimetre wide, he often remarked that she wasn't finished off right. It was dark pink, almost, but not quite red and it looked as though the skin had merely been recently grazed.

She turned towards him again and took off her glasses folding the arms in such a way that she was able to slide them down the front of her blouse and clip them there. She pulled off her scarf with her right hand quickly followed that by running her left hand up through her hair to tousle it gently, shaking her head as she did so.

'What did you bring me back?' she said wickedly looking at his cases.

'Me.' came the playful reply, as he raised his eyebrows twice in quick succession and they both laughed.

'I've missed this,' she said softly, walking towards him and taking his hand again after he dropped the cases once more.

She gave his hand a long squeeze as though to prove to herself that he was really there and likewise he squeezed her hand in the same way.

'Can't you get a job where you don't have to go away again?' There was a pause as she walked through into the kitchen. 'After all, it's like I work for that company. And they don't pay me to be alone at night. All the profit goes into Abbot's pocket.'

'I may not be there for much longer,' Tom remarked seriously.

'Why? Have you resigned?' Madeleine asked, also in a more matter of fact tone.

'No,' replied Tom, 'but something happened on the plane last night.'

Madeleine started to make a pot of coffee as Tom leant against the doorway. Swilling out the jug with a blast of water from the tap, she glanced back at him.

'Did you get much sleep?'

'Yes. I did quite well, but that's not what I meant.'

'Oh,' she remarked pulling a filter paper from the packet. 'I assume you'd like a coffee?'

'Yes. Yes please.' Tom was distracted, but he didn't know how to begin.

Madeleine filled the pause and Tom was happy just to hear her voice. 'As it's such a nice day I thought maybe if you're not too tired we could go out this afternoon, eat out perhaps, get some fresh air.'

Tom smiled 'Why? What have you been up to?'

'I've found a new garden centre,' she replied. 'They stock orchids. It's near the coast and they're looking for help.'

Madeleine was a marine biologist by trade if that was the correct phrase, but in reality she had a way with flowers that was more than luck and although she didn't go out to work— with Tom's salary she didn't need to—she enjoyed trying to nurture and grow difficult types of flowers.

It seemed to Tom that it was a criminal waste of her talent for her to work in a flower shop or a garden centre. Having done the hard work for her doctorate in the subject, living near the coast seemed like an excellent idea.

'Where is it?' He asked.

'I'll show you this afternoon.'

She added the water to the coffee maker and placing the jug underneath, it was only moments before it began to brew.

'I've got something to show you first though,' she said, wiping her hands in the towel. 'Come with me. See if you can guess what it is.' She took his hand and led him out of the kitchen and into the back garden.

Even though it was a modern house, the garden was reasonably large. Madeleine had insisted on that when they'd bought the place, so that she could grow a whole menagerie of tropical plants.

'What is it that I like more than anything else?' She asked emphatically as though Tom would know the answer without even thinking.

'I can't answer that,' he said looking surprised.

'Not that!' she in mock indignation.

The late morning sun felt good and made the place look exotic, colourful and a haven of peace as she took him towards the greenhouse, the various fragrances of the flowers mixing in the air adding to the rich depth of feeling he was given from this scene.

He thought carefully about her question. 'Chocolate!' he declared with a triumphant smile.

'Yes,' she replied ambivalently, 'but that's not it either.'

'Moving furniture around?' He queried, knowing now that she was probably intending to show him what she'd meant, but he enjoyed toying with her.

'Try again,' she demanded with a hint of frustration in her voice, raising one eyebrow as she looked back at him.

He thought for a few moments as they both stepped inside the greenhouse; but due to Madeleine's exuberance with growing things that would make triffids look normal, there wasn't much room to move.

Then once Tom had stopped looking around she pointed at three potted plants and almost squealed in delight. 'What do you think?'

Bending over to scrutinise each one in turn, Tom then stood up and looked at her closely and gave his considered verdict. 'I think they're plants.'

'Yes,' she added shaking her head. 'Your powers of observation do you credit. They're dendrobium sulawesiense.'

'And in English that would be?' he asked squinting at her and waiting for the imminent answer.

'Pretty flowers to you,' she replied. 'Orchids: tricky to grow.'

'Tricky to say even,' he remarked, 'although I'd be happy just to be able to spell it,' he added, trying to read the label more closely. The flowers were attractive though, he thought to himself; and somehow seemed to be perfect for Madeleine. Tom wasn't quite sure how or why, but this flower was her flower, if any such thing existed.

He looked at her again. 'As you're a marine biologist why do you keep forgetting the marine part and remembering the biology part?'

'You mean you don't like the biology part?' she said wickedly, sidling past him and rubbing her body close to his as she did so.

'That's not quite what I meant,' he replied.

'I know. That's why I want to go to this new garden centre, it's near the coast. We can go after lunch. As it's Friday it won't be as crowded as the weekend and you can see for yourself.'

'Okay,' replied Tom. 'You drive though. I've already done a hundred miles today.'

'You wish to live dangerously? And let me drive?' She remarked, slightly surprised at his suggestion.

'No. Actually, I want to get drunk in a few minutes and I thought letting you drive would be the quickest way for me to get sober again.' He laughed and moved out of reach as she tried to thump him gently, biting her lip as she did so. But in the end she took his hand again and pulled him back outside.

Tom didn't find the opportunity that morning to raise the subject with Madeleine about Selway's chat the previous night. Those things just seemed too intrusive and he didn't want to spoil the atmosphere by letting them surface just yet.

Before long they were in her car, driving off towards the new haunt that she'd discovered. The clouds had thickened slightly since his arrival home, but there was still plenty of blue sky and the temperature had progressed from warm to hot.

Madeleine owned a bright red soft top and they drove with the roof neatly folded back into it's container, with a picnic basket wedged behind the front seats, packed with various assortments of food and drink for later.

The journey took them along the country roads and they couldn't speak to each other because of the noise of the wind, so every now and again they turned to face each other momentarily and smiled.

Tom allowed his thoughts to drift back to Selway, and had there been any doubt in his mind, he now resolved to tell Madeleine everything that had happened—regardless of any fear she may have had to show about being photographed without her knowledge. This whole thing was too important. Madeleine wasn't known for irrational behaviour, probably as a result of her background in science; and else or anyway she was a logical thinker. Tom had often remarked to her that if she wanted to move into information technology he knew she would do well in the field. But she had shown no such interest, usually telling him that she was more interested in the living and not the dead, which was her way of referring to computers.

The car slowed and they turned into the car park of a garden centre; above its large warehouse style entrance its name boldly painted, 'Flower Barn'. Turning off the engine, Madeleine stepped out of the car and began walking away. Tom had also stepped outside and closed the passenger door. He looked at the car and then at Madeleine as though to say something, but Madeleine interrupted his thoughts.

'I'll tell you what,' she said with a smile, walking back towards him. 'I'll lock it if you put the roof up for me.' Tom moved back towards the canopy that had been neatly put away. 'Don't you dare!' she exclaimed. 'Lighten up!'

Tom turned and sheepishly walked towards her. Holding out his hand for her, she slid her hand into his as they walked in.

They meandered around the building looking at the flowers, bulbs and seeds until they found the orchid section.

'They haven't got as many as they had the other day,' Madeleine remarked. One of the female assistants overheard her and as if from nowhere popped her head up. On her badge the name 'Gaby' was clearly printed. 'It's quite an art growing them, and no one here seems to have the knack,' she interrupted.

'It's not too difficult once you know how.' Madeleine assured her; and this kicked off a lengthy conversation between the two women, giving Tom the opportunity to drift off once more.

As if in autopilot, when the conversation had finished, Madeleine took Tom's hand again and asked him 'Well what do you think?'

'Oh yes,' he said, not really concentrating but looking back. 'She was really nice.'

Madeleine stopped dead in her tracks and faced him. 'I wasn't talking about her, I meant working here part time?'

'Eh,' replied Tom, 'I'm sorry can you run that by me again?'

'You're still thinking about that assistant aren't you?' Madeleine continued.

'Oh you mean Gaby,' Tom replied.

'Gaby?' said Madeleine. 'You heard that part then.'

'No,' Tom replied pointing to the upper part of Madeleine's chest he added 'She had her name badge there.'

'And why were you looking at that part of her body?'

'To see her name,' came the cool reply. 'I was just being polite.'

'And in your politeness did you notice what colour eyes she had?'

'Of course not,' he replied looking into Madeleine's eyes. 'I only have eyes for you. To have looked in her eyes would have been staring and that would have been impolite.'

'So you just kept your eyes on her chest then?'

'Exactly,' he said nodding.

'Well if you'd exceeded your 'politeness' a little and bothered to look at her left hand you would have seen a ring there.'

'Would I? But why would I have done that? After all I only wanted to know her name. I wasn't interested in her for any other reason.'

They smiled at each other and Tom almost walked into a hardware rack that he hadn't noticed on the way in. Luckily with careful guidance, Madeleine managed to stop him.

'I thought you said my driving would sober you up?' she laughed.

'Yes I did. You're obviously improving and not scaring me as much as you used to,' he told her.

Stepping back into the open, they walked into the wall of heat from the afternoon sun and made their way back to the car. Tom leapt in without opening the door and placed his arm around the back of the driving seat. Madeleine took deliberate care with getting into the car and moments later she started the engine and drove off, with Tom looking behind and checking for the picnic hamper.

Within a short time they entered a village with a winding main street and veering off, Madeleine took them past an old church that was fronted by lawns with a long curved wall next to the pavement. The wall had two entrances for cars—one either side of the church front—and both led to small gravel laid car parks.

Driving beyond the church, Tom could see in front of them there was rough gorse, beyond which were sand dunes and then the sea, all too apparent from the fresh sea air now engulfing them, driven slowly by a balmy breeze. Madeleine turned left.

The road followed the coastline and about half a mile from the church, they came to another car park. It was more of a barren patch of land, separating fields on one side, from the gorse-laden dunes on the other.

There were only two other cars present. An old couple apparently eating ice creams sat in one of the cars; and a man reading a newspaper sat in the other. The man looked up briefly as they pulled in, but then returned to his paper, shaking it to fold it together to turn the next page, all the while holding it with both hands.

Once she'd stopped the car, Madeleine turned off the engine after a few seconds of letting it idle, and then she stepped out. She leant over to pick up the hamper, but Tom grabbed it first.

'Where to?' he asked.

'This way,' came the reply as she strode off into the pasture.

Towards the back end of the field were trees, enough to be classified as a small wood. The meadow itself sloped up hill and two thirds of the way up and about three hundred yards from the car, stood a large oak tree.

The two of them trekked across and sat down in its shade. They opened the picnic hamper and laid out a carefully packed tablecloth. After rummaging in the hamper for a few minutes, Madeleine had pulled out various items of food, drink and plates along with a bottle of wine.

'For you,' she said waving the bottle at Tom as he stood surveying the woods then the field and finally the sea beyond, which was now quite visible due to their greater elevation.

Tom sat down and taking the corkscrew that Madeleine had packed, he peeled back the metal shroud from the bottle and extracted the cork.

'There's only one glass,' he said frowning.

'I can't drink that stuff. Remember? I'm driving,' she said.

Shrugging his shoulders and then pouring out a glass of wine for himself, he looked at Madeleine and was about to speak when she took hold of the conversation again.

'Wouldn't you just love to live here?'

'What right here in this field?' he replied.

'No of course not, but perhaps nearby in a cottage or in the village we just drove through.'

He didn't answer her, but he began to weigh up the possibility. 'There's a nice view here and the air is clean too. But where would I work?'

'You could stay at home and let me work,' she replied half biting into a roll at the same time and now almost lying down and leaning on one elbow. She shook her head as if to clear her hair out of her eyes and carried on. 'Seriously though, what's happening with your job? It sounds like you think you may be leaving soon. Or did I misunderstand you?'

Tom shifted around and began looking down towards the ground. Then he gazed at his glass for a few seconds before taking a sip from it. It was another few moments before he finally answered.

'You remember I said that something happened on the plane coming home?'

'Yes,' she replied.

'Well, I was given an envelope that contained news cuttings about Steve, Jim and Martin,' Tom added, now looking down intently at the wine glass, gently swirling the wine.

'They were in the news then? What did they do?' Madeleine inquired, only slightly intrigued.

Still looking at his drink he continued. 'According to the information in the cuttings, they all died.' As he finished speaking he looked Madeleine in the eyes. It was clear from the expression on her face that she wasn't certain whether to believe him or not.

'There's something else,' Tom added. 'There was a photograph of you taken on Wednesday outside the supermarket, getting into the car with your shopping.'

'Someone's been photographing me?' she asked.

'Yes,' he replied.

'What's going on? Why would anyone want to photograph me?' Madeleine pressed him for an answer, thinking that he knew. She finished her food and sitting up, she brushed her hands together to remove any remaining crumbs. Leaning over to the hamper, she pulled out a can of diet coke and after opening it she took a sip.

'I don't know,' came Tom's reply, 'but the package was given to me by one of the airhostesses and there was a note on the back of the last page, inviting me upstairs if I wanted to find out more. When I got there, I met a man who introduced himself as Bob Selway.

He claimed he worked for the government and said that Steve, Jim and Martin had all been murdered, and that the one thing they had in common was that they had all worked on the development of the Elektra software.' Tom stopped to let Madeleine take this in. By now, she was sat cuddling her knees in front of her and facing at right angles to him. She thought about this for a few moments.

'It sounds too far-fetched,' she said. 'Are you certain about the deaths? I haven't heard anything,' she paused and thinking for a moment she then continued, 'but then again why should I? Unless it was in the national news?'

Tom agreed. 'That's what I thought and that's why I didn't bring the photograph and cuttings back with me, although this man Selway said I could if I wished.'

'Why was I photographed and by whom?' Madeleine asked.

'I don't know why, but there's a clear implication that you're being watched.'

'But that doesn't make sense. Does it?' she added. 'Think it through. The bad guys—if there are any—photographed me and then sent a copy to the good guys. Is that what we're saying here? Why would they do that and why or how would it get into Bob Selway's possession?'

Tom could see the logic of it.

'Or the good guys photographed you, to show me how vulnerable you are to get me to do something,' he added almost tripping over every word as he thought on it.

'You're right, it doesn't make sense,' he continued. 'Everything else looks plausible except the photograph of you. Selway, or one of his people, must have taken it and then included it with the cuttings.'

'Okay,' said Madeleine, 'so what's going on here? Some guy that you don't know has a photograph of me taken by someone else we don't know to try and get you to do what?'

'Selway did apologise for something quirky that he said he had to do because he was short of time, and that it was no big deal. Maybe that was it. The photographs of you were the quirky thing.' Tom remarked as he cast his mind back to the conversation. He began to remember the other parts of the meeting with Selway.

'He asked me if I'd worked on Elektra and although I didn't actually tell him, he told me that it was unimportant what he knew, or what anyone else thought, other than the killer. If the killer believed that I'd worked on the project, then that would be enough to put my safety in jeopardy.'

'And you did didn't you?' Madeleine asked, already vaguely remembering that Tom had been involved in the early days.

'Yes,' he replied.

'What did Selway want you to do?'

'Nothing. He just said that I would be contacted about it.'

'Okay then. First of all we need to check on the web, to see if we can find out about those deaths,' Madeleine suggested. 'In the mean time let's finish our picnic.'

She stood up and raising her hand to shield her eyes she could see the sun about to disappear behind an approaching cloud. 'Come on!' she declared, 'lets get the edges!'

'What do you mean?' asked Tom standing up. Madeleine started running. 'Try and stay in the shadows,' she shouted back at him, 'didn't you ever do this when you were young?'

Her voice began to fade as she ran up the hill towards the wood, laughing as she did so. Tom began to chase her and just before the tree line he caught up with her as they both tumbled over, out of breath and laughing. He took her in his arms and kissed her. As he looked up into the wood his expression suddenly changed.

'What's wrong?' she said worried by his look and checking behind her in the direction Tom had been facing.

'I saw a man there, with a tripod and camera. He's running away through the trees.' Tom bobbed his head around trying to see through the wooded area, but he stopped as soon as they both heard the sound of a car engine starting, quickly followed by the car moving off at high speed. He stood and caught sight of the last digit and the last three characters on the licence plate: '2 THJ,' he said.

Madeleine stood up. 'So some man was photographing trees or birds. So what?' she asked.

'Why did he rush off so quickly when he saw me looking at him?' Tom replied still looking in the direction of the car.

'Because you look threatening,' she added, smiling at him. 'He was scared of you!'

Neither of them said anything for a few moments and then Madeleine tried to put it in perspective. 'Have you considered paranoia? He was probably just some weirdo who gets off from photographing couples.'

'Maybe,' Tom agreed, but events were beginning to distort his view of the world and to some small extent her question was well timed.

'Come on,' Madeleine added. 'We can sort this out. Let's get the picnic stuff and go and see the beach.'

They walked back to the oak tree, but as each cloud came by so Madeleine taunted Tom to chase her and the clouds again and again. By the time they'd reached the tree, they were both well out of breath and laughing almost continuously.

They packed up their things and strolled back down towards the car tossing the hamper into the back. With Madeleine making the most of the conversation and giggling at her more serious husband, they then meandered hand in hand along the beach looking out across the water and listening to the lapping sound of the soft swell of the sea.

Before too long they returned to the car with Madeleine driving them back home. Tom noticed the cloud shadows as they raced across the fields and looking over at Madeleine every now and again, he smiled as he reminisced over what they'd been doing only a short time earlier.

DEADLY RENDEZVOUS

The following day, Madeleine rose early, as Tom soon found. When he rolled over in bed and reached out, there was nobody there, but there was a vaguely warm patch instead.

He got dressed and then made his way downstairs and saw that Madeleine had already got the coffee brewing: so helping himself to a cup, he followed the noises coming from the clicking keys of their laptop computer, until he tracked her down in the lounge.

'Hiya sleepy head,' she said, smiling at him, 'I've been looking for news reports in the papers. With some success too—I'm afraid.'

'How? I mean, what have you found?' Tom replied, sitting beside her on the sofa.

'From the web,' she said, pointing at the screen, with a serious look.

Tom placed his coffee on the table and looked at the laptop display. It was showing web pages of recent articles from a newspaper based in Basingstoke. One of the stories was about Steve Mills—a colleague of Tom's who had been a programmer on the Elektra software development team.

'Can you see the screen okay?' she asked him, watching Tom peering at it.

'Yes thanks,' he half answered as he continued reading the article.

It detailed a car accident, where his associate's car had been found in a ditch and completely gutted by fire damage. The police hadn't yet found a cause for the accident, but burned remains were found in the wreckage, after a fire crew had managed to douse the flames.

Tom looked at Madeleine as he confirmed what she already knew from reading it a few minutes earlier. 'It is true then, at least this one. The car was on fire and there seems to have been no other vehicle involved.' Tom read further. 'According to the police there were no skid marks, or adverse road conditions, and the impact didn't seem to justify a cause of ignition. I wonder how they know that?' Tom was really thinking aloud and didn't expect an answer.

'Forensic science,' came the reply from Madeleine. 'Remember. The police see these all the time, much more so than you or I at least. So it's safe to assume they used their expert opinion based on a lot of experience.'

'So why did it burn, or burst into flames? Why did Steve have to die?' Tom added in some disbelief. 'It's not sinking in. It's too much too soon. I can't visualize being at the office with seeing Steve there, laughing and joking the way he always used to— annoying us all.'

Pausing momentarily, Tom stopped thinking about himself and his thoughts went to Steve's family. 'When's the funeral?'

Madeleine pointed at the screen. 'This all happened two weeks ago on the day after you left for South Africa, the 27th July. No doubt the funeral has already been done.'

Tom raised one eyebrow and nodded slowly, as he thought about it.

'So why didn't anyone at the office tell me?' he asked, not really expecting an answer.

Madeleine shrugged her shoulders, not knowing what to say.

'Shall we try and find out about the other two?' she asked him gently. 'I think it's important.'

'Yes,' replied Tom, very distracted by the news, knowing now that it was true.

'Try Martin next if you can; he died at home apparently and he lives… or I should perhaps say he lived in Swindon.'

Madeleine turned towards her husband and placed a hand on his knee. 'I know that you know…' she stopped, 'that is, knew him quite well, but we'll solve this thing, if there's anything to solve.' She smiled at him to give him some reassurance. Strangely though Tom wasn't in fear of his own life: not even in the slightest way. He was consumed by his thoughts of how to guarantee Madeleine's safety.

'I know the odds are against it,' she continued, 'but just because of that it doesn't mean something is impossible. When I was a girl I used to wonder what the odds were of all the teachers telephoning in sick to school on the same day.'

'Really?' said Tom frowning and smiling in disbelief, 'you do have some funny thoughts.'

She raised both eyebrows at him as though to say, 'what's wrong with that?' but before she could actually begin to speak Tom continued. 'Did you ever calculate the answer?'

'No,' she replied. 'I always assumed that I couldn't be that lucky. But no matter how great the odds were against it happening, it was always possible. And that's the point. So even if three of your colleagues have died, it doesn't necessarily follow that something sinister lies behind it. It may have just happened. There are long odds against it, I know. But nevertheless it's still within the bounds of what's possible.'

Again Tom nodded. But he was unconvinced and he flashed her a glance that reinforced his view. Then as if to try and mask his feelings he stood and picking up his coffee for a sip, he began to look out of the patio doors at the vibrancy of the plants and flowers in their garden, attempting to reconcile his reality— all the safe things he was familiar with and relied on to confirm the universe was in order—with the reality now being thrust on him. It just wasn't sinking in. It didn't seem real to Tom the two worlds didn't mesh together.

His attention was pulled back to the sound of Madeleine typing. Tracking down the web site for the local newspaper in

Swindon, she scanned through days of news entries until she found one dated Wednesday 6th August 2008.

'It's here,' she said reluctantly.

Tom sat down beside her as she read out the report.

'Martin Tunbridge was found dead at home just before dawn this morning police reported today. The alarm was sounded by a neighbour, who was woken in the early hours by a noise sounding like a door crashing closed in his own house. The neighbour investigated, and on walking outside into his own back garden, noticed smoke pouring out of the back door of Mr Tunbridge's kitchen. Fire, ambulance and police were called but Mr Tunbridge was pronounced dead at the scene. No one else was involved. Police and fire officers are working on a theory that there was a gas leak that caused the blast and subsequent fire.'

Madeleine stopped and turned to look at Tom.

'How did Jim die?' she asked softly.

Tom now had a far away look in his eyes, just staring ahead of him. His face muscles had relaxed and he appeared expressionless, almost trance-like. Remaining motionless for a few more moments, the only sounds breaking the silence being the whirring noise of the computer's fan and the coffee maker still dripping in the kitchen and sizzling as each drop hit the hot plate beneath.

'In a boat,' Tom answered, still trying to come to terms with this onslaught of news.

'What was his surname? And where was the accident? Do you know?' Madeleine asked.

'His surname is...' Tom stopped and corrected himself '... was, Alexander.'

He leaned back in the settee, gazing into the distance and holding the coffee cup with his left hand he placed it on his left thigh to steady it. 'It was near his home in Southampton. The Solent perhaps,' he added.

Madeleine began typing and soon enough she'd tracked down a shipping report for the Tuesday eleven days earlier dated 29th July 2008.

'I think I've found it,' she said.

As the web page loaded on the screen, they huddled forward again, reading through the report.

Jim Alexander, his wife and two children had been killed in what was described as a freak accident. Flames were seen from a nearby yacht, following an explosion on board his cabin cruiser. The debris was limited to small parts of the hull, that themselves had been subjected to intense heat from a fire. No bodies were found. The only eyewitness thought he'd heard two explosions, the second one fractionally after the first, but admitted that he may have misheard it, or it could have been an echo of the sound bouncing off the Isle of Wight. But there was no one else nearby.

'Three for three,' Tom commented.

'Yes,' replied Madeleine. 'But think about these one at a time. Steve was in a car and there was no evidence that he had been in a collision.'

'Yes,' replied Tom, 'but a bullet hole or a being driven off the road by a larger vehicle wouldn't necessarily leave much evidence.'

'Okay,' said Madeleine. 'Let's do it your way. Instead of me trying to prove they were accidents, why don't you try and prove they were murders. All of them mind, not just one or two, but all three. If you can't do that then there's a good chance that they were accidental, wouldn't you say?'

'Okay,' said Tom, standing once more with his coffee and then pacing up and down.

'Steve could have had his car tyres shot by a gunman,' he began, 'or he could have been driven off the road.'

Madeleine thought about this.

'For his car tyres to have been shot then the man would have needed to have known that he would have been on that road;

and he would have needed to recognise him and take aim, to hit a small moving target. Why not just shoot him at home or somewhere where he was a bigger more stationary target. No. Shooting isn't reasonable.'

'Okay,' Tom replied, 'and if he'd been driven off the road then there ought to be marks on the car, unless the other vehicle had exactly the same paint colour. Again, that's an awful lot of trouble just to kill someone, when it could have been done much more easily.'

'Accident then?' Madeleine asked.

'Probably,' Tom nodded resignedly but not with complete belief. 'What about Jim and his family?'

'Can't have been a shooting,' Madeleine remarked.

'Why not?' Tom asked unconvinced.

Madeleine began to think out loud. 'Well the marksman probably had to shoot the fuel tank in the boat for them all to die. Remember the whole boat exploded and according to the eyewitness, he was the closest to the boat and he thought he heard two bangs but couldn't be sure.'

'And a rifle shot is very distinctive,' Tom added.

'How do you know?' Madeleine asked with a puzzled look on her face.

'It's in those old cowboy films. Rifles always have a ring to them, I suppose it's due to their long barrel.'

'It sounds like sabotage was the only possibility,' said Madeleine, 'but if so then the saboteur was very clever with the boat at sea a long way from witnesses when it happened.'

'But why kill the whole family,' Tom asked. 'If it was deliberate then that was unnecessary surely?'

'It was certainly messy from a murderer's point of view. But effective,' Madeleine added.

'How about a bomb on the boat, detonated by remote control?' Tom suggested.

'No,' replied Madeleine. 'That's not good enough. It would explain the two bangs, but the murderer would have to be sure that Jim was on the boat and the bomb could have been detonated anywhere once they had put to out sea. Remember in these circumstances the murderer—if there was one—didn't care about innocent bystanders. So he or she would have been confident of the kill once they'd seen Jim get aboard. They could have then just blown the boat up straight away.'

Tom nodded again.

'Accident then?' Madeleine asked.

'Accident,' Tom paused. 'Probably. So how about Martin?'

'Gas leak? What's wrong with that?' Madeleine suggested.

'Nothing at all and yet everything,' Tom replied, stopping dead in his tracks. 'We're missing something here I'm sure. We must be. It doesn't feel right.'

'And you with your logic too,' Madeleine remarked. 'It may not feel right, but the science is okay. They each had a rendezvous with death that wasn't fate but was accidental. Besides, to prove murder, shouldn't there be a motive?'

'Yes,' Tom replied turning to stare out to the garden once again, 'and that's a problem. I feel certain that the motive is staring me in the face. What's happened now is that only Geoff Abbot and myself know anything about the Elektra software.'

Tom paused again. 'Selway suggested that Geoff was going to sell it along with the French software—Vitesse Acquise 4. But firstly he doesn't necessarily have a copy of it; because the whole idea was that the two companies wouldn't have access to each other's software; and even if he did have both parts then he wouldn't need the developers to be dead.'

Madeleine then finally sided with him. 'Still, someone thought there was a connection, because that's why you were contacted in the first place. So what happens next?'

'You've just solved it,' declared Tom with increasing certainty.

'What?' replied Madeleine, 'I've solved what?'

'The entire thing,' said Tom.

'It's obvious that they're murders.'

'Why?'

'Because…' he stopped momentarily and raised his hand to cover his eyes to focus his thoughts again, 'It's gone!' he added in annoyance. He placed the now empty coffee cup on the table nearby. 'Now what was that thought process again?' he said aloud to himself, as he paced up and down the room. 'It was something you said,' he added 'something about someone else seeing a connection, what was it you said?'

Madeleine tried to remember her exact words. 'Someone thought there was a connection, because that's why they contacted you.'

'Exactly!' declared Tom. 'It's not the part about someone else thinking there was a connection, it was the part about me being contacted.'

'And?' Madeleine asked eagerly awaiting illumination.

'48 hours,' Tom muttered to himself.

'What about it?' Madeleine asked.

Tom shook his head as if to try and clear his thoughts because they weren't quite coming out right.

'It was something Bob Selway said on the plane. I didn't query it at the time, but he said something about me being dead within 48 hours.'

'What if he did?' Madeleine asked now puzzled.

'You're the scientist,' Tom remarked.

'Yes,' Madeleine replied, 'but even scientists need evidence we can't just use guesswork. Give me something more to work with.'

Tom stood in front of her now with his arms folded and began to think carefully about Bob Selway's approach to him.

'When I went upstairs on the plane, it was empty apart from Bob. No one spoke to me so I turned around and began to walk back downstairs when he said, 'come in number four, your time is up,' he then carried on and asked me how I would approach someone to tell them that their life was at risk and the person in question would be dead within 48 hours.'

Madeleine sat thinking about this for a few moments weighing up what Tom had said before she spoke. 'You're sure that he said 48 hours, that he actually said the man would be dead within 48 hours?'

Tom nodded.

'What you're saying is that you believe that he told you his exact problem.'

Tom nodded again.

'That he asked you how to tell you that you would be dead within 48 hours?'

'That's right,' Tom replied still in deep thought.

Madeleine paused for a few moments to reflect on this again. Finally after much thought and wrestling with herself over the evidence, trying not to make too much or too little of it she answered.

'You want to know how he was able to say that he knew you'd be dead within 48 hours.'

'Yes,' Tom replied moving back to the settee and sitting down. 'In my business small details make a big difference. When I left Bob I felt sure there was something else I should have asked him but I didn't know what. This has been nagging at me ever since.'

'What does it mean?' Madeleine asked him.

'I don't know,' Tom told her, 'but could it be that Selway knows the killer or has hired…or in fact is the killer. The issue about Steve, Jim and Martin is unhelpful other than to suggest a pattern: three deaths, which in reality are three murders. It seems to me that Bob Selway didn't tell me everything he knew.'

'Perhaps he said too much and he didn't want to panic you.' Madeleine added, not sure herself of whether Tom was in mortal danger. 'But if he is the killer then why would he warn you? Why would he meet with you? Why not just kill you on the way home? Meeting you must surely clear him of suspicion.'

Tom thought about this and nodded slowly.

'So Bob Selway knows something, but he's not the killer.'

Madeleine nodded this time. 'What there anything else?'

Tom looked distracted. 'Yes,' he paused, 'the 48 hours. How does he know the time frame? Was it a guess, a mistake or a lie perhaps? Perhaps he's got the suspect under surveillance and tracking him, or them.' Tom added, 'maybe that's why he did nothing on the plane, but told me to wait until I was contacted.'

'Or maybe the 48 hours is the quirky thing that he apologised for. Perhaps he just wanted you on side quickly to reduce the risk of you getting killed,' Madeleine remarked thinking aloud.

Tom nodded but now he had more questions.

'So what should we do?' Madeleine asked him.

'We wait and see if I get contacted again. Until then we act normally.' Tom answered still deep in thought.

'You mean like a pair of fools, like we usually do?' Madeleine asked with a mischievous smile trying to change Tom's mood, but only because of her own fears about his safety.

Tom smiled too. 'You're mad!' he softly remonstrated as she stood. He got up to stand with her and placed his arms around her waist clasping his hands behind her. 'I'm not mad,' she replied. 'I'm Madeleine! Haven't you grasped that yet?'

They looked into each other's eyes for a few moments not saying anything but each wondering how long they would be with the other.

Madeleine spoke first.

'When's the 48 hours up?'

'Tonight,' Tom replied. 'If I want to be pedantic, it's by a quarter to one tomorrow morning. But I don't know how accurate Bob Selway was being. It could be anytime really. Even if we get past the 48 hours, who's to say we'll be free and clear?'

'We're not exactly difficult to find,' Madeleine remarked, as her look changed back to a more serious one, the concern showing in her eyes.

'But perhaps difficult to get to: I have been overseas—Abbot knew that so in some respects he's off the hook too.' Tom added.

'You can't be certain of that.' Madeleine suggested, before continuing. 'All this speculation is getting us nowhere. What we need is more information. How do you think you'll be contacted?'

'I don't actually know,' Tom replied raising his eyebrows and shaking his head, 'someone could visit, or I could get an e-mail or simply a phone call.'

'Well in that case,' Madeleine added, 'have you switched on your cell phone since you've been back? I know you didn't take it, because you didn't think it would work in South Africa, but you may as well do it now hadn't you?'

'I don't see the point,' Tom remarked. 'It's a company phone and I don't want any company calls. Not until I go back to work anyway.'

'If you go back,' she corrected him, stressing the word 'if'. 'But it's not just for business calls. You may as well use it. After all there may be a message on there for you.'

Tom hunted around for it, and found it in his favourite casual jacket that was hanging on a coat hook in the hallway. He switched on the phone, but there were no messages. It was a small compact Nokia and as a general rule he detested carrying cell phones, but he placed it back in the jacket anyway, as he couldn't be bothered to find a more permanent home for it. He returned to the lounge and before he could say anything else, an e-mail arrived at the laptop, heralded by a pinging noise.

The two of them turned to look at the screen together and sitting down, Tom moved the laptop in his direction and selected the mail room option. Madeleine sat beside him, perfectly still, in anticipation.

The new message's title appeared at the top of the list. It was now a familiar phrase to Tom and it read. 'Come in number four'.

They looked at each other.

'Open it,' Madeleine urged him with some anxiety in her voice.

But Tom had already started to double click the touch pad, he needed no prompting. The e-mail opened.

'If you wish to make sure you're not number four then come to the Lamb and Flag at 17:00 today'. There was no sign-off but there was an attached map. Opening the attachment, Tom could see the location, east of Swindon.

'I know this place,' he said. 'I've been there before.'

Returning to the e-mail, Tom looked for the originating address.

'It's from a dot gov dot uk site,' he declared.

'So it's genuine?' Madeleine asked.

'Who knows?' he replied, 'now all I have to do is decide whether or not I'll go. Could it be a trap?'

'No. It won't be a trap,' Madeleine replied, pointing at the screen. 'It's a public place and we have evidence of where the e-mail came from. Besides which, we have the problem that if you don't go, you might become number four and you'll wonder when exactly that will happen: for the rest of your life maybe.'

'Only for the next few hours,' Tom remarked. 'After all, the 48 hours will be up by then.'

Madeleine shook her head at him vigorously, tears welling up in her eyes. 'No you don't,' she said, her voice beginning to falter. 'We have to find out what's happening.'

It was clear that she was deeply concerned, not just about Tom's long-term safety, but also about the meeting. She looked into his eyes and spoke more gently. 'You take care now. If anything happens to you I'll beat you up.'

Tom smiled from one side of his mouth and Madeleine buried her head into his chest as they embraced again. This time though, Tom cuddled her and kept her close to him.

'I don't want to go either. But as you said, we have to find out what's happening.' He paused momentarily and looked down at her head, but her face was still buried, trying to hide the tears from him.

'Promise me this,' he continued, 'if anything does happen to me, promise me that you'll leave here and go and stay with your parents, or a friend, or someone that you know but haven't seen for ages. Just get away from here.'

Madeleine was silent. Fear had engulfed her as the reality of the situation began to build. Eventually she lifted her head and looked at Tom again, playing with the feel of his hand, her eyes were still glassy. 'No matter where you are we're a couple, do you understand?'

'What do you mean by that?' Tom asked her gently not wishing to sound stupid.

'Wherever you are I'm going to be there too,' Madeleine answered.

'I'm not sure I follow what you're saying,' Tom continued.

She shook back the hair from her face and through tearful eyes she looked at him seriously as she spoke.

'I can't live on my own and I won't.'

He looked at her, waiting for her to elaborate.

'When you leave this world I want to leave with you, so that we'll never be apart, not even in death.'

Tom leaned his head back slightly and frowned but the words burned their way into his memory. He smiled and kissed her. 'I love you,' he said softly, 'and I've no intention of leaving you at all—ever.'

He looked at his watch and checking the time he commented, 'barbecue?' Wiping her eyes and sitting upright she remarked, 'what, now? In the morning?'

'Yes,' he said, 'why not? We can sit and watch a chicken on the rotisserie until it's burned to a frazzle.'

Getting up from the settee, he opened the patio doors and said. 'Okay. Now where's that lighter fuel?'

Tom spent the next fifteen minutes setting up the barbecue. This was a ritual that almost had a purpose in itself without the need for food to be cooked. He lit the charcoal, having carefully arranged it and the two of them had a long and slow lunch of odds and ends, waiting for and watching a whole chicken burn to a crisp. Tom could never quite get the timing right and as always it ended up being over cooked—just to be on the safe side. This in fact usually made it thoroughly inedible. So it had become a tradition just to watch it burn to a cinder, without actually eating it, even though it wasn't the intended goal.

Finally the time had arrived for him to leave. They spoke few words: almost everything passing between them being said by looks alone. He held Madeleine and kissed her, each one wondering whether they'd see the other again. Then he gently released her as she extended her arms, almost not letting go and he walked out of the house. Grabbing his favourite casual jacket on the way, he tossed it into his car and reversing out of the drive, he roared off waving briefly at Madeleine as he did so.

She remained rooted to the spot until the car had turned out of view. Wondering whether either of them were under surveillance she remained stationary for some time. Then finally dropping her gaze she ambled back in doors.

Tom had taken the opportunity of writing down a brief list of directions, but they weren't so complicated that he couldn't remember them.

He headed north and east towards the M4 and then getting off just east of Swindon, he proceeded along a dual carriageway until he found the road that led to the pub. He still had a number of miles to go but it was an 'A' class road and was easily negotiated.

The thought crossed his mind that he might die the same way that Steve Mills had, and because of this, he was more alert than usual of other cars and vehicles. He eliminated the thought in his own mind of a marksman trying to shoot out his tyres. Now that he was driving, this seemed too far-fetched to be true, although the pub could only be reached by this one long road, and if the gunman were near the pub, then that might have been a possibility.

Tom dismissed that thought too though, because if a gunman were to be that close to the pub, then Tom would be driving much slower and therefore have much more chance of controlling the car with a blown out tyre.

These ideas soon evaporated when Tom caught sight of the pub in the distance as he drove over the brow of a hill. He indicated to pull into the car park and as he parked, he noticed that he was still a few minutes early. But he reached for his jacket and taking it, he got out of the car, slung the jacket over his shoulder and pointing his keys at the car, he pressed the fob and was given the confirmatory signal from the car's indicators that it was locked.

There were other vehicles already there, but only a handful. There was a Ford with someone sat inside reading a newspaper. This looked familiar Tom thought, but he wasn't sure why. After a few moments he realised that it had looked like the man that he and Madeleine had seen the previous day reading the paper at the beach car park.

A few parking bays away from Tom's Audi was a silver Mercedes. It was a new model and fairly majestic in its own way, exuding power with every curve of its expensive looking body.

Tom sauntered across to the pub door, he lifted the latch and pushing open the door, it creaked as he walked in.

At the far end of the bar was a log fire roaring away, which was particularly strange as it was August and very warm outside. There was an old couple sitting near the fire, working their way through a dish of food each. Near to them were three men in their early twenties drinking and talking and laughing. A young couple sat nearby with a large golden retriever tethered to the bench. The man was feeding peanuts to the dog, from his hand.

At the bar was a man in his forties dressed in a sports jacket that had leather elbow patches. He had dark hair, a slight paunch and was apparently struggling with a crossword or so it appeared to Tom. He was leaning on the bar scrutinising a folded newspaper laid out in front of him on the bar's surface, gently stabbing his chin with the button of a ball point pen, repeatedly clicking it as he did so. The man stopped the action with the pen as he tried to evade smoke from his own burning cigarette, by moving his head back, wincing and screwing up his eyes slightly.

He looked over at Tom briefly. Tom wondered whether his contact was there already and stepped across to the bar to be served.

The publican was elderly and severe looking. Tom ordered a pint of Guinness and paying for it, he straddled a bar stool and checked his watch.

The man at the far end of the bar stubbed out his cigarette and picking up his pint glass, gulped down the remainder of his drink. Then, grabbing his newspaper and pen, he walked across to Tom and placed the paper on the bar next to him.

Tom looked at the man, who by now had held out his hand. 'My name is Norman King. I work for Bob Selway. It's a pleasure to meet you Mr Brady.'

Tom shook the man's hand and the man gestured to a table close to the window. Tom got off the stool, picked up his drink and followed. As they sat, a noisy group of people entered the bar.

'Fortuitous,' Norman said as he shuffled around and unfolded the newspaper. 'There shouldn't be too many people listening in.'

Tom said nothing for a few moments while he looked the man over. In every respect there seemed to be normality, yet Tom sensed that there could be a sinister edge to the man sitting opposite him—a dark side that yielded nothing of its nature, unless he were to be pushed to a given point.

Breaking the silence between them, Norman continued in a swift yet powerful voice. There was a definite sense of presence to him that carried unquestioning authority. For many people Tom realised that they would feel compelled to carry out his instructions, merely from the way in which he spoke. 'My friends call me Bill. I know that sounds odd but it's true.' Still Tom remained silent.

Bill leaned back in the chair. 'As you're here, can I assume that you are convinced that you're colleagues deaths were murder?' He looked around briefly—making subtle eye movements only—as the words left his mouth, in case he'd been overheard. But the noise level was high enough for his comments to have gone unnoticed by anyone else in the bar.

'You can assume that you have my interest. I checked about their deaths as Bob Selway suggested, and I know that part is true,' Tom replied. 'But what do you want from me?'

'I want you alive and protected,' Bill answered, now taking out a cigarette and lighting it. 'Do you mind?' he casually added, referring to the cigarette. Tom shook his head as if the question was not just irrelevant but also an unnecessary intrusion on the conversation. Although he wondered how this was allowed in public places believing it to have been banned.

'I don't know how much Bob told you, but he and I work for the treasury and we've had information about Geoff Abbot for some time now. Particularly that he's got a spiralling debt problem and an expensive habit.' Bill produced a photograph from inside the folds of the newspaper and continued. 'Do you know this woman?'

Tom looked at the picture. 'Yes,' he replied. 'That's Vicky, or rather Victoria Kennedy. She's the office receptionist.'

Bill nodded. 'She's also Abbot's sleeping partner, when he's not sharing his bed with his wife. Which, according to our information, is now hardly ever.'

'And your point?' Tom asked.

'Any man that cheats on his wife can't be trusted with state secrets,' Bill added.

Tom frowned. 'That's a bit harsh wouldn't you say? But anyway, he doesn't have any state secrets. Does he?'

Bill leaned back and looked Tom in the eyes. 'You've had security clearance before haven't you?' Tom nodded. 'Then,' continued Bill, 'you know that you can have any sexual orientation you like, but secret trysts or affairs aren't allowed. Have a mistress. That's fine. Have six if you like, but your wife has to know. You know that and so does Abbot.'

'So tell his wife,' Tom remarked.

'We don't actually care if his wife knows or not, it's the fact that any man with such a secret can be blackmailed and we think that Abbot is going to try and sell Elektra along with Vitesse Acquise 4—the French software—to an eastern European government.'

Tom waited for further information but he didn't have to wait long.

'Frankly, my department views these recent deaths as highly suspicious, even though we can't yet prove murder. Our suspicions were first aroused because we thought that the deaths might have been a method of demonstrating to Abbot that he was vulnerable. Now we believe that someone is systematically wiping out all the expertise in Exterra—your company—that can work on or develop the software further.' Bill stopped briefly to take a puff on his cigarette.

'We know that you're the last person—other than Abbot— who knows anything about the software, so we can't afford to have you killed too. Something sinister is going on here and if you die, her majesty's government could be held to ransom over its own software.'

'Why?' Tom asked. 'Get a copy of the source code and give it to another company. Where's the problem?'

'We don't have the source,' Bill continued. 'It's gone missing and even if we found it, we wouldn't recognise it from a program to predict the lottery.'

'You want me to find it for you then?' said Tom.

'Not really,' Bill answered now stubbing out his smoked cigarette, 'we'll find it and when we do, we'll want you to confirm what it is.'

'But I can't,' Tom replied. 'I only worked on it briefly and that was some time ago. If you merely find an old version then I wouldn't be able to tell the difference between that and the latest version.'

Bill thought about this for a few moments before continuing. 'The software is delivered to us in what has been called executable format? If that means anything to you, so we have that. Does that help?'

'Yes,' replied Tom. 'If we could get the source then it can be compiled and checked against the executable version you have. If the executable from the compiled output matches yours, then it's the right source. But any competent programmer could do that for you.'

Bill saw the validity of Tom's argument but there was a hole in what he'd said. 'We need someone we can trust, who is security cleared that can actually look at the program code and recognise it. I'd say that limits us to someone who has worked on this.'

'Okay,' said Tom. 'But what about the murders? If they are murders. How are you going to stop me from being number four? And more importantly I want my wife protected.'

'No problem,' said Bill. 'Even as we speak I've arranged protection for Madeleine. Around the clock, she won't even know it's there.'

'So what do you want me to do now?' Tom asked. 'Is that it? Do I just go home and go back to work again as usual?'

'No,' replied Bill, 'that won't work. It's far too risky and we believe that you'll be dead if you do carry on as normal, that's why we need you here tonight.'

'So what do I do then?' Tom asked again.

'First I have to know. Are you with us?' Bill asked him.

Tom looked out of the window and thought for a few moments. Then he looked back and answered 'What do I have to lose?'

'Your life,' Bill replied.

'Possibly,' said Tom.

'No,' Bill continued, 'definitely.'

Tom's face took on a puzzled look.

Bill looked down briefly and took out another cigarette and lit it. He kept it in his lips as he spoke. 'There's only one safe way to stop someone, anyone in fact, from trying to kill you. If you agree to this there's no going back. Ever.'

'What do you mean?' Tom asked, now looking suspiciously at Bill.

Bill said nothing for a few moments and then still with the cigarette in his mouth he answered. 'If you agree to help, then Tom Brady dies tonight.'

Tom let the words sink in, but gradually he could see the sense of it. Bill elaborated slightly and added. 'You'll be given a new identity that will be yours for the rest of your life. You won't be able to be Tom Brady again.'

'Okay,' he said, 'but Madeleine is going to be safe isn't she?'

'Yes,' Bill replied, 'but there's something else.'

'What?' Tom asked.

'For your safety and hers she can't know,' Bill replied.

'Can't know what?' Tom said, somewhat more concerned.

'She can't know that you're really still alive but with a new identity. There's a leak—we believe—and if Madeleine were told that you're okay, that may put you at risk again.'

Tom realised the impact that his 'death' would have on Madeleine. He knew that she may never forgive him when he got to see her again, but most of all he knew she would be desperately heartbroken.

He agonised over the decision, wanting to tell her somehow that he wasn't really going to die. His thoughts returned to the possibility of just walking out, but then Madeleine's safety would be placed at risk. But he couldn't put her through it.

'There has to be another way,' he said unyieldingly.

Bill shrugged his shoulders.

'Give me another way,' Tom insisted.

'We're too far in and they're too close,' Bill insisted.

Tom looked down at the table, closed his eyes briefly and then began to stand as he opened his eyes again.

'I can't do it,' he said and then turned towards the door as Bill slowly leaned back in his chair.

Tom walked out and noticed a large van parked next to the driver's side of his car. He walked slowly towards it with a heavy heart, feeling that he'd just done the wrong thing. What he wanted was for both him and Madeleine to be whisked away. He couldn't go alone.

He drew up to the side of his car and unlocked it. His hand made contact with the outer door at the same instant that a cloth-covered hand was placed over his mouth and he heard the van door being slid open just before he was bundled into it. His keys were wrenched from his hand and the door of the van was slammed closed from the outside. His eyes adjusted to the light and all he could see was a man in black standing over him with a gun pointing at his head.

'Time to die,' said the figure.

MAN WITHOUT A PAST

The gunman held on to the inside of the van as it began moving. Tom couldn't understand why he hadn't been shot yet, but he was still being held firmly by a second man whose grip didn't loosen.

In a matter of minutes the van began to lurch more violently as they turned onto a dirt track. He estimated that they'd only covered about a mile since leaving the pub. Then the driver switched off the engine and following voices from the outside, the van door slid back.

Bill gestured at the standing figure who handed him the gun. Tom tried to struggle free from his captor, but Bill aimed the gun at his head and pulled the trigger.

The metallic click made Tom jump. But the gun wasn't loaded.

'It would be just that easy,' Bill remarked, 'if we'd wanted you dead.'

Tom didn't know what to think, his heart was racing and he was angry with himself at being caught so easily.

Bill took out his cell phone and placed a call.

'Keep the line open, our man is about to decide whether he wants his wife to enjoy our protection.'

Bill flashed a glance at the man holding Tom who then released his grip.

'You're no good to us dead,' Bill added as he passed the gun back to its owner.

'What's it to be? Are you a willing recruit who wants our protection for his wife, or are you going to try and escape, forcing us to leave her to whatever fate your hunter has for you?'

Tom said nothing, leaving Bill to try and add weight to his own argument.

'Can you protect her?' he asked, his eyes almost burning into Tom as though it was a foregone conclusion that Tom couldn't.

Still Tom remained silent, although clearly struggling with the choice that lay before him, uneasy with both options.

'They haven't missed yet and I know I can keep her safe, but it's got to be done my way,' Bill added with increasing intensity.

Tom needed no reassurance regarding what Bill was or was not capable of, and as he looked around at the men standing with him, he realised that Bill had indeed helped him, if only by taking most of the decision away from him. He did briefly wonder whether his three dead colleagues had faced the same situation and had all said no. The ease with which Tom's captors had acted and secured his abduction was the overwhelming influencing factor. The previous few minutes had meant that the decision had been made a lot easier for him, which was now more apparent from his noticeably less strained appearance. Then, after a few more moments struggling with his conscience regarding Madeleine, and the fact that she would soon believe he was going to be dead, he relented.

'I'm with you,' Tom finally sighed, feeling slightly sickened as the words left his mouth.

'Move in now,' Bill said speaking into the phone. At that moment the other men began working industriously in a clearly well organized fashion to a plan that Tom had no knowledge of whatsoever.

'I want your wallet, your watch and other personal items please,' Bill demanded clicking his fingers at a bewildered Tom.

'Why should I?' Tom remonstrated.

'Think of it as a mugging,' said Bill, 'I can use real bullets if you wish,' he added cynically glancing at the pistol.

Tom said nothing but handed over the items and stood up to step out of the van. He caught sight of the Mercedes parked directly behind and at the rear was his own car. Tom's heart began to race. Was this it? He thought to himself. He turned to look at Bill.

Bill smiled and placed a hand on his shoulder.

'I know how strange this must all look. But if you want Madeleine to live you must agree not to contact her. Not until this business is over. If she finds out that you're still alive then you may have signed her death warrant. Do you understand?'

Tom nodded, 'yes,' he said quietly.

Bill glanced at him and then at the activity taking place around Tom's car. They were on a track parallel to the main road and what looked like a dead body was being loaded into his Audi.

'Don't worry. It has to look realistic. You can't just disappear.' Bill gestured at the car.

'What are they doing?' Tom asked.

'They're about to complete the illusion.' Bill replied. Seeing the look of concern on Tom's face, he tried to elaborate without making it sound too criminal and without scaring him into flight. 'Unidentified dead bodies arrive in most major mortuaries around the country. We have to put one in your car with your things; wallet, watch etc. Ideally, the body will be a close match for you in age, weight and origin; prepared before hand so that he won't look too dissimilar from you.'

'But anyone who checks will see it's not me if they know me,' Tom exclaimed as though Bill hadn't thought of this.

'As it stands currently,' replied Bill, 'but burned beyond recognition is exactly that. The only way to identify the body will be from dental records, and we've done our homework there too. They've already been changed.'

'You assumed I would agree then,' said a puzzled Tom, 'but why?'

'We didn't. But I couldn't take no for an answer. Even so, even if we had accepted your answer and you somehow evaded murder, then one day your dentist would find your records were badly out of line and would merely redraw them. There's nothing sinister in that is there?'

Tom was impressed that Bill had thought of so much in advance, and realised the preparation that had gone into this venture was a lot greater that he might have first imagined.

He could see the dead man sitting in the driving seat of his Audi. Bill's helpers—as Tom thought of them—began to pour petrol around it, and leaning inside the driver's window one of them restarted the car's engine. Another man was crouching by the front passenger side wheel and had been letting the air out of the tyre, apparently with a screwdriver type device, just stuck in the valve. Then, when the tyre was flat he took out a large hunting knife and began to carve chunks out of it.

Bill gestured to Tom to follow him to the Mercedes and to get in the back with him. Meanwhile one of the men preparing the Audi returned to the Mercedes and got in. Bill merely introduced him as Roger.

After the introductions, Roger started the engine and he then turned the car to face in the opposite direction and began driving back towards the main road. As they passed the Audi, Tom looked back at the van. The driver had already turned it around and the front passenger door was open.

Having now made significant gashes to the tyre on Tom's car, the man lit the spilled petrol and ran to the awaiting van and leapt in, quickly slamming the door shut, moments before the van accelerated away leaving a cloud of dust from its spinning rear wheels.

The Mercedes had by then returned to the main road. They'd travelled about six hundred yards when there was an almighty explosion. Tom turned around in his seat to see flames dancing above the hedge and already a plume of black smoke was rising up beyond it.

'Now you're number four,' Bill commented, 'but don't worry, we've got a new identity for you.'

Tom's mind wandered to his dead colleagues. 'Is it possible that one or more of the others went through what I just went through?' he asked Bill.

'Not from our doing,' he replied, 'although the bodies were either unrecognisable or just not recovered, so at least one of them could still be alive. But if someone did that, they would need a great deal of resources.'

'An inside job then?' queried Tom.

'Not necessarily,' Bill replied. 'We didn't do anything that was particularly special. That part could have been done by competent outsiders, the next bit gets tougher, although still not impossible for outsiders.

For the moment we haven't even entertained the idea that one of your dead colleagues could still be alive. If we were to consider it, then I don't know which one I would choose, if I had to choose just one. Perhaps all three are still alive, but I find that difficult to believe. We have to proceed with facts and evidence. There are no facts to support such a theory and no evidence, let alone proof.'

Tom was still curious about the possibility of Jim, Martin or Steve still being alive, so he neatly filed the thought away for future reference.

Bill reached into the magazine compartment of the driver's seat in front of him and pulled out a whole series of items from inside a thick padded A4 envelope.

'You'll be needing some new papers and identity,' Bill remarked as he poured the contents on his lap. He handed Tom a new passport. 'This is who you are from now on. I only came up with the surname. It was chosen as something forgettable.'

Tom opened the passport and looking at the picture, he could see that it was a recent one of himself, taken from a security database from the MoD, he thought to himself and underneath was the name, 'Michael Pierson'. Bill looked at him whilst he studied the photograph. 'Get used to it Mike.' Still holding the Passport, Tom now tried to think of himself as Mike Pierson. 'It'll do,' he said, thinking to himself that at least he wasn't going to suffer a series of traumatic encounters as the result of a strange name.

'Why 'Pierson'?' he asked Bill, 'spelled in this way?' he added showing the passport to Bill.

'A play on words,' Bill smirked. Pierson looked on puzzled, but Bill continued. 'You'll probably have to spell it to everyone you meet. That will add to the authenticity and help you remember it.'

Pierson looked at the home address but didn't recognise it. He wondered if it was real and whether that's where they were heading now.

'Is this where we're going?' Pierson asked turning the passport to Bill with his thumb under the address as a pointer.

'No,' replied Bill. 'You're a man without a past, so were not going to expose you by placing you where someone might look.'

Pierson looked at the address again. The house had a name and not a number and the village name looked familiar, even though the road name wasn't: but he didn't know why. There was too much going on in his head.

Bill passed a large piece of paper to him. 'You're wife's name is Hilary. Your date of birth has changed and I'm afraid you're slightly older now as is Madeleine, who will become Hilary.'

Pierson smiled, being thankful that Bill's department was thinking of her too.

Bill passed a wallet to Pierson. 'Your credit cards, bank guarantee card, driving licence with three points on it. The cards are all empty and valid; and they've been pre-signed for you.'

'How could you know my signature?' Pierson asked.

'We didn't,' Bill replied, 'remember we gave you the new identity and we had no signature of Mike Pierson's. We looked at hand writing samples and extrapolated it. Make sure you practice it before you draw any money.' Bill raised an eyebrow as he said this looking at Pierson.

Pierson checked the back of one of the credit cards and the driving licence to see the new signature. 'Why did you give me three points?'

'Creative anomalies,' came the reply. 'We can't have you too pure now can we?'

'Anything else I should know?' Pierson asked.

'No. Everything else is just fine,' Bill answered, rummaging through the other items.

'Do I own a car?' Pierson half asked and half suggested.

'We didn't get that creative,' Bill added, 'but even if we had, then it wouldn't do you any good. Not where you're going anyway.'

Bill handed Pierson a security pass for multiple sites within the MoD. It had Pierson's photograph and the new signature on it. 'Keep this safe,' he told him, checking the number on the pass with a list in front of him. 'Because you were cleared with a list X company and only three years ago, your records were relatively easy to create. That would have been difficult for an outsider to do.'

Pierson's curiosity was understandable as he continued with his questions. 'How much money is in the bank account?'

'Fifteen thousand Euros. But I'm not sure what you're going to spend it on, your accommodation will be paid for and transport will be easy, you'll be able to walk to work. The credit cards have a limit of three thousand Euros each and there are two of those along with two charge cards. You won't starve and although we've kitted you out with a modest wardrobe, you essentially have nothing except the clothes on your back.'

Pierson finished looking at the contents of the wallet and there inside were two thousand Euros in cash, in large note denominations.

'You said work? And why is everything in Euros?' Pierson inquired as he closed the wallet and placed it in his pocket, having already slid the MoD pass into it.

'Where's the best place to hide you in England?' Bill pressed Pierson while turning to face him.

'Give me some time and I'll come up with something,' Pierson replied.

'Fine,' said Bill, 'but in the mean time I think the best place is going to be outside of England. That way, anyone with even a slight suspicion that you're not really dead will probably start looking for you close to home, or by checking the airports or passport control. A big operation, even for internal government departments.'

The last comment wasn't lost on Pierson. 'You suspect another department in the government?'

There was a gap in the conversation as Bill looked at the back of Roger's head and wondered whether he should say too much in his presence. Giving in to his own judgement he continued though.

'Suspect is too strong a word. Let's just say that there's a lack of trust, and I don't wish to show my ace just yet.'

'What's your ace?' Pierson asked.

'Who is my ace,' Bill stated in a more matter of fact manner, still looking at the contents of the envelope.

'And?...' Pierson inquired again.

'Mike Pierson is my ace,' Bill replied, looking up from the mess on his lap and at Pierson. 'The only living person who knows Elektra other than Geoff Abbot.'

'So where are we going?' Pierson asked again.

'The best hiding place in England,' Bill replied with a wry smile. 'I'm taking you to Paris. You'll be working with our counterparts in France. For one of the few occasions in history, we'll trust the French more than our own people. They know all about you and have been expecting you—as Mike Pierson of course. They see your involvement as instrumental in cracking this case, although they have their own theories I'm sure.

You'll remain there until this is over, it should only take a few weeks, and by the end of the month at the latest, you'll be able to move on with your life again: safely this time.'

Pierson looked out of the window and could see some temporary buildings and a small car park to his left. The sun was now on his right and behind him and as he looked to his right he could see Stone Henge. They had been travelling south for some time. He was familiar with the area, because he'd been there when he'd worked for the MoD.

Stone Henge was surrounded by army barracks, camps and garrisons, and at least two airstrips, neither of which was marked on any map.

Bill handed Pierson what appeared to be a watch and some instructions for it. 'Having taken your watch you'll need a new one perhaps. Look closely and learn how to use it. It's actually a cell phone and you'll see that my number is programmed in memory zero.'

Pierson checked and the watch face displayed an analogue watch with hands in a liquid crystal display. The strap had been manufactured from metal and contained some of the electronics for both the phone and watch elements, with send and receive buttons, along with mute, memory, menu, up and down.

'You won't want to dial numbers with this one, it'll take too long, but there's a menu system and using the up and down keys you can store up to a hundred numbers,' Bill told him, as Pierson tried to put the watch on.

The strap was self-adjusting and seemed to just pull itself in to the right size. This surprised Pierson and as usual he wore the watch with the face down and his cuff slid over it, placing it out of view.

Before too long, the road they were on ran parallel with high fencing and every now and again they could see security signs mounted on the fence stating that it was an MoD site. As the Mercedes pulled up to the gate, the security guard raised a barrier and walked towards the car, but outer gates still barred the car's entry. Unlocking the gates, the guard pulled one of them open. Roger, Bill and Pierson held their passes up for him. Having scrutinised each one, he waved them through and then closed and locked the gates again.

There were officers and ranks from all three services moving around the site. Pierson had been here before, but it was unlikely that anyone would recognise him. There was a long one-way system from a certain point on the route. Roger drove the car along that part and they doubled back on themselves, but this was the only way to get to their next stop. Roger then turned the Mercedes left and was about to enter the apron, where various aircraft were sitting.

Being Saturday, little work was being done there, but there was a large plane with four turbo prop engines to their right outside a huge hangar. The car had stopped for traffic lights at the entrance to the apron.

Pierson and Bill peered around through the windows into the sky to see if they could find a reason for the delay. Both had assumed that an aircraft of some form must have been nearby and about to land.

It was the noise that they noticed first. It sounded like the air was being beaten repetitively with a huge bat. The noise was coming from almost directly above. As the sound got closer, so the source came into view. Like the instrument of Armageddon, it lowered itself menacingly and landed on the far side of the apron. It was a Chinook helicopter on a test run.

The noise was overwhelming. A steel dumping skip had its door blasted shut from the force of the twin contra rotating blades of this enormous helicopter.

'That's loud,' Bill remarked almost as an understatement squinting as if closing his eyes would reduce the noise.

'Twenty five tons of downward force,' Pierson replied. 'That's why they kept us back. It would have blown this car to Kingdom come.'

'How do you know that?' Bill asked.

'I have a friend who works in the aviation industry. Although I admit that he knows more about engines than planes.' Pierson replied.

'What's that over there?' Bill asked pointing to one of the jets inside the exposed hangar.

'Tornado. Codenamed MRCA or Multi Role Combat Aircraft. Twin RB 199 engines,' Pierson answered without really thinking.

Bill was impressed. 'And that's a Harrier isn't it?' he added trying to show that he could recognise at least one of the aircraft there.

'Yes,' Pierson replied 'Pegasus engine, vectored, 42,000 pounds of thrust.'

Bill stopped before he got sucked into a plane spotting fest.

The lights turned green and Roger parked the Mercedes to one side of the apron.

Bill led the way to the plane that was stationed there, with the four turbo prop engines. He gestured to Pierson to follow, and getting to the base of the steps for the aircraft Bill showed his pass to the aircrew man standing guard. The man saluted and stood back for Bill and Pierson to climb aboard.

Just before entering, Pierson looked down at the Mercedes only to see it being driven away.

Once inside, Pierson could see that it was crammed full of electronic equipment near the front, just behind the pilot's and co-pilot's positions. There were four other seating positions located immediately behind the crew, two on either side of the aircraft and each of the four positions had monitors and computer keyboards positioned in front of them.

Towards the rear of the plane were other seating positions. Bill pointed at them. 'Choose one,' he said, 'there's plenty of room.'

Pierson sat on the port side.

The crew were already aboard. Getting out of his seat, the co-pilot walked to the outer door and gesturing to the ground staff, he waved as if to confirm that the steps could be withdrawn. Pierson buckled up and the co-pilot then closed the aircraft door; and moments after the door engaged, he pushed down a large lever to lock it in place.

Approaching Bill, the co-pilot called across to him. 'Ready when you are sir.'

By now Bill had sat across the aisle from Pierson. 'Any time that suits you,' he replied. Bill looked at Pierson and pointing at the seat belt he added, 'you don't need to bother with that.'

The co-pilot squeezed into his seat again and then he and the pilot began to start each of the four huge turbo prop engines.

The aircraft seemed to be a Hercules type aircraft converted for weather observation, Pierson thought to himself.

After a few minutes the plane began to move and turned slowly on the apron and then only moments later it manoeuvred past the Chinook that had landed earlier. The runway was south of the apron and ran in a north east to south west direction.

Pierson could hear the pilot talking to the control tower above the noise of the engines, as there was surprisingly good sound insulation within the aircraft. They taxied towards one end of the airstrip, and as they approached it Pierson could see the yellow markers with black numbers 25-07 indicating the runway direction.

The plane waited for a few moments as two alpha jets roared along the landing strip in parallel takeoff ahead of it. The pilot then turned the plane and as it sat at the end of the tarmac, Pierson looked out of the right hand window to see the dropping sun beginning to take on a red glow. He at least knew now that Bill had no intention of killing him, as there had been many opportunities to do it by that stage. But his thoughts returned to Madeleine and the anguish she was about to go through. His heart was heavy as he was overcome, all be it briefly, with the guilt of causing her that much pain.

Pushing the throttle levers, the pilot and co-pilot made all four engines roar and the plane was jolted slightly because the pilot still had the brakes applied. Then within moments he spoke into his headset microphone and released them. The plane hurtled along the runway and eventually took to the skies.

Pierson could see the ground dropping away from him and caught sight of the other main airstrip at the base. Scattered around the airfield were a series of concrete domed hangars for fighter bombers, such as the Tornado and newer Typhoon. As they rose further into the air, the hangars seemed to just melt into the ground.

The plane circled the airfield to the south and then began to head towards the coast.

'You need some further updates,' said Bill interrupting Pierson's thoughts. 'Your contact in Paris is a man called Henri, and working for him is an operative called Francesca.'

'Why Paris?' Pierson asked.

'As well as getting you out of England it's the base for what the French call the R.G.,' Bill replied. 'It's like one third of their secret service and keeps files on French citizens, and others in fact. The other two parts of their secret service are known as D.G.S.E. and the D.S.T. It all stemmed from what they used to call the deuxieme and cinquieme bureaux. Don't concern yourself about what they do, other than to understand that they are similar to M.I.5 and M.I.6.'

Pierson merely nodded, trying to take all of this in.

'Henri is like my opposite number. His family own a vineyard, although he didn't wish to crush grapes for the rest of his life,' Bill added raising his eyebrows and smiling. 'He likes his drink though. You may find it tough keeping up with him.'

'What do I do when I get there?' Pierson asked.

'Henri will fill you in on that part. They're keeping a lot of this from us, with good reason I suspect, although it's always in the nature of secret service personnel to keep secrets.'

There was silence for a moment, interrupted only by the sound of a cell phone ringing. Bill quickly checked his pockets and then realised it wasn't his. He had an older style cell. But it was silent.

The co-pilot shouted back. 'You know the rules gentlemen. Switch the phones off.'

Pierson looked at his watch but it merely showed the time. Bill had by now moved across to look at the face of Pierson's new timepiece. Then Pierson suddenly remembered, just as Bill was homing in on the source of the ringing. It was coming from his jacket. It was his Nokia from work. It had slipped into the jacket's lining and as he pulled it out, so the ringing got louder and Bill just held his hand out. 'Sorry, Mike, if it's Madeleine you can't answer. And on top of that you simply mustn't telephone her.'

Pierson looked disturbed by the remark and handed it to Bill.

Bill stared at the face. It was showing the incoming number. 'Who's that?' he asked incredulously, looking and sounding extremely concerned and turning the face for Pierson to see and register the number mentally. 'It's coming from Paris. Who do you know in Paris?'

Pierson shook his head and shrugged his shoulders but concern snatched at him mildly, with an immediacy that he couldn't ignore. 'Of all the places it could have come from,' Pierson began, 'it can't be a coincidence that that's the very place we're going to now. It wouldn't be Henri by any chance?' But even Pierson didn't really believe that it would have been Henri.

Bill said nothing, he took note of the number and scribbled it hastily into his diary note pad. 'It's not Henri,' he retorted deadpan.

'Come on gentlemen. You can use the consoles here to make calls. Switch off your cell phones,' the pilot shouted back at them as the ring tone continued to get louder.

Bill switched off the power to the cell. It didn't switch off immediately and the ringing continued, so he turned it over and disengaged the battery by unclipping it and sliding it out.

'What the Hell!' he exclaimed, standing up and looking at the inside of the phone.

'What is it?' Pierson asked. 'What's wrong?'

Bill smelled the phone and walking carefully with it, he took it to one of the console desk positions. He gingerly sat down and placed it on the desk in front of him.

Pierson got up and walked across. He peered into the guts of the electronics and saw two small flashing lights and a chip with two wires leading into something that looked like a small lump of putty.

Bill remained silent and gently pulled the wires from the putty-like substance, very carefully and one at a time. Then lifting the cell, the two flashing lights extinguished.

'I could be mistaken, but I think you'll find that this is plastic explosive,' Bill stated calmly, 'keep the battery separate from it, but give both parts to Henri when we get to Paris. Get his people to find out how this thing works.'

'Okay,' Pierson replied gingerly, taking the battery and placing the phone and battery into separate pockets on his jacket. The plane lurched briefly in turbulence and Pierson stuck his arm out to steady himself.

'You're not worried that the call came from Paris?' Pierson offered Bill the chance to reveal any troubling thoughts concerning his French counterparts.

'I'm very worried.' Bill replied curtly glancing at him.

Although Pierson was uncomfortable about pushing the point, because the matter concerned his own life, he went ahead anyway. 'It goes without saying that I'm grateful that you've saved my life—twice—but I have to ask. Are you about to place me in the hands of someone who wants me dead?'

Both of them remained silent and the plane jerked again in more turbulence. 'Sorry about that gents,' the pilot shouted back, 'we'll soon be past this. I'll try to find a better altitude.'

Pierson didn't know whether Bill couldn't answer or simply didn't wish to, so as he waited for the answer he took the seat behind Bill and swivelled it around. But instead of pursuing the point, they independently reached the same stark realisation as they looked at each other. But it was Pierson who voiced their collective deduction.

'That phone call was supposed to kill me.'

Bill nodded slowly, 'I can't see any other possibility, especially as you don't recognise the number of the caller. In the circumstances, it would probably have killed us all.'

'Yes,' Pierson added thoughtfully as he reflected on the deaths of his colleagues.

'That's how it was done,' Pierson remarked almost with relief in his voice, because now he believed he knew how he might have been killed. 'The boat accident, the car crash, and the apparent gas blast.'

Bill nodded in agreement but was clearly in deep thought too.

'We all had Nokia's like mine, loaded with explosive,' Pierson continued, 'but why didn't mine go off?'

Bill shifted his train of thought momentarily. 'It could be that yours was faulty. Let me see it again.'

Pierson took it out of his pocket and handed it to Bill. Taking out the plastic explosive, Bill scrutinised it. 'What's its number?'

'I don't know,' Pierson replied, 'I've never telephoned it.'

'How long have you had it?' Bill asked, turning the phone over and looking at the face.

'I was given it just before I left for South Africa,' Pierson replied.

'Has it been out of your sight much since then?'

'Yes,' Pierson answered, 'I didn't take it to South Africa because it wouldn't work out there and I didn't need it.'

'How do you know it wouldn't work out there?' Bill continued, turning it over again to examine the back in more detail.

'I just assumed, and anyway I could always get to a land line if I needed to phone the UK, so I didn't take it.'

'So it's never been out of your sight or your home?'

'No. Not to my knowledge.' Pierson then spoke more slowly taking deliberate care over each successive word as the next thought dawned on him. 'Which means the explosive was in there when I got the phone.'

'Apparently,' Bill remarked, 'and whoever put the explosive in didn't think you'd take the battery out and find this stuff.'

Bill took out his diary note pad and copied the serial number of the SIM card, then he started typing at the keyboard of the terminal in front of him.

Pierson wondered how accessing the system on a weather plane was going to help. But he didn't have to ask the question, nor did he have to wait long for an answer.

'This just looks like a weather plane,' Bill commented nonchalantly, glancing up at Pierson, as though Pierson should have realised that it was really used for another purpose. 'You might say that it also helps with meteorology.' He paused before returning to the main subject. 'I want to track this thing down and find out more about it.'

After a few moments of tapping on the keys during which the plane continued its sporadic lurches, the screen flashed up historical information about the phone.

'How can you do that?' Pierson asked, looking impressed.

'You'd be surprised at just what we can do,' Bill replied before pointing at the screen. Displayed in front of the two men was an entry there for the telephone's call log history. 'Let's see what this shows us shall we?'

As the screen came up there were more than fifty calls that had never been received.

'Every one of them the same,' Bill remarked. 'Someone in Paris wants to contact you it seems. The first call is for 23rd July.'

Pierson was now perplexed by the new revelations.

'So the others were murdered then,' Pierson said almost in resignation and in realisation of the true nature of their deaths.

'What I really want to know is who gave you the phone?' said Bill, now looking at Pierson directly, 'and we need to find out why you're still alive.'

'You mean why Tom Brady survived until a couple of hours ago,' Pierson remarked.

'But they or he or she doesn't know that yet,' Bill mused, 'so that's perhaps why you got the call—assuming it was the killer.'

Pierson nodded realising the importance of what Bill had just said. For some reason, news of Tom Brady's 'death' hadn't reached those seeking it. But it had only been a couple of hours.

'Give it all to Henri and let his people check.' Bill continued, now partly intrigued. 'But tell me. Who gave you the phone?'

'Abbot's receptionist. Vicky Kennedy. She said that Abbot had ordered them specially.'

'Them?' said Bill returning the Nokia to Pierson, along with the plastic explosive, which he affixed to the back of it.

'Yes them,' Pierson affirmed. 'But she didn't say who else was being issued with one, or why they were being handed out. None of us were travelling salesmen, we generally worked from the office and only I really spent a lot of time at other locations, and just about everyone else always knew where I'd be.'

'But better than that,' Bill added, 'they didn't need to know where any of you were, all they had to do was get someone to dial the number and then who gets blamed for the murder? Especially if the dialler did it from abroad.'

'But they had to guarantee that the owner would have the phone on or nearby and switched on.' Pierson remarked, slightly puzzled and trying to figure out if there were any gaps in the growing theory.

'Which is exactly what a cell phone is for. Wouldn't most people take it with them? Were all the calls free for example?' Bill asked.

'Yes,' Pierson replied. 'That's right. Vicky mentioned that all outgoing calls would be paid for by the company.'

'Which might appeal to anyone looking for a freebie, which is usually just about everyone,' Bill remarked, looking at Pierson. 'Anyone it seems except you my friend.'

'I hate the things,' Pierson replied, 'I usually only switch them on for outgoing calls.' Bill and Pierson then both realised why he hadn't been killed. It appeared that his hatred of the device had been instrumental in saving his life.

'They say those things are bad for your health,' Bill remarked, shaking his head. 'If only they knew how. What a resourceful way to kill someone.'

'What's really going on here?' Pierson asked Bill, trying to see the bigger picture. 'Now that we're more certain the others were murdered. You don't need to kill someone to steal software.'

'No,' Bill replied. He gestured back to the other seats and they both moved towards the rear of the plane again.

'We don't think that software theft is the only thing happening here. We're not sure what else is about to happen, but murder usually implies a lot of money at stake. The software theft is worth millions of Euros to an individual trying to steal it and sell it; and tens of millions to our two governments, but these are desperate actions taken to silence people.'

'What else could be happening?' Pierson asked.

'Look to the money markets and watch closely,' Bill replied 'I've got no proof, but someone is toying with us I believe.'

'Why the money markets?' Pierson asked.

'I work for the treasury and believe it or not, banks are lined up like dominoes ready to topple and currency is volatile—even the US dollar. If I'm wrong then no harm will be done, but if I'm right then that may lead you in the right direction,' Bill replied.

Pierson was unhappy with the answer, but Bill wasn't about to divulge anything further. Even Pierson could tell this from the look on his face.

'We're approaching your destination gentlemen,' the pilot called back.

Pierson looked out of the window and saw the lights below. It had got quite dark now, especially as they had been travelling east. Checking his watch, Pierson could see that they'd been in the air for almost two hours.

'What about Henri though?' Pierson was troubled by the call to the cell having come from Paris. 'You're asking me to trust him and his organisation with my life.'

'I know,' said Bill. 'But think of it this way. No matter what I tell you about how far back Henri and I go and how much I trust him. If he was behind the murders, why get you to France first. The caller just made an attempt on your life without the need for you to be anywhere specific—except within signal range.'

Pierson was unconvinced, as was Bill. Neither of them voiced further concerns. But they both knew that if Pierson didn't get off the plane in Paris, then the alternative would have been to return to the UK making his new identity slightly pointless, and leaving him at risk to the mole in the UK. Pierson resigned himself to getting off the plane in Paris, even though he was uncomfortable with the prospect.

They touched down at a commercial airport, but not being familiar with this one, Pierson was unsure which one it was.

As the plane drew to a halt, mobile steps were wheeled up to it and the co-pilot swung the lever to open the outer door and then pulled it back to reveal the fresh night air of Paris, scented with the slight perfume of aviation fuel.

Pierson could hear footsteps resonating on the metal staircase leading to the aircraft, gradually getting louder and slower as the person ascending became increasingly fatigued.

Just as the sound of the footsteps stopped, the co-pilot stood back, and in climbed a man with a bushy moustache and a huge smile, wearing a khaki brown coloured suit with the jacket buttoned, mopping his brow with a slightly soiled handkerchief with one hand and holding the side of the door frame with the other.

THE BEST HIDING PLACE IN ENGLAND

Bill stood up and walked towards the sweaty visitor. 'It's good to see you my friend,' he said, reaching out to shake the man's hand. 'This is Mike Pierson,' he added gesturing for Pierson, who was by then standing too. 'I'd like to introduce you to Henri Pinvin—my opposite number and your new boss.'

'Nice to meet you,' Pierson said, shaking Henri's hand.

'What news do you have for me Bill?' Henri asked, as he fumbled to place his handkerchief in his outside jacket pocket.

'Not a great deal. But there's something you can start with, although this may not be news to you, it was certainly a shock to us,' Bill reached inside his pocket and taking out his diary sized notebook, he tore off one of its pages and gave it to Henri. 'I think you should try and track down this phone number. Whoever owns it made the call to Mike's cell phone.'

Henri took the paper and shrugged. 'Why should this be interesting?'

'Because,' replied Bill 'someone has been desperately trying to reach Mike's cell number and it looks as though that may trigger some additional electronics.'

Pierson pulled out the Nokia and the battery and showed Henri its guts and the other extras in the back of it. Henri opened his eyes wide, blinked in amazement and stepped backwards slightly as if in fear, 'Mon Dieu!' he declared, 'That's no way to greet a friend.'

Taking the phone and the battery he examined the putty-like substance. Looking at Pierson he continued. 'It appears that someone wants you dead too. How is it that you're still alive? Just good fortune perhaps or something else?'

'I don't know,' said Pierson.

Henri smiled. 'Then we'll find out and perhaps we can let you face your would be assassin. What a pleasant surprise that will be for him,' Henri looked again at Bill. 'Are you staying or must you return to that cold little island of yours?'

'I have to go back,' Bill replied.

'And the other matter?' Henri asked.

'We don't know yet,' said Bill dismissively, looking slightly embarrassed that Pierson had heard.

'What other matter?' Pierson asked.

'Nothing of any great importance,' said Bill. 'Perhaps even nothing at all.'

Henri and Bill shook hands again.

Pierson gave Bill a puzzled look.

'Come with me Mike,' said Henri, as he made his way back down the stairs towards a waiting car at the base of the steps.

'Don't worry,' said Bill. 'I'll be in touch and if you need me, press memory zero.'

Pierson looked at his watch.

'I assure you that phone is safe, but don't use it underground,' Bill added.

'Why not?' Pierson asked.

'Because,' came the reply, 'it won't work underground. I'll be back soon. I'll see you then.'

Pierson acknowledged this and held out his hand. 'Thank you,' he said.

'For what?' Bill replied.

Pierson smiled. 'For keeping me alive.'

'You're welcome,' said Bill, holding on to Pierson's hand with both of his own.

He let go of his grasp and watched him make his way down the steps. As soon as Pierson was on solid ground, so someone dressed in ground crew overalls pushed the steps away.

Pierson remained on the tarmac, watching as the door to the plane was slammed closed again.

The aircraft's engines started one at a time, coughing and spluttering into life, each ejecting thick grey smoke that drifted off out of view into the black beyond. Henri came and stood next to Pierson placing his hand on the young man's shoulder. 'We'll look after each other my friend,' he said as they watched the plane slowly turn and taxi back to the runway.

The engines roared into life and the two men stood almost mesmerized by its green, red and white flashing lights. Then, as the pilot released the brakes, the lumbering plane hurtled along the runway, eventually lifting into the night sky and off back towards the cold little island as Henri had referred to it. Before they could hear the plane's engines disappear, that sound was drowned by the noise of an approaching jet coming in from behind them, lights ablaze.

Turning around and concentrating on the present again, Pierson could see before him a white convertible sports car with its roof down. Sitting inside was a beautiful brunette with a smile that belied a wicked humour and a look in her eyes that promised mischief.

'This is my niece. Francesca,' said Henri, 'and this is Mike Pierson.' He added gesturing from one to the other of them. Francesca caught Pierson's gaze full on. As he approached her, so her upper body revealed that she was wearing a wrap-around blouse, held tight to the well-sculptured curves of her torso. The blouse came together below her neck in such a way that although there was no cleavage shown, it declared that she was not afraid of her sexuality; but neither did she flaunt it.

She had the perfect mix of femininity, casual friendliness and confidence.

Pierson wondered whether the term niece was a euphemism for something more intimate. Not that it mattered to him, for all her attractive qualities, his heart belonged elsewhere.

Henri pretended to whisper to Francesca in a voice loud enough for Pierson to overhear. 'He's married. So he's on loan. Nothing permanent here.'

Francesca turned around and placed her arm across the top of the front passenger seat. 'Ignore him,' she said, still smiling and now looking at Pierson. 'He's the black sheep of the family. Bad genes on that side, my mother spent years trying to train him, but he's beyond help.' She cast her eyes back to Henri as he slid into the back seat. 'Please get in,' she added, 'otherwise you may find yourself with a very long walk.'

Francesca leaned over to open the passenger door and as she did, Pierson could see that she was wearing a mini skirt showing the curves of well-exercised thighs. Trying to keep his eyes on the door and then mentally telling himself to look her in the eyes, he got in, almost falling over in the process.

Revving the car's engine, she pulled away the very instant that he'd closed his door; and immediately both Pierson and Henri were thrown back in their seats from the fierce acceleration. 'Slowly please 'Cesca,' Henri declared. 'Your Italian blood makes you too desperate, too frantic. I wish to light my pipe.'

Pierson looked back to see Henri with the device in his mouth, leaning forward in his seat with a cigarette lighter in one hand and shielding the pipe with the other trying to light it, but the flame kept being extinguished by the wind rushing by.

'How do you expect to give up uncle Henri if you don't make the most of this fresh air?' she asked him, looking in the mirror and seeing him struggling to get a flame that would stay lit for more than a moment. Turning to Pierson she winked and then raised her eyebrows at him.

'I had sufficient fresh air on the way here,' Henri replied. 'Now I'd like to relax a little.'

Francesca pulled the car to a halt and Henri almost head butted the back of her seat in the process, but at least he was able to get his pipe lit. He sucked a few times and the tiniest puff of smoke came out of the end. Taking it out of his mouth, he looked disparagingly at the pathetic looking lump of tobacco gently glowing and fading in the bowl. He used his lighter once again with a vengeance. Sucking on it much harder and faster. He soon had enough smoke that he needed to waft the air to keep it out of his eyes.

'Now mademoiselle: proceed,' Henri declared, waving his pipe triumphantly at her and rearranging himself in the seat so that he was more comfortable. 'But there's no rush: let's take in the sights for our new guest,' he added.

'At night?' she asked pulling off gently.

'There is no more beautiful place than the city of lovers at night,' Henri continued, 'allow us to experience it, at something less than the speed of light.'

Francesca raced through the manual gearbox and still smiling she looked at Pierson. 'I'll take it slowly for the old one.' Reaching top gear, she held it at a steady fifty kilometres per hour until they neared the perimeter fence and the security gate.

Henri waved at the security guard standing there, who was drinking something from a mug and hadn't noticed them approaching, because he was looking for people trying to get in, rather than people trying to get out of the airfield. Henri's wave was a kind of half salute and half wave. The guard rushed to put his drink down without spilling it. Then equally quickly, he raised the barrier by hand, applying his own weight to the end nearest his shack. The barrier lifted briefly as Francesca gunned the engine and raced through. She then brought the car to a screeching halt, only yards away, in readiness to join the main road outside.

They were very much on the outskirts of Paris and Pierson wasn't sure which way they were heading, other than for the bright concentration of lights ahead.

''Cesca put some music on, we can't talk with all this wind,' Henri shouted out as he leaned forward to speak to his niece over her shoulder. She switched on the car radio, and within seconds, music that Pierson could only describe as French came over the speakers. It was good, but he knew he had better things to do than just look and take in the view.

Already Pierson felt at home, but he cast his mind back 48 hours and he considered how much things had changed. He wondered how much more would change in the coming weeks and what it would be like to conclude this thing, this project or task that lay ahead. He hoped it would be over within days, but he had to let it all unfold in whatever way it was going to happen.

He also realised that if he'd done nothing, he might now be dead along with his late colleagues. The fact that his company had not contacted him about their deaths made it look like a big conspiracy. Although Pierson realised that only Vicky Kennedy or Geoff Abbot would probably have felt the need to call, yet they hadn't called him.

Pierson checked his watch and saw that it showed the time as being just after eight. Realising that it was an hour out, he spent a few minutes—largely by trial and error—attempting and finally succeeding in setting it forward by one hour.

Before long, they came to the city limits and into the outskirts of Paris. Pierson looked for signposts to get a fix on his position, not that he was familiar with the French capital, but more as a matter of interest.

The radio was still playing and Pierson noticed that Francesca was wearing no rings on her left hand, but he reminded himself that he wasn't interested anyway. He turned away before she sensed him looking; and in any case he didn't want Henri to think he was taking an over enthusiastic interest in his niece.

One street looked much like another and the street names were difficult to read. Pierson looked to see if he could recognise a landmark such as the Arc de Triomphe or the Tour Eiffel. Instead a huge tower block appeared ahead and slightly to their right. 'That's the Tour Montparnasse,' Henri said as he leaned forward and tapped Pierson on the shoulder. 'It's the tallest tower block in Europe.'

'Second tallest,' Francesca corrected him. Pierson looked around to his left at Francesca again and in the distance he could see the illuminated Tour Eiffel. It seemed to dart in and out of view as they passed the buildings leaving the Montparnasse district and moving on into Invalides. A few more minutes passed by and Henri pointed out other landmarks including the Ministere de La Defense and then without warning they were driving across the Seine and on towards the Place de La Concorde.

Francesca had slowed the car now and at last Pierson could see the name of the street they were in, it read 'Rue Royale' and moments later they drove into a place called La Madeleine. 'This is your closest Metro station,' Henri pointed out. 'I think you should be able to remember the name don't you?' Pierson began to think this had been specially done for his benefit. He hadn't realised until then that Henri knew his wife's name, but clearly he'd been updated thoroughly on Pierson's background.

They turned left into Rue de Surene and slowed to a halt outside some apartment buildings.

'Voila!' Francesca declared as she switched off the engine. 'This is where you'll be staying,' she said waving in a Gallic manner at the block on their right. They got out of the car and standing on the pavement Pierson looked towards the end of the road.

'Along there is the Ministere de L'Interieur,' Henri pointed at the buildings.

'That's where we go tomorrow?' Pierson asked.

'No,' Henri replied 'that's where I go tomorrow to get your Nokia examined. I'll expect to see you on Monday.'

'Do I need a pass or something?' Pierson asked. 'They won't just let me walk in will they?'

Henri shrugged his shoulders. 'Perhaps,' he said laughing, 'It's okay. Francesca will go in with you. I'll sort out the final clearance tomorrow. First though let me have your passport.'

Pierson handed it over without question. 'Good,' continued Henri. 'Now something the French are world famous for. When was the last time you ate?'

'Some time ago,' Pierson replied.

'Then it sounds like a good time to try some real food, cooked by people that know how to cook.'

Francesca sat back in the car and turned the ignition key. She pressed a button on the dashboard and the roof came up out of its holder and engaged to cover the car. She switched off the ignition again and stepping out, she walked around the car to its boot. Opening it, she revealed there was a small luggage space, big enough for a ladies handbag Pierson thought to himself.

'It's as well you brought no luggage with you, or you might have had to walk here,' Henri commented pointing at the small compartment.

Francesca leaned in and balancing on one leg Pierson noticed her curves were equally sumptuous below waist level as well as above. Her tight skirt had just enough room for her to manoeuvre and reach in for her jacket—a small white leather bomber jacket. He looked down at her calves, and noticed the calf of the leg she was standing on had contracted to the coiled position showing the soft inverted "vee" outline of the muscles. She was clearly very fit and kept herself in excellent shape.

Henri began tapping his pipe out on his hand and placed the still warm contraption in his pocket, he quickly brushed his hands free of the carbon and ash that it had deposited there.

Francesca closed the boot and swung her jacket on. Pointing the keys at the car, she pressed the alarm fob to arm and lock the vehicle.

The three of them walked back the way they had just driven and although it was approaching 21:30, the air was surprisingly warm. At the end of the road they turned right into the Rue Boissy d'Anglas, all the while Henri and to a lesser extent Francesca, pointing out individual buildings to Pierson.

They were now in one of the main eatery and shopping areas, and street cafes were still thriving with both tourist and local business.

Pierson looked across the street to see a McDonald's and further along a Burger King. Now at last, this felt more familiar to him and he relaxed slightly because of it.

Passing one café after another, Henri, with Francesca by his side, led the way whilst Pierson looked all around, taking in the views. He could see couples sitting at tables drinking wine and laughing aloud. They passed an oriental looking group who were in heated conversation, each with a camera around their necks and one of the younger men had two cameras, one of which he was trying to strip down. It looked as though he had some sort of problem with it.

A quiet family were sitting nearby, with the parents attempting to help their very curly haired blonde two or three year old daughter make her way through an ice cream, whilst another daughter sucked loudly on a soft drink through a spiral straw, making the drink go up and down the tube, stopping it partway to see how long she could keep it there.

An old man wearing a cap sat reading his newspaper by the light of the lamps and the café behind him; just in front of him a slim, elegant, middle aged lady sat dreamily staring along the street; just along from her various groups of teenagers were laughing and joking; and to one side were seven men walking in single file, with heads shaved, dressed in bright orange saris playing miniature cymbals as they walked speechlessly by.

The noise and the view completely contrasted with the road where the car had been parked, yet they were physically adjacent.

The traffic was light but fast. French drivers weren't comfortable with speeds less than 60 kilometres per hour it seemed, but the pavements were not a completely safe haven as they were fouled extensively with dog faeces.

Henri and Francesca turned to go through a doorway to one of the restaurants, which happened to be named 'Henri's'. Henri walked straight in, but Francesca stopped and turned to make sure Pierson was following.

'Mike,' she said, nodding her head towards the door. She held the door open for him, but by the time Pierson had got there, a couple were on their way out, so standing back he let them through.

On entering, the first thing that struck him was the change in lighting, which in concert with the décor, gave an over all dull orange glow to everything. The next thing that Pierson noticed was the rich mix of smells, coming predominantly from the kitchen, but was augmented by burning incense and scented candles on various tables.

Pierson could see Henri talking to the Maitre d' who, nodding quite excitedly, gestured towards the back of the restaurant.

Francesca took hold of Pierson's hand, to indicate that they should follow. Pierson thought it strange, but such a touch wasn't as alien or forward in Europe as it might have seemed in England. She led him through to the back and as she was about to sit, so he pulled the chair out for her. She thanked him and smiled.

Sitting down himself, he had his back to the door but the adjacent tables were empty; others though near the entrance were occupied. The large glass frontage afforded a good view outside for Henri and to a lesser extent Francesca.

The Maitre d' gave each of them a menu. Opening his, Pierson wasn't surprised to see it was printed in French. The name 'Henri's' was emblazoned across the top in a hand written script style. Pierson mustered up his entire recollection of schoolboy French to attempt to understand what was on offer, but he was curious about the restaurant's name.

'Your restaurant?' he asked Henri.

'No,' came the reply, 'I'm not the only Henri in Paris, but the owner is a friend.'

The Maitre d' returned momentarily with three large wine glasses and a bottle of red wine that he opened for Henri to taste. He poured a little into Henri's glass and stood back, still holding the bottle as Henri picked up the glass and swirled it gently, first of all inhaling deeply over its rim and then holding the glass up to the dim light available, he then moved it to his already expectant lips and slowly tipped it into his mouth ensuring it covered his tongue before rolling off to the sides. Placing the glass on the table, he pouted his lips and following two or three deft sideways movements of his jaws, he swallowed. Nodding at the Maitre d', Henri watched as he filled his glass.

Moving around to Francesca's side, the Maitre d' then continued to pour a glass for her. She smiled and quietly spoke, 'merci.'

He moved on to Pierson and poured out the third glass and then placed the wine in an ice bucket next to the table.

No sooner had he gone, than Henri pulled out the wine to show it to Pierson. 'It's good,' he said turning the label so that Pierson could see it. 'Chateau Pinvin' it read. Pierson guessed that this was from Henri's family vineyard. He picked up his glass and first pointing it towards Henri and then Francesca as if to toast them, he tasted it, nodding in appreciation.

'Now to business,' Henri spoke more seriously. 'What would you like?' Pierson thought they were going to discuss the matter at hand but Henri was referring to the ordering of the food. 'Something simple and palatable no doubt. We have red wine, so a red meat to match it I think,' Henri remarked, scanning the menu.

'Uncle Henri,' declared Francesca, 'our vineyard produces only red wine. We should let our guest choose regardless of the limited offering from our family business,' she looked at Pierson. 'It's late. Perhaps a chicken dish?'

'That's fine with me,' Pierson replied, amused by all these events.

Calling the Maitre d' across, Henri ordered for himself, and Francesca ordered for herself and for Pierson too.

'I've chosen something without too many sauces, so it shouldn't disagree with you,' she said to him.

'No sense of adventure,' Henri remarked. He leaned forward on the table almost meeting his face with that of his guest's.

'What do you know? Eh?' he asked Pierson. Pierson looked at Henri and then Francesca.

'I'm sorry. What do you mean?' he replied.

Henri continued, scratching his temple. He fixed Pierson with his stare. 'In your head there is some secret there; some piece of knowledge. You know something, but as yet you don't know what it is.'

Pierson thought on this. 'Such as?'

'Aaah!' exclaimed Henri leaning back, then picking up his wine glass he drank a small amount. 'That's the problem. We don't know.'

He put the glass down. Francesca took up the conversation.

'We've been working with your government, with Bob Selway and Bill to find the connection between Exterra and Vitesse Acquise.'

'How do you know someone is trying to sell the software illegally?' Pierson asked. 'After all if you know that, then the question begs itself that you already have the lead.'

'Not true, I'm afraid,' Francesca replied. 'You see, this matter only came to light recently and we were asked to look into it because…' she tailed off and looked at Henri. Henri nodded. 'It's okay. He has to know.'

'Because,' she continued, 'we were selling or trying to sell the software to the Polish national railway as a complete package. The two companies have been paid up front for development and the trains running on the Channel Tunnel are fantastic ambassadors for the sales. Interest was high. The

Polish government was going to buy the software and rolling stock, now they appear disinterested in the software and say they have another solution. But we know there isn't one.'

Pierson drank from his glass. 'Unless,' he surmised, 'someone has a copy of Elektra and Vitesse Acquise 4.'

'Precisely,' Henri interrupted, 'So our suspicions were naturally aroused and we vetted Vitesse Acquise and its employees thoroughly.'

'How?' Pierson asked, 'How can you be sure?'

'We have more powers in the R.G. than your secret service in England,' we can tap into phones and place listening devices in people's homes more easily than you can in your country. Trust me. Vitesse Acquise and its employees are clean.'

Francesca picked up the conversation. 'We had doubts about Exterra because of your boss and more recently because of your colleagues' deaths and also because of your trip to South Africa.'

'Why? What did I do?' Pierson asked, puzzled by the interest in him.

'You tell us,' Henri replied.

'I was training out there,' Pierson answered.

'What did you learn?' said Henri, fixing Pierson's stare as if trying to look into his very being.

'Nothing,' Pierson responded. 'What I mean is that I was giving courses to a customer out there.'

'You have South African customers?' Henri asked.

'Well, one now. But they came to England looking for someone who could give some courses and I had the skills and I was happy to go.' The conversation stopped and the Maitre d' began serving a soup dish. Once he was out of earshot again Pierson continued. 'Why the interest? What's so special or worrying about South Africa?'

'Maybe nothing,' Henri replied, 'but we've been watching things over there. Especially the money markets and the state of the rand, I'm sure even Bob Selway hasn't missed that.'

Pierson thought back to Bill's comments about watching the money markets and realised that Henri's comments were on the mark. Perhaps, Pierson thought to himself, Selway had been watching him during his final day in South Africa, or maybe even for longer. The photograph of Madeleine could have been sent as an e-mail attachment and just printed there in Johannesburg. Selway himself could have been watching him closely the entire two weeks that Pierson was there, to vet him completely before approaching. A picture began to build in Pierson's mind but there were still more questions than answers.

'Surely no one has to visit South Africa just to buy rand?' Pierson asked as he began his soup.

'No,' Francesca replied, 'but it's more difficult to trace if it's bought out there than in one of the major centres such as Europe, the US, Hong Kong, Japan or Germany.'

'I can't prove that I didn't buy any. Well no more than I had exchanged for me before I went,' Pierson remarked.

'It's okay,' said Henri, 'we were suspicious of you, but once we found that Bill was trying to get you here, our suspicions were allayed. And now of course it seems that there's been at least one attempt on your life. So we take the rest on trust.'

'What do you know about Elektra?' Henri continued.

'I can recognise the programs and even show you some of the code that I wrote, if we can lay our hands on the source,' Pierson replied, but Henri didn't seem overly impressed.

They finished their soup and the conversation changed again to other topics as the other courses were served and consumed.

At the end of the meal, Henri looked at the other two. 'I believe it's time to bid you goodnight,' he said, standing up. Francesca and Pierson stood too. 'I'll take care of the bill and I'll see you on Monday,' Henri added checking his watch and then feeling in his jacket for his wallet.

'Goodnight then,' said Pierson, 'and thank you for the meal. But how will I get into the apartment?'

Francesca pulled out a key ring with a number of keys and waggled them at him. 'With these,' she said. Pierson reached out for them. 'I'll have some cut for you tomorrow,' Francesca added and then thought on her statement for a moment. 'If we can find someone to cut them on a Sunday.' Pierson looked confused, was he going to be locked in he wondered?

'Goodnight uncle, I'll see you on Monday,' Francesca said as she pecked Henri on the cheek. She looked at Pierson. 'Are you ready?'

'Yes,' Pierson said in a clipped fashion looking at her and then back at Henri. Henri gave him a warm smile.

Walking outside behind Francesca, Pierson looked back into the restaurant as the door closed gradually shutting off his view. 'Where's Henri going?'

Francesca turned to him. 'He stays over the restaurant when he's in town. He has a room there, it's quite convenient for the office.'

They walked back the way they'd come earlier, passing the signs for Madeleine. Before long they were outside the apartment building and Francesca led the way. Pierson expected to be given the keys, but it didn't happen. Unlocking the outer door Francesca still led the way in and Pierson walked through too, letting the door close of its own accord and locking behind him.

She pulled back the metal lattice concertina doorway for the lift that ran centrally through the apartment block, after stepping in with her, Pierson then pulled it shut. 'Third floor,' she said to him waiting for him to press the right button. As he did, so a high-pitched whirring noise began, followed a few seconds later by a jolt of the upward thrust of the lift motor. The lift itself was merely a cage that could be looked into from any side, so as they ascended, he could see the counterweights passing them on their way down.

The lift stopped and wobbled slightly, in unison with a clunk from the motor and braking mechanism. They were at the third floor and Pierson tugged on the gate to open it, allowing Francesca to step out. As he left the cage he stopped briefly and then swung the lift gate closed behind him making it re-engage.

Francesca walked along a short corridor affording Pierson the opportunity to look at the décor. The building itself was quite old, but inside it was decorated in bright and modern colours and was very clean. There were flowers in a vase on a table that they walked by and he bent over to smell them as he passed. There were no windows on this part of the building though; and the light came from a complicated looking lighting fixture some two floors or so above.

Francesca stopped by the door to one of the apartments and unlocking it she then opened the door and stepped inside. Pierson was still looking up at the lights and as he turned, he couldn't see her any longer, so he walked along the corridor; and then noticing the open doorway he stepped inside, closing the door behind him.

As he entered, Francesca was walking over to a large picture window. She took off her jacket and draped it onto the sofa that backed onto it.

'Your room is over there,' she said, pointing to Pierson's left. 'Mine is that way. The bathroom is there and the kitchen is over here.' Pierson was surprised. He'd thought he would be alone.

'This is your place then?' he asked.

'Not really,' she replied, making her way into the kitchen and turning on the light. 'It belongs to the government, but I make use of it for the moment. Anyway the rent's pretty good and it's close to work.'

'Do I owe you for rent?' he asked as he looked around the lounge area.

'No,' she laughed. 'It's paid for by the government.' She appeared in the doorway. 'Would you like some coffee?'

'Yes please,' he replied, taking off his jacket as he approached the room that she'd pointed out as his.

'I thought I'd show you around the city tomorrow if you like and then we can get started properly on Monday.'

'Fine,' replied Pierson. He looked at his bed and sat on the edge. It was soft and warm. There was a large window in his room too, which he gazed out of briefly. Laying back, he looked up at the ceiling and felt the bed snuggle into him.

'Do you take sugar or cream?' Francesca asked from the kitchen, slightly raising her voice. But the question remained unanswered. After a few minutes she reappeared in the lounge with two coffees, a jug of cream and a bowl of sugar cubes on a tray. Placing it down on the coffee table in front of the sofa, she turned and quietly made her way to Pierson's bedroom door.

She could see him laid asleep as she leaned on the door pillar. Turning the light out on him, she closed the door as quietly as possible, whispering, 'good night,' just before it engaged.

Pierson slept solidly through the night, but the following morning, the sun shone in and its light caught on a large wall mirror, bouncing on to the bed and inching across until it made contact with his eyes. After a short while it was enough to wake him.

It was strange. For a few moments he didn't know where he was or how he got there. So he checked his watch, but he had to wait for his eyes to remember how to focus.

Eventually he could read the time displayed on the watch's face. It was two minutes after seven o'clock. Pierson couldn't remember his own name at first let alone anything else. So he sat up for a few moments and tried to remember the events of the previous day. He concentrated on the new watch and this helped him piece together the story. Then the full details of the previous 24 hours slowly came back to him.

He could hear water running from the shower in the bathroom. He decided to familiarize himself with this new life. Surveying the room, he opened the wardrobe and found two suits, jackets, trousers and shirts all neatly hanging inside and all surprisingly in his size. A chest of drawers to one side held items of underwear, again in the right sizes and on top was an overnight bag containing soap, deodorant, razor, toothbrush and other toiletries.

The running water stopped and there was a knock on his door a minute or so later. Opening it, he saw Francesca standing outside in a white cotton flannel dressing gown; her short wavy hair still dripping as she vigorously rubbed it with a towel.

'Good morning,' she said smiling at him. 'I didn't want to wake you last night. But the bathroom's free if you wish to use it. I'll make some coffee for when you're finished.'

'Thank you,' Pierson replied as he walked into the lounge noticing the coffee she'd made the previous evening. 'I'm sorry. I must have dropped off last night, I don't remember much after we got here.'

Francesca walked off. 'That's okay, men don't usually fall asleep on me that quickly,' she commented and as she turned her head back towards him she winked cheekily before entering her bedroom and closing the door behind her. Moments later Pierson could hear the hum of a hair dryer coming from within.

He got the toiletries and availed himself of the now empty bathroom.

Emerging some fifteen minutes later with a towel wrapped around himself, he could see Francesca was already in the kitchen preparing drinks.

Once he'd got himself dressed with the new clothes, he then folded the ones he'd worn the previous day. He caught sight of himself in the mirror and saw a cut on his face, caused by shaving with a mirror steamed up by the bathroom's previous occupant.

Finally, he too emerged ready for the day, placing his towel back in the bathroom before he made his way to the kitchen. Parking himself on one of three stools at a central bench that extended from the window wall he watched Francesca as she poured out two coffees.

'Do you have any plans today?' she asked him as she sat opposite him on the other side of the bar. She was asking more out of politeness than anything else; but he laughed at the idea.

'I hadn't planned anything,' he told her, 'except perhaps to get keys for this place.'

'Good,' she said, glancing out of the window and then back at him, 'Maybe I can show you around the city.'

Nodding in agreement, the two of them continued with leisurely small talk for the next hour and a half at which point they left the apartment. Pierson had learned from her during that time that it was her mother who was the sister of Henri and that her father was Italian but had died some years previously. Even though she was brought up in Italy, on her father's death, her mother was begged by Henri and the rest of her family to move back to the family vineyard, situated in the countryside to the west of Paris.

She had managed to get a job in the French foreign office due to being able to speak fluent French, Italian and English. Following a series of moves she now worked for her uncle in the R.G.

Her training included firearms and self defence and she was a qualified pilot, which itself had extended from amateur—and illegal—flying experience from crop spraying at the vineyard.

Outside the apartment, once they had walked to the end of the road and returned to café area again, Pierson could now see some of the shops beginning to open, even though it was Sunday. They had to walk much further than the previous night to track down a locksmith and they found themselves by the banks of the Seine by the time they were able to locate a hardware store with a key cutting facility.

After a short wait, Francesca presented Pierson with his own keys. It was as they meandered by a newsagents shop moments later that Francesca noticed the headlines, which intrigued her sufficiently to encourage her to buy a copy of Le Monde. With their initial objective for the day achieved they took the opportunity to relax for a while and at the next street side café they ordered coffee and croissants.

Francesca took great interest in the news and largely ignored the scene around them. She attempted to spread open the paper on the rather small table, but the gentle breeze kept working against her. It was only her coffee cup and plate that kept it from turning the pages.

It was a beautiful day and there were boats of varying kinds on the Seine and in the distance Pierson could see the Ile de la cite—the home of Notre Dame.

'You seem very interested in that article,' he remarked, speaking to Francesca as he sipped his coffee, only really half noticing her and half concentrating on the river.

'Uh,' she said looking up. 'Oh yes, it's strange.'

'What?' he asked her. 'What's strange?'

'According to this, someone has stolen a new submarine from a high security Naval port near Cherbourg. It happened yesterday.'

'Why? What was so special about it.' Pierson asked.

'It's secret, according to this, but two Naval officers on duty were killed during the robbery. It cost four hundred million francs to build, so it's a major source of embarrassment,' Francesca replied.

'Should we be interested in this?'

'I don't think so,' she answered, moving the cup and plate to allow her to fold the paper closed. 'But it's a strange thing to steal. Don't you think? Why would anyone want it for themselves? And if not for themselves then who would buy it from you?'

She drank some coffee and began to chew her way through the freshly baked croissants only interrupting her eating briefly to speak again.

'Okay, first l'Arc De Triomphe I think and then across to Notre Dame and then le Tour Eiffel, with a ride on the Seine on the way.'

'Sounds great,' Pierson remarked watching her return to finish devouring the croissants.

'And,' Francesca continued, gently using her finger tips to wipe the crumbs from her lips, 'I must show you Le Metro so that you can find your way around the city.'

'Okay,' Pierson answered.

'The first thing to learn is that there are 14 Metro lines, numbered 1 to 14, so that makes 28 final destinations. Remember their names and you will be most of the way to understanding how it works. The other important thing for you is that you have to get back to Madeleine.'

'I know,' he replied, thinking of his wife and looking slightly curious.

'The place,' Francesca added, 'not the woman. Madeleine is the name of the nearest Metro station to the apartment.'

'Oh yes,' Pierson nodded, putting his hand to his head as though he'd been a complete fool.

They got up to leave the table and with the newspaper now folded exhibiting the front page once more, Pierson looked down at the photograph of the stolen submarine. It was small and strangely shaped, perhaps only big enough for a crew of four and some cargo. He thought nothing more of it though, as Francesca beckoned him to walk by her side; and they made their way together to the nearest Metro station.

They spent the day as she'd suggested. The penultimate visit was Notre Dame and finally the Eiffel tower.

As they stood on its highest vantage point looking out over Paris, Francesca noticed a distant look in Pierson's eyes. 'Beautiful isn't it?' she commented.

'Yes,' he replied, watching a couple arm in arm nearby engaging in a kiss. She looked curiously into his eyes. 'You miss your wife. Don't you?' she remarked softly, looking away as she said it. He nodded, and as an afterthought when he saw she wasn't looking at him, he quietly spoke, 'yes.'

A few more moments passed before he broke the silence. 'I thought that I would somehow feel God's presence in Notre Dame. Maybe not God, but, well it's difficult to explain. But if he's anywhere, then he's here.' Francesca looked at him again and saw him slowly surveying the horizon and looking at the clouds.

'You feel more religious here?' she asked him.

'No,' he replied. 'More serene; closer to heaven; I feel alone and yet not forgotten in a strange way. Up here my, my heart feels less heavy; I feel less guilty.'

'Why should you feel guilty?' she asked him. He turned to look at her. 'I gave my word that I wouldn't tell my wife that I was still alive. It was for her safety and mine,' he replied.

'She'll know soon enough what the truth is.' She watched him as he seemed to drift and then she brought him back into her world.

'Let me take you down from heaven to eat.'

'Okay,' he smiled, 'food it is.'

They descended from the tower and then walked the rest of the journey to the apartment, stopping by a burger bar en route, where he was able to indulge in food less unfamiliar to him.

Pierson felt as if he'd had a full workout that day from all of the exercise, so throughout the evening, he made the best possible use of his time by practising his new signature, managing both to perfect it and to do it without really thinking about it.

THE PARISIAN TELEPHONIST

Arriving at the ministry of the interior the following morning, the entry was easy, as Henri had obviously made all the correct arrangements. Pierson was given a pass allowing him ready access, from that day onwards, to the whole building via any of its entrances; but only certain rooms and floors within the building. He chose to wear a suit, although Francesca thought this was amusing as she was wearing a tee shirt and jeans. She implied that it must be because he was English.

She led the way, beginning with the lift, where she selected floor minus five. This took them below ground—as the number suggested—and within a few moments the lift doors opened revealing a foyer, with a large green triangle on the wall above the doorway in front of them. The green triangle identified a sector within the building, and the only signs present were all written in French, so for Pierson, the colour coding was the most helpful location clue.

'You have to make your way back to the green zone to get to these lifts,' Francesca said, pointing at the large coloured triangle. Pierson nodded, just trying to absorb the environment. The walls themselves appeared to be metallic; they were a silver colour, in matte finish, possibly stainless steel he surmised. It was clear that some considerable expense had been made in the construction of this part of the building, but before he could ask about it, his thoughts were interrupted.

'The walls are this colour to reflect the lights,' Francesca remarked, trying to pre-empt Pierson's next question.

The doorway ahead of them housed a pair of doors with large translucent glass panels, allowing the artificial light through. Francesca pushed through and held them open for Pierson as he followed closely.

Pierson noticed the floor was a hard tiled surface enabling footsteps to be clearly heard. In addition, the tiles were a matte finish too, also in a metallic silver shade; and as he glanced upwards to see the lighting, he couldn't fail to notice the continuance of the metallic décor overhead. The lights were recessed into the ceiling itself, and comprised groups of fluorescent tubes arranged in two rows along its entire length: making it appear as one continuous fitting.

They walked a great distance, following each meandering twist of the corridor. Every now and again they could hear approaching footsteps as groups of people drew closer and then walked by. Pierson's presence, even being a new face, did not distract the confident single-minded purpose of any of these people.

Solid double doors on each side of the corridor were marked with numbers and a green triangle, like the one in the lift foyer, but the numbers were not consecutive and followed no apparent sequence. On top of that, they were eight digit numbers and consecutive rooms had the digits slightly rearranged.

There was a large selection of pictures on the walls showing abstract art. One picture hung between each set of doors for the offices off the corridor, and each of the pictures was a distinctive set of lines and colours.

Eventually they found themselves at a point in the corridor where a large blue triangle appeared on the wall, indicating a new zone. Francesca pointed this out to Pierson. He could then see that all the rooms off the corridor beyond that point also had blue triangles above them with a number, but again the numbering system seemed random.

'Why aren't the room numbers sequential?' he asked her.

'In case we get infiltrated,' she replied. 'It's there to confuse a would-be spy or someone who is unfamiliar with the place. It has the added advantage that if one of us is retired, or switches to an unfriendly power, it is virtually impossible to remember where a particular room is. Most of us will use only four or five rooms during our normal work and although we often remember those room numbers, that isn't useful information, because they are not set in sequence and so unless you look at all of them you won't find the one you want.'

'Isn't that really inefficient though?' Pierson asked not sure whether to believe her.

'No,' Francesca replied, 'because most people remember where they are by the zone colour and the wall picture. Each one is specially designed and is different to all the others in the building. It relies on people looking for the room number the first time and then remembering the picture on the wall for the other times. That's why the numbers are eight digits long. They're too hard to remember and easily rearranged subconsciously to an incorrect one.'

Pierson shook his head in disbelief. 'It's true,' Francesca added, smiling, 'people remember things visually.'

'What about the mail person, doesn't he or she get confused?' Pierson continued.

'Not at all,' Francesca replied, 'It's all handled by computer.'

'Handled by computer? How?' Pierson persisted.

'E-mail of course!' Francesca declared.

They carried on walking and finally they got to the red zone where Francesca stopped outside a pair of doors to their left. Using her pass she swiped it down a card reader on the wall. A red light at the top and to one side of the card swipe channel extinguished, and a green light underneath it illuminated, following which, the doors clicked, electronically unlocking.

'You'll have to swipe too,' she added pointing at the card entry mechanism. 'Or you won't be able to get out again.' The doors were solid, like the doors for all the other rooms off the corridor. Pierson looked at the number above the room. He then swiped his pass through the electronic lock.

As they stepped through, he had a quick glance at the picture hanging to the left of the door. It had a yellow grid like a portcullis, and three diagonal red stripes partly cutting across the front of the grid. In addition there were seven blue and purple circles trailed around the edges. He blinked at it as if to burn it into his memory.

Stepping inside, the doors closed behind him. Sitting at desks at the far end of the office were two young men, both of whom were casually dressed. To their right was a slightly older yet still dark haired gentleman sporting a light grey business suit. The office itself was large and had sufficient space to have squeezed in enough desks for ten people without much effort. In the corner to the right was another door, with an equally long number above it, but no picture on the wall.

The door to that room was ajar, and from within Pierson could hear Henri speaking. He and Francesca walked in to meet him.

'Ah welcome,' he declared his entire face lighting up as he spoke.

'Good morning Henri,' Pierson replied feeling very much the new boy and a guest in the strange surroundings.

Henri was sitting behind his desk and had been looking at a computer screen. He was dressed in a brown suit, which made Pierson feel a little more relaxed. It appeared that he had been talking to himself, Pierson thought, as he wasn't using the phone and there was nobody else present.

Henri gestured to the two of them to sit down at chairs next to a small round conference style table. After getting up, he walked around his desk to join them.

'So Mike; we have much to do today,' he said. 'Bill has been busy and has sent through some details.' Henri leaned over to his desk and picked up a small and untidy pile of paper resting there. He handed the papers to Pierson. They were copies of call logs for cell phones; including the Nokia that Pierson had been given before he departed for South Africa.

'If you look closely,' Henri began, 'you'll see that Mr Mills was called on Sunday 27Th from a caller in Paris. Please take note of the telephone number.' Pierson took out a pen and Francesca walked out of the office for a few moments and returned, having briefly rifled the drawer of one of the desks. In her hand was a post-it pad. She handed it to Pierson. 'Thanks,' he remarked as she took her seat again. He wrote down the number of the caller and the time.

Pierson then looked closely at the call log. 'Is this a call log or an invoice?' he asked Henri.

'Does it matter?' Henri asked.

'It might,' Pierson added.

Henri stepped over to his desk once again and looking at one of the other many pieces of paper there he declared, 'it's a call log, of all calls to and from the phone regardless of whether they will be billed.'

'Thank you Henri,' Pierson said, quietly thinking about the log. He looked at the call log for Jim Alexander. Scanning down the list he saw the same incoming call from Paris and it was dated and timed at 13:35 on Tuesday 29th July.

'Good grief,' he declared. 'It's Jim's last call too and it's the same number.' Pierson tilted the log so that Francesca could see it.

Selecting the next call log, he saw the one for Martin Tunbridge. There were four calls every day from the same number in Paris, the last one being at 01:38 in the early hours of Wednesday 6th August.

'The caller was persistent,' Pierson declared. He looked back at all of the other logs too. 'There's a pattern.' He declared. Henri nodded in agreement as he watched Pierson reach the same conclusions that he had already arrived at. 'The calls are coming through every six hours or so.' Pierson remarked further.

'Four times a day,' Henri added.

The calls were slightly disguised at first, because of the outgoing calls made, but closer inspection revealed the pattern.

Francesca looked at the logs, 'they're coming in at 01:35, 07:35, 13:35 and 19:35. But some are a minute later than others.'

'Steve Mills's came in at 01:37, 07:37, 13:37 and 19:37, at six hour intervals starting at 37 minutes past the hour. Why?' Pierson asked, not expecting an answer. He shuffled the papers and looked at his own call log and the first four calls from the same number. They came in at 19:36, 01:36, 07:36 and 13:36.

Francesca and Henri passed a glance at each other looking perhaps for inspiration, while Pierson sat back in his chair. 'It's done by computer,' he stated in a matter of fact manner, betraying a wry smile. 'The calls have precise regularity.'

'Hardly precise,' Henri replied raising his eyebrows. He stood up and to his left was a large white board. He asked Pierson for the daily call pattern for each call and wrote them next to the four names, Jim Alexander, Steve Mills, Martin Tunbridge and Mike Pierson.

They looked at the sixteen sets of times. 'All of Mr Alexander's calls came at 35 minutes past the hour,' Henri mused, 'and Mr Mills's all came at 37 minutes past the hour, with Mr Tunbridge's at 38 and finally yours Mike at 36 minutes past the hour.'

'Not true,' Pierson remarked. 'Tom Brady's calls came at 36 minutes past the hour. Put that name between Jim Alexander and Steve Mills and they become alphabetical.'

Henri did as Pierson suggested and then it was obvious, that the calls had been made alphabetically to Alexander, Brady, Mills and Tunbridge, on consecutive minutes.

'What does that tell us?' Henri said.

'They were made by a computer program hence the precision. Each number was dialled and then a minute later the next one was dialled. But what I want to know, is why my phone didn't explode?'

'Ah,' replied Henri, replacing the white board marker pen in the small rack at the base of the board. 'I have the answer for you.' He walked over to the door, 'Jean-Pierre, bring the phone please.'

One of the three men outside of Henri's office stood up, and picking up the Nokia, he walked in. 'This is Jean-Pierre, he's been working with our people in electronic surveillance.'

Jean-Pierre appeared to be in his early thirties, had ginger hair, wore silver rimmed glasses and appeared studious and well read. The goatee he was growing somehow endorsed his appearance.

Pierson stood up and shook his hand as the two men were introduced. Jean-Pierre then looked at Henri. Henri sat, and without saying a word, it was as though his eyes gave Jean-Pierre the instruction to continue. Jean-Pierre having paused briefly to register Henri's look, pulled up a chair, placing the Nokia on the table. He turned it over and pulling off the battery, he exposed the chip, some small bulbs and plastic explosive.

'The bomb would be enough to destroy a boat made of wood or fibre glass, or to cause extensive fire and burning in a car or a house,' Jean-Pierre began.

'The chip controls the detonation and is triggered by a pulse sequence from the phone.'

'From the incoming number?' Pierson asked.

'Not the incoming number as such, it was quite clever. Detonation is actually caused by a sequence of complex tones that when emitted audibly begin a trigger sequence, which in turn detonates the explosive either after thirty seconds of continual play, or when the incoming call is answered once the tones have started.'

'Do you know what the sequence of tones are?' Pierson asked.

'Do you like Mozart?' Henri quizzed him.

'Some,' said Pierson.

'But what about as a ring tone for a cell phone? Would you like Mozart's fortieth symphony?' Jean-Pierre asked him.

'No,' replied Pierson, 'I hate those quirky phone sounds. Actually, now that I think about it, Mozart's fortieth was one of them, and anyway I changed it on the phone as soon as I could.'

'Then,' continued Henri, 'that's what saved your life.' Pierson looked both surprised and sceptical, turning his head to Henri and then to Jean-Pierre. Jean-Pierre nodded to confirm Henri's statement.

'Someone set this phone up when it was distributed,' Jean-Pierre added, 'it had a pre-programmed detonation chip, and when the incoming number matched the caller from Paris, then Mozart's fortieth would have played. Thirty seconds later the phone would have exploded, or if it had been answered after Mozart had begun to play, then it would have detonated, killing the user. Assuming the other three were wired up the same way then that explains the deaths.'

'Ingenious,' Henri remarked, 'and deadly.'

'So it was definitely murder,' Pierson remarked.

'Prove it,' said Henri raising his eyebrows.

Pierson nodded, 'You mean all of the evidence that they were murders has been destroyed.'

'Vooomph!' said Henri gesturing with his hands like a bomb going off. 'Blown into a million microscopic pieces.'

'So who is the caller?' Pierson asked.

'We're still tracing it,' Jean-Pierre replied. 'We know where the phone line is but we're trying to get a list of the other calls made from it during the last month. Marcel is doing that right now.' Jean-Pierre nodded his head sideways as if to point to one of the remaining men in the outer office.

'Why did they choose Paris as a base? I wonder,' Pierson mused aloud.

It was Henri who finally answered.

'Vitesse Acquise are located here in the city. What better way to cast suspicion over them than to arrange for a base to be set up nearby? If it had been done in England then that might have left Vitesse Acquise looking clean and would have made it easier to investigate. There would only have been a need for a single police force. Or at least with all of the investigative problems of this matter contained in England, it would have simplified the investigation.'

They all listened intently and as there was no criticism of his theory, Henri augmented it.

'In addition, it gave the murderer an extra level of safety by placing him in a second country. The chance of successfully prosecuting for murder is even more slender by doing that. In fact if it was murder then who is the murderer? What if the person who wrote the program had no knowledge of the effect of the telephone calls?'

'What about Abbot?' Pierson asked. 'Did he have a phone? And was he telephoned too?'

'It's unlikely,' Henri replied. 'You're alive by luck. Did you know for instance that your phone would have worked in South Africa?'

'No,' Pierson replied. 'So it's as well that I didn't take it with me then.'

Henri nodded slowly. Silence fell once again for a few moments and then Henri got to his feet. 'I'll arrange for some coffee while we try and figure out these strange times,' he added.

'What are you going to do with the Nokia now?' Pierson asked Jean-Pierre.

Looking at the phone and then at Pierson he replied. 'It's yours. You may keep it if you wish. But don't use it in here. The metal walls stop cell phones from working, apart from interview rooms and one or two others. It's a security thing. And anyway we wouldn't want to clear up the mess.'

Pierson picked it up and studied it closely. 'So if I program this to receive an incoming call and play Mozart's fortieth symphony for that number, then it will explode,' he finished his words by looking at Jean-Pierre.

'Yes,' Jean-Pierre replied slightly alarmed and backing off, 'but I suggest you remove the chip while you're setting it up,' he paused briefly and then continued 'but of course try not to ring it when you have it your possession!'

Pierson smiled and nodded. Taking out the chip and explosive he looked at his watch with the built-in phone. He checked its telephone number and set it into the memory of the Nokia. The Nokia was quite small and neatly fitted into the palm of the hand when closed. Once he'd finished the operation of programming it, Pierson ensured that that specific incoming number and only that number triggered Mozart's fortieth symphony. He then replaced the chip and plastic explosive to Jean-Pierre's satisfaction and after switching it off he then slid the Nokia into his pocket.'

Playing with his watch further, he set up memory one to store the number for the Nokia. He then realised that what Bill had told him about trying to use the watch as a phone was true. It was very difficult to dial new numbers, as the entire number had to be entered with up and down keys and then the send button would have to be pressed.

Eventually though, he managed to program the phone correctly. A few moments later, Henri himself wheeled in coffee and biscuits on a trolley. Pierson looked bemused at this site, but said nothing. He realised that perhaps the coffee had been delivered to the outer office door and that Henri wheeled it in the rest of the way, security preventing the coffee waiter from bringing the trolley all the way in.

'So these times?' Henri asked, looking at Pierson as he tilted the tap of the coffee urn and poured himself a drink. 'Are they significant?'

'I don't think so,' Pierson replied, 'you have to add an hour on to each of them to make it local time in France, but I don't think there's anything significant about them. There's far more significance to the call logs.'

'Why?' Henri asked. Pierson selected the call log for his phone and showed it to the others. 'Look at the last page,' he said to them as he pointed towards the end of the entries.

Henri shrugged, 'they stopped yesterday at 12:36' he commented.

'Precisely,' Pierson noted, 'yesterday was Sunday.'

Jean-Pierre, Francesca and Henri all looked at each other as if to see if any of the others knew what Pierson was driving at.

Pierson could see their confusion. 'Look at the last call for each of the others,' he added, trying to get them to see it for themselves.

Rummaging through the sheets, they found the last call from the Parisian caller, and Henri stood and placed the time on the whiteboard next to each of the correct names.

'They all coincide with the time of death,' Pierson added.

Henri and the others nodded. 'That's why they died,' Henri replied.

'Yes,' said Pierson, 'but the calls stopped once they were killed.'

'Because they were dead,' Henri added laughing incredulously.

Pierson looked a little perplexed but continued anyway, wondering whether he had seen something that wasn't there. 'But how did the caller know the victim was dead. How did the person making the calls know they didn't need to ring again? The phone didn't send a message back did it?'

'These are billed calls,' said Henri, 'so only those with a charge will be seen,'

'You don't get charged for incoming calls,' Pierson replied and you already said it's a call log. It's not the billed calls, it's all call attempts.' He paused momentarily for them to see and realise what he'd said.

'Yet in my case,' Pierson continued. 'Or in Tom Brady's case; the calls carry on long after he… I mean I… I mean after death, three more calls and then they stop.'

Francesca understood what he was saying. 'You mean the caller was told after each successful murder by some other means; phone, e-mail or somehow, yet in your case, the caller wasn't told until over eighteen hours later.'

'Exactly,' said Pierson. 'So why were the dead people never called after they were killed? The phone company logged all connect attempts. It seems that someone was nearby watching and updating the Parisian caller, except in my case, when the information became public or was in the hands of the police.'

Henri nodded at the subtlety of Pierson's point and sat down. 'I'm sorry my friend I didn't see the importance of what you were saying. But I see it now.'

None of them could fault Pierson's point, or explain it, but they made a mental note of it for the future.

Henri finished his coffee. 'An answer will come,' he added, 'maybe not quickly, but anyone who's carried out surveillance knows that patience is a virtue.'

Henri paused, as though he were making sure that no immediate answer was available, and then changing the subject he spoke again. 'Come and meet the others.'

Stepping outside his office he introduced the other two men there who were diligently working at computer terminals. 'This is Antoine and Marcel,' he gestured to the two of them. Pierson went to shake their hands, 'and this is Mike Pierson from England.' He added. 'What do have for us today gentlemen?' Henri continued looking at Antoine.

Antoine seemed to have had a lapse in his dental work with holes and missing teeth an obvious characteristic to his less than complete smile. Like Jean-Pierre he too wore glasses and was bearded, but his beard was more wayward. His personal hygiene looked as though he dressed and maybe even slept in dustbins before arriving at work. He had a kind of 'been up all night' look to him. His hair was almost red, but almost brown too. Being neither one thing or another it seemed to glint in the light as he turned his face. Unlike Jean-Pierre who gave the impression that he still lived with his mother—largely due to the wearing of a plain grey pullover—Antoine was more of a free spirit who seemed to be more flustered and far more liberal in his facial expressions, as though he were continually conducting facial aerobics as he spoke. Pierson concluded that Antoine was in his late twenties, but through alcohol, or substance abuse, or at least over use, looked somewhat older.

Marcel sat quietly nearby, and although happy to speak, he was in fact more jovial than the other two as Mike found out over time, but Marcel's apparent confidence—largely inferred from his striking black hair and good looks—was undermined by a tic and occasional stutter, that resulted in heavy blinking from time to time, keeping everyone spellbound waiting for the verb. He was also visibly older than the other two as Pierson viewed him close up; possibly in his late forties, Pierson concluded.

Antoine stroked his beard as he smiled mischievously. 'The rand got stronger a few days ago, temporarily, but it's settling back down again.'

'I've got it here,' Marcel declared, pointing at his screen, blinking profusely and almost uncontrollably. 'I'll just print it and we can see the log.'

'You have what?' Henri asked as he watched Marcel hobble slightly over to the laser printer, just as the first sheet was being ejected. 'It's the call log of our murderer,' he replied. Marcel's walking problem arose from a motorbike accident when he'd been in his teens and this had left him with one leg slightly shorter and stiffer than the other.

The printer spurted out more than one sheet. It produced the output so fast that it had finished before the others had a chance to gather round. Marcel though was already scrutinising the output.

'This is strange,' he remarked. '34 minute calls on the hour every hour.'

'That partly explains why the calls to the Nokias started at 35 minutes past the hour,' Pierson remarked.

'Who is being telephoned for exactly 34 minutes every hour and why?' Henri asked.

'Data?' Pierson suggested.

'What sort of data?' Henri asked.

'It could be anything, but the data are files of the same length each time,' Pierson added. 'It's the same amount of data each time and that's why the calls last the same length of time.'

Henri nodded in agreement even though it was speculation on Pierson's part it sounded plausible.

'What data and why?' Henri asked without expecting an answer, but musing over his own question. The others looked at him and waited for him to announce the answer. 'We'll have to raid the place to find out,' he added. 'Is there anything else there of interest?'

'Yes,' Marcel answered, looking at one of the other pages. 'A whole series of phone calls from many different telephone numbers.'

Henri leaned over Marcel's shoulder to have a look.

'They're all English. Every one of them comes from England,' Pierson remarked.

'Okay Marcel: list them for me and trace them if you can,' Henri continued. 'This is getting bigger than I'd originally thought,' he shook his head in anticipation of a growing research problem.

'I need to get out of here and think for a while…take some time to look at something else.'

'He wants to smoke his pipe,' Francesca said smiling and nudging Pierson in the ribs.

Henri turned to Pierson. 'Would you like to see our server room?'

'Yes, actually I would. But what about this stuff?' he replied pointing at the phone lists.

'Leave it to them. They're good at this sort of thing. Come with me and I'll show you the nerve centre of this building.'

Pierson followed Henri out of the outer office and walked with him back towards the lifts. Once in the lift, Henri selected level minus seven. The doors closed smoothly and the two men descended.

Stepping out of the lift, Pierson noticed that the corridors looked like the ones they'd just left.

Henri led the way and turned towards a pair of doors on the right just beyond the lift foyer. He swiped his identity card as did Pierson and they both entered. It was an outer room for the server hall, a bridge area as Henri called it. Passing by a couple of the staff there, Henri spoke to one briefly and the man nodded and gestured for them to walk on through into the main server area.

The server hall was enormous, but it was only about one third full.

'When we had this place built, computers were much bigger,' Henri explained, gesturing to the vast expanse of open space. 'But we use the space from time to time for experimental equipment. Do you recognise this?' he asked pointing to a rack of equipment.

'RS 6000 running AIX if I'm not mistaken,' Pierson replied, 'I've worked on this technology myself and this operating system too.' Henri nodded.

'And this?' he pointed at a series of consoles.

'OS/2,' came the reply.

'What's running here?' Henri asked again, pointing to some other equipment,

'Solaris. If I'm not mistaken,' Pierson answered, looking closely at the screen.

'And here?' Henri pointed again as they walked on further.

'Windows—obviously.' Pierson replied with a wry smile.

As they walked beyond the first group of equipment there was a section with black boxes over six feet tall. Henri pointed again. 'But what about this, do you know about this one?'

'z/OS,' Pierson replied. 'I've worked on that too.'

Henri was disappointed 'You know your systems, yet you can't be an expert in all of them.' It was both a statement and a question, but Pierson merely shrugged his shoulders and remarked almost under his breath, 'if you say so Henri.'

Pierson retraced his route. Henri followed and as they passed back through the outer office, where Henri turned right.

'The operators all smoke. Well, most of them smoke; it's in their nature. Perhaps they're bored. They're certainly lazy, so the smoking room is down here; close enough so they won't have to go far.' He walked up to a pair of doors and opened them. There was no card swipe mechanism, but there was good air conditioning. The room reeked of stale tobacco, even though nobody was present except the two of them.

'It appears to be an opportune moment,' Henri remarked, looking around and choosing a table near the back of the room.

Within the room were eleven round tables, each with either four or five chairs. Ashtrays placed in the middle of the tables were full of cigarette butts. At the far end was a soft drinks machine and next to it one that vended coffee and beyond that was a cigarette vending machine.

Henri pulled up one of the chairs and Pierson sat adjacent. Henri spent a few minutes loading the bowl of his pipe with tobacco and eventually lighting it. 'We've been monitoring the communications of a man called Konstantin Dobrowiecki. According to our information, he works for the Polish government and has been the official contact for the sales of Elektra and Vitesse Acquise 4. A short time ago he pulled out of negotiations, but we know he's been in contact with Geoff Abbot.' Henri paused briefly before picking up the conversation again. 'Do you know how the software is going to be licenced?'

'No idea,' Pierson replied.

Henri puffed at his pipe and continued. '1600 Euros per journey per train.'

Pierson mulled this over in his mind for a few seconds.

'But that's enormous per day, for all the trains used in one country or by one company.' Pierson remarked.

'Exactly,' replied Henri, 'so if it could be bought for a lower price, then that would benefit everybody except the real owners of the software. Even a one time fee for 10,000 journeys would be cheap for the buyer and lucrative for the seller. Especially so if the seller didn't have the rights to it.'

'Is that the selling price then: 16,000,000 Euros?' Pierson asked, having calculated the number quickly.

'Through piracy it is—according to our information,' Henri replied.

'Where have you got such detailed information from?' Pierson asked wondering about its authenticity.

'This part came from Bob Selway, if I recall correctly,' Henri remarked almost as a throwaway comment not appearing concerned about it.

'So why the interest in the money markets?' Pierson pressed him.

'Because,' Henri replied, 'a hiccough was noticed a few weeks ago as a routine check by our treasury. They notified us. It may be nothing, but there may be some directly or indirectly related activity.'

'Is that what you meant on the plane on Saturday when you spoke of the other matter to Bill?' Pierson asked.

Henri took a long puff and then slowly exhaled, looking wistfully at the pipe before answering. 'Soon it will be no secret that there's a huge banking crisis looming. We've already seen the first signs, and so as you English say, that muddies the waters. On top of this, Bill indicated that he believed there was a leak in the higher echelons of your country's civil service, and that's partly why you're here instead of England.'

'But we know the deadly phone calls came from Paris,' Pierson remarked.

'Yes,' Henri answered again puffing on his pipe, 'but your colleagues were all in England when they died. Do you want to go back there and risk the same fate?'

'No,' Pierson replied.

'There's a curious part of the problem that we don't understand. It may be nothing,' said Henri as he weighed it in his mind, waving his hand dismissively, 'but it may be key information,'

Pierson waited for Henri to finish.

Finally he took another large inhalation on his pipe and exhaled slowly before speaking again.

'Have you heard of the Pareto Principle?' he asked.

Pierson shook his head.

'Vilfredo Pareto, 1848 to 1923. He was an Italian who carried out a survey in Italy and established that 80 per cent of the country was owned by 20 per cent of the people. The Pareto Principle is commonly known as the 80/20 rule.'

'I've heard of that,' said Pierson emphatically.

Henri nodded. 'As I said it may be nothing, but we've seen references to it more than once in this matter.'

Henri revealed nothing further; and clearly wasn't sure whether this so called Pareto Principle was of any importance.

'Okay,' Henri continued, 'let's go back and see if we can track down our Parisian caller.'

They returned to the office where Jean-Pierre, Francesca and Antoine were still looking at the reports that Marcel had printed.

'Any more information from the phone companies?' Henri asked them.

Marcel looked up, 'none,' he said, shaking his head and blinking profusely.

'Let's pay the computer a visit and find out who is operating it,' Henri continued. 'What's the address?'

Marcel passed him a sheet of paper and Henri took it and walked into his inner office. Picking up his telephone he dialled the number for and then spoke to a senior officer in the gendarmerie and arranged to meet at the address that evening at eight pm.

'Why so late?' Pierson asked.

'We can arrest them, sling them somewhere quiet for the night and go for a meal. Assuming there is anyone to catch, and if they only work during the day then we'll have a nice easy visit and we'll be uninterrupted. It might be that the place is merely a switching centre, just a modem connected from somewhere else, but if people are around I'd rather not have a street fight, this address is a market street,' Henri said, waving the sheet of paper with the address written on it. 'Remember, the French gendarmes carry guns. The fewer innocent bystanders we shoot, the better it will look. These people are clearly not afraid of killing. That much we already know. On top of which, at eight pm it will still be daylight and if there is anyone there trying to make a getaway we have a better chance of seeing them.'

The time passed quickly and soon after five pm they each left the buildings. Francesca and Pierson walked back along the Rue de Surene to their apartment. Pierson got changed and as he walked into the lounge he saw Francesca with a gun. Looking surprised he pointed at it, 'I didn't know you carried one of those.'

'It's just as well you didn't try anything then,' she replied smiling at him. 'I'm well prepared.'

'What now?' he asked still half watching the gun and trying to look at his watch. Noting it was almost six in the evening he moved carefully around the room, never completely taking his eyes of the pistol as Francesca expertly finished off her maintenance of the weapon.

'We can go and get there early if you want to see the raid. It's in the Rue Mouffetard in the Jardin des Plantes quarter.'

'Whatever you say,' Pierson replied. 'Are you taking your car?'

'No,' Francesca replied, 'it's a market street and parking will be difficult. We'll go by Metro.'

They left the apartment a few minutes later and made their way to Madeleine Metro station. As they descended, there was a map of the Metro on the wall next to the ticket machines. 'We need to get to Censier Daubenton and we'll have to change at Pyramides from metro line 14 to line 7,' Francesca remarked having quickly checked the map.

Pierson nodded and felt uneasy, as was betrayed by his almost continual watching of everyone that went by. The fact the Francesca had a gun didn't make him feel any more comfortable.

She paid for the tickets and giving him one of them, led the way through the automatic barriers and then onto the platform for destination Boulevard Massena.

It was warm on the platform and they both sat down waiting for the next train. It took more than 20 minutes. Pierson meanwhile checked his watch continuously and playfully kicked the ground trying to lever up chewing gum that was stuck in place.

As Pierson looked towards the tunnel where the train would emerge, he saw a blonde haired woman standing on the platform nearby. Wisps of her hair began to rise gently. Then, as the invisible breeze increased, so more of her hair began to dance uncontrollably. Even Pierson himself was soon enjoying the cool wind from the rush of air being pushed through into the station.

It wasn't just the wind, but the growing noise of the approaching carriages on the rails that encouraged the awaiting travellers to step towards the platform edge. Within moments, Pierson and Francesca stood and watched as the rolling stock passed by, gradually decelerating and finally halting with a squeal of its brakes.

Hardly anyone disembarked and only a few people were already on board when they entered their carriage. The doors swished c ~d behind them a few seconds later. Pierson remaine'   ng whilst Francesca sat. The train lurched forwar'   .ɔn slowly and relatively smoothly it accelerated, with only the occasional subsequent erratic surge.

It took only two minutes to get to Pyramides, and as they disembarked Francesca led the way through the labyrinth of tunnels onto the platform for line seven, bound for Mairie d'Ivry and Villejuif-Louis Aragon. Either destination would have been fine.

It was only a five-minute wait on this occasion before the next train arrived and then once aboard, Pierson checked the time, but there was still almost an hour and a half before the raid.

Eight stops later and they emerged at their destination and made their way to the surface. After the heat of the Metro, it was a pleasant evening air that greeted them. Being now almost seven pm, they sat at a table of one of the street side cafés and ordered drinks whilst waiting for their colleagues to arrive.

Pierson and Francesca chatted for some time. She told him some more of her background and her family. He couldn't help noticing her gun as her jacket opened slightly while they were talking.

With only twenty minutes remaining Henri arrived, and he made his way to the table next to theirs. Like Pierson, he was now dressed casually and he too kept checking his watch.

After a further 15 minutes the gendarmes arrived and Henri made himself known to them. Waving at Francesca he beckoned her to join. Pierson got up too.

'Not you,' she said. 'You're not trained for this I'm afraid.'

Pierson was taken aback, but realised that argument was futile. They were right. He wasn't trained for it. After all, he thought, even Henri had got the police involved. In any case,

Henri was looking his way and just nodded as if to confirm what Francesca had said.

The gendarmes entered the building, with Henri and Francesca in tow. On the third floor of the building, lights went on as Pierson watched from the café table outside. A split second later a gunshot rang out. There was a scream but from a woman in the street, near to where he was sitting. Pierson's body went rigid as his eyes flashed from the apartment lights to the woman and then back to the door of the apartment building. People in the street were running indoors or taking shelter where they could. Pierson was glued to the spot, partly by fear and partly by his own rational thoughts prevailing. He didn't wish to present his back to the gunman and give him a big target, so he remained in place. His heart began to pound stronger and stronger.

There were two further shots and then shouting. A man burst out of the building and began running along the now empty street, chased by two gendarmes. He turned and shot one of the gendarmes who instantaneously fell in agony. The other gendarme dropped to the floor behind a market stall that was still present from earlier in the day. The gunman fired at the second gendarme but missed. Then Pierson saw Francesca coming out of the building, checking for the man. She had heard the shots, but didn't know from which direction they'd come.

The adrenalin was now coursing through Pierson's arteries as he gradually stood, not wishing to attract the gunman's attention with any sudden movement.

The man was slowly walking backwards, watching the doorway he had just run out of, and he was now closing towards Pierson. On seeing Francesca, the gunman raised his gun a third time, Pierson shouted out, 'Get down!' and ran the few steps towards him, using superhuman power, willing himself there before the gunman could shoot. In an instant he took a flying leap at the man, his throat now dry and his heart almost pumping out of his chest.

The gun discharged again and both men fell to the ground with Pierson lying on top, blood beginning to trickle down the cobbled street.

Francesca had thrown herself to the floor, but was now rising to her feet again. Her hair began dangling partly in front of her eyes, she was still crouching, with her gun held firmly in both hands pointing at the two bodies laid on the street in front of her.

Continuing to keep a small profile she walked carefully towards them, never once taking her gun or her eyes off the target. The uninjured gendarme began to mirror her, walking in a curved path towards the head of the gunman, keeping his gun firmly targeted on the man.

As they reached the two men, Francesca could see the gun was laid on the ground nearby. She picked it up. Crouching near the two bodies, she looked at the gendarme now holding his gun and aiming it at the head of the perpetrator. Francesca reached for Pierson's limp body and she could see the blood now running from underneath him. She rolled him over.

Pierson slowly opened his eyes and looked at her. 'He had you in his sights. It was the only thing I could do,' he sat up and she helped him to his feet.

'Thank you,' she replied gently as she placed her arms around him and kissed him, realising that he may well have saved her life and at some personal risk. 'You've been shot,' she continued. As she stood back and looked at his left arm, she could see blood oozing from it.

'These clothes were new,' Pierson declared, trying to make a joke of it but wincing at the same time. 'I've never been shot before, it's really painful,' he added, trying to stop the blood.

The gendarme handcuffed the gunman, stood him up and led him away. Henri had appeared at the doorway and was using his phone to get medical help on the scene, he then placed his phone back in his pocket and came across to where

Pierson and Francesca were standing. 'You were supposed to stay here,' he said angrily, pointing at the café tables.

'I did,' Pierson replied. 'Well, almost. I had to do something.'

Henri raised a single eyebrow as if to indicate that he wasn't really buying the story. But it was clear that he understood.

Medics arrived within a few minutes and treated Pierson. The bullet had passed through his lower arm missing vital tendons and arteries, so it was relatively simple to clean up, although there had been quite a lot of blood. 'It will be sore for a few days,' Francesca told him, translating for the paramedic who seemed bemused that Pierson could not speak French.

After the attention, Pierson saw the shot gendarme, but in fact he wasn't critically injured, he'd fallen as a result of being shot. He'd been hit near his right shoulder and the bullet had passed completely through his body.

'Who was our Parisian caller?' Pierson asked Henri. 'Was it a computer?'

'Oh yes,' Henri replied. 'You were right; come and see.' Henri led the way again, back up to the third floor where another gendarme was standing guard.

'What are these people protecting that needs guns?' Pierson asked.

'A lot of money,' Henri replied.

They walked inside and Pierson saw the apartment brimming over with computer equipment. There was an IBM RS6000 running AIX like the one at the ministry of the interior.

He studied the equipment and saw the extensive array of disks.

'What do they need all this for?' he asked slowly as he surveyed it all; really directing the question at himself more than anyone else. 'There's a huge amount of data storage capacity here. It's in the order of terabytes.'

'Terabytes?' Henri asked.

Somewhat distracted by what he was seeing, Pierson replied slowly to Henri, as though he had many other things on his mind. 'A terabyte is 1,000 gigabytes.' There was a pause as Pierson continued to examine the equipment looking closely at the console, 'Well actually it's 1,024 gigabytes if you wish to be precise, but there's loads of it in this array,' he added, pointing at the stack of electronic boxes to one side of the console and then standing back to take it all in.

'We'll have it shipped to the ministry and re-assembled there for close study,' Henri remarked.

'Why not just leave it here?' Pierson asked.

Henri pointed at Pierson's shot arm. 'I will, if you have a spare for this. I don't want any surprise visitors.'

Pierson smiled. 'Okay, let's do it your way.'

ASK NO QUESTIONS

The following day Pierson got up earlier and noticed that Francesca had already left. It seemed more comfortable to dress casually and he was about to put on the jacket he'd worn the night before, but the hole in the sleeve going in one side and out of the other made it look shabby.

His arm was still painful. Although it had only been a flesh wound, the bullet had separated the tissue as it travelled through, rather than pushing a cylinder of it out. It had felt to him at the time as if the limb was being ripped off, but within seconds the sensation of searing pain had taken over. Now though, it ached instead, but as he thought about it, he realised how lucky he'd been not to have been killed the previous evening.

The wound itself was in his forearm, and had needed stitches that left an ugly reminder of that violent moment, not that the pain left him needing any kind of visual memory jogger.

He chose another jacket; and then with some care slipped his left arm into it, and then manoeuvred it around his shoulders sliding the other sleeve onto his right arm. Leaving the apartment soon afterwards, he began walking towards the ministry of the interior, but he couldn't fail to notice the gloomy signs of deteriorating weather.

It had begun to rain: but only a little at that time. The overcast sky made a depressing view, and for Pierson, somehow, it exacerbated his loneliness. His desire to wrap his arms around Madeleine was very much on his mind. Just to see her and tell her that everything was okay was all that he wanted to do at that moment.

He tried his best to push the thoughts of her away. But he realised it would be tantalisingly easy to get a taxi to Orly and fly home. He could have been with her within six hours. It was then that he remembered the danger was still present. The fact that someone had photographed Madeleine on the 6Th August from a distance was worrying. So too was the mystery photographer on the previous Friday, when he and Madeleine had had their picnic.

He was unhappy that in his view, between him and his new colleagues, they had made such little progress on the case. Even though he knew about the exploding cell phones, he sensed that the people who'd set that up probably wouldn't stop there. Until he knew why they wanted him dead, he couldn't be certain of how to stay alive. He was simply an amateur— although an amateur by definition does something for the love of it. There was no love here—just fear.

His thoughts returned to the problem at hand and he consoled himself with the thought that within a few weeks at most, the consensus was that it would all be sorted out, and safe for him to return. The fact that the Parisian caller had been tracked down was a big plus, hopefully the interviewing of this man would reveal, if not everything, then enough to move the investigation forward.

Pierson started to make a mental list of the points in the case that perhaps were loose ends or needed closer scrutiny. One of the first things that stood out was news of a possible leak in the UK government department, and who it might be, and whether it was limited to one person, or if it was a group of people. He was also curious about the money markets and the rand, and how that impacted the case, if in fact it had any bearing on it at all. As it had been Bill who'd suggested keeping his eye on the money markets, perhaps he knew something that was troubling him, but not enough to provide hard evidence of any criminal acts. After all Pierson thought, what if someone had been buying foreign currency, that wasn't a crime—so it had to be some peripheral matter. How could the illegal selling of software to an Eastern European country tie in with buying currency from South Africa? The jump between the two was beyond logic, or at least beyond the facts in his possession at that time.

The photograph taken of Madeleine was strange too, as she herself had said. If the bad guys took the shot then why—and how even—did they give it to the good guys; or did the good guys take the photograph to scare both of them? This was eating away at him. It gnawed at Pierson's subconscious mind, but perhaps that was the quirky element that Bob Selway had mentioned and apologised for on the plane.

Most of all though, there was Henri's remark about what Pierson knew that was so dangerous: what hidden secret did he have that he didn't realise he possessed. Or what did they— whoever they were—believe he knew that could threaten what they wanted to do. And, in addition, what was being done that was worth killing four people?

He couldn't see any answers crystallising out of these questions, nor could he see an overall picture developing.

As he mused over these points he'd failed to properly notice how close he'd got to the ministry, and he suddenly found himself standing on the plaza immediately outside the main building.

On entering the complex, he managed to get in just before a large group of people dressed in raincoats came rushing through, umbrellas in hand. This was immediately followed by the same people at varying stages desperately catching their breath, laughing loudly and gesturing wildly at the weather outside and each other, looking very pleased with themselves that they'd made it into the safe haven; all of them talking at high speed and of course in French.

Pierson got into the elevator and selected his floor. His thoughts floated in and out as he waited to descend completely, being slightly distracted by the lift's electrical noises.

Once the doors opened at his destination he stepped out and followed the labyrinth of corridors towards Henri's office, remembering much of the route as Francesca had described it the previous day. He found the picture of the yellow portcullis grid, and using his pass, he entered.

Henri was already in the swing of the day's business, reading some documentation in the outer office. As Pierson walked in it didn't distract Henri immediately, but after a few seconds he looked up.

'Good morning,' he said with a beaming smile.

'Hi everyone,' Pierson replied smiling and glancing around to see who else was present. Francesca came out of Henri's office and greeted him warmly.

Coffee had already been made and delivered and—as she was by now familiar with the way he took it—she offered Pierson a mug. He stood quietly sipping his drink waiting for Henri to speak again.

'We have all the parts from the computer downstairs. They were delivered overnight. Maybe you can help us to get it operational and then see if you can find the source code for Elektra on it.'

'Okay,' said Pierson.

Henri led the way down to the seventh basement floor. They walked in silence towards the lifts and then down to the computer hall again; and at the far end, in pieces, was the IBM computer that had been housed at the raided address the previous evening.

Marcel, Antoine and Jean-Pierre were already busy trying to reassemble and rewire the equipment. Antoine began to lift the floor tiles, revealing a half metre void underneath and showing that the entire floor stood on metal stilts. Such an arrangement was common in many computer rooms, and Pierson was sufficiently familiar with the sight not to be intrigued by it.

Henri looked a little surprised on seeing the floor being taken up. 'I have other work to do. I'll be back later. It seems that the computer was switched off without knowing the password for the main login account. If the man we brought in doesn't know the answer, then we're in trouble, unless you know a way around it.'

Pierson shrugged.

'I'll catch you later,' Henri added as he walked off.

Pierson carefully took off his jacket and started to help the other three to assemble the racks of disks, even with his arm aching so badly. The movement involved seemed to be therapeutic and diminished the pain somewhat, so he was keen to continue.

Henri made his way up one level. On that floor were situated a whole suite of offices that included conference rooms for formal meetings; informal and ad-hoc get-togethers; social gatherings with bars available; interview rooms for suspects ranging from non violent ones who could be interviewed without great security, to interview rooms that had the highest level of security and were packed with electronic surveillance equipment.

Henri found himself in a corridor that was not well lit, deliberately so, to put off the interviewee should he or she escape. He entered one of the rooms by using his swipe card to let him in. The electronic lock clicked and he pushed the door open.

As he stepped inside he could see a seated male operative wearing headphones. The only clue to the man's authorised presence was the identity pass loosely dangling from his neck. In front of him was what appeared to be a large window, but was in fact a two-way mirror, the other side of which was a very secure and brightly lit interrogation room; and sitting at right angles to the vantage point from the observation room, was the gunman who'd been arrested the previous evening.

On the console area below the viewing window and next to Henri was a whole series of recording equipment for sound and vision, fed from a microphone and camera in the interrogation room. A video tape recorder was running; recording the silence.

Henri's colleague removed his headphones.

'Ca va?' Henri quizzed.

'Oui, Ca va,' came the reply, as the man looked up again from his monitoring activities.

Henri looked at the console area and to its right was the gun that had been used by their captive, neatly placed inside a sealed plastic bag. A report stapled to the outside gave details of the weapon and its registered owner. Henri picked up the package and studied it.

Interrogation was his least favourite task, but the four people who worked for him were mainly involved in research and were incapable of interacting with much other than computers. Extracting vital information from a hostile subject was not something he could ask any of them to do and expect success. Francesca—although vastly different in personality to the three men that reported to him due to her background and training— was in Henri's opinion guilty of having too much personality. Her approach was best described as fearsome and as such generally counterproductive.

So it was Henri who was left with the short straw. He placed his hand on the shoulder of his seated colleague and just sighed, nodding resignedly. His colleague smiled and Henri turned to leave the room as his colleague replaced his headphones and resumed watching the silent detainee.

Having walked the short distance along the corridor to the door of the interrogation room, Henri paused briefly before entering. Above the door was a band of lights. A green one was illuminated, indicating that it was safe to enter. Henri used his pass to swipe the entry control mechanism. The door lock clicked and he opened the door. Unseen by Henri the light above the door changed to amber, now indicating that an interview was in progress.

Inside the bare, wood-panelled room were two chairs and a single table. The gunman occupied one of the chairs. His arms and legs were bound to it with thin cord. He was in his twenties, had dark curly hair and was now sporting a day's growth of beard. His eyes were sunken and he had a slightly wild look about him. Henri noticed that he smelled bad too, but perhaps that wasn't his own fault. The interrogation room had a cupboard-sized annexe comprising a stainless steel toilet and wash basin. But clearly the prisoner was unable to use it at that time.

Henri pulled out the other chair, lightly scraping two of its legs across the hard ceramic tiled floor. The sound bounced off the walls, and the ceiling's acoustically enhanced suspended panelling. This was enough to distract the gunman from his apparently self imposed stupor, and he briefly looked upwards catching sight of the fluorescent lights recessed into some of the overhead panels. But he soon turned his attention back towards Henri without actually looking him in the eyes. There was a distant vagueness to his expression. Even when Henri dropped the gun on the table in front of his captive there was no further reaction, so Henri began speaking to him in French.

'We've checked this gun. It's registered to Rene Sebastien. Is that you?'

The man still refused to make eye contact.

'You're in a great deal of trouble.' Henri continued 'That computer of yours has been telephoning some people in England and when they answered they were killed. We know about the cell phones and the explosives fitted in them. We also know exactly how it was done—by the unique tones of Mozart's fortieth symphony.'

The gunman looked into Henri's eyes as though there was a glimmer that he was now worried by Henri's knowledge.

'Ah,' said Henri. 'You're wondering how we know?' His captive looked away. Henri leaned across the table. 'You missed one,' he added, 'one of your targets is still alive.'

Again the gunman looked into Henri's eyes and now looked slightly more concerned but still he said nothing. 'Unfortunately for you, he didn't like Mozart, so he changed the tune,' Henri continued. 'Think about it. How else could we know? The phone calls were traced back to your computer and we know you telephoned the three men that died.'

The gunman's expression changed almost imperceptibly but Henri didn't let it slip by unnoticed. It looked like there was growing fear in his face; the only problem for Henri was why?

Henri stood again and walked around the room, still talking, 'now that's interesting isn't it. If the people were killed in England yet the phone number was dialled in France by a computer, then who is the murderer?'

Henri paused and looked across at the mirror at the end of the room. Then he continued again. 'The English have no jurisdiction, which is good. No one carried out a criminal act there. Do you know why it's good?' Henri paused again, allowing the man to speak but not really expecting him to. 'Because the English don't have the death penalty for murder,' he added. 'Of course few civilised nations do that now. But in France we still have certain colonial interests and because jurisdiction is a problem, we can elect to send you there.'

Then leaning down to the ear of the man he whispered, 'and of course some of those colonies still use the guillotine.' The man struggled slightly at the sound of the word 'guillotine' but said nothing, the look in his eyes was now definitely fearful. Yet something still stopped him from saying anything.

Henri picked up the gun and left the room, giving the man a chance to think on his words. He left him for a full thirty minutes and deposited the gun back in the observation room.

When he entered the interrogation room again, the man's eyes met his; and Henri continued the questioning as he sat opposite him. 'Tell me your name and who you're working for. We have all the evidence we need against you for murder, so telling me that won't hurt you, but it might help you soften our attitude.' But the man was still silent, apparently fearful based on the look in his eyes, yet still defiant: in a fragile way, yet defiant anyway.

'Do you think you can escape from here?' Henri continued, calmly gesturing around the room, 'is that what's going through your mind? Believe me, that won't happen. And if your friends— if you're not working alone—if they are planning to get you out, it won't happen. Do you know where you are officially at this moment?' The man's eyes changed and he flinched as though he was about to shrug his shoulders, but stopped himself. 'You're still officially free, there's no record of your arrest, because we have you. This is the ministry of the interior and nobody knows you're here. There will be no phone calls and no help on its way. No legal advisors.'

Still the man didn't speak.

Henri looked into his eyes and without revealing any of his frustration he got up and walked to the door again. The exit mechanism needed his pass swiped to let him out—which he did. Seconds later the external security light returned to green as the spring-loaded hinges forced the door closed making the resounding clang behind him.

Back in the observation room his colleague passed on a message from the reception on the ground floor. Bill had arrived from England and Henri proceeded to collect him, hoping for some inspiration against his silent adversary.

While Henri had been interrogating the gunman, Pierson, Antoine, Marcel and Jean-Pierre had been steadily working in the computer room.

It took over an hour to just get the computer components and racks in the correct arrangement and vicinity to each other. However, all of the equipment had been neatly packed into cardboard boxes with protective material to safeguard against damage whilst in transit. But this operation had been carried out by civil servants who merely numbered the boxes from one upwards, and the inventory was inaccurate to the point where it just described the contents in French as sundry electronics or electronic racking in most cases, so all the boxes had to be opened before a complete picture could be seen.

Jean-Pierre, Antoine and Marcel had been busy doing all of this before Pierson arrived. But now pieces seemed to be missing. Pierson checked every box, looking for the missing components. There were over a hundred packages and they'd been strewn around with no regard to their original order—not that that would have been of any help.

Gradually, he tracked down some loose components and handed them to the nearest of the other three; and depending on which one he gave this new component or part to determined their reaction. Marcel generally blinked a great deal at the item looking confused and wandering off with great purpose after a few seconds without saying a word; Jean-Pierre invariably mused over it by gently stroking his goatee and would then nod to himself and utter a long sound—probably the French equivalent of 'hmmmm' Pierson assumed; Antoine though was far more demonstrative and often louder, always enthusiastically taking the item and declaring in great delight that it was just what he was looking for by announcing a very noisy 'Oui!' or a less dominant but equally loud 'Voila!', on some occasions he would exclaim something in French that was obviously akin to eureka, but once or twice he just stood there and scratched his head looking at the component, sometimes in awe and sometimes in confusion, turning it and moving it between his hands to see if that made it look any more familiar.

Even with all of these trials they did complete the assembly satisfactorily, but it was almost lunchtime before the equipment had been totally reassembled, and it was early afternoon by the time that the final cabling was underway to connect the machine to the mains and telephone outlets. They'd arranged with the French telephone company to provide a telephone line with the same phone number as was given for the equipment when it had been in the apartment—where they'd found it the previous night.

Marcel replaced the removed floor tiles and then sitting at the console, he powered up the computer. The boot process took a few minutes, in which time the racking for the disks emitted flashing green lights like some frantic display at a discotheque. Eventually the console issued a message to prompt for someone to login to the system with a valid account. Marcel halted and left it in that state.

'We can't go any further,' he explained to Pierson, 'until we have the account and password we need.'

'I know,' Pierson replied, viewing the equipment and wondering whether any of its users from the previous day were trying to connect to it. 'If there's nothing else to be done, then I'll find Henri and Francesca and see if they've made any progress.'

Marcel moved his eyes to focus on a spot just behind Pierson and pointed. It was Henri.

Pierson turned around to see that Henri was sporting an uncharacteristically serious look, so severe was his expression that all the joviality that was usually just underneath the surface was now buried much deeper. He was clasping a piece of paper in his left hand that appeared to be an official report of some sort.

Pierson began walking towards him and frowned slightly in a quizzical fashion. Henri looked at the paper and back towards Pierson as he began to speak quietly and slowly. 'We have some very bad news I'm afraid.' He looked almost ill with concern.

From behind Henri, Pierson could see Bill, who slowly stepped to one side and beckoned Pierson to go with him.

'Hi Bill,' said Pierson cautiously checking Henri's expression again. But Henri had cast his eyes toward the floor.

Bill had a troubled look that indicated something terrible must have happened.

'What is it?' Pierson asked now with some concern in his voice.

Bill carefully took the paper from Henri. as Henri slowly released his grip on it and then stood back.

'Let's go somewhere we can talk,' said Bill.

Without a word, Henri ushered them to the outer room of the computer hall, he whispered to the operator sat at the consoles, whose face turned ashen and then he quickly got up and left.

Pierson sat down. He wondered what the problem could be.

'Although I have it in writing I need to tell you myself,' Bill continued.

'It's Madeleine,' Pierson said slowly as though he knew and didn't want it to be true. He couldn't stop himself from saying the words.

And Bill slowly nodded. 'I'm afraid so. I'm deeply, deeply sorry…'

Pierson said nothing and began to get a sickening feeling inside, from the pit of his stomach. His mouth went dry and his heart began pounding. His eyes blurred from shock and he felt as though he was about to pass out.

Placing his arm on the table next to him to steady himself he looked at Bill and with his other hand he reached for the paper Bill was holding. It was clear. It was a police report detailing an explosion at his house during the early hours of that morning. It was blamed on a suspected gas leak and the charred remains of a man and a woman were found in the debris. The woman had been identified as Madeleine Brady.

Pierson said nothing. His eyes lost their spark as though his soul had just been extinguished. A mass of jumbled thoughts swamped his mind. None of them clear, just too many questions, and a devastating sense of loss. He felt empty.

From that moment on nothing mattered. The purpose behind his French excursion had evaporated. He'd lost his sense of being and couldn't function. He just knew he had to leave the building—that was the only thing he could think about.

He rose from his chair and giving the paper back to Bill he spoke softly. 'Thank you for coming here in person.' Without another word he turned and left the room before he lost the last remnants of his composure.

Pierson made his way back to the lifts. He couldn't work out what was happening. He didn't feel anger: he felt nothing. His mind wasn't functioning. It was like he was in a different reality, as though he'd been plucked from his own life and plunged into this empty existence: an existence over which he had no control and one that he didn't even understand. There was nothing familiar about it and all his connections to the past were now irretrievably severed.

The next few minutes were a haze and although he couldn't remember how he got there, he soon found himself outside the building complex. The weather had now got much worse and the rain was falling in torrents. Within seconds he was soaked. He began to walk towards the traffic and briefly considered stepping out in front of any fast moving vehicle. But as he reached the kerb it was as though autopilot cut in and he stopped and found himself hailing a taxi. In his schoolboy French he was able to give the driver adequate instructions to get him to his destination.

Henri and Bill were both deeply shocked by the news, but they waited before they followed Pierson, wondering, but neither actually saying, whether they'd lost their best chance at unlocking the enigma at the heart of the case.

On leaving the computer room, Henri took Bill back to the lift and they went up the two floors to Henri's office.

'Hello Bill,' said Francesca, greeting him warmly. When she saw his reaction though she backed off a little, glanced at Henri to see a similar cool response and then noticed that Pierson wasn't with them. She quickly assumed that whatever the problem was, it was about him.

'I thought Mike was in the computer room?' she added quizzically, looking at Henri and trying to be helpful, as she guessed Bill would want to see him, but she didn't know that he already had.

'He was,' Henri replied.

'Until we showed him this,' Bill added glancing first at Henri for his approval. Henri nodded.

Francesca read through the report and then looked at each of the men in turn.

'Is this true?' she asked.

Bill nodded this time.

'Oh no,' she exclaimed putting her hand to her mouth and handing the paper back. 'Where is he now?'

Henri shrugged his shoulders and Bill shook his head as if to say he didn't know.

'Aren't you concerned about him?' she asked them in a voice that was speeding up by the second and getting louder too.

'Yes we are,' Bill replied, 'but no one can deal with counselling straight away. I've never had to do this in the field before with any agent.'

'He's not an agent,' exclaimed Francesca emphatically. 'He's just a man that's lost his wife; and it shouldn't have happened. How could you just let him walk out?' she demanded. 'You don't know what he might do. This news…it could destroy him and you just let him walk out of here without watching him or following him?'

Both men looked sheepish as she began to vent her temper on them. 'What if he does something stupid, who will check your precious software then? Did you think of that?'

Neither of them replied.

'I'll have him picked up,' said Henri after a few moments looking shaken, 'I'll get in touch with the gendarmerie and get them to track him down. But he needs time to grieve, to be alone, that's why I didn't stop him.'

Francesca stood with her hands clenching into fists as her eyes flared at Henri, waiting for him to say anything that she could argue with. Although he thought of many things to say he dismissed them all except one, 'your passion is strong but you don't know what goes through the mind of a man in this situation.'

'And you do!?' she declared.

'I know something of it. I can imagine. Let him be. We'll find him.'

Francesca picked up her coat. Henri was about to enter his inner office when he saw her disappearing. 'Where are you going?' he shouted, 'you may be my niece but you still work for me and you still obey my orders!'

Francesca said nothing, but stormed out of the outer office.

Henri picked up the phone on his desk and made a quick telephone call. Bill was standing in the doorway of his office and as Henri put the receiver down he looked at his English counterpart. 'Sometimes we get complications we didn't look for.'

Bill merely nodded slowly.

'I gave him my word I would take care of Madeleine.' Bill remarked with some remorse and a hint of controlled sadness in his voice.

'This comes at a bad time. It's a terrible thing,' Henri observed shaking his head with a look of thunder on his face, but then he continued more philosophically and with a slightly worried expression.

'However, I can't afford to lose two people in one day.'

Quickly checking for his car keys in his jacket pocket Henri left hastily.

Francesca ran to the lifts, jabbing the buttons over and over until it arrived and then rushing in just as the doors had opened wide enough to squeeze through, she repeatedly selected floor zero, angrily shouting in Italian at the electronics to hurry up.

It didn't take long, but held captive in the confined space she paced around like a predatory feline, occasionally beating the doors with her fists accompanied by further vocal outbursts, only interspersed by her loud breathing that signalled her attempts to control her anger. On arrival at the reception area, she dashed straight outside, leaving behind a trail of people whose heads turned at this young woman's obvious urgency.

For all of her sense of purpose and determination, she hadn't gained much advantage. She attempted to hail three taxis which themselves were scarce due to the severe weather conditions. Shouting at each one that ignored her and drove on by as though she had been invisible, she refused to give up.

She remained standing—all be it impatiently—by the kerb, frantically trying to get a lift, until a cream Citroen pulled in by her. The driver leaned across and opened the door. 'Get in, we'll get him together.' It was Henri. Francesca slid into the car and Henri pulled off into the afternoon traffic while Francesca was still closing the door.

'Where will he be?' Henri asked.

'I don't know?' she replied with a murderous look in her eyes and desperation in her voice, 'I'm trying to think.'

'The airport?' Henri suggested.

'No, not the airport,' she replied. 'He's not running away. He's rushing to be somewhere. The airport's a place to go when you're leaving.'

'He'll want to be alone,' she continued, 'away from people. Just him and his thoughts.'

'A church: the Notre Dame perhaps?' Henri asked accelerating and beginning to head east.

'Perhaps,' Francesca replied. She paused for a few minutes and remained silent as Henri fought his way through the traffic.

'No he won't be there,' she eventually remarked. Turning to Henri the sudden realisation of where he would be struck her like a bolt of lightning. 'Le Tour Eiffel. That's where he'll be.'

'Are you sure?' Henri asked disbelievingly.

'Oui,' she replied. 'Very sure. Turn around.' she demanded.

'Why there?' Henri asked.

'Just do it!' Francesca shouted.

Henri wasn't convinced.

'Please,' she asked him more softly as she gently touched his arm and looked her uncle in the eyes.

Henri nodded and did a 'u' turn and began heading west and then south past the ministry of the interior again and on towards the Eiffel tower. Even with the weight of traffic, Henri had managed to get them there within just a few minutes, driving like a maniac.

As the car screeched to a halt, Francesca leapt out and began running towards the entrance. She waved her pass but the rain made it virtually impossible to read and she ran through to the first set of elevators forcefully squeezing in only as the doors were closing.

She wasn't alone as she began her journey to the top of the tower, although she was just as oblivious to her fellow passengers as they were to her, moving from one leg to the other and looking up, muttering under her breath to get there quicker. She checked her watch every few seconds in between repeatedly slipping her hands into the pockets of her raincoat. Finally when the cage halted, she rushed out pushing her way through the preoccupied sightseers in her hurry.

She dashed to the next set of lifts and waited, checking her watch again as she stamped her feet; but even though it caught the attention of other people getting in, she didn't care what anyone else thought of her actions, her mind was set on one goal: finding Pierson. The second elevator started moving, but her impatience grew exponentially it seemed with each passing moment, until the point when she reached the top, and as the doors opened she burst out with almost explosive force.

Now she found herself at the observation point at the very top of the tower. She ran from one side to the next, slowing down as she saw each new person or group of people. She tried hard to look at everyone's face, wanting and hoping that one of them would be Pierson and then finally, in one corner, standing in the open and getting soaked by the rain, was the lonely sight of the man she was seeking, briefly looking towards the heavens and then towards England.

She slowed as she drew closer. As soon as she was standing beside him, she reached out to touch him but stopped midway and placed her hands back in her pockets instead. She said nothing. He sensed she was there and turned to look at her and with the rain pouring down his face she realised she didn't know what to say.

She reached for his hand and took hold of it. She squeezed it tight and he responded and looked at her. 'She's gone,' Pierson said, as their eyes met. Francesca said nothing but just nodded gently. Pierson looked back out and then turning to look at Francesca he noticed her smiling at him faintly as she gently tugged him.

He took one last look at the view as though he was saying goodbye to Madeleine. Taking a deep breath he relaxed—but only slightly—and turned to walk away.

Pierson let his thoughts drift for the next few minutes as Francesca slowly took him to the base of the tower.

Henri was still waiting, but now he was arguing with a gendarme about his right to park his car there. Pierson hadn't noticed his new boss, but Francesca waved across to indicate that they would be walking back.

She took him to a nearby café, finally getting themselves out of the rain. As he sat at a table she got the coffees while Pierson continued to gaze out at the view of the Seine. It was more than a few minutes before either of them spoke, and then taking a deep breath Pierson was the one who broke the silence.

'What next?' he asked clearly distracted.

'Well,' she replied softly, holding her cup with both hands but not making eye contact immediately, 'I think we should get out of these wet things.'

She looked up and glanced at him briefly with a friendly half smile.

Pierson wanted to respond likewise, but merely flinched. However his eyes said enough to her to know that she'd connected with him.

'What do you want to do?' she asked him gently.

He took a few moments before replying, watching as she placed her cup back in the saucer.

'Stop the killing,' he said with a distant look in his eyes. 'I just want it to stop,' he added emphatically placing his hand across his forehead and closing his eyes as though he was trying to work out how it could be done.

'What about the people who did it?' Francesca asked him as she took a sip of her coffee, but immediately realised it was the wrong question. She closed her eyes and looked down—angry with herself at being so stupid.

'I want to find them,' he replied. 'It's them I want to stop.'

Silence followed between them again before he continued. 'I can't do this. I can't carry on like this. Thinking about Madeleine's death is slowly killing me.' As he finished speaking and he'd realised what he'd said, he paused before continuing. 'I never thought I would hear myself say those words.'

Francesca kept looking down, now holding her coffee cup with both hands she turned and then gazed out of the window.

'I want to find Madeleine's killer. I want justice,' said Pierson, 'Is that possible? Or am I being really naive?'

Francesca put her cup down and reaching out she touched his hand as he continued to talk, almost indicating that it was good for him to let his thoughts emerge.

'Perhaps I was stupid to come here. I should have just taken Madeleine away somewhere. What was I thinking? We could have gone trekking in the Himalayas or something. Gone somewhere remote. By the sound of it we only needed a few weeks or even days. We could have gone on a boat and still been alive.'

'You are alive,' Francesca declared looking at him and this time not turning away.

'I'll help you,' she added softly but with unyielding sincerity. 'Together we'll make this thing right again. We'll find the people who did this and put a stop to it. Believe me when I say they don't know what they're up against. They have badly underestimated us.'

Strangely, Pierson began to believe her conviction. There was something about her tone of voice and her Italian nature that engendered a belief of its own—like it was her personal vendetta.

A full hour passed by before they finished their drinks; then walking slowly they made their way back to the apartment. Francesca loosely slipped her arm through Pierson's: more to guide him in the right direction than any other reason, but it felt comfortable to them both.

No further progress was made that day on the case and the following day, Pierson and Francesca entered Henri's office in the morning. Bill was already waiting and standing as though he was nervous about seeing Pierson and what he would actually find.

They all noticed the empty look in Pierson's eyes. No further mention was made of Madeleine though.

'What have you learned from our guest Henri?' Pierson asked him in his now flat and emotionless voice.

Henri was quietly pleased that Pierson seemed keen on business as usual so he responded with as much normality as possible in the circumstances.

'Nothing,' came the reply. 'We know from other means that the gun belonged to a man called Rene Sebastien. But that's it. The man we have won't speak to us.'

Pierson thought on this for a few moments. 'Then I have an idea,' he said to Henri and took Henri into the inner office and closed the door behind the two of them. A few minutes later, Pierson and Henri walked out of the inner and outer offices. Henri looked aghast.

Bill turned to Francesca. 'Should we follow?'

'I don't think so,' she replied. 'Not this time.'

Henri and Pierson made their way to the observation room next to the interrogation room where the gunman could still be seen, sitting tied to his chair. He'd been released under guard for certain periods to use the toilets and to be fed, but was tied up again after each occasion.

'What do you want to know from this man more than anything else?' Pierson asked Henri with deadly earnest.

'His name, the most powerful account and password for the system and who he is working for,' Henri replied.

'Then,' said Pierson. 'Go in there, say nothing else and just ask him those questions, to burn them in his memory and then leave. Just ask him once that's all. Do nothing else to distract him.'

Henri looked at Pierson closely. Pierson's eyes seemed now to be a window on his empty soul. The muscles in Pierson's face had dropped and relaxed, and even Henri felt chilled from the view of the tormented man standing in front of him. He turned and placed his hand on the door handle to leave the room and closed the door behind him.

After reaching the correct point in the corridor, he reached out for the swipe mechanism next to the door of the interrogation room. He had his pass in his hand already. As he swiped it through, so the light above him changed from green to amber and the door lock electronically clicked releasing it. Henri opened the door and saw the gunman, who didn't even bother to look at Henri as he entered. Even the clang of the door closing again made no difference to the man. He remained emotionless. Henri spoke to him in his native tongue and then for Pierson's benefit in English too.

'I want the answer to four questions. I will ask you now one final time and then I will not ask you again. What is your name? What is the main account on the AIX system that you have been using? What is the password for that account? And who are you working for?'

The man slowly moved his eyes towards Henri and gave him a defiant almost patronising look. He uttered a single short sigh but made no other noise. Henri turned and left the room.

Entering the observation room again Henri looked at Pierson. 'What do you need?'

'Carpet tape, scissors or a sharp knife and a cell phone that will work in that room,' he replied, pointing to it at the mirrored glass.

Henri held out his hand. 'Give me the Nokia. The rooms will stand explosive blasts of a certain magnitude, but not too much.' Henri guessed what Pierson was going to do.

'You have no problem with this?' Pierson almost told Henri rather than asking him.

'Killing a witness? Yes. I have a big problem with it, but accidents do happen don't they?' Henri replied, fiddling with the back of the Nokia before returning it to Pierson.

Pierson said nothing. He made no acknowledgement. His eyes merely stared back at Henri without emotion.

Henri left the room once again and ten minutes had passed before he returned with the items. Handing the additional cell phone to Pierson he gave him the requisite instructions.

'This one has a large display and even though you'll be in an interview room all cell phones will work in that particular room, but the call will take longer to get through because your Nokia works from England. That will give you plenty of time to get out.'

Pierson nodded and took the phones, the knife and the carpet tape. He left the observation room and moments later he entered the interview room.

The prisoner looked up on this occasion, directly at Pierson. Pierson though made no eye contact, he pulled the table to one side along with the unoccupied chair, leaving the way clear for him to move his captive around the room more easily.

Yanking the chair, Pierson turned his prisoner through ninety degrees, dragging him across the floor—and in so doing, making the occasional grunting noise. Once complete, the man was sitting with his back to the mirror such that any observers could no longer see his face. The prisoner was now worried looking and made more head movements in those few moments than the entire time he'd been in the room up until then.

Pierson placed the table in front of the man once more. He then took the carpet tape and unwinding short lengths of it, he cut them and placed them over the man's arms and legs and wrapped them firmly around the chair.

Pierson then placed the cell phones on the desk and sitting to one side of them he looked at the man and spoke to him in English. 'They let me in to talk to you: to interrogate you. They believe I've got a good chance of making you tell me what they need to know.' He paused and turned away. The man glanced at Pierson briefly and then looked impassively forwards again, no longer making so many energetic head movements as he settled in this new position.

'Trouble is, I have no interest in making you talk. So why am I here you're asking yourself? Except that you're not, because it seems you don't speak English. Which is why I know you won't talk to me and I think they know it too.' Pierson pointed at the mirror behind the man.

'Three of my friends died recently. Someone was calling them, on phones like this.' Pierson held up the Nokia. He switched it on and leaning forward he placed it in the man's inside jacket pocket.

'You should try it some time. In fact why don't I call you now?' Pierson added smiling. He picked up the other cell and started to type in the number for the Nokia. Once complete he showed the number on the display to his captive.

'Recognise this number?' The man didn't look, he deliberately turned his eyes elsewhere. Pierson placed the phone on the desk. 'Just to make sure that you understand what is happening here; my real name is Tom Brady, or at least it was until a few days ago. But of course you knew that. You tried to phone me over fifty times and failed. Apparently my dislike of Mozart saved my life.'

Pierson paused again as he picked up the reel of carpet tape. He pulled out a small piece and the man looked at him. 'Oh this?' Pierson asked as he cut it. 'This is for your mouth. I meant what I said. I have no intention of trying to make you talk. That's why your back is to the mirror.' The man started to struggle as Pierson put the tape across his mouth.

He tapped the man on the chest with his forefinger. 'Of course if you can think of a way of switching off the phone, then it won't redecorate this room with your inners.' Pierson walked to the wall mounted microphone and switched it off. The man's eyes glared at him as his face grew redder with each desperate struggling move.

Pierson moved to the door and the man was trying to make noises. By this time, the wooden chair was rocking violently.

'Oh I almost forgot,' Pierson remarked, 'they're probably wondering how we're getting along,' he nodded and smiled at the mirror.

He leaned forward to the man and spoke close to his ear.

'Killing my wife was the last mistake you'll make. But I know that if I ask no questions I'll get no lies.'

Pierson looked at the cell phone on the desk and pressed the send button. The man's eyes almost exploded with fear. Sweat was now running down his brow as he tried to fling the chair around. Pierson swiped his card and opened the door to leave. Without looking back, the door clanged shut behind him.

Trying to jump the chair around and gasping for breath only being able to breathe through his nose, the captive managed to partly turn the chair but then the Nokia began to ring.

Almost instantly the prisoner's blood pressure shot up as he recognised the tune. It was Mozart's fortieth symphony.

Within seconds, Henri opened the door to the interview room and walking over to the man he ripped off the carpet tape from his mouth. In plain English the man almost shouted the words out, 'I'm Rene Sebastien, TN is the account on the AIX machine, tauqmuc is the password—it's cumquat backwards—and I work for Sir Henry Young.'

Henri pressed the end button on the cell phone on the desk and reaching into the pocket of Sebastien he pulled out the Nokia and switched it off too. Sliding off its battery he placed the chip and plastic explosive back in that he had taken out in the observation room.

'Next time I won't take the explosive out,' Henri remarked in English. 'Now I want everything or I'll let Pierson—the man you know as Tom Brady—try again.' He waved the Nokia at Sebastien.

Sebastien started talking and almost didn't stop for breath, as he told Henri as much as he knew. The interview took hours and they discussed his recruitment, how long he'd been in the apartment using the machine and why it was used. Sebastien still held back some details, not deliberately though and only one really big one that they would be able to work out for themselves sooner or later.

WEB OF DECEIT

Now that the account and password for the imported system was known, Pierson was able to throw himself into his work for the rest of that day, and in fact for the following two days too. He didn't leave each day until gone midnight and on the Thursday and Friday he arrived at six in the morning, having had less than three hours sleep each night.

On waking in the mornings, for the first ten seconds, everything was perfect as his mind did its best to figure out why it shouldn't be so, and then it hit him like an express train. The stark realisation yet again that Madeleine was dead, every day the pattern was the same, serenity for a few brief moments and then crushing loneliness. For those few seconds each day, before his brain had figured out what was wrong, he was able to exist without the anguish of her not being alive, but after that, the sickening feeling remained with him at some level until he fell asleep again. It was almost too much for him to bear, and he did everything possible to take his mind off it, and not dwell on her permanent absence. It was like she just kept on dying day after day.

Even after he'd got past his initial morning shock, every time he stopped working his thoughts returned to Madeleine. So he tried to push the thoughts out of his mind by filling it with other things. The only thing available was work.

Henri ordered Francesca to keep Pierson supplied with food and drink, an order to which she happily acceded in the circumstances and would have done anyway. But neither food nor drink were allowed into the computer room, so they compromised and attached a new terminal in Henri's outer office where Pierson could sit and carry on his work and consume food.

Although he drank most of the coffee put in front of him, he didn't eat once. In fact by Friday lunchtime Francesca was sure that he hadn't eaten anything since he'd heard the news of Madeleine's death. Pierson was working like a man possessed.

He set grief aside but was burning himself out, and it was in this light that Henri decided to steer matters on a new course.

He invited Pierson to his vineyard that weekend, starting from the Friday evening and returning on the Monday. Francesca placed herself near to Henri as he made the invitation. She was standing with her hands behind her back, her fingers crossed, smiling, almost coyly, like a young girl too embarrassed to ask for a date with a boy she was besotted with, and therefore getting a friend to do it for her.

Pierson stopped typing long enough to listen to Henri. Then his look became one of frustrated disinterest, like a husband that had just been asked to choose some new wallpaper and show some preference for one of two very similar but dull patterns. Glancing back to his keyboard though he returned to his typing.

'I forbid you to come in the office this weekend,' Henri stated thumping the desk and trying to jar Pierson from his preoccupation, 'and I may get the locks changed on the apartment too.'

Pierson stopped typing once more and swivelled his revolving chair to look at Henri directly. He hadn't noticed Francesca standing there at first, but when he cast his eyes to one side and caught a brief glimpse of her, he could see that Henri was not the only one wanting to get him out of the office.

'Who else will be there?' he asked in a matter of fact manner.

'My wife and daughters; Bill, and of course, I'll be there; and some hands from the vineyard,' came the reply.

Francesca couldn't contain her self. 'I think I might go too. To see mama again,' she added, trying to look and sound vaguely nonchalant.

'There will be wine and good home cooked French food,' Henri added, 'there may be dancing and picnics and the chance to relax.'

'Dancing?' Pierson queried looking worried. 'Oh no. That's not for me,' he turned back to the terminal.

Francesca's face dropped.

'We won't force you to dance,' Henri continued, 'we might let you sit there and watch the stars.'

'But what about this?' Pierson asked gesturing at the screen.

'I can get you a laptop to connect to the system. If you must,' Henri replied.

'In that case, I'd love to come,' Pierson answered, 'but how do I get there?'

In unison Henri and Francesca answered, 'you can come with me.'

Pierson smiled faintly. It was hardly noticeable, yet it was definitely a smile and it was his first for nearly three days. 'I'll go with the non smoker, if that's alright,' Pierson replied, referring to and then looking at Francesca.

Francesca nodded, almost too enthusiastically and moments afterwards nearly danced off to get Pierson a refill of his coffee, wearing a huge smile that she couldn't stop as she turned away from him. But, as she revolved, she saw Antoine, Marcel and Jean-Pierre, all of whom had stopped what they were doing, and all of whom were almost hypnotised by Francesca's display of uncharacteristically affable behaviour, especially coming from such a Mediterranean volcano, which is how they thought of her, their pet names for her usually being Etna or Vesuvius. Her demeanour immediately changed and she even cleared her throat as a kind of distraction, before she returned to her normal more demure and slightly more self-controlled nature.

They would have laughed, except they knew the return barrage would have involved some words spoken at high speed, at high volume and in Italian, such an onslaught was definitely not welcome anytime and especially not at the end of a working week, when they all felt drained.

Henri looked at the three of them sitting there. 'Like the three wise monkeys, wouldn't you say Bill?'

Bill just smiled from another desk, where he had only been half watching. 'Yes,' he replied after a few moments, trying to show some level of politeness by responding to Henri, but not really listening to the question.

Bill had stayed on in Paris, as it had seemed sensible to be near the heart of the only leads coming from the case so far. He was using the opportunity to work with Henri and his team, to try and make some headway.

Antoine's research had confirmed to a certain extent the point raised by Bill about the money markets, especially in light of the ever-looming banking crisis on both sides of the Atlantic. The fact that Marcel had traced a series of calls made from many different phone numbers in England to the computer they were now looking at, only deepened the intrigue of the true purpose of the computer.

Francesca sat beside Pierson as he struggled through the huge amount of data stored on the system looking for the Elektra software.

In an attempt to keep everything under close control, Henri had authorised the creation of other accounts on the system for Antoine, Marcel and Jean-Pierre in addition to extra terminals in the office, so that they could hunt down the program that carried out the automatic dialling and find out when it was written, and by whom. Henri had also tasked them to find out why 34 minutes of transmissions took place every hour and why those transmissions had restarted, tying up the phone line for that amount of time every hour. Although it wasn't important to the ministry, because they could get as many phone lines as they wished and it was an additional line anyway—hijacked from the apartment from where the computer had originally been located.

There was very little talking in the office, until just after two in the afternoon when Pierson declared, 'I think I've got it!'

Bill looked up, as did Henri, who had been inside his inner office. He was sufficiently interested in Pierson's outburst to stroll out and then lean over Pierson's screen.

'It's Elektra; the software. The source code is here,' Pierson continued.

'The latest copy?' Bill asked.

'I don't know,' Pierson replied, 'now what I need is to compile this stuff and compare the output to the copy you have.'

'In that case I'll get my people to transmit it,' Bill replied.

'Perhaps,' said Henri stroking his chin, 'but maybe that wouldn't be such a good idea. Not until we've found the leak in your department.'

'If one exists,' Bill replied, leaning back in his chair. 'You're right though, I would like a copy of that source taken off the machine and written to CD along with any executable you can create from compiling it.'

'Leave that with me if you wish,' Jean-Pierre replied. 'I can do that for you.'

Henri turned to look at the others, 'Okay everyone; update meeting at three, before we leave for the weekend,' Henri checked his watch as he said it.

Pierson went to take a sip of the latest drink that had been put there, but in his absentmindedness he had already drunk it. Francesca shot up to get him a refill, but he stopped her by placing his hand on hers and mouthing the words, 'thanks, it's okay.'

Helping himself from the urn that had been wheeled in earlier, he sat down again and began looking through the system once more. Something curious had caught his eye and he wanted a closer look.

Henri spent the time on the phone and waited for information to come through on his fax machine and Antoine seemed to hit on a moment of genius, which he then revealed to Bill, beckoning him over to sit beside his desk and look at his screen, which appeared to be displaying web pages.

Jean-Pierre had disappeared to manufacture the CD copies of the software, leaving Marcel to work on tracking down the incoming phone numbers that had dialled the computer.

At twenty to three a deliveryman walked in with a box clearly marked, showing that it contained a laptop computer. He handed it to Henri, who signed for it. The deliveryman then made his exit.

Henri just handed it to Pierson. 'Your toy has come,' he remarked.

Pierson looked up from his screen but hadn't taken much notice of the package. 'Thanks Henri,' he said placing his coffee on the desk to his left as he then gave the new arrival a quick once over. 'I'll unpack it later.'

At three o'clock they entered Henri's office and wheeled in additional chairs to make up for the shortage. Henri had cleaned the larger white board on the other side of the office to the one he had used earlier in the week.

'So,' Henri began. 'Mike's found a copy of the Elektra software on the computer. Jean-Pierre, have you taken copies of it?'

'Yes,' Jean-Pierre replied 'I've also compiled the code and there are quite a lot of programs, but it's a fast machine and the program source and executables are on these disks,' he added, waving three CDs at them and giving two to Henri and one to Bill.

'Why three?' Henri asked.

'Three copies,' came the reply with the word 'copies' being emphasised. 'We can keep a safe copy here, as well as one each for you and Bill.'

'Good,' replied Henri. 'Mike. Have you got anything else to add.'

'Yes,' Pierson replied. 'I've found twelve more accounts on the system and whoever configured it set up a mail server there. Someone, in fact twelve people, have been logging on to the system over a period of months if not years and sending mail to each other.'

Henri looked surprised. Bill looked concerned, but the rest of them remained unimpressed by the information.

'I think Antoine may have found something that fits in with that,' Bill added. 'He's found that most of the data on the disks are, well...' Bill stopped and thought for a moment before speaking again. 'It's not for me to say, I'm not an expert. You tell them Antoine.'

Antoine picked up the story. 'They're web pages; thousands of them. Web pages of financial markets and in particular monetary figures and exchange rates, precious metals, broker details, buying and selling prices too. Changed hourly.'

'Hence the hourly transmissions,' Pierson added.

'Yes,' Antoine replied. 'But set up in advance, like someone is trying to manipulate the markets. I'm not sure yet, but this stuff contains information that could be cascaded to hundreds of web sites if the sender can hack in, creating a false picture of money markets and prices of precious metals, gold, silver and platinum and the like. There's also a recurring number that I keep seeing regarding merchandise of figs and it's lot 8233 but I can't make any sense of it,'

Henri and the others thought about this for a few moments but nothing new occurred to any of them. 'Marcel,' Henri spoke, 'what have you found?'

Marcel had some paper with him, detailing telephone calls. 'It looks like the computer has been dialled by telephones or certainly telephone lines and then connecting to actually look at those web pages.'

'Or the e-mail system,' Pierson remarked.

'Yes,' Marcel replied, 'that's more likely. Much more likely, but the phone numbers all originate in England and I've had trouble tracing them. I've found one so far and it's odd. It's from a building that's called...' he stopped as he rummaged through the paper work until he found it, 'it's called the Royal Courts of Justice.'

Pierson and Bill looked at each other. 'Someone in the judiciary?' Pierson said.

Bill wasn't sure, but he shrugged his shoulders as he answered, 'it's possible but difficult to believe and even harder to prove, it could be a civil servant or someone who works for the courts. It's not necessarily someone in the judiciary itself.'

'Let me see if I can add some pieces to this,' said Henri. 'The only name I have from interviewing Rene Sebastien is that of Sir Henry Young.'

Bill's face dropped immediately. Henri was still writing the name on the large whiteboard, but he still managed to catch the embers of Bill's look as he turned. 'You know him?' Henri asked.

'I know of him. He's a high court judge,' Bill replied.

Pierson looked at the name on the board, 'Just a moment Henri, I've got some information on the accounts from the system that may help.' Pierson walked out to the outer office and then at his terminal after typing in a command, the display gave him a list and he wrote down twelve sets of letters. He walked back in to Henri's office where they had all been waiting and he sat down again. All eyes were on him.

'Well?' Bill asked after a few moments. Pierson looked up. 'Oh I'm sorry,' he said. 'They all seem to be initials. I've got one person here called R.S.'

'Rene Sebastien?' Francesca replied.

'Yes,' said Pierson. 'I've also got S.H.Y.'

'And,' replied Bill.

'Sir Henry Young? Perhaps,' Pierson replied.

Bill just looked at him astonished. 'The evidence is difficult to ignore.'

They examined the initials of the other ten names on the list that Pierson had, but nothing stood out about any of those.

Henri, still standing by the whiteboard wrote the letters SHY next to Sir Henry Young and then wrote the letters RS against the name Rene Sebastien.

'Now I have something for you all,' Henri added. 'We have no record of Rene Sebastien.'

'He has false documents then?' Francesca asked.

'He has no documents other than credit cards,' Henri replied.

'So deport him,' Antoine declared.

'That is why I don't let you interrogate suspects,' Henri remarked looking at Antoine incredulously. 'He's guilty of murder by proxy yet you want him deported for not having all his documents.'

Henri paused and looked at the others. 'I've been trying to track him down through fingerprints, but to no avail.'

'Just in France?' Bill asked.

'Yes, but I've now got Interpol checking too.' Henri replied.

'What if he really is Rene Sebastien though?' Francesca asked.

'What do you mean?' replied Henri quizzically.

'Well let's suppose he's foreign but he has a name that sounds French, that would explain why he has no documents,' she replied.

'When you say he has no documents, do you mean no passport or driving licence either though?' Marcel asked.

'You mean this?' said Henri, leaning around to his desk and pulling out a Dutch Passport. He showed it to the others. 'It's a fake,' he added, 'a very good one, but still a fake.'

Each of them began looking at one another again, mainly for inspiration but none came.

Henri turned to Bill. 'Anything to add?'

'Yes,' Bill replied, pausing for a few moments but remaining sat down as he looked around at the others, he began speaking. 'We've got a man called Geoff Abbot who has a copy of two pieces of software that's going to be sold illegally to a foreign power, we believe. This is a small deal but a major embarrassment for your government and mine. Yet we have had three…' he stopped himself briefly as he looked at Pierson and then at the floor, 'that is, four deaths caused directly as a result of something connected with this, not to mention other deaths that occurred at the same time in a peripheral manner,' Bill was referring to the man's body found with Madeleine's as well as the bodies of Jim Alexander's family.

'We think this software is going to be handed over somewhere in return for money, but as yet we've not moved forward on that.'

Pierson looked around the room before he asked his question. 'Is the software in use yet?'

'In use?' Bill queried.

'Yes. You know Elektra and Vitesse Acquise 4, have they been implemented on the systems on the trains?' Pierson continued.

'Yes,' Bill replied. 'They were put into use on the morning of August 1st. Exterra and Vitesse Acquise delivered the final copies of the software in mid July. A two week testing period preceded the live implementation at the beginning of this month.'

'About the same time as the killings began,' Pierson added.

Bill nodded.

Pierson had a puzzled look.

'What is it Mike?' Henri asked.

'I've had a chance to read some of the e-mails on the system; and that name 'Pareto' pops up from time to time, but with no discernable pattern of reference, more often as a codeword than anything else and it seems to carry some importance. One of the references makes it clear that target percentage must be achieved before completion of the contract. Whatever that means.'

'Target percentage of what?' Antoine asked. But there was no answer.

Henri nodded and shrugged at the same time and Bill quickly threw him a quizzical look to check if Henri seemed to know something that Bill was in the dark over. Henri looked back at Bill without any acknowledgement of Pierson's comment or Antoine's question. 'Can you get traces on those English phone numbers to get precise locations, to help Marcel before we leave this afternoon? Hopefully we can have the answers for Monday.'

'I'll get our people on it,' Bill replied and walked out to a phone in the outer office.

'The rest of you may go. Until this evening at Vineyard Pinvin, Au revoir,' said Henri.

The others replied in unison.

Francesca and Pierson left together within a few minutes, although she had to virtually stand over him. She was attempting to endorse her presence by remaining in his view and therefore on his mind. Pierson though was still examining the e-mails that had been sent between the various parties of users on the computer. But finally, he logged off and grabbing his coat he picked up the laptop box as Francesca almost dragged him away.

As they strolled back to the apartment, the sky was unblemished by clouds. The sun declared its presence by the clearly defined shadows of the apartments on the pavements as they passed each one; and dancing through the gaps it beat down at every opportunity, only to disappear again behind the next building.

On entering the apartment, Francesca packed just a few items in a carrier bag. Pierson on the other hand had no luggage, but was able to find some bags and took what he could for the weekend.

'Why so little?' he asked her, on seeing the single carrier she had with her.

'You forget,' she said to him, as they tried stuffing his hastily acquired bags of clothes into the small boot of her car, along with the laptop computer. 'I live there. I already have clothes at the vineyard.'

'Of course,' he replied as they got in; and within seconds Francesca had begun to drop the roof of the car and fold it back into its compartment at the rear of the vehicle. Then after getting in, she started the engine and the car roared off west towards the ministry again, but this time heading beyond it and towards the Arc de Triomphe, and then on towards the countryside.

The journey into the rural France was a pleasant distraction. Pierson was able to take in the views, and he still found it slightly odd that he was sitting in the passenger seat of a car that he would be expecting to be in the driving seat, if in England.

With the roof down, the wind rushing through their hair, there was no chance for conversation.

For one road after another he saw field upon field separated by hedgerows and trees.

The traffic gradually disbursed and instead of the majority of other vehicles being cars, the general trend was that more lorries and farm vehicles began to dominate the highways.

Pierson noticed that the smells changed too, from the traffic fumes of the city that he had got used to, he could now smell manure and on occasions almost sickly sweet aromas coming from the trees and shrubs, but only in fleeting moments. On one occasion he picked up the smell of burning tyres as they passed by a farm with a huge pile of them that had erupted into flames. The fire was spewing out the thick black smoke that had the familiar and unwelcome stench of burning rubber.

A few miles further on, Francesca slowed the car and turned right onto a rough gravel and mud track, splashing through puddles as they rocked on the uneven surface of the lane. After a short distance, they pulled into a large courtyard.

This was the Pinvin vineyard as shown by the dilapidated and barely legible sign outside that had endured many seasons of weathering.

The courtyard was surrounded on three sides by roofed buildings of the same height, all of which had two floors, but there were skylights in the dark tiled roofs, indicating further rooms were present in the attics.

The first part of the buildings on the left stretched for some forty yards. They then turned to the right for another section of building of about the same length. Finally that section was connected to a smaller part jutting along the third side of the courtyard for about twenty yards. This third piece was the most active at that time, as it housed stables.

There were six slots for horses that Pierson could count along that section. Outside was a long tethering bar where one horse was tied and being groomed, whilst its stable was being cleared out by someone that Pierson could only see the back of.

It was like a small community going about its daily business and Pierson wondered why anyone would wish to leave this place and work in the city.

Francesca parked the car on the opposite side to the stables. Two other cars were already parked there at an angle to the buildings. As she pulled in to park the car, it splashed though a puddle on the cobble stone courtyard and added yet more dirt to the formerly white vehicle.

None of the others had arrived yet, but Francesca was about to take Pierson inside, when her mother walked out to meet her. Pierson could see the family resemblance although their hair colouring was quite different. Francesca's hair was much darker than her mother's, yet the likeness was obvious. Her mother however had a much softer demeanour and exuded serenity, in her late forties or early fifties she was well rounded but not fat, she had voluptuous curves that would have turned any man's head.

Her hair had wisps that had blown out of place and she was wearing a dress of a simple floral design with pale yellows and greens that might have been mistaken for camouflage had she been working in the fields. She too spoke English, but with quite a strong French accent and it seemed that she spoke Italian too.

Within moments, Henri's wife had arrived, along with his two teenage daughters who were at home, being that it was the summer holidays. Pierson tried to remember all of their names but it was no good.

'Let me take you to your room so that you can unpack,' Francesca said to him as she stepped back towards the car, 'and then I can show you the gardens.'

Pierson nodded and smiled. 'Okay.'

Getting their things, she led him into the block of buildings on the left and through some dark corridors on the ground floor, Pierson almost having to feel his way, but with hands full he brushed the wall every now and again with his elbow and tried to follow the smell of Francesca's perfume. She took him upstairs and into a large bedroom big enough for four people, and with it's own bathroom.

'Voila,' she said triumphantly. 'You can clean up and I'll see you downstairs in a few minutes,' she paused, 'or when you're ready.'

'I'll be down soon, as long as I don't get lost,' he replied trying to peer back through the door.

'It's okay,' she added, 'my room is three doors down on the left,' smiling at him she closed the door behind her as she walked out. He could hear her footsteps as she walked along the landing and then he heard another door close.

Pierson wondered why it was necessary for him to know where Francesca's room was, but he didn't spend much time pondering it.

He gazed out of the window and his spirit was uplifted by what he could see. There were miles of rolling countryside, although there hadn't been much impression of the stunning view that he now beheld when they had been driving along the entrance lane a few minutes earlier.

The land gently dropped away from the house and led down to hundreds of acres of vines, neatly planted in rows and columns, even though he didn't know how much belonged to Henri's family, it seemed to go on forever. The fields of vines were separated, sometimes by other hedgerows and sometimes by lanes winding between them. To one side were woods that themselves must have held some secret promise to any child growing up in that place; and to the other side the dropping sun was now beginning to glow slightly more orange than yellow, but it was still producing enough warmth to encourage anyone in its path to stay there. Not that it was cold in the house, but the sun added to the entire scene.

Pierson found himself leaning on the windowsill and just soaking up the wondrous vista before him. Checking his watch, he could see that it was by then almost six in the evening. He showered and changed and returned to his window once again, where he could hear the noise of talking and laughter from below.

He made his way downstairs but got lost, and began to try and remember the route he'd taken when he went in. He did this successfully enough to find himself back by Francesca's car in the courtyard. Walking around the buildings he picked up the noise of the talking once more and this time he saw Bill, Henri and the others, all of whom had now arrived.

Henri's wife—Michelle—was preparing a large meal. The smell was magnificent, Pierson thought to himself, and outside of the back of the house, on a small courtyard style patio, was a long trestle table. Wine had already been poured and was being tried by several of the already noisy revellers. Pierson was offered a large glass of it from one of Henri's giggling daughters. He took a sip and its effects were almost immediate.

Sitting down on the bench seat, on the side of the table away from the house, he looked out into the distance to the countryside. Only moments passed before the familiar smell of Francesca's perfume wafted nearby, as she came and sat next to him. Like her mother and aunt she too was wearing a dress, a kind of gypsy style off the shoulder type. Somehow he thought, this suited her perfectly.

He was amazed that the woman now sitting next to him could have been the same one, who armed with a gun four nights earlier, had raided the apartment in Paris and was involved in a shoot out in the streets. Yet there she was: beautiful and very distracting, almost too distracting.

Serving the meal to cheers and applause from everyone present—all of whom had by now taken their places—Henri's wife place two large joints of meat on huge platters equidistant along the length of the table. Henri stood up and carved from one while one of the male vineyard workers carved from and served from the other.

Although there was much talk and laughter, Pierson remembered little of the rest of the evening and with help from Francesca, made his way to bed some hours after the meal and fell asleep properly for the first time in four nights.

The following morning Pierson awoke as the sunlight shone in the window onto his face. Checking his watch he saw that it was just after seven o'clock and having showered and dressed he made his way downstairs again. He wasn't the first to rise and Henri was already standing outside the back of the house looking down across the vineyard.

'Now I can let you into a secret,' Henri said, as he noticed Pierson arriving.

'And?' Pierson asked.

'This is the weekend that we harvest the crop, so extra hands are welcome.' Before he could say anything, Francesca arrived, dressed in jeans this time with tee shirt and headscarf. She grabbed Pierson's hand and led him to the barn.

'So early?' he said to her as they entered.

'To pick fruit of course,' she replied, selecting a large wicker basket with straps and placing it firmly on his back.

'I haven't agreed to anything to yet,' he protested mildly, but he didn't mind. 'How heavy does thing get when its full?' he asked her as they left the barn.

'Too heavy for a woman,' came the reply as she laughed at him and began leading the way to the vineyard.

In the absence of other activity, apart from trying to set up the laptop he'd been given by Henri, Pierson was happy to be a part of the action. Soon enough the other employees and family members and friends joined them and by mid morning there were over twenty people in the vineyard, cutting and collecting the bunches of ripe grapes.

It was too hot for Pierson to think of much other than the task in hand and working with Francesca all day, she showed him how to cut and then collect the fruit. He hadn't realised that there was any great skill involved, but a certain amount of care was needed.

Between them, they filled a basket every twenty minutes or so and Henri had brought hundreds down to the vineyard, on the back of a wagon, drawn by a horse that Pierson would have described as a shire horse. As each basket got full, so they were taken to the same wagon, which was walked back up to the barn next to the house when full.

At lunchtime, the wagon was brought down with supplies of food and refreshments. The food was simple in nature, including such items as apples, cheese, bread and strangely, chocolate. Michelle had explained that the chocolate was for energy, but Pierson assumed that was merely an excuse.

At the end of the day, they returned to the house and watched the setting sun as they ate another well supplied home-cooked evening meal. Shattered for the second night in a row, Pierson said his goodnights to the others and made his way to his bed.

He thought briefly about setting up the laptop but fell asleep fully clothed before he could do anything about it.

On the Sunday, the day unfolded the same way as the previous day, but this time the work stopped at four in the afternoon giving them chance to clean up before the evening meal, which was going to be a barbecue with music and dancing.

Pierson found that the aches and pains of the previous day's work had caught up with him, and there was no way he would be able to dance that evening, even if he'd wanted to.

A group of them sat around the trestle tables talking and watching the sky change through its myriad colours as the sun set. Francesca was sitting at the end of the table with Pierson on her immediate right, next to Pierson, Bill was sitting, smoking a Gitane cigarette having decided to try the French brand, but taking it out of his mouth every now and again, curious at its taste and then taking a swig of wine as if to remove the flavour of the cigarette.

Henri was sitting opposite Pierson and was playing with his pipe, trying to light it. Marcel, Antoine and Jean-Pierre had all begun the drive back to the city so that they wouldn't be late for the morning.

The tables were positioned near to the brick built barbecues and there was some dancing taking place for those showing off that they had enough energy to freely fling it around after working in the vineyards for two days. The sound of the music and laughter was not so much that it drowned the talking at the table, and once his pipe was lit, Henri sat back to engage in this more cerebral activity.

'Have you remembered yet?' he began, looking at Pierson. 'The secret that's hidden in your mind?' he continued.

'No,' Pierson replied shaking his head and gazing at the dancers.

'We'll have to find a way to unlock your memory soon if we're to get an advantage from it,' Henri added.

Pierson stared up and the stars were now clearly visible and checking his watch he saw that it was nine in the evening. His gaze wandered over to the barn. 'What happens to the grapes, now Henri?' he asked his host.

'They'll be crushed and then we take the juice and place it in barrels for a while with some secret additives,' he winked at Pierson.

'When will you crush them?' Pierson asked him, curious that they hadn't yet been crushed.

'We have a tradition here,' Henri replied, 'and we believe it helps the flavour, so we always pick the harvest—weather permitting—on the day of the full moon.'

'So why did you do it differently this year?' Pierson asked.

Francesca had an expression of bewilderment on her face as she turned to look at Pierson. 'But we didn't,' she responded, 'the full moon was yesterday.'

'Yesterday?' Pierson quizzed.

'Yesterday,' Henri confirmed. 'What's wrong with that?'

'The moon was full on the sixth, so how could it be full ten days later?' came Pierson's reply.

'Come with me,' Francesca said to Pierson, standing up and walking a few yards from the table. 'What do you see?' she asked pointing to a brightly illuminated cloud passing over the barn.

Pierson watched as the cloud moved by, revealing an almost full moon. 'But that can't be right,' he commented trying to think why, but not being certain.

Sitting back at the table, the others were laughing at the fact that Pierson hadn't seen the celestial body in all its magnificence that night or the previous two nights.

'There's something wrong,' he remarked.

'With the moon?' Bill asked.

'Not as such,' replied Pierson 'I know there was a full moon on the sixth but there can't have been. I just can't remember why it's significant.'

'Remember, you were in South Africa on the sixth,' Bill commented.

'I don't think that makes a difference,' said Henri sucking on his pipe and wafting the smoke away as it hovered near his eyes.

The conversation moved on to other subjects for a few minutes, but the issue with the moon bugged Pierson, until finally he remembered.

'It was the picture of Madeleine,' Pierson blurted out looking at Bill. Nobody there wanted to cause Pierson more pain by talking about her, but with the pregnant silence, Bill felt obliged to ask the obvious question.

'What picture Mike?'

'The one in the package that Selway showed me,' came the reply.

'I don't understand,' Bill answered, looking confused. 'You're saying that Selway had a picture of Madeleine?'

'Yes,' Pierson replied. 'It was a photograph of her shopping at the supermarket. In the background it showed some offer running from the third to the ninth of August and had three days to go, clearly indicating that it had been taken on the sixth.'

'And?' said Bill.

'And,' repeated Pierson. 'There was a full moon which in fact it was very large, so the shot must have been taken from a distance using a zoom lens.'

Bill and Henri thought about this for a few moments. 'So clearly it was a fake shot,' Bill replied. 'Why would Selway show you a fake?'

'Madeleine said about that,' Pierson replied, 'she said it was strange, because it meant that the bad guys photographed her and showed it to the good guys. Which didn't make sense.'

'Why put the moon on it if it wasn't there?' Henri asked.

'Because,' Pierson replied, 'perhaps just to make it look as though it were taken from a distance.'

Bill thought on this. 'Then why not use the moon in its correct phase?'

'Two reasons,' Pierson replied, 'firstly it's correct phase must have been a crescent moon and therefore there would have been little to show and secondly,' he paused, 'anything less than a full moon may not have sufficiently caught my eye to encourage me to conclude the photograph was taken from a distance.'

'But why show you anyway? Madeleine was right,' Bill said, thinking aloud more than anything else.

'You're missing the obvious, my friend,' Henri commented.

'I am?' Bill replied.

Henri nodded. 'It may be that you don't wish to believe it, but if the bad guys took the photograph, then they wouldn't hand it to the good guys to help persuade the good guys to protect one of their own.'

'It would never leave the hands of the bad guys,' Francesca remarked.

'So Selway is the leak?' Pierson asked looking first at Henri and then at Bill.

'I hope not,' Bill replied, 'it doesn't make sense.'

'Doesn't it?' Henri asked, 'Are you sure?'

'No,' Bill replied. 'I've known Selway for many years and although I don't know everything about his background, I would trust him with my life.'

'You work for him. Maybe that's loyalty speaking,' Henri added.

'What I don't understand is why he would waste time at the airport showing you a photograph of Madeleine and not just the reports about your colleagues,' Bill continued.

'He didn't,' Pierson replied, 'he didn't waste any time at the airport other than dropping his case. He didn't approach me until we got on the plane.'

'Plane?' Bill queried. 'What plane? You'd just landed, why were you both getting on a plane?'

Pierson looked at Bill curiously now, but answered anyway. 'It was the flight back from Johannesburg. I saw Selway in the departure lounge before we actually met on the flight home.'

'Selway went to South Africa?' Bill spoke aloud again. 'I didn't know he was out there. Why didn't you say anything before?' Bill asked incredulously.

'Nobody asked and I assumed you knew; and anyway it wouldn't have occurred to me that it was important.' Pierson replied.

'What was he doing in South Africa?' Bill asked, again thinking aloud and not really expecting an answer.

'I thought from what Henri had told me that he was watching me,' Pierson replied.

'No my friend. I think you may have offered up some useful information, not the secret that you have in your head, locked away, but still it's vital information.' Henri added and then speaking to Bill he continued. 'He was buying rands. That's what he was doing.'

Bill was shocked by the news. But he had to think carefully on the next steps and how it tied in with everything else on the case.

'Why did he let me see him on the plane?' Pierson asked, 'and then he let me live?'

'Perhaps,' Henri replied 'you've answered your own question from Monday about how someone knew to stop making the telephone calls to the Nokias. Perhaps his trip was twofold, to buy rands and to see if you were dead. As you suggested for your colleagues, the deadly phone calls stopped after their phones exploded yet yours continued for three more calls after your 'death'.'

'Does Selway think I'm dead or alive?' Pierson asked Bill.

'Dead,' came the reply.

'Then,' Henri added 'we may have an advantage after all. Tomorrow we can review the impact of this and we must find out

Selway's role. It seems that Marcel's discovery of thousands of web pages set to deceive the markets is not the only web of deceit here.'

KEEP YOUR ENEMIES CLOSE

Monday morning found Pierson back in the offices, in the Ministry of the interior. Francesca had arrived before him and was reading a copy of Le Monde. Pierson leant over her shoulder and bid her good morning, and then saw the headline on the paper. Even with his very limited understanding of French he could see that it was making a reference to dead fish.

'What's that about?' he asked her, pointing at it.

'Something strange is happening to fish near Calais,' she replied. 'Thousands of them have turned up on the beaches in the mornings, and they've all died for no apparent reason. Scientists can't find any disease or anything wrong with them, but it's been happening for a week now.'

Pierson thought nothing more of the comment, and immediately went to get himself a coffee from the urn that someone had already so thoughtfully brought in. He sat at his terminal and logged in to the system as he collected his thoughts.

Bill had decided to return to England, he'd be contactable, but something needed his attention and he had chosen not to say what that was to his French friends. There were some things that were of national interest that couldn't be repeated— even in front of this ally.

Pierson spent time musing over the locked away secret that he had in his head. What was it he could do, he wondered, that made it important that he should be killed? Or what was it that only Geoff Abbot should be able to do? And in fact who wanted him dead? Was it Geoff Abbot? His initials weren't amongst the twelve accounts that Pierson had found on the system.

He delved through the e-mails of those users and found a reference from SHY—whom they now believed to be Sir Henry Young. There were further references to lot 8233 and Pareto but not in any discernable context, even though some references used the words 'shipment' and 'aboard' when referring to the figs. There was something odd about it all. Some missing element, but Pierson couldn't get his head around it.

He found a reference to the entire group of twelve users as 'Jury' a nickname for them—a criminal cartel perhaps, but without faces and names, the initials gave little insight into the identities of the people to whom they referred. In addition, even if their names were known, then it was unlikely that they would involve themselves directly in the software swap; and would probably employ minions or go betweens to do that for them.

Looking closely at the e-mails present on the system, it did indeed appear that the user known as SHY was the main author of e-mails, often sending them to the group known as Jury: meaning that everyone got a copy.

Henri eventually arrived and Pierson entered his office with the new information just as Marcel was cleaning the whiteboard.

Pierson added the word Pareto and the phrase "lot 8233 figs" underneath.

Henri looked at the information and raised a single eyebrow before shaking his head and turning away, appearing less than impressed.

Marcel finished by diligently adding the date to the top of the board.

Henri was fidgety and was looking for inspiration but he didn't need to wait long. Just as he was clearing his throat for the third time and about to point at the whiteboard, so a fax came through and he wandered across his office briefly to collect it. He pulled it out of the machine and looked somewhat troubled as he read through it, finally showing it to Pierson.

Pierson looked at the fax but it was in French. He managed to make out that it was from the Surete in Paris, but beyond that there was nothing he could understand. 'Can you read it for me please Henri?'

Henri took it back, 'I'm sorry,' he said. 'I keep forgetting that you're English. It's from the Surete.' Pierson nodded. Henri continued, 'Interpol checked with many agencies in Europe, and Scotland Yard have a positive match on Rene Sebastien's fingerprints.'

Pierson looked surprised as Henri read further and paraphrased what he saw. 'According to this, Rene Sebastien is really someone called Trevor Norris.'

'Trevor Norris?' Pierson repeated quizzically. 'How can that be true?'

Henri shrugged his shoulders. 'Why not? It may be that he really is who he says he is and Trevor Norris is an alias. There's a way to find out though. Let's ask him and see how co-operative he'll be today.'

The two of them made their way to the interview room where Sebastien was still in residence, Henri passed the fax to Pierson and then whilst Henri entered the room directly, Pierson went into the observation room.

A man was already sitting there, controlling the recording of the video and audio equipment.

Pierson sat and watched through the large mirror, the other man turned and nodded at him in acknowledgement, prompting Pierson to do likewise.

Rene Sebastien now looked more dishevelled than when Pierson had spoken to him the previous week. He hadn't bothered to shave, even though there were facilities to do so. He was still tied to his chair, but this time he gave away a look of trepidation as Henri entered.

Henri sat opposite him, and both of them were positioned sideways on to the mirror once again, the furniture having been rearranged following Pierson's encounter with Sebastien.

'What's your real name?' Henri asked him in English.

'I've already told you,' came the reply to Henri's question with slow deliberation, 'Rene Sebastien.'

Pierson hadn't heard the man speak before. He hadn't been in the room when Henri had removed the carpet tape from Sebastien's mouth. So when Sebastien had blurted out the answers to Henri's questions trying to save his own life, only Henri had heard him. On hearing his voice for the very first time, Pierson recognised there was something wrong. He ran out of the observation room and swiped his pass on the door of the interview room and burst in.

Henri looked alarmed and turned to see Pierson standing at his shoulder, anger flaring in his eyes, as though Sebastien was still playing a role in some devious plan.

'Read this,' demanded Pierson as he shoved the fax from the Surete in front of Sebastien. He then walked away from the table as though disinterested but waiting to pounce, still looking at Sebastien and visibly seething with anger.

Sebastien looked at it, and then at Pierson briefly and then at the fax again. 'You can't read it can you?' Pierson declared spitting out the words with venom as he moved forward and leaned on the table. 'You're English!'

The fear in Sebastien's eyes grew. 'Yes,' he declared, his voice beginning to break with the prospect of being blown up again, 'of course I'm English.'

'How did you know?' Henri asked Pierson, who was still leaning over the table with his face only inches from Sebastien's and Sebastien trying, but not succeeding, to move his head back and away from Pierson.

Pierson answered Henri without even turning his head away from Sebastien. 'It's his accent, it's false,' he replied, 'he sounds like an Englishman trying to impersonate a French man speaking English. He can probably speak rudimentary French, and understand more than he can speak, but it seems that he can't read and understand it.'

Henri raised one eyebrow. 'Is this true?'

The man nodded. 'You never asked me my nationality before,' he shrugged his shoulders as best he could with his arms tied down.

'True enough,' replied Henri nonchalantly.

Sebastien continued, 'you spoke to me mainly in French. I could only understand the odd word like guillotine. The first time I really understood you was when you asked me those four questions in English the other day.'

Henri just nodded silently, smiling slightly.

'So what's your real name?' Pierson asked him, still venting his anger.

'My real name is Rene Sebastien,' the man replied.

'Then how do you explain that Scotland Yard have your fingerprints on file under the name Trevor Norris?' Pierson continued, still looking as though he was trying to bore a hole into the man's head with his eyes.

'Because I was,' Sebastien replied.

'What do you mean? Is Rene Sebastien an alias?'

'No. I changed my name by deed poll. My name really is Rene Sebastien. Well it is now. It's completely legal so I've been telling you the truth.'

'You've changed your name?' Pierson said almost under his breath trying to see if there was anything significant about it.

'Why?' interrupted Henri.

'Why what?' said Sebastien.

'Why did you change your name, and why the Dutch passport?' Henri asked.

Sebastien looked at Henri and flashed his eyes quickly at Pierson but then back to Henri again.

'You can't change your name in Holland without permission of the Queen, the monarch,' Sebastien began. There was a pause for a few moments, 'so I changed my name in England to something that could pass as French, or Belgian or not seem too out of place in Holland and because it's so difficult to change your name in Holland, then it seemed an obvious choice for my nationality.'

'Obvious for whom?' Pierson asked.

'The man who set all this up, back in England,' Sebastien replied.

'So you really are English then?' Henri continued.

'I already told you,' came the emphatic reply.

'And this was all done, why?' Henri asked further.

'It was part of the deal,' Sebastien answered.

'What deal?' Henri asked now losing his patience.

'What does your information tell you?' Sebastien asked him nodding at the fax.

'In my business, one of the first things that you are taught is never to give up any information. Now just answer my question if you wouldn't mind, or I'll let my friend here continue,' Henri gestured at Pierson.

Sebastien exhaled long and slow as though he was about to release some great secret that might have precipitated his own death.

'Two years ago I was caught by the treasury—in England— hacking into web sites and trying to pull a scam,' Sebastien began.

'Scam? What is scam?' Henri asked, bemused by the word. Although his mastery of English was excellent, this was a term he'd not heard before.

Pierson explained for him. 'It's a confidence trick, usually a criminal act.'

Sebastien looked at each of them in turn and nodded.

'What sort of scam was it?' Henri asked. Pierson stood up straight and began to walk around the room, but only behind Sebastien, pacing slowly back and forth. Sebastien felt uneasy but carried on talking, his eyes moving from one side to the other as Pierson moved into view each time.

'I found a way to hit certain web sites at certain times with copies of their own pages. I downloaded the originals and then using Java I modified the text on the pages and sent them back.'

Henri nodded and gestured for him to carry on with a wave of his open hand.

Sebastien continued. 'Well it was just a gas a first, you know, a joke, just a bit of fun, and then I found I could make money from it, by buying money through certain dealers, getting them to sell when it reached a certain price and all I had to do was upload the wrong prices and that was it, I made a killing.'

'Pardon me?' Henri asked.

'I made a lot of money,' Sebastien replied.

'But where did you get the money to begin trading with?' Pierson asked him from behind. Sebastien swung his head around to try and look at him. The tension in Sebastien's voice increased noticeably every time Pierson asked him something, and this was evidenced by a slight croak as he replied, 'you don't need any. All you do is create a credit limit with the broker.'

Pierson interrupted. 'Which no doubt you hacked online.'

Sebastien nodded. 'And then you pay the bill at the end of the month if there is one, or you collect your payment,' he added.

'So how did you get caught?' Pierson asked him.

'I didn't collect any money for months and then tried to collect it all at once,' Sebastien answered.

Pierson laughed aloud, 'and that's how they tracked you down, because you asked for a cheque.'

'Yes,' Sebastien replied. 'I should have just got it transferred electronically, but I wanted to see it in my hands. I wanted to hold it.'

'How much money was it?' Pierson asked.

'One hundred and seventy thousand pounds,' came the reply, 'give or take.'

Henri interrupted them. 'So what happened then?'

'My house was raided, I was arrested and charged with computer fraud.' Sebastien replied and beginning to look less scared but more agitated as he began to shuffle as best he could, whilst tethered in place.

'And then?' Henri prompted him.

'Could I have a drink please,' Sebastien asked. 'My throat's dry.'

'No,' came the swift reply from Pierson.

Sebastien paused and swallowed before continuing.

'And then the case went to court, but just as it was about to start, my counsel,' Sebastien paused, 'my barrister, you know, lawyer, gave me a message that I had to see the judge in chambers.'

Pierson had by now walked around to stand next to Henri. Sebastien stopped as he watched Pierson again, and then picked up from where he left off. 'Well, the judge told me that if I pleaded guilty, then they could make arrangements for my rehabilitation, but it would have to be abroad, probably Paris.' Sebastien smiled with a wry smile. 'He was a sly old fox.'

Both Henri and Pierson said nothing but waited for Sebastien to continue.

'He told me that if I was found guilty he'd give me the maximum sentence and that would be seven years. I didn't want that. I hadn't hurt anyone. It was only money. It's typical in England, beat up an old lady and they let you off; steal from the establishment and that's different, they lock you up for taking the mickey.'

Sebastien paused again. 'Well I had no choice did I? They set me up with a new identity, and told me to change my name by deed poll to Rene Sebastien. They told me about the Dutch passport and all that stuff, but it didn't make much sense to me at the time, I didn't care though. I was going to be in Paris, I would have a new name, but so what? I was free.'

'What did you have to do in return?' Pierson asked him.

Sebastien swallowed hard before answering. 'Exactly what I'd been doing before, except they'd would e-mail me now and again telling me to do specific things. Like those phone numbers. I knew the phones exploded because the judge told me, saying that if I knew about it up front I'd want to make sure it was done right or I'd be caught. If I refused there was still the seven year jail sentence hanging over me.'

'The judge told you?' Pierson queried.

'Yes, the judge.'

'But what about that seven year sentence, I thought you said they dropped that, didn't you?' Pierson asked.

'No they didn't,' Sebastien replied, 'no sooner had they got me here, than they put out a newsflash that I'd been convicted with a seven year sentence and that I'd escaped. So you see; if I try and run they'll get me and I didn't even get a trial.'

'But what about your barrister? He couldn't have agreed to this surely?' Henri asked further.

'Oh really? Lovely people barristers aren't they?' Sebastien replied, 'he was a dodgy character too. I suspect he was paid off by the judge or the other guy with him, so I won't have any chance. They're all bent.'

'Who was the judge?' Pierson asked.

'Sir Henry Young. Impressive wouldn't you say? A Knight of the realm carrying on like that. I won't forget him in a hurry.'

'And your lawyer?' Henri asked. 'What was his name?'

'Um, George something,' Sebastien paused for thought. 'Yes that's it, George Bannister: a real sleaze bag. I couldn't afford anyone better. In fact I couldn't afford anyone at all.'

'What? Not even with two hundred grand?' Pierson remarked.

'Well that's the point, isn't it? I never actually got the money so I don't know where it is now. By the time it arrived, I was already under arrest. I never even had it in my hands. So in the end I needn't have bothered.'

Pierson looked at Henri and nodded knowingly, but Henri wasn't sure why just yet. Neither of them spoke openly in front of Sebastien at that stage though.

'You mentioned they,' Pierson remarked. 'Who are they? Do you mean the judge and the barrister?'

'Yes and the other guy,' Sebastien replied.

'Who was he?' Pierson asked him.

Sebastien sat there in thought for a few moments. It didn't look as though he was trying to remember the man's name: it just looked as though he didn't want to say it.

'What was his name?' Pierson pressed him further as he leaned on the table once more.

Sebastien swallowed again and now looked Pierson in the eyes. 'Norman King,' came the reply. 'But it's funny, he said everyone calls him Bill.'

The blood drained from Pierson's face. He could hardly believe his ears. He looked at Henri and then back at Sebastien. 'When was the last time you met him?'

'I only met him the once, but he's called me since and e-mailed me too.'

Henri took over the conversation, now surprised by the revelation that his friend had been identified as the inside man.

'What does Pareto mean to you?' Henri fixed Sebastien with his own steely look.

'Nothing. But I did see references to it. It was like it was a joke—you know an in-joke.'

Henri didn't understand but Pierson explained it for him and Henri merely nodded.

'What about figs lot 8322?' Henri continued.

'8233,' Sebastien corrected him.

Henri gestured nonchalantly that Sebastien could have been right.

'It was like public school boys and their own private game,' Sebastien continued, 'I don't know what it meant.'

'Or means,' Pierson remarked.

Pierson took over the questioning again. 'Who wrote the program to telephone the cell phones?'

'I did,' Sebastien replied. 'It wasn't very difficult. A trained monkey could have done it.'

'How did you know to make it stop ringing certain numbers?'

'I got a phone call each time,' he replied.

'From Bill?' Pierson asked.

'I don't know,' Sebastien replied. 'I mean people can sound different over the phone can't they? He never said who it was, but thinking about it, Bill never knew about the phones, only the judge knew that. You know I think it was the judge who called me. Anyway, whoever it was called after each death and said that I should change the program to stop making calls to one of the numbers.'

'Did you have any other instructions about the computer?' Pierson asked.

'Yes. I was supposed to upload a series of web pages on Tuesday 19th August to keep the rate of the rand as level as possible,' Sebastien answered.

'Tomorrow,' Henri and Pierson said in unison looking at each other.

'Why?' Pierson asked.

'I don't know. I told them that the rand was a dodgy currency and they should stick to US dollars, but they gave me the prices that I had to show in the web pages and I set them up to run, automatically, except I suppose you've switched the thing off by now,' Sebastien replied.

Henri and Pierson looked at each other again and Pierson began walking around the room once more.

'Anything else?' he asked Sebastien.

'I was supposed to run another set of programs on the 19th August to drop the value of the Euro and then send a message to various brokers that when the Euro hits a certain level to buy them with the rands,' came the reply.

Pierson muttered something unintelligible to himself as he looked at Henri. Henri tried to listen closely but he'd missed what Pierson had said. 'So what's going to happen to the Euro this week?' said Pierson.

'I don't know,' Sebastien replied 'They wouldn't tell me, but if you ask me they're about to lose a lot of money.'

'How much?' Pierson asked.

'An awful lot,' Sebastien replied.

'Give me an idea here. A ball park figure.' Pierson continued.

'It may as well be a ball park,' Sebastien replied. He stared down at the table and then looking at Henri he gave them the answer. 'Two hundred million dollars worth.'

'How low is the Euro expected to drop?' Pierson asked.

'The trigger for the brokers is set for when it reaches fifty cents, you know US cents,' he replied, 'by the time I've finished manipulating the prices that's what will happen, or at least it would have happened.'

Pierson and Henri both churned the numbers over in their mind.

'So they expect to make a profit of two hundred million dollars,' Pierson remarked.

'Or thereabouts,' remarked Sebastien.

'These programs for tomorrow, are they set to run automatically?' Pierson asked him.

'Yes. If the computer is up and running and tied in to the same phone number,' Sebastien replied.

'So why have you been uploading the web pages every hour for the past few weeks?' Pierson continued.

'Practice,' came the reply. 'I've been grabbing their pages and sending them back.'

Silence followed for a few moments.

'No you haven't,' Pierson commented thinking about Sebastien's past.

Sebastien looked down at the desk again.

'That doesn't make sense, that would warn too many people of system problems,' Pierson continued, 'old habits die hard don't they?'

Sebastien said nothing as though he realised Pierson was on to something.

'I've looked at what you've been doing and you've been manipulating platinum prices for your own ends,' Pierson added.

Sebastien looked at him. 'So what if I have?'

'So your partners wouldn't like it if they knew you'd been playing away so to speak, would they?' Pierson added.

'They don't know and anyway all I got out of this thing was my freedom, I thought that a little extra,' Sebastien paused to find the right words, 'you know, pocket money, wouldn't harm at all.'

Henri laughed. 'Inspired,' he said. He looked at Pierson and nodded for them both to leave the room with their additional information. Pierson shook his head indicating he had further questions.

'What about Elektra?' he asked Sebastien.

'What?' replied Sebastien.

Pierson frowned with incredulity. 'The software: what's it doing on your computer. Why have you got it and when did it come?'

'I don't know why its there. It was sent to me in the post, air mail from England, with a note from Bill saying that I should upload it and keep it safe,' he replied.

'What about Vitesse Acquise 4, the French side of it?' Pierson asked.

'I got that about the same time,' Sebastien answered.

'Where from?' said Pierson.

'Same place,' came the reply. 'Sent in from England, by Bill.'

'How on Earth did they get that?' Pierson asked not expecting an answer.

Sebastien said nothing.

'So what's Abbot's role?' Pierson said aloud not really expecting an answer.

'Beats me,' said Sebastien. 'I heard about him before, and he was mentioned in some of the e-mails, but I've never met him.'

'If you've already got the latest software then, I don't understand where he fits in,' Pierson continued.

'To demonstrate it perhaps?' Sebastien suggested.

'What do you mean?' said Pierson, not wishing to reveal even to Sebastien that he had what might be described as intimate knowledge of the software.

'It does more than just run the train's systems.' Sebastien began, 'some of the functions wouldn't normally be used on a typical journey. Go and look at the code. The software there allows overrides to slow the train in case of fire, and to separate it whilst moving. All sorts of stuff that you wouldn't think is necessary. It can even split the train between passenger and freight compartments.'

Pierson gave him a disbelieving look to elicit more from Sebastien. But it was Henri that supplied the answer.

'Because in the case of a fire, they changed the safety protocols a few years ago. When a fire was found aboard they used to just carry on driving the thing out of the Channel Tunnel and extinguish it at one end or the other. But after that incident a few years ago, they changed the procedures. Driving the train out of the tunnel takes about thirty minutes, and the flames are fanned by the moving air and the ready supply of oxygen. So they took a new approach. The next step was to stop the train and then try and fight the fire as soon as it was found. More recently they've changed the procedure again. They now believe the best way is to slow the train to about ten kilometres per hour but keep it moving and then split it into three parts. The part with the fire would remain stationary whilst the front and back would move in different directions away from the burning carriages.'

Pierson looked impressed at Henri's knowledge. 'So why do they need Abbot to demonstrate that. Why don't they just get the driver to do it?' He said without really thinking.

'Yeah right,' said Sebastien, 'you can imagine that can't you. 'Excuse me driver could you interrupt this service to demonstrate splitting the train into three parts. Oh and don't worry about the schedule or panic to the passengers, that's a bit like asking a plane to simulate a crash dive so the passengers would know how it feels.'

Pierson took the point, but as for demonstrating what the software could do, he was unconvinced that demonstration would be necessary—especially on a live service with passengers. In his opinion it was more likely to be demonstrated at the point of sale, and this brought his thought back to the French part of the software. 'Where's the Vitesse Acquise 4 software?' he asked.

'It's in the same directory as Elektra, I put it all together as it's really all the same stuff, dovetailing into each other, look for a directory called Elektra. It's all there,' said Sebastien.

'One more thing,' Pierson said, 'why did you need a gun?'

'I didn't,' Sebastien said, 'but I was left instructions to destroy as much of the system as possible if I was raided. I was given the gun to hold at bay anyone trying to get in, whilst I destroyed it.'

'You know how to use a gun then?' Pierson asked.

'I used to go to a firing range when I was a kid. My dad used to take me. I was quite a good shot,' Sebastien replied.

'So why did you only wound the gendarme instead of killing him?' Pierson continued.

'I'd been running, I turned and didn't have too much time to steady myself. Basically I didn't think I'd get him at all, I was trying to fire a warning shot to slow down the gendarmes and the woman.'

Pierson took all this in and nodded slowly.

'How were you going to destroy the data on the computer, there's so much of it?' Pierson continued.

'With a shell script I'd written. One command and every disk would have had the files erased and overwritten with binary zeros,' Sebastien replied, 'but they kicked down the door and I wasn't ready for them.'

Henri looked at Pierson as though to ask him if he were ready to go. Pierson nodded and they began to leave.

'What about me?' Sebastien declared. 'I've given you what you want, so when can I leave?'

'Even though it was murder by proxy, it was still murder.' Henri replied, 'for what you've given us, I only guaranteed to let you live, if you want freedom then I can't imagine how you can earn that. Perhaps you can think of something yourself. Tell us what Pareto is or 8322,'

'I keep telling you it's 8233!' Sebastien shouted in exasperation as he watched them leave the room, waiting for the door to make its resonating clang behind them.

Both Henri and Pierson were silent as they made their way back to Henri's inner office. Henri signalled for Francesca, Jean-Pierre, Antoine and Marcel to follow them in and he closed the door behind them.

Inside the office, Henri walked to the large whiteboard and wrote up three names, Sir Henry Young, Rene Sebastien and Norman King.

Francesca looked shocked. 'Why have you put Bill's name up there?' she asked Henri and then she looked at Pierson to see if he would enlighten her, but he waited for Henri to give her the news.

'It seems that Rene Sebastien is an Englishman who changed his name from Trevor Norris in a deal with Sir Henry Young and Norman King. If he refused then he would have been sent to jail for seven years.'

Francesca now looked troubled. 'But Bill knows everything.'

'And he has been a good friend,' Henri commented.

'Didn't you ask him to send you details of Sebastien's fingerprints from London?' Pierson asked.

Henri nodded. 'That's why I'm concerned. I got the information from the Surete, originating from Scotland Yard, Bill should have got it to me much quicker. The fact that he still hasn't sent anything causes me grave concern.'

'Couldn't Sebastien be lying?' Francesca asked.

'Possibly, but why?' Henri replied. 'When Bill was here he didn't take part in any of the interviews. Sebastien never saw him, or even knew that he was here. He has no reason to lie and everything else he's said seems to check out.'

'So where does that leave us with Bob Selway?' Pierson asked.

'It may be that he is your guardian angel,' Henri replied and that he went to South Africa to watch you, to make sure that you returned alive, instructing Bill to give you the new identity. Once he'd done that, then Bill couldn't have killed you unless you were ever truly alone with him.'

Pierson thought carefully, 'No, only in the pub and then there were a lot of other people around.'

Henri looked at Pierson and continued. 'Unfortunately it may also explain your wife's death.'

'Why?' Pierson asked.

'The death of a family member is no easy thing to get over, who ever did it perhaps wished to make you ineffective. It certainly…' Henri stopped.

'What?' said Pierson thinking back to Madeleine.

'I was going to say that it certainly distracted you,' Henri continued, 'but instead of grieving and turning in on yourself you threw yourself into your work. That takes a lot of self control.'

Pierson's look became morose as he now considered that he may have caused Madeleine's death by dealing with Bill.

They all sat silently for a few moments and Henri tried to change the mood. 'That lawyer, George Bannister. The one that Sebastien mentioned, are his initials amongst the twelve accounts on the system?'

Pierson nodded. 'Yes, that's what I wanted to tell you, but I didn't want to say anything in front of Sebastien.'

Henri added the name George Bannister to the list on the whiteboard.

'What about Bill? Do any of the accounts have the initials NK or BK or even WK?' Henri continued.

'No,' came the reply.

'So we have some new things to consider,' Henri began.

'We have nothing but a consignment of figs. Lot 8233 being transported somewhere, but we won't know when and we have Pareto as some sort of joke,'

'Pareto?' queried Jean-Pierre.

Henri wrote 20/80 on the whiteboard next to the word Pareto.

'Why figs?' Antoine asked jokingly, 'I prefer dates myself.'

Henri shook his head as Antoine slumped in his seat silently. Henri gestured to throw the whiteboard marker at him. But it was Pierson's change in demeanour that caught everyone else's attention.

'That's it!' he declared.

Nobody said anything as Pierson stood and gestured for the whiteboard marker.

Henri passed it to him and as Pierson slowly took off the top he walked almost trance-like to the whiteboard counting to himself as he did so.

'It's not figs,' he exclaimed, 'it is dates,' he added emphatically.

He turned to the others. But all he got was blank faces.

'It's an English thing. An in-joke if you like.' Pierson continued. 'That's why the merchandise is moving but there's never a delivery date in all the e-mails. Nobody once asks which day it's on.'

'Or even where it's coming from or going to,' Jean-Pierre pointed out.

'That doesn't matter,' said Pierson, 'they all know where it's coming from they have a master copy of the merchandise on the computer here that Sebastien's been looking after—it can be downloaded anywhere in the world and then either carried or electronically sent. The delivery method is unimportant it's the date that's missing.'

'It's all going to take place on Wednesday. The whole thing: the market shake-up; everything is being lined up for 20th August 2008.'

Henri was baffled. 'Where did you get that from? I don't follow you,' he remarked.

Pierson turned to the board as he replied, 'it's been here all along.'

Henri waited, looking less than impressed.

Pierson took the consignment number 8233 and prefixed it with the digits 200 so that it read 2008233. He turned to Jean-Pierre and posed the next question for him specifically.

'If this number is a date then when would it be?'

Jean-Pierre tried to work it out. 'You mean it's the Julian Date?'

Pierson nodded.

Henri and the others looked confused again.

'You're saying that 8233 means day 233 of year 8 or year 2008,' Jean-Pierre elaborated.

Pierson merely nodded as Jean-Pierre did the arithmetic.

Well this year is a leap year, so the first four months have a total of 121 days instead of the usual 120. On top of that add in 31 for May, another 30 for June and that gets us to 182. July adds on another 31 giving a new total of 213 and that leaves the final…'

'Twenty,' said Francesca as she could see the answer looming. 'This can't be coincidence,'

'Okay,' said Henri pausing slightly, 'but what will be happening on 20th? The software is being delivered perhaps. Maybe a demonstration or some special run of one of the Eurostar trains?'

Everyone remained quiet as Henri thought on until he broke the silence once more.

'Marcel, get the passenger manifest for all Eurostar trains for Wednesday: both directions.'

Marcel blinked a few times before rising and then quickly nodding and scurrying out.

'You two,' Henri pointed at Pierson and Francesca, 'find out all you can about the Eurostar, the Channel Tunnel, the stops, air vents, emergency procedures, everything including the number of rats infesting every mile of tunnel, and do it before the end of the day. I want no surprises. Familiarise yourself with every aspect of the tunnel's construction, cost, length, depth and escape routes.'

Pierson nodded and left with Francesca.

'Cesca,' Henri stopped her as she left, 'I want you to guard him with your life—do you understand? With your life.'

She nodded and gave her uncle a look that reassured him, although for her part, she saw something in his eyes she didn't recognise, and this was the start of a niggling annoyance for her. She felt a strange chill that he was holding something back.

With remarkable swiftness Marcel returned almost panting. He's on Wednesday's train from London.

'Who is?' Henri demanded irritably.

Marcel began to stutter and blink much more rapidly. 'Geoff Abbot,' he replied passing the manifest to Henri.

Quickly scanning down the list of names Henri saw another name he recognised Konstantin Dobrowiecki.

Francesca had still not left his office and Henri again spoke to her. 'Get yourself on the overnight ferry tomorrow. Pick up the train in Dover. Brief Mike on usual protocol for surveillance with extreme prejudice.'

Francesca nodded.

'Go,' said Henri, 'I want an update from everyone at 16:00 today.'

There was suddenly huge impetus, even though Jean-Pierre and Antoine had no specific instructions, they busied themselves for Francesca as she passed on her own directives to them.

Pierson was making use of the time to fill his head with as much detail on the Channel Tunnel as he could. The office was absent of humour as silence dominated, broken only occasionally by an incoming fax or arrival of another coffee urn.

At 16:00 they gathered in Henri's office once again for a final brainstorming. Pierson updated Francesca on Rene Sebastien's web uploads and told her about the automated programs.

'But that's been happening already hasn't it?' Francesca asked them.

This time Henri nodded as he sat down with them, 'especially as the computer system is active and there is an automatic program to do it,' Henri remarked.

Pierson continued. 'It appears that tomorrow another set of programs will run and upload further web pages to distort the price of the Euro and the rand. A set of trigger conditions will be sent to the brokers to buy Euros at a much lower price.'

'But that's not very clever,' Francesca remarked. 'How do they know the Euro will increase in value again?'

'Because,' replied Pierson, 'they will have falsely shown the price of the Euro as much too low, so when the real price is shown from the genuinely updated web pages—when they're uploaded by the usual refresh process—they will have made their money.'

'So all the murders were carried out just to manipulate the money markets? That doesn't make sense,' Francesca remarked.

'We agree,' Henri interrupted. 'There's still something missing, even though the bad guys have spent two hundred million US dollars buying South African rands.'

'Why not just invest in dollars?' Francesca asked.

'We don't know,' replied Pierson, 'that seems odd, but perhaps not in the current climate. The dollar is usually so stable that it would make a good choice for investment, but not if a banking crisis is looming on both sides of the Atlantic.'

'What if...' Henri began but stopped himself. 'What if the dollar was hit in the same way? After all, whatever they're doing is only going to last for a day. What if some event were to take place that would seriously undermine the dollar too?'

'Like what?' Pierson asked.

'Well don't they say that when America sneezes the world catches a cold?' Henri remarked.

'Yes...' replied Pierson, 'and?'

'Well what would happen if the UK sneezed. Would the dollar remain steady?' He asked.

'Conceivably. But I'm not an expert; and it would depend on the magnitude of the event,' Pierson replied. 'So what you're suggesting is some economic catastrophe that would hit the UK for a day and hence anyone investing in currency outside Europe and America would be safe and possibly could make a profit?'

'Perhaps,' replied Henri, 'especially a country whose economy was based on gold, platinum or other commodities such as diamonds. If they knew in advance what was about to happen. We just have to find out what that is.'

'So where does the Elektra software fit in to all of this?' Francesca asked.

'I don't think it does,' Pierson replied.

'It does,' replied Henri, 'and when you realise what your secret is. That thing that you can do, or that thing you know. Once you remember or realise what it is, that's when we'll be a step closer to solving this case.'

'What about Abbot?' Pierson asked, 'and Dobrowiecki. Is their meeting real?'

'We'll only know that on Wednesday,' Henri replied. 'At the moment it seems from what we know, that the copy of the software here is a real backup, and can still be sold, so Abbot may well be trying to sell it illegally.'

'And they're exchanging the software and the payment for it on the train, so that Abbot can demonstrate what it can do?' said Pierson out loud, but more for his own purpose, just to hear what that thought sounded like to listen to, as if someone else had spoken it. 'That doesn't make sense though. No demonstration is needed. If there were, then to whom and why?' He continued to ask himself.

There was a knock at the door.

'Entrée,' Henri said distracted by the thoughts flying around in his head.

In walked a young woman carrying a thin brown A4 sized envelope. She passed it to Henri, along with a clipboard that had a piece of paper on it, which seemed to contain a list of signatures. She spoke to him in French and clearly asked him to sign for the envelope.

'Merci,' she said as she departed, closing the door behind her.

Henri opened it and read the contents of the single page inside.

Both Pierson and Francesca watched the look on his face change as he merely muttered to himself, 'oh,' a few times and then looking up he raised his eyebrows at them.

'Enfin,' he said, 'now the speculation ends. We have an answer,' he paused as he wondered whether to impart the information he'd been given, glancing briefly at each one of them as his thought processes evolved. But he didn't wrestle with his conscience for more than a few moments. 'What I'm about to tell you cannot leave this room,' he paused, 'not yet anyway. But it's vital for you to know. I know why they had to kill you Mike.'

Henri started to paraphrase the information, reading to himself silently in French and then speaking aloud in English.

'Because of the growing Euro zone banking crisis, the UK will be joining the Euro in January,' he began.

Francesca and Pierson sat in silence, hanging on Henri's every word, but Pierson definitely looked the more alarmed of the two. 'It seems that the UK economy cannot continue without its trading partners in the Euro zone, and that won't continue if the Euro crashes. In order to…' he stopped to read the note properly. 'In order to consolidate banking functions and centralise them in Europe, all UK gold reserves will be transported to the European central bank in Berlin.'

Pierson and Francesca looked at each other.

'And the first shipment is Wednesday,' Pierson remarked, guessing what was coming next. Henri nodded.

'So now we know what Abbot can do,' Henri remarked almost as a throwaway line before adding, 'finally we know the special skill he has.'

'What can he do?' Pierson asked still confused.

'Apparently he can stop the train,' Henri remarked.

They all looked at each other.

'And can you override that and start it again Mike?' Francesca asked.

'Yes,' he said with a dawning realisation.

'Voila!' said Henri. 'That's your secret. That's why they wanted you and the others dead. When Abbot is there to stop the train, he can no doubt override the control of the software, and someone was afraid that if any of you or your three dead colleagues were there, that you may have left some back door in the software to let you in and start the train again.'

'To what end?' Pierson asked. 'Why could stopping the train be such a big deal, and why should my knowledge of overriding the systems be such a problem to those who wish to stop the train—if in fact they do? The driver could simply restart it...' Pierson thought for a few moments, 'provided Elektra allowed him,' he added purposefully, as the realisation dawned on him.

Henri leant forward on the desk and with his steely look he continued. 'Did you leave a back door in the software, some secret override command that lets you in?'

'Yes I did,' Pierson replied somewhat sheepishly, as though he was about to place himself in deep trouble. He didn't tell Henri, but when he had worked on the software he'd left himself two ways in, although he could have told Henri this fact, he decided to keep it to himself for the moment.

'I still don't understand why stopping the train could be so important—why not just get the driver to do it?' Pierson was clearly dissatisfied with the theory.

'Perhaps it's guaranteed to stop if Elektra disables the train. Maybe not even the driver could start it again without Elektra having been reset.' Henri suggested.

Pierson nodded. 'You're right. That's exactly what Elektra can do. In theory it could block out the driver's attempt to restart the train if the software gets locked out or hangs indefinitely. A simple subroutine, or even a few well placed lines of code could cause that.'

'And anyone who can control Elektra could interfere with what may become the biggest heist of all time.' Henri added. 'Unless of course we stop them.'

'How's the gold going to be moved?' Francesca asked trying to refocus on the more important elements of the matter in hand.

Henri read further before answering only moments later.

'It says here that it will be in unmarked and unescorted lorries on the Eurostar, transported in anonymity.' Henri added, 'this information has been sent to me from the French Minister of the Interior himself, following a top secret communiqué from your government Mike.'

'That's not a very secure method of transport though is it?' Francesca asked.

'Why not?' said Henri. 'This isn't the Wild West, nobody will hold up the train, but if they do then where will it happen?'

'In France,' replied Pierson.

'Exactly,' Henri replied poking his finger at him. 'In France, and you can imagine how upset the UK would be if it was stolen whilst en route in France.'

'Very,' replied Pierson.

'Wars have been started over less than this,' Henri remarked, and it gets worse, the UK holds more than just its own reserves of gold in the bank of England. It keeps gold there that's owned by America, and Europe and other countries.'

'So stealing it would mean stealing from the UK and from America or Europe or the Middle East,' Pierson commented.

'Precisely,' said Henri.

'How much gold is being shipped?' Pierson asked.

'One hundred and fifty metric tonnes,' Henri replied, at eight million US dollars per ton, that's one point two billion US dollars worth of gold.'

Again silence fell on the three of them for a few moments.

'Where does France start?' Pierson asked.

'What do you mean?' Henri asked.

'In the Channel Tunnel, where does England end and France begin. Where does France have jurisdiction.' Pierson qualified his question.

'Oh I see,' said Henri. 'I'll check, but I believe it's half way.'

'So what you're saying is that it will be an embarrassment for France if the gold is stolen from halfway in the tunnel and not before.' Pierson added.

'Yes. But nobody would steal it in the tunnel,' Francesca remarked. 'There are only two ways out.'

'At the moment,' said Pierson. 'I've seen the statistics and there's an average of forty five metres of chalk above the tunnels and to get through from the sea you'd need a group of criminals who were well financed, had access to a submarine, and knew how to rig explosive charges under water to blast a precise hole most but not all the way through.'

Pierson stopped as Francesca and Henri looked at each other.

'The Nouveau,' they said together.

'The Nouveau?' Pierson asked.

'Yes,' replied Henri 'it was a secret submarine stolen just about a week ago from the French Navy.'

'You think that this is why it was stolen? To rob the train and take the gold on a submarine. That's crazy. Anyway if they had been blasting holes in the chalk ready for this, then there would have been some evidence like a lot of dead fish washed up on the shore,' Pierson replied.

Without realising what he had said until he'd said it, Pierson turned to Francesca and said. 'The newspaper—Le Monde.'

Francesca dashed out to get it and showed Henri the headlines about the dead fish.

'I agree with you Francesca,' Henri said. 'I think there are only two ways out of the tunnel and one of those is in England and the other in France. Get all the information you can on the Channel Tunnel this afternoon and download it to that laptop. Take it with you and see if the two of you can learn as much as you can before Wednesday.'

Henri stroked his moustache for a few moments as he paused for thought and then he continued. 'Mike, before that, I want you to find the trigger program and make some changes. I'll tell you what to change later.'

'Okay,' Pierson replied.

TRUST NO ONE

Having spent much of the afternoon tracking down the automatic trigger programs that the criminal cartel was planning to have activated the following day, there was little time to make the actual changes according to Henri's new instructions, but Pierson managed it. This meant that he had most of the next day available to collect data on the Channel Tunnel and download it to the laptop. He did take time out to begin monitoring the consequences of the program changes that Henri requested, and check on what Henri had referred to as the 'interesting effect' of running the programs with those changes implemented.

Leaving the office together on the Tuesday, Pierson and Francesca had been told by Henri to look like tourists whilst on the ferry, and on the train the day after, in an attempt to dissolve into the background.

They returned to the apartment, collected some overnight things; and with Francesca driving she got them to Calais with plenty of time to spare. The general idea of these particular overnight ferries was to travel most of the way towards the destination, anchor overnight nearby and then finish the last few miles of the journey in the morning itself.

The two of them were dressed casually and having dropped their bags in their remarkably luxurious cabins, they met in the corridor outside.

'Where now?' said Francesca, looking somewhat bored.

'The shops,' Pierson suggested. Francesca's eyes lit up briefly and Pierson hoped to himself that there weren't any shoe shops or jewellery shops, or he might find himself stuck there for hours. Although, Francesca wasn't like any other woman he'd ever known, and so he couldn't be sure that she would be afflicted with the same bug for shopping for those items that most women seemed to have—but in the circumstances, he figured that it would have added authenticity to what he saw as their thin disguise.

He led the way up to the top deck to work through the ship methodically, trying to locate the shops or even just a diagram that pointed out where they could be found. The ship was generously adorned with maps and having chosen one, the two of them then spent five minutes or more trying to work out where the shops were, and how to get to them.

They noted that the ship had at least ten restaurants and places to eat; and six bars—two of which were club style discotheques. Planning their route, they stayed out in the open air as long as possible. This also meant that they were able to enjoy the longest view of the by now orange setting sun.

Finally stepping inside, they made their way along two corridors, the second of which was at right angles to the first. Then, without warning they'd arrived; and found themselves standing in front of a large tax-free shop: selling everything from sun tan lotion to computer games.

Most of the outlets were open plan like those at many airports, their borders merging seamlessly with the walkways between them.

As they meandered in and out of the racks and displays, Pierson caught a chance sighting of another passenger walking almost within reach, but oblivious to his presence—as he had been partially obscured by rotating sunglass racks.

His heart missed a beat and he turned to Francesca. 'I know him,' he said as he nudged her gently. Francesca was looking at some personal hi-fi equipment. 'What?' she said as she turned.

'That man over there; see him?' Pierson asked her.

'What the old man with the grey hair?' she replied vaguely pointing to another one.

'No,' Pierson continued.

Francesca looked at Pierson closely as he craned his neck and bobbed and weaved around the racks, almost walking in to one in his attempts to try and see the man again without being spotted in return.

'Who was it?' she said, walking over to his side.

'I'm not sure,' he replied, 'it looked like someone called Roger.'

'Roger who?' she asked.

'I don't know. I just knew him as Roger,' came the answer.

'You knew him well then?' Francesca remarked sarcastically as she turned away.

'No. He was one of the one's that arranged my death,' Pierson continued, but as he said it, he was overheard by a young woman standing nearby. She turned and gave Pierson a look like he had just escaped from a mental institute, so he just smiled and shrugged at her.

Francesca giggled. 'Would you like to chew your other foot now?'

Pierson shook his head, but he wondered whether he'd actually seen the man that Bill had introduced as Roger; and if so, then what he was doing aboard?

Finding himself standing by the camera section, he began to study the various types on offer.

'Come on I'm bored now,' Francesca tugged at his arm. 'Let's get some food or drink.'

'You're on duty,' Pierson replied, 'besides which Henri told us to look like tourists. So how can we do that without a camera?'

Francesca sighed, and began to look extremely disinterested, with her arms folded, standing mainly on one leg, she tapped the foot of the other on the floor, looking around just trying to kill time.

'How much for this one?' Pierson asked the male assistant.

'Eleven hundred Euros,' came the reply.

'I'll take it,' said Pierson, trying to read the details on the box as the man put it into the bag. Pierson got out one of his credit cards, remembering to use the correct signature when presented with the invoice.

The assistant handed the bagged goods to him and then looking at Francesca he asked. 'And for you madam?'

'Oh no I'm not interested, thank you,' Francesca replied, uncrossing her arms and waving one hand at him to emphasise her denial.

'Where's your sense of adventure?' said Pierson. Then turning to the assistant he continued, 'She wants a digital video camera with USB or firewire output.' Francesca threw Pierson a look of disdain. She followed this up with a single yet slow and forceful deliberate blink of her eyes, and finished the gesture by opening her eyes wide as if in disbelief, tilting her head sideways slightly.

The assistant showed Francesca a particular model. 'The tape is already loaded and the battery is charged, so you can use it straight away. You know; to capture your experience.'

'Wonderful,' Francesca remarked derisively.

'That'll be nice darling, won't it?' Pierson continued, smiling at the assistant 'Come on I'll buy it for you as an anniversary present.'

'That comes to fifteen hundred Euros please sir.'

Pierson selected the other credit card and paid with it.

'Any more in there?' Francesca asked almost under her breath looking in his wallet, but then worried that the assistant may have heard her, she gave him a beaming smile. 'That's such a nice gesture,' she said loudly for the assistant's benefit, turning to look at Pierson as she spoke.

As they walked away she added. 'Remind me to buy you some vegetables some time.'

Pierson frowned.

'So you can watch them grow and have as much fun with them as I'll have with this,' she said, holding the carrier bag containing the video camera out at arms length, as though it contained some foul smelling decomposing animal.

'It's all part of the plan,' Pierson said.

'Oh. Forgive me. So now we have a plan do we?' Francesca replied, playfully though, rather than with cynicism.

'Let's take some 'holiday' shots and see if I can spot that man again,' Pierson remarked.

'What are you going to do? Photograph the entire ship?' Francesca asked loudly, her Italian accent becoming more apparent. But it was one of those moments when everyone else around her had gone silent and now she was the centre of attention.

'Why not darling? Can you think of a better way to have fun here tonight?' Pierson replied, grabbing her hand and whisking her off as she just slinked along as quickly as possible, head down, not trying to cause another scene.

They slowed to meander past the other shops and Pierson saw a copy of the Times and bought it. He'd missed the English news, and thought this might make him feel less homesick.

Just beyond the shopping area they found one of the bars, where, sitting at a window side table, they could watch the sunset and talk, while Pierson did his best to work out how to use the cameras.

He began taking shots of Francesca, ensuring the background was well in focus and with the particular resolution of the camera, after four shots, he had the entire bar photographed.

'Would you mind trying this one?' Pierson said to Francesca getting the video camera out.

'Okay,' she replied, 'why the sudden interest in cameras?'

'You have something better to do?' he asked.

But she gave no reply.

'I've got an idea,' he said.

'That many?' she said toying with him.

Pierson merely flashed her a serious look that made her giggle at her own ingenuity, which out of politeness she attempted to stifle, clearing her throat in the process and looking at him more solemnly—or at least trying to.

'If Roger is aboard,' he continued pokerfaced, 'then I want to know if it's for business or for pleasure. It's too much of a coincidence; and if it is business then perhaps he won't be alone. Call it a gut feeling, but there's been so much going on so far with this case, that I'm beginning not to believe in coincidences. The more people I can capture on film, all be it digital,' he picked up the still camera and waved it slightly to endorse his point, 'the better our chances later of seeing who might be working with him. After all what's the down side?'

'None.' Francesca agrees. 'It may help our cover even though we haven't needed it so far, but you're right about looking like tourists.'

'Until someone recognises me,' Pierson added.

Francesca just flicked her eyes up at him and began to smile but stopped herself.

'What?' he asked her. 'What was that look for?'

'Nobody knows you're alive. So how could anyone recognise you?' she remarked.

'Roger could,' Pierson replied gravely.

Francesca ignored his comment but began using the video to record the events in the bar. She placed the camera on the table next to her, and just let it run while the two of them sat there drinking and chatting. Every now and again, Pierson took another photograph of something or someone. Even in the artificial light, both cameras were sensitive enough to get excellent images.

'What have you found out about the Channel Tunnel?' Francesca asked.

'I downloaded lots of stuff, but it's on the laptop. I'll need to go and get it. If you want to stay here and order some more drinks, I'll do that now.'

She nodded in agreement.

'No talking to strange men,' he added as he stood, picking up his copy of the Times.

'I'm sorry,' she replied, 'not even you?' she turned her head and followed him with her eyes as he walked off. Then as he finally disappeared she raised her arm to catch the attention of the waiter and ordered two coffees.

Pierson's thoughts returned to Roger and whether he'd actually seen him. But his mind just went around in circles wanting proof, feeling paranoid and then concerned as to why Roger was there, if indeed he had been.

As he passed the retail outlets again, he stopped at the tax free shop and bought himself a bottle of Jack Daniels—for personal indulgence he thought, as he paid for it.

It took Pierson no more than fifteen minutes to do the round trip to his cabin, dropping off the whiskey and newspaper when there, and then getting back to the bar with his laptop. As he returned, so Francesca used the still camera to photograph him.

He placed the laptop down and took it out of its case. Opening the lid he powered it on.

'What do you think of the camera?' he asked her.

'Nice colour,' she replied nodding at it.

He frowned and raised one eyebrow at her.

'No it's good. I've taken a few shots while you were out. As I don't know Roger and he presumably doesn't know me, I thought it would be worth me taking as many shots as possible,' she remarked.

'We'll upload them in a minute,' he replied, 'and get a better resolution.'

As the laptop got close to finishing its power on sequence, Pierson noticed how much busier the bar had become.

'What about food?' he asked.

'There's bound to be something open most of the night. We can eat any time,' she replied in a matter of fact manner.

She picked up the camera again and took a shot. Pierson watched, and then he saw her wave at someone.

'Who was that?'

'Nobody,' came the reply.

'So why did you wave?'

'To remove suspicion; if you wave at someone, or in fact nothing when someone has just watched you take a photograph, it makes them look away and makes you look less suspicious.'

'It's like when you enter a room,' she added.

'What do you mean?'

'Well I've noticed that when you walk into a room, you look like you're going to kill someone, so nobody trusts you. Everyone is wary of you,' she commented as she took his photograph, 'but,' she continued, 'I was taught to smile as I enter a room. It puts people at their ease, they think they know me, but can't remember where from, and they don't see me as a threat. You should try it. It works.'

Pierson smiled.

'That's it,' Francesca remarked, 'now just keep practising until you can smile properly and not grimace,' she laughed before continuing. 'I know, you think you look foolish, smiling at everyone, but it's not true. Do you think that people who smile at you are foolish?'

'No,' Pierson replied.

'Good,' Francesca added with a smile, as if to demonstrate it. 'Even an enemy can be put off balance when you give them a genuine smile, and the worst thing that will happen is that your enemy will think you're a fool.'

She paused for a moment. 'If you can't smile then try and think of paradise: you know, somewhere nice where you'd like to be and keep that thought in your mind.'

'Why?' he asked her.

'Because it helps relax your muscles, including your face muscles and give you a look of serenity; and that too is seen as non threatening.'

Pierson nodded again and looked at Francesca in a different light. 'Was this all part of your training?' he asked.

She just looked at him ignoring the question. 'Remember it works both ways.'

'What do you mean?' Pierson asked her.

'Anyone that smiles at you is not necessarily your friend,' she said and then gave him a large smile, 'watch people who smile at you because they may have something to hide.'

'What are you hiding?' he asked her.

She pulled back her jacket to reveal her gun and what appeared to be a pair of handcuffs.

'Don't try anything tonight,' she added, looking at him seriously and raising one eyebrow.

'How did you get that aboard?' he asked her, looking surprised that she had the gun.

'Does it matter?' she replied, 'I obviously did.'

Pierson agreed. He thought briefly about trying to work it out, but he had better things to focus on.

He looked at the laptop screen and started to browse the downloaded files. 'Are you ready for this?' he asked her, just as a waiter approached with their drinks.

'Yes,' she said to him and quickly thanked the waiter and paid him.

Pierson began to paraphrase the information from the laptop.

'There are three tunnels in all, two for trains and one for access between them. In case of emergency a train can be evacuated, and the passengers can get into the access tunnel between the two main tunnels.

Access to the central tunnel can be found every four hundred metres. There are piston valves every two hundred and fifty metres to allow air from oncoming trains to escape. The central tunnel is pressurised to keep fire out.

Only one track is laid in each of the outer tunnels, and so trains cannot pass each other directly other than at crossover points.'

Pierson stopped and looked at Francesca 'Are you taking all this in?'

'Oh yes,' she replied, 'its riveting.' She threw him a look that indicated she was completely with him and then leaned forward to try her coffee.

Pierson just continued regardless.

'There's electrical power in the tunnel for lighting, air pumps and for the trains. A supply of one hundred and sixty megawatts exists.

The tunnel itself reaches its closest point to the water—in the channel above—five sixths of the way between Britain and France.'

'Or one sixth of the way from France to Britain,' Francesca interrupted, 'it all depends on where you start from.'

Pierson paused again to looked at Francesca and then carried on.

'The trains are made from an alloy that can withstand fire for thirty five minutes without warping. There are three different types of carriage on the rolling stock; one for passengers, a shuttle for cars and a shuttle for lorries.'

'How long does it take to get through the tunnel?' Francesca asked.

'Thirty minutes at normal speed,' Pierson replied. 'There's more data if you're interested, but it's mainly about the way the tunnels were built and how much rock they moved and other stuff like that, so it's probably not useful to us.'

Francesca nodded and took another sip from her coffee. 'Let's go back to my cabin and talk,' she suggested. 'Maybe we can upload the pictures and see if you recognise anyone.' Raising one eyebrow, she flashed Pierson a look as though it was highly unlikely.

They picked up their things and Pierson packed away the laptop in its bag. Getting back to Francesca's cabin, he noticed that her bathroom was full of all the strange potions and liquids that women seem to use to improve their skin, hair, nails and sundry other parts of their body. Many of these dubious looking liquids were in small brightly coloured containers. But regardless of this, or possibly because of it, the bathroom smelled sweet.

The power in the room wouldn't work without the credit card style key in the door lock. This was a feature found in many hotels, but Pierson found it odd that it should work the same way aboard a ship. Yet in some ways it made sense, because it saved on electricity—not that it was metered.

Francesca took the laptop computer out of its case and began to get it to power up. She connected the still camera and waited for it all to start.

She hunted through the camera bag finding and then installing the upload software, after which, she restarted the computer and then with the camera connected, she triggered the upload process.

'I hope your hard disk is big enough,' she commented as she watched it.

'It should be,' Pierson replied without boring her with the details. They watched the progress bar on the upload and after a couple of minutes it had completed. Pierson squeezed in beside her as Francesca set the picture library viewer to automatic.

Each of the photographs was displayed on the screen for a few seconds at a time. They looked closely and soon Pierson could see the shots taken by Francesca.

'What's that!' he declared disbelievingly, as he saw a shot of a man bending over who had dropped his wallet.

'Cute,' she replied with a smile, 'don't you think?'

Pierson raised his eyebrows and looked at her in horror, 'It's not a toy,' he said referring to the camera.

'Yes, I know,' she replied, 'but look what fun we can have,' she added wickedly.

'You can have,' Pierson remarked soberly.

They viewed the other photographs, until they got to the one where she had waved at the imaginary person in the bar.

'Stop there!' Pierson exclaimed. But it was too late. The software continued to display the next photograph in the sequence, which actually was the first one again. Francesca pressed the touchpad of the laptop and displayed the entire list of shots. Clicking the last one, she selected the option to display it again, in full screen size.

'That's him,' declared Pierson. 'That's Roger. I'm certain. There's no doubt about it.' Pierson pointed at the figure, just to the right of the centre of the photograph. He was standing with another man, and both of them were looking at the camera, but the face of the other man was slightly obscured.

'I did see him,' Pierson remarked, now troubled by the sight of him.

'He works for Bill, or at least he was with him on the day that my death was set up, you know, staged.'

Francesca sat quietly and looked at him for a few moments before glancing back at the screen briefly, and then shrugging her shoulders she attempted to allay his fears. 'It's August, perhaps he's on holiday.'

Pierson was unconvinced.

'Zoom in on him,' he asked her.

She found the correct icon, set it on his face and it doubled in size.

'That's definitely him,' Pierson added. 'And my belief in coincidences is fading fast.'

'What would prove to you that he's on holiday?' Francesca added, trying to dispel what she considered to be Pierson's paranoia.

'If he were alone, or with his wife—not that I know who she is,' he replied. 'But if he's with someone else I know, or someone else there that day that I...' Pierson tailed off, 'that is, the day Tom Brady died. Then I'd be certain he's here on business.'

He scanned the photograph closely but he couldn't see anyone he recognised. They spent some time looking in detail at the other photographs too, but to no avail.

'How about this?' Pierson asked Francesca pointing at the bag containing the digital video camera.

'I don't know,' she said looking at the box. 'It's not too difficult to use, but I didn't see the part about uploading it to PC. You figure out that part and I'll order some food. Is Pasta okay?'

'Yes, fine.'

Pierson found the media for the video camera software installation, performed the install and then uploaded the film.

Francesca watched as he connected the camera to the laptop. Minutes passed by as the film played and uploaded. 'Is it working?' she asked him.

'It seems to be, but we'll know in a few minutes,'

Once the upload process had completed, he played it back on the PC. They watched and listened. Most of what they heard was their own conversation, and then after about twenty five minutes, the film lined up with the still photographs that Francesca had taken. The camera having been recording all the time on their table showed the film at a slightly different angle to the still shots, but it had a wide-angle lens that captured most of the important activity in the bar.

'There,' Pierson declared pointing at the screen, 'there's a second man with Roger.' They could see Roger standing away from the bar, smoking a cigarette whilst another man walked away from him.

'Was he with him or did he just walk by?' Francesca asked.

'He was with him,' Pierson replied, 'I think.' he added, looking at her. They waited a few more moments, but the man was hidden from view. Then as he came back into the camera shot, he walked towards Roger and handed him a drink, but Francesca and Pierson still couldn't see his face.

The flash went off and the man turned around. 'Sorry about that,' said Francesca, 'that was me taking a picture with the other camera and the flash was set to automatic.'

'I'm glad it was,' Pierson replied, 'I know him too. He was one of the other men there the evening Tom Brady died. They're here on business.'

Pierson lunged at the touchpad.

'What's wrong?' Francesca asked.

Pierson stepped the film backwards frame by frame and then she could see too. Roger's jacket had spilled open briefly revealing some hardware of sorts.

'Do treasury men always drink on holiday, with their guns in place?' he inquired.

She just looked at him and said nothing. At that moment there was a knock at the door. It was room service. The steward smiled at her as he wheeled in the trolley.

'Pasta for two?' he asked.

Francesca nodded. 'Thank you,' she replied.

He left and closed the door behind him. As the door engaged, Pierson noticed the electronic lock flash through a sequence of lights. He walked over to it and withdrew the card and immediately the power stopped and the lights went out. The only thing still illuminated was the laptop PC, now running from batteries. Pierson tried the door handle but it wouldn't work, it was locked.

He noticed that his watch glowed brightly in the dark—a fact he hadn't realised before—and this distracted him momentarily. Replacing the credit card style key in the lock, the lights came back on, as did the power, the bathroom light flashing it's fluorescent circular tube a few times before it settled to a constant illumination.

'What was that for?' Francesca asked him.

'I was curious.'

She shook her head in mild disbelief and then removed the silver domed cover from the food, and passed some cutlery wrapped in a paper napkin to Pierson.

They took one small tray of pasta each and began eating as they talked.

The food was hot and Pierson had to stop quickly; and breaking open a can of diet coke, he took a swig before he was able to carry on.

'How did they know I was here?' he asked her, pointing at the screen with his fork.

She just looked at him unable to answer, but then asked him a question. 'Did we find them by accident?'

'Yes,' he replied after a few moments thought.

'No we didn't.' she said seriously, looking at Pierson.

'What do you mean?' he asked her.

'There are six bars on this ship, two of which are clubs or discotheques and they happened to be in the one we chose,' she said. 'And you think that was accidental?'

'Are you certain?' he continued, 'that bar is the closest to the shops, it's on the port side of the ship and had a brilliant view of the sunset.'

'It had a brilliant view of you,' she added, 'we didn't find them, they found us,' she continued, 'they were in clear view of the camera, most of the time, because they were watching us. But they obviously didn't recognise me, or more would have happened when I took their photograph with the flash. They would have disappeared. As for the video, only you and I knew it was recording.'

Pierson nodded. 'So they were following us. But who sent them and why?'

Francesca shrugged her shoulders as she had just taken a mouthful of hot pasta.

'Okay. Let's start this another way.' Pierson continued. 'Who knew we were going to be here tonight?'

She shrugged her shoulders again and carried on eating.

'Henri knew,' he said answering his own question and fixing her in his stare as he did so.

Francesca ignored him and put her plate down, then, wiping her lips with her napkin, she opened one of the other soft drink cans. Pointing at the screen and shaking the hair out of her eyes, she spoke. 'We knew too.'

Pierson finished his pasta and put the plate back on the trolley. 'You're evading my question,' he said.

'You didn't ask one,' she replied defensively, 'you just said Henri knew.'

'Who else knew?' Pierson asked her.

Again she shrugged her shoulders.

'Are you hiding something?' he asked her.

'Yes,' came the reply.

'What?' Pierson continued, 'what are you hiding?'

'I don't know where to begin,' she said, but the tone was sarcastic. Even Pierson was beginning to recognise that much. He knew he'd touched a sore point, but he wanted the truth. Suddenly he was beginning to have doubts about her.

'If it wasn't Henri then who?' Pierson asked.

'These men work for Bill?' she said to him.

'Yes,' he replied.

'Then it seems obvious to me that Bill told them to come. Do you think that Henri has employees in the treasury department in Britain?'

Now Pierson didn't answer, not wishing to offend Francesca, as it was her uncle that they were talking about.

'Why didn't Henri come aboard with us?' Pierson asked. 'He said he'd be on the train with us tomorrow.'

'So ask him tomorrow,' she said unhelpfully. 'You know as much as I do.'

There was a pause and they both said nothing.

'Let's start at the beginning,' Pierson suggested.

'They're here and they're not on vacation, because one of them is armed,'

Francesca nodded. 'I agree,' she said.

Pierson then continued. 'It's likely that Roger has a gun in order to use it. Specifically to use it on me as they were watching me. It seems unlikely that he's on board with a gun to shoot me just to wound me. So I'm led to the conclusion that he wants to kill me,' Pierson added.

'Possibly,' Francesca replied. 'Maybe they're here for another reason that we don't know.'

'Such as?' Pierson asked, trying to be more open-minded.

'Such as coming back from France having viewed Rene Sebastien's apartment and seen a Gendarme on guard.'

Pierson hadn't thought of that.

'But why tonight?' he continued.

'Because they have to be on tomorrow's train,' she replied. 'Or may be they're here to keep you safe from someone else, another unknown assassin.'

This was something that Pierson hadn't thought of either. 'Why do you assume that everyone wants to kill you?' she asked him 'There could be other equally, or better fitting explanations for this.'

'Because until a couple of weeks ago when anyone said they wanted to kill me, I knew it was a figure of speech. Now though, I realise they probably mean it,' he replied. 'I like the way you think though. You're good,' he remarked, 'very good, but Henri isn't off the hook yet.'

'Trust me,' she said looking at him in earnest. 'Henri is straight and honest.'

'Why should I trust you?' Pierson asked her. But he didn't really mean what he said and as soon as the words had left his mouth he regretted it.

'Okay,' Francesca shouted at him. 'Do what you like! We've tried to help you. But if that's what you wish, then do as you please!' she paused but only briefly and she then continued, 'trust no one!'

Pierson could see there was very little point in arguing with her. 'I'm sorry,' he said genuinely.

She moved to the bed and sat there hugging her knees like a fuming teenager, looking as though she'd had some great wrong committed against her.

Pierson spoke softly to her, 'I'll leave now. Thank you for a pleasant evening.'

He left her cabin closing the door behind him and returned to his cabin.

After a few moments her anger bubbled over and she threw the first thing she could grab at the door. It was a glass ashtray and she watched it as it shattered into countless splinters showering the carpet by the door with its crystal rain. Her anger though was with herself and not with Pierson, and after a few moments she walked towards her door, and avoiding the broken glass as much as she could, she went outside into the corridor.

She stepped carefully towards his cabin and placed her ear at Pierson's door. But she could hear nothing. Moving her head away from it she reached out with her hand and touched it gently with the tips of her fingers. Her face saddened as she slowly pulled her hand away. She turned her back to it, pressed against it gently and looked toward the handle as she carefully slid down, bending her knees as she did so, tears of anger and frustration in her eyes, finally bringing her clenched fists up to cover her face as she rested her elbows on her knees.

She remained there for a full fifteen minutes reflecting on her thoughts as her emotions consumed her. Then moving her hands away from her face she looked upwards. She wiped the tears from her eyes, slowly stood and faced his cabin door once again. Then kissing the tips of the fingers on her left hand, she gently placed them on the door, with a distant look of longing in her eyes. She whispered the words, 'good night,' and then lowering her head, slowly she turned again, to return to her own cabin.

Pierson lay on his bed and opened his copy of the Times and began trying to read, but couldn't. He reached for the Jack Daniels and not being able to find a glass he opened the bottle and took a swig from it.

It was only about ten in the evening and he tried to get some sleep, but couldn't. The only friends he seemed to have in the world either wanted him dead, or he'd managed to alienate. Now the loneliness began to set in. He looked at the Jack Daniels in his hand, but instead of drinking from the bottle again, he replaced the top and put it on the shelf next to him.

Thinking about someone trying to kill him, he couldn't see how anyone could break into his room, unless they had a master key, but he took some precautions anyway, knowing the resourcefulness of the people he'd been dealing with.

There was a chair in his cabin, one of a pair, a kind of boudoir or highly decorated dining chair, with thick upholstery. It was quite heavy for its style and he placed it on its side on the floor, with its legs pointing at an angle to the door, then he took the credit card key out of its holder in the door and carefully made his way back to the bed, making sure he avoided the chair.

After some thirty minutes he fell asleep.

He didn't notice the lights on the lock of his cabin door beginning to flash at one in the morning, as he was well and truly asleep by that time, even though he'd failed to get undressed. The door opened but there was no light.

A man slowly entered, and taking a gun from the holster inside his jacket he stood inside the room. He remained within the radius of the doorway, peering over to Pierson who was still lying on the bed. The only thing the gunman could make out properly was the illuminated display from Pierson's wristwatch. He pulled out a silencer from his inside pocket and began screwing it to the end of the gun.

'Come on!' said a voice from the corridor in a loud whisper. 'Do him now.'

The man finished screwing on the silencer and then moved forward into the room beyond the radius of the door instantly jamming his shin into the end of the chair leg. He cried out immediately and fell into the mangled shape of the chair, hitting his head on the table in front it as he fell. Pierson woke with a start, his heart pounding and the adrenalin suddenly coursing through his arteries. By reflex alone he leapt back on the bed and then dived on the man and punched him hard in the side of the head, knocking him out. As he looked up though, a second man stood in the doorway. It was Roger's accomplice from earlier that evening.

'What a mess,' he declared looking at Pierson. 'Back off,' he added waving his gun at him. The man remained in the corridor, looking into the dimly lit cabin, the only light actually coming from the corridor where he was standing, but his view was obscured by his own shadow.

Pierson saw his silhouette clearly and gambled from the man's movements that he couldn't see Pierson properly if at all, so he kept moving slowly out of his assailant's direct view and towards the side of the door.

Pierson carefully picked up the bottle of Jack Daniels by the neck. And raised it ready to strike. He gradually slid off the other side of the bed and moved to the wall sidling smoothly towards the door.

Pierson was ready for the second man to enter. He must have had a master key Pierson thought to himself. Yet the second gunman dare not risk placing it on the inside lock to switch on the lights for fear of giving Pierson the brief advantage he would need while the man's back was turned.

The gunman was about to step in to the room and Pierson's whole body became taught as he raised the bottle higher. From the man's outline Pierson could tell he was about to move in, but then just as he was about to enter, the man was distracted by a noise from his right.

Unseen by Pierson, Francesca had heard the commotion of the first intruder falling and crashing. She had opened her door and was standing in the corridor dressed only in her underwear, one bra strap hanging down on her arm. As she stood looking at the gunman with her left hand holding a bloody handkerchief to her face, she spoke. 'Can you help me please?' she implored. The man stepped into Pierson's room, briefly placing himself out of her view. 'Just a moment,' he said putting his gun away, and, as he turned to step out again and offer her help, she'd produced her gun which she'd earlier slid into the back of her briefs but was now pointing directly at him. Holding it with both hands, the handkerchief still dangling in her left hand and could be seen hanging below the gun she gestured for him to enter Pierson's cabin.

'No tricks,' she said uncompromisingly.

Pierson got up and took the man's gun. 'There's one on the floor too,' he remarked as he put the key card in the door and closed it. The lights came on.

Francesca gestured for the second man to lie on the floor. 'Face down, hands on your head,' she said to him.

Pierson could hardly take his eyes off her. Dressed in only her bra and briefs, he could see she was in beautiful shape, with a body that must have been carved in heaven. The curves were precisely formed and the underlying muscle structure was sensual and magnificent all at once. Her shapely lower legs led to thighs whose curves and muscular beauty shimmered in the room's light. She held her tummy muscles tense and the smooth lines led to her rib cage where the individual ribs were covered, but still slightly visible. The curve of her breasts created an overhang that might have been considered an engineering marvel in any other circumstance, and with her arms outstretched their shapely contours added to a complete picture that left Pierson almost breathless with admiration and desire. The crowning glory of all of this though, was her pouting look, exuding killer confidence, her eyes fixed to her quarry as she stood there without blinking, keeping her target on the borderline of that split second between life and death.

Pierson shook himself mentally from the vision and looked at the first intruder. Finding his gun under the bedside table, he reached for it and then stepped across to Francesca. 'Show me how this thing works and I'll watch them while you get dressed,' he said offering it to her.

'Safety catch here,' she said pointing at it. 'It's off now so the gun can fire. This is the dangerous end, point it at your target and then squeeze here,' she said pointing to the trigger. 'Use both hands to steady the gun it will kick back. Try it on him first.'

'No lady! Please.' Came the voice of the still conscious second intruder.

'Okay,' she replied. 'If they're good, then don't shoot them yet.'

'Get the cameras please.' Pierson asked her.

She left the room and went back into her own and cleaned herself up. Returning only minutes later, she had the cameras. She also had the handcuffs, but unfortunately only one set. But she'd got dressed into her jeans, tee shirt, trainers and jacket.

'What now?' she asked Pierson. 'Would you like them dead?'

'Yes, but not yet.' He replied.

'We don't play games with assassins,' she added, 'you just shoot and that's it. They don't have any information, they just have orders, letting them live just gives them another opportunity to kill you.'

'These men were instrumental in saving my life. I can't believe that they were doing anything other than following orders,' Pierson replied, as he sat on the bed. 'I won't kill them unless they do something stupid, but I have a gut feeling that whoever ordered them to do this, is the one we need to kill.'

Francesca looked at Pierson with disdain. 'This is a mistake, but it's your life,' she said.

Pierson bent over the unconscious man and started to strip his clothes. It took a few minutes, but he was left wearing only his underpants. 'Are you some kind of pervert?' The other man said.

'Don't speak again, unless you have some useful information for me,' Pierson said with deadly calm. The man turned his face back to the floor. Pierson dragged Roger in his almost completely stripped state to the middle of the room. He had a cut on his head from falling over the chair. Pierson stood the chair upright and with Roger face down, he spoke to the other man.

'Okay, now get up and strip. If you say one word out of place, my friend here has her own idea of what to do with assassins.'

The man stood up. He was fatter and shorter than Roger and began to remove all of his clothes with his back to them.

'Underpants too?' he asked turning his head around slowly, hoping they'd say no.

Pierson shook his head. 'Now lie down on the floor next to your friend and place your left wrist next to his left ankle'.

Slowly, the man did as he was told.

'This isn't going to be one of those homosexual set ups? Is it?' the man asked.

Pierson said nothing but gestured for the handcuffs from Francesca. He stepped on the man's left arm, holding it down. Pierson then placed one of the cuffs around Roger's left ankle and the other around the man's left wrist clasping them shut.

Picking up Roger's gun again, Pierson spoke to the man, 'Now wake up your friend.'

The man pushed Roger back and forth and tried to roll him over which just made things worse, as he ended up laid on top of him.

Pierson swapped the gun for the camera and started taking photographs. 'Remember, I know who you work for. Just think how good this will make your career look Roger, when I post these shots on your web site.'

Roger opened his eyes. He'd been conscious for a few moments but saw no reason to give that away until he saw the flashes and heard Pierson's comments.

Pierson laid out the copy of the Times on the floor so that it opened on the middle pages. 'Stand up,' he said to them. But it was almost impossible and when they finally managed it, Roger had his left foot slightly raised trying to balance on one leg while the other man was crouching trying to pick his arm up, but he had his back to Roger.

'Stand on the paper!' Pierson barked at them. Francesca still held the gun on the two men and remained statuesque and motionless. 'Move or say a word and your dead,' Pierson added. He then picked up the bottle of Jack Daniels, and looking at the two men dressed only in their underpants, one looking like an incontinent cripple, and the other like Quasimodo, he began to pour the whiskey onto their underwear and soaked them thoroughly. A great deal of the whiskey ran down their legs and onto the newspaper.

Pierson put the bottle back and then feeling around in the pile of Roger's clothes on the floor, he pulled out something from one of the pockets. 'Off the paper,' he said to them and they moved off. He picked up the soaking edition of the Times and folded it closed. With the gun in one hand covered by the paper, he ushered them out.

Taking the card out of the door lock he and Francesca walked behind them as they made their way onto the deck.

There was complete silence, apart from the swell against the ship, which had by now anchored within sight of the English coast. The moon was almost full and as they got to the deck, the sight of the two would-be assassins was extremely funny and Francesca couldn't stop smiling.

Roger had to walk with a hop and a skip because his colleague couldn't keep his arm low enough; he in turn swapped between walking backwards with a slouch and walking forwards and looking like a gorilla. No matter how he tried to walk it was always extremely awkward.

Pierson moved them towards the railings. 'If you have anything you'd like to tell me then say it now,' he said.

Neither of them spoke. He pushed them against the railings and with Roger's back to Pierson, Pierson gestured to Francesca to point her gun at the other man's head, which she did. The man cowered briefly trying to shield his face from her. Pierson placed Roger's gun on the deck out of reach of the two men and then pulled out of his pocket the item he'd taken from Roger's clothing. It was a cigarette lighter and with it he lit the copy of the Times newspaper that was now well and truly soaked with Jack Daniels.

With only a brief thought of the morality of his actions he watched the flames lick their way down the paper, then he placed it by Roger's underpants. They immediately caught fire and he began screaming and jumping around.

The other man looked in mortal fear of his life. A simple assassination had turned into the fiasco he now faced. Roger began to leap about and yell as he tried unsuccessfully to extinguish his burning underwear on the railings.

Pierson bent over towards the second man. Francesca still held the gun to his head. 'No please, no!' he yelled as the flames caught him and began to race up his hairy back, burning it.

Pierson stood there impassively. 'The water is that way gentlemen,' he pointed at the sea. Roger by now was screaming and yelling and trying to fling himself over the side of the ship. The other man resisted but Roger succeeded in jumping overboard, only to end up dangling from a great height above the water, underpants alight while almost dislocating the other man's shoulder as they were still handcuffed ankle to wrist. The second man was now screaming, as Roger shouted obscenities at him. He tried desperately to climb over the railings with Roger's weight still on his left wrist.

The flames now beginning to lick further up to the hair on his head, he channelled all of his desperation to clumsily scramble over the railings and let gravity do the rest, taking him and Roger into the cool channel water.

Pierson tossed in the remains of the burning newspaper after them.

'Can they swim?' Francesca asked him, open eyed and in stunned amazement at what she'd witnessed.

'I hope so,' Pierson replied, 'for their sake. If nothing else it will teach them a lesson in humility. Anyway it's only about a mile to the shore, and then they can walk naked to the Police or wherever.'

She stood gazing over the side for a few moments longer and mentally thanked God that Pierson was alive. Turning to him she waited for him to look at her. 'I'm sorry about what I said earlier,' she said to him putting the gun away and then taking his arm with both of her hands.

Pierson picked up Roger's gun from the deck and tossed it over the side along with his lighter. 'It was my fault. Thank you for saving my life,' he said as he looked at her face to face, gently sliding his hand from her grasp and moving to hold her upper arms.

'You were right,' she added.

'What do you mean, I was right?' he replied.

'About trusting no one, you should trust no one,' she continued.

'No Francesca,' he replied, 'you were right.' Pausing briefly he continued as he looked her in the eyes. 'I trust you.' They held each other's gaze and then moving his head towards hers he kissed her; and although she was surprised initially, she responded.

After a few moments he pulled away. 'I'm sorry,' he said, 'I shouldn't have done that.'

'Don't be sorry,' she said softly, looking deep into his eyes and then looking down. Before either of them could say anything further though, the moment was shattered by a man shouting along the deck from where they were standing.

'Oi, you two! What's all that screaming about? Was that you?'

'No,' Pierson replied, 'it wasn't us. It looks as though someone's stag night got out of control.'

It was one of the stewards. 'What happened? Where did they go then?' he continued talking, all the while walking towards the two of them and leaning over the railings trying to peer into the water, shading his eyes from the moon as if that would help him see.

Pierson waited for the man to catch his attention again and then gave the steward something new to think about. 'One of them said something about racing the other to the shore, you know what these young people are like.'

'Idiots,' said the steward. 'How do they think they'll get back on board? Oh well; sorry to have interrupted you.'

He walked off, shaking his head and left Pierson and Francesca to themselves.

'What now?' she asked.

'Now we scavenge for a few minutes,' he replied.

'What do you mean scavenge?'

'We've still got their clothes in my cabin. I wonder whether there's anything useful, you know, like passes or ids that can be changed,'

'Now you're thinking more deviously,' she commented, 'are we corrupting you perhaps?'

'A little,' he answered flashing her a quick but serious look as he held the door open for her to walk inside again.

Back in his cabin, the two piles of clothes were strewn around and there was a stain on the floor from the Jack Daniels where it had seeped through the newspaper.

'Check out Quasimodo's clothes, see if there's a wallet or something,' said Pierson pointing at the pile of clothes from the shorter man.

Pierson looked through Roger's jacket and trousers, pulling out car keys and a wallet. The wallet contained a photographic pass for the treasury.

'Have you got one of these yet?' he asked Francesca, waving the pass at her.

'Yes,' she replied, 'his name is Leslie Garrett.'

'Good,' Pierson said, nodding and smiling.

'Why good?' she said, 'do you know him?'

'No. But, Leslie is what you might refer to as an androgynous name, not quite certain whether it's a man or woman.'

'And you want to put my photo in here instead of his,' she said realising what he was thinking.

'All we need is a passport photograph, a knife or something to cut this open and some glue,' Pierson remarked.

'We just need Passport Photos, I've got the rest,' she said to him as she stood up.

'You've got glue?' he asked incredulously.

'I've got clear nail varnish. It'll be as good as glue,' she replied, 'what about their clothes and other things though?'

'Well it looks like we won't need a taxi when we arrive,' Pierson replied shaking the car keys at her, 'let's take the money and anything else that could identify them and we'll get the clothes to the laundry. But throw away one sock from each pile somewhere.'

'Why?' she looked at him and frowned.

'Everyone loses socks,' he answered with a smile.

Even though it was still the middle of the night, they did as Pierson suggested, disposing of the clothes in the laundry chute first. Tracking down the passport machine in the mall, they paid for and waited for the photographs. Back at Francesca's cabin, she doctored the two passes, while Pierson cleared up the broken glass from the ashtray.

'What did you do in the corridor to distract Garrett?' he asked her, picking up the glass and noticing blood on one of the pieces.

'That's a trade secret.'

She smiled at him briefly as she put the finishing touches to the second pass. Pierson watched as she packed away the scissors. 'Why did you cut yourself with the ashtray rather than the scissors?' he asked.

'Because it was already there,' Francesca replied, not looking at him.

'Oh,' he commented wondering whether she meant it was the first thing she thought of, or whether it was already broken and if it was, then why was it broken? She clearly didn't seem to want to go down that avenue with him, he thought to himself.

Then a thought struck him. 'They didn't come after you? Did they?' he said slowly and gradually turning to face her.

'I don't think so,' she said.

'They didn't even seem to know about you though,' he remarked still really just thinking out loud.

She shook her head. 'Then that puts Henri in the clear,' she added.

'Not really,' Pierson replied, 'in fact, not at all. It makes him look more guilty.'

'How?' she asked carefully, using all her self control, not wishing to repeat the earlier argument and trying to stop herself from erupting.

'If Henri had wanted me dead, then he certainly wouldn't have you killed, he wouldn't even tell the hit men about you. He would have kept you safe and given them instructions to just kill me and absolutely forbid them to kill anyone else.'

Francesca could see the sense in this, but she told Pierson about Henri's instructions to guard him with her life. Pierson's mind was beginning to overload. But he continued thinking aloud to at least see how it sounded.

'Bill however would probably have wanted both of us dead and so the gunmen would each have entered the two rooms at the same time, or they would have tried to kill you first as you would be more likely to be armed. But Bill didn't know we were aboard.'

Feeling tired, Francesca realised she couldn't work out what had happened either, they needed more evidence, but more than anything now they needed sleep.

'Can I go to bed now?' she asked him.

'Yes,' came the reply. He got up to leave, but she looked at him and spoke. 'It'll be safer if you stay here now.'

He looked at her and thought about how close they'd both come to being killed. He had no intention of letting his only friend in the world die and as he was feeling more protective towards her now, so he stayed.

'I'll take the floor,' he suggested, 'shame about those clothes though.'

'What do you mean?' She asked.

'Well they would have been something soft to lie on.'

Regardless of the hard floor, the slow rhythmic rocking of the boat had him asleep in minutes.

Francesca lay there on the bed, just listening to Pierson's gentle breathing pleased she had smoothed things out with him. Soon, she too fell asleep.

SOMETHING UNEXPECTED

Francesca awoke a few hours later by a morning call that she'd prearranged. She showered and dressed and then woke Pierson. He returned to his room and cleaned himself up. Tidying his cabin, he picked up all of his things—this now just amounted to his clothes and the cameras—and he took them in a bag into Francesca's cabin.

Checking his watch he could see that it was seven am.

'There are some things I need,' he said to her as she was making the finishing touches to cleaning her gun, 'maybe we can have some breakfast and then on the way back visit the shops.'

'No problem,' she replied as she held up the barrel to check it for blockages.

He saw the laptop computer was still switched on, so he packed it away along with the cameras before leaving for the restaurant. Finding they were amongst the first ones there, they helped themselves to coffee, but neither of them could stomach a full breakfast.

Pierson felt the anticipation and fear building up within him. He knew this was to be the big day, and now for the first time he wondered whether he would get through it alive. But strangely he was beginning to sense a certain excitement about the entire thing. Francesca seemed much more relaxed as she stared out of the window looking at the calm waters of the channel.

'What do you want from the shops?' she asked only half paying attention.

'A bag: a rucksack or something similar for the cameras and laptop, and my clothes too,' he replied.

She nodded as if to say 'good idea'.

'We'll get two,' she eventually remarked. 'Was that it?'

'Sunglasses too,' Pierson added as he surveyed the restaurant.

'There won't be much sun,' she replied, looking at him curiously, 'we'll be underground.'

'I just want something to disguise myself a little so that I won't be recognised straight away,' he continued. Adding cream to his coffee and stirring it rhythmically, he placed the spoon back in the saucer and picked up the cup to take his first taste; then, thinking back to the events of the previous night he changed the subject.

'I've been thinking about our traitor, our inside man,' he said, pausing while Francesca turned to him. He became distracted by how good she looked in the morning and he found himself indulging in the opportunity to study her symmetric beauty and the carefree look she seemed to exude so naturally. After waiting for him to continue but with no avail, she raised one eyebrow as though to prompt him to carry on with his commentary.

His previous thoughts evaporated and the piece of impeccable logic he thought was forming in his mind suddenly eluded him. He shook his head in frustration. 'Never mind. It's gone. I'm sure there's something I'm missing.'

'In many ways we now have the upper hand,' she almost casually remarked, 'I think today will hold some surprises for a number of people. Someone is going to be sorely disappointed about last night and the fact that you're still alive. We'll have to think on our feet; and as long as we trust each other...'

'I do trust you,' Pierson interrupted her, deliberately flashing her a look so she could see into his eyes. 'Only you,' he declared seriously like he was giving her his solemn oath. 'Right now there's no one else that I do trust.'

He turned away briefly before carrying on. Then from the moment he continued speaking he never took his eyes off hers.

'I know that I'm not trained for this kind of work: the stuff that you do. But you won't find me holding back. Whatever you need, if I don't know how to do it just show me, or tell me how to do it and I'll do it. No matter what the cost I want to stop these people; and if that's not realistic then I'd like to at least throw a spanner in their works.'

There was a pause as she weighed up what he said.

'Spanners happen to be my strong point,' she remarked, with a mildly mischievous look in her eyes, but her tone made it believable: like she was about to carry out some act of revenge and nobody was going to be able to stop her. 'And remember,' she continued, 'there's a hundred and fifty tonnes of merchandise. That won't be easy to move or to hide.'

Pierson mused on this for a few moments, realising that the logistics involved were going to be barely credible. So he began to carry out the calculations aloud, speaking slowly and purposefully as he deliberated on every new point.

'The bars weigh twelve and a half kilos each; so that's eighty bars per ton and twelve thousand bars in all.' He thought about this for a few moments, and then picked up the commentary again. 'They've got to move twelve thousand bars and do it within thirty minutes.'

'Why thirty minutes? You don't know that?'

'I'm assuming they're going to steal it in the tunnel itself and thirty minutes is the longest time it will take the train to get through.'

'Your point?' Francesca continued.

'Even eighteen hundred bars would have to be moved at the rate of one a second to achieve moving them in thirty minutes, and there are twelve thousand bars, so that would mean moving them at the rate of seven a second from the lorries or transport to wherever. They're going to need an army.' Pierson declared.

'Unless you've missed something,' Francesca added.

'Such as?' Pierson prompted her.

'What if they just steal the trucks?'

'From a moving train? In a tunnel wide enough for one train only? How's that going to be possible?' His answer was almost a reflex, but he was beginning to see her point.

'You're assuming their going to just take the gold from the current transport—whatever that is and move it to a different transport. Why? How could you make such an assumption?' Francesca took a final swig from her coffee and waited for his reply.

'I don't know. It just seems that stealing the trucks could be done anywhere and by moving the gold from the trucks to another place or off the trucks is going to make it more difficult to track down.'

She nodded, but still looked unconvinced.

'There's going to be a lot going on. If you're right then either there will already be a small army on the train or if they're not already there, then they will be about to get in position soon.'

'We have a software swap taking place for money and we really have to watch Abbot, although I don't think he knows what he's getting himself into; and then there's the movement of the merchandise and the possibility of Selway appearing; and we don't know whose side he's on.'

She paused again. 'There's something else too,' she added.

'What?' said Pierson.

'I don't know yet, but believe me there is always something else,' she continued, 'like your visitors last night, there will be something unexpected today. It always happens.'

Pierson checked his watch again. It was time to move, they finished their drinks, visited the tax-free shop to buy the two rucksacks and sunglasses; and then returned to the cabins to pack their things properly. In a matter of minutes they found themselves on their way to the vehicle deck below, having handed in their cabin card keys. The ship was now moving again and they were standing at the entrance to the deck, while Pierson looked around.

'What are you looking for?' Francesca asked.

'A BMW,' Pierson replied, 'but I don't know what colour or model.'

'We could wait until every one else leaves,' she suggested.

'I don't think so, not with one of these,' he said holding up the car's electronic security fob.

They weaved their way through the vehicles starting at the bow. Pierson kept pressing the button on the fob, firing it in different directions as they walked hand in hand, trying to look like tourists.

Near the stern they heard the magical sound of the doors of a car unlocking. Pierson pressed the fob again and it locked the car, flashing its indicator lights and identifying itself to them.

It was a dark blue five hundred series; and as he approached he pressed the fob again to unlock it and then he walked around to the rear of the car, lifted the boot and placed their bags in, allowing Pierson to take the opportunity to look around and see who, if anyone, was watching him. He was temporarily relieved to find that he wasn't under obvious scrutiny. But his paranoia didn't let him feel easy about what he was doing. He'd never stolen a car before and he felt like a fugitive.

He took the driving seat and began to adjust it to fit, as Francesca got in the passenger side. There was a smell of stale cigarettes and the ashtray was full which didn't help. In the foot well he noticed ash as though someone had been sat in the car smoking while it had been stationary, but had been preoccupied. In the back were discarded polystyrene coffee cups strewn across the floor along with some fast food packaging.

Francesca reached around and picked up one of the cardboard tray covers, having noticed some hand written message on it. Across the top hastily scribbled in biro was the word 'Pareto' along with a note underneath. 'Final 20%—Wednesday 20th'. She showed it to Pierson and he frowned at it wondering what it could mean.

'A pay off perhaps?' he suggested.

'Who knows?' she replied.

Shrugging his shoulders he put the keys in the ignition and switched on the radio.

The ferry docked some minutes later and passengers took to their cars, coaches and lorries in readiness for departure. Pierson started the engine and switched on the air conditioning with the airflow kept on internal, to spare the two of them from the smell of the exhaust fumes of the other vehicles.

It took fifteen minutes to finally get off the ship, and then following the signs they took the route to the Eurostar embarkation, near Shakespeare cliff.

Once free of the traffic, they were able to open the windows and drive for a while, getting some fresh air.

They arrived at the terminal embarkation area for the train, and finding the long-term car park, Pierson parked the vehicle and read the ticket. 'Remember where we parked,' Francesca said to him jokingly as he looked back at the car. But they both knew that they wouldn't be coming back for it. He looked at the keys and studied them for a few seconds, but he decided to keep them and not discard them somewhere.

Pierson put the ticket in his inside jacket pocket, and then together he and Francesca walked towards the station buildings.

He checked his watch. It was 08:40. They found seats that overlooked the marshalling yards for the trains. They could see shuttles being loaded and then being attached to their train, which was already sitting on tracks parallel to the main line, waiting to get all of its rolling stock attached. There were four carriages for passengers and these were positioned at the front; followed by one carriage for cars and then three for lorries.

Pierson screwed up his eyes to try and focus more clearly— but it didn't help, so he took out the camera and began snapping shots of a series of tankers that had already been loaded. Zooming in he could see they carried markings of hazardous product warnings and they were all bearing the same name: Constantinou Pharmaceutical Company.

It was some fifteen minutes later that five refrigerated lorries arrived in convoy. Each lorry carried a different brand of food according to the labels on the outside. One was for ice cream, another for meat pies, two had frozen fish and seafood products and the last carried yoghurt—if their labels could be believed.

Then Pierson noticed something curious, the lorries were being rearranged with one of the refrigerated lorries on the same shuttle as a tanker. But they were being placed with their backs to each other so that the tankers faced France and the lorries faced England.

'Why are they doing that?' he said to Francesca.

She merely shook her head.

Pierson found this curious. He took the video camera and began filming and with its powerful zoom he closed in on someone standing nearby, while the lorries were being repositioned. It was Bill; and he was talking in an animated fashion to two of the marshalling stewards. Pierson watched the scene and pointed it out to Francesca, 'our traitor perhaps?'

'Who knows?' she replied looking at the small LCD screen for the camera, 'but, it looks as though he's got something to do with the transportation arrangements. Which means he probably knows about the cargo. I wonder whether he'll tell us about it when we see him?'

There was nothing the two of them could do at that stage, and with time for departure fast approaching they made their way into the passenger terminal and waited there for embarkation.

By 9:25 Pierson was already wearing his sunglasses. A large format television screen tuned to a 24 four hour news channel started to broadcast images from the alien asylum settlement camp at Sangatte on the French side of the tunnel. The breaking news was broadcasting film showing riots beginning, with asylum seekers running amok from the camp, towards the channel tunnel entrance, even though it was two miles from the camp. The authorities were preparing to ward off a siege in the tunnel, but they hoped they could quell the chaos long before the rioters reached that point.

Pierson and Francesca gave each other a look of intrigue and Pierson wondered whether this too could be a coincidence. 'Well?' he said looking at her.

'Something unexpected?' she remarked. Pierson raised one eyebrow as he looked back at the screen. The time had come to make their way to the to the passenger carriages in order to board, so that was the last the saw of the news item.

The train had finally been assembled and Pierson could now see there were ten carriages or shuttles: four for passengers and one shuttle for cars, followed by five shuttles for lorries, each of which had the one refrigerated food lorry facing backwards and a tanker facing forwards. As he scanned the length of the platform, Pierson could see Bill in the distance, still talking to a marshalling steward, but less animatedly than before. He seemed just to be nodding and then he momentarily raised the palm of his hand to the steward as if in agreement, followed by him pointing at his watch as he continued speaking. The steward then walked off towards the rear of the train without any acknowledging gestures or comments.

Pierson took out his camera to take some shots within the departure area, he wasn't quite sure what he might achieve by doing this, but as he hadn't seen Abbot, he was hoping—all be it an extremely unlikely possibility—that Abbot's face might show up in the crowd when he scrutinised the photos later. Once he'd finished, he then switched the camera off again and replaced it in his rucksack.

There was a clear cloudless sky, and the heat of the day was already becoming apparent. Pierson's sunglasses didn't look out of place at this stage. But like an airport, he had to show his passport and ticket to the woman standing at the terminal door. She had already checked Francesca through—who was now waiting ahead of Pierson—and as she looked at Pierson he dropped his sunglasses slightly so she could confirm his identity from the passport photograph.

Pierson looked around to see if he could recognise anyone else. Then suddenly he did a double take. He'd spotted Selway. He turned away quickly, smiled at the check-in woman and took his ticket and passport and followed Francesca, pushing his sunglasses back up fully.

Francesca stepped into the carriage and Pierson followed immediately behind, holding her left elbow to help her in. Again he lowered his sunglasses briefly to the end of his nose and peered over them as his eyes adjusted to the light inside.

The seats were pre-allocated just like with an airline and they found themselves in the second carriage from the front, facing backwards. Stowing the two bags, Pierson retrieved his still camera and this allowed Francesca time to take her seat by the window, and then Pierson sat next to her.

Henri arrived moments later and as he sat, he greeted the two of them. They both smiled and greeted him warmly— Pierson having remembered what Francesca had told him about smiling more readily.

A minute or so later, Bill walked along the aisle looking troubled and Pierson smiled at him as he took his place next to Henri. The four of them spoke briefly about the weather, the departure time, the number of passengers aboard and whether there were any refreshments available. During this time they could hear the whistle outside and the first jolt as the train began moving.

Pierson checked his watch. It was 9:40 to the second. The train was on time. Pierson felt like he was in a game of poker without the cards as the four of them sat in silence.

Looking at the camera, now on the table in front of him, Pierson picked it up and switched it on. He aimed it at Bill to take a shot.

'New toy?' Bill commented.

'I'm a tourist,' Pierson replied, 'smile please,' he added.

The camera took the shot and after a few seconds was ready for another. Pierson pointed it at Henri. Henri smiled readily and Pierson took the second shot. Then looking at Francesca he took one of her too.

Just as the camera finished saving away the photograph images, the train entered the tunnel and the interior lights flashed up brighter.

There was an instantaneous change in sound. The noise of the train got louder. They were now travelling downhill, as they traversed the first stretch of the tunnel. It was almost imperceptible, but nevertheless Pierson and the others did notice the shift in angle.

Bill checked his watch and Pierson saw it was of the same style that he was wearing.

The train was full and its passengers were a mix of business travellers and families. As this was a main route to Disneyland Paris, the number of families on board was large, but didn't seem out of place.

Pierson decided it was time to open things up a little, he was uncomfortable and had no idea what to do next, but he felt even more uneasy at the thought of something happening without him being ready. He was convinced that if something were to happen then it would be during the time they were going to be in the tunnel.

'Has anyone seen Abbot yet?' he asked. Bill and Henri shook their heads, 'we know he's booked on the train, did anyone find out which seat?' Pierson continued. Bill and Henri looked at each other as though the other one might know the answer.

'What about Dobrowiecki?' Pierson asked again, 'does anyone know what he looks like?' There was silence again as a smartly dressed woman in her thirties walked by, towards the front of the train. She had a cell phone in her hand but had a frustrated look on her face, as she scrutinised its display, obviously not aware that it wouldn't function in the tunnel.

Then a high-pitched tone emanated from the front of the train, but only a matter of feet away, as though someone had struck a note on a glockenspiel. Pierson was distracted by the sound, but as he checked, he noticed that it was the occupation signal for the toilets behind him as was also confirmed by an illuminated sign above the gangway.

He decided to search and got out of his seat, camera in hand. He took off his sunglasses and placed them on the table.

'Where are you going?' Francesca asked him.

'To find an old friend,' he replied as he winked at her.

Bill looked up and gave him a serious and almost concerned look, but didn't say anything, as though he was preoccupied with other matters. Francesca began to move out of her seat and moments later she was standing next to him.

'One carriage that way,' Pierson remarked pointing towards the front of the train, 'and two more this way,' he added pointing backwards. 'Let's try the back way first.' People in the nearby seats were looking at them, their heads tilting up from their newspapers and books.

Francesca and Pierson walked along the carriage, casually observing the other passengers, some with laptops, some playing with cell phones, others drinking and eating. One lady was sat knitting whilst others sat around her were asleep. Children were sitting in various groups with their parents, staring out of the windows, but only seeing flashes of light every now and again; and from time to time the enormous cross over point chambers came into view. This was made more apparent by the sudden change in sound, dropping the noise levels of the train and then just as suddenly increasing again back to its former levels.

Pierson and Francesca arrived at the intersection between their carriage and the third one. He looked through the glass doorway and saw a familiar face. 'There's Abbot,' he exclaimed to Francesca. She stood looking with Pierson. Abbot was fat and had a greasy look to him. His dark eyebrows pointed down towards his nose and made him look as though he was both underhanded and weak. Just from his body language he appeared untrustworthy.

Abbot shifted in his seat, but he kept looking up to the overhead locker.

'He's got the software with him,' Pierson remarked.

'How do you know that?' Francesca asked.

'It's in his case in the overhead locker,' Pierson replied, 'he used to tell me about keeping his eye on his property all the time when we travelled together.'

Abbot turned his eyes and looked their way. Pierson moved his head forward to kiss Francesca, turning both himself and Francesca around so that he was facing away from Abbot.

'Sorry,' he said, drawing back from her slightly and trying to move his head a little to give her a better view over his shoulder.

She just cast her eyes up at him and smiled, although he didn't notice. Keeping her arms wrapped around him, she was about to speak when he interrupted her thoughts.

'Is he still looking?'

'Yes,' she replied. 'But he's standing up now. What do you want to do?'

'Raise his blood pressure,' Pierson replied, 'I want to walk through the carriage as though I never knew him and walk right past him. I want him to see me. Like he's seen a ghost.'

'He's sitting back down again,' she said, 'all he did was open the locker and check his case was still there.'

Pierson smiled knowingly and pulled back from Francesca. As her hands slipped away from holding him, he held them both with his and looking at her earnestly he made a suggestion.

'As we walk through I want you to talk to me incessantly in Italian? I won't say anything, but you lead the way walking and speaking to me. I'll just smile and nod. Lead me through by the hand.'

'Why?' Francesca asked.

'Because he speaks French perfectly, and German too, but not Italian. I want him to think he's looking at Tom Brady, but I also want him to be uncertain and scare him into finding his contact or blowing someone's identity,' Pierson replied, 'like you said, let's put a spanner in their works. Oh, and when we walk through check him out from time to time to see his reaction.'

'Okay,' she replied and taking his hand she began to gabble at him in Italian, just as he had asked; and then they walked through the carriage. Abbot was sitting at the far end on the left hand side of the train, which was on their right as they were about to pass him. Pierson made no eye contact with him, as though he was invisible. They walked right past Abbot and into the gangway at the end of the carriage.

Francesca noticed the elderly gentleman sitting next to Abbot. He was smartly dressed and had a look of affluence. For a brief moment she thought he had spoken to Abbot, but she couldn't be sure. But in that moment there was something that indicated to her that the man was doing more than pass the time of day. It looked as though he and Abbot knew each other, just from their body language.

'What happened?' Pierson asked her, still not looking behind.

'He looked shocked,' she said with a smile, 'he's getting up now and he's opening the locker and taking out his case.'

She embraced Pierson again as she watched further. 'He's taking out some computer media, a DVD perhaps and putting it in his coat pocket.' Pierson watched Francesca closely, indulging himself in studying her face again as she relayed to him every minuscule detail of Abbot's actions. Her own attention was focussed on Abbot and so she didn't know what Pierson was doing, until she flashed her eyes back at him and she was about to look at Abbot again, but was hooked into Pierson's gaze.

Pierson was now remembering how she looked in his cabin in her white bra and briefs the previous night.

'That's better,' she said looking at him closely, 'you're thinking about something nice aren't you?'

'Yes,' he replied completely mesmerized by her.

'What are you thinking about?' she frowned curiously as she asked him.

'Something nice, something very nice,' he replied, 'keep telling me about Abbot.'

'He's gone from the carriage,' she said, snapping him back to the present.

Pierson leaned around to see Abbot walking through the automatic door at the far end, his light brown mohair coat flapping due to the speed of his step.

'Thank you for that,' Pierson remarked, 'let's see where he goes.'

'Why?' Francesca replied. 'He can't go anywhere and Bill and Henri are there anyway. They can watch him for us.'

Pierson hesitated momentarily. He didn't see any point in checking the last carriage but then he remembered about Selway. 'I haven't seen Selway yet,' he remarked.

'Why should you?' Francesca replied.

'I saw him in the departure queue for train,' Pierson added, 'so he's got to be aboard somewhere.'

Francesca turned and led the way into the fourth carriage, scanning the faces of the passengers, but without really trying look as though she was. She got half way along and turned to look at Pierson.

'Well?' she said.

Pierson shook his head 'No. He's not here.'

'Let's go back then,' she added, trying to turn.

'While we're here let's see what's out the back,' Pierson nodded as if to gesture towards the rear of the carriage.

They made their way to the end and found the outer doorway sealed. But through the glass of the door they could see the first shuttle containing cars.

'There are people sat in them,' Francesca declared, trying to see clearly in the dim light, getting a better picture as each set of fluorescent lights briefly flashed by and illuminated the first car.

'That's quite normal,' Pierson replied.

'Yes I know,' she said, 'but look at them closely. What do you see?'

'Men,' he said peering through the glass, but he could only see into the first car.

'What are they doing?' she asked him.

He paused, trying to focus his attention on their activities, as they were clearly moving. They're getting changed into different clothes; black outfits or uniforms.'

'Wet suits,' she said looking back at Pierson, 'we're in trouble.'

'That's stupid, with wet suits on, they'll fry if they do anything vigorous,' he remarked.

'Yes, but what's the temperature in the tunnel? Didn't you say something about all the air being pumped through?' she continued.

'Yes,' he replied, 'they try and keep the temperature at ten degrees Celsius.'

She raised her eyebrows at him as though to indicate that he had just answered his own question.

They began walking back up the carriages and beyond their own. As they entered the first carriage they saw two hostesses serving drinks and refreshments. Pierson squeezed past each one in turn and made his way to the front of the carriage. They still hadn't seen Selway at all, not on any of the four passenger carriages; worse still, Abbot was now missing too.

'I'm sorry sir you can't go through there. It'll take you outside,' said the hostess who'd watched Pierson walk by.

'I'm sorry,' he said 'I was looking for a friend of mine, he came this way a minute or so ago; wearing a light brown mohair coat?'

'Yes I did see him, but he must have walked back, there aren't any more carriages that way,' she added, pointing towards the front, 'just the engine and driver,' she continued.

Pierson thanked her and he and Francesca began to make their way back to their seats. Pierson checked the toilet sign at the very front of the carriage, but it wasn't illuminated, so it was clear to him that Abbot wasn't hiding within.

As he and Francesca took their seats again, Pierson looked at Bill and Henri 'Did you see Abbot?' Pierson asked them. They both shook the heads. Bill leaned forward. 'I wouldn't recognise him anyway,' he added. Pierson just held his stare wondering whether he would tell the truth on anything now.

'He walked by a few minutes ago in a brown mohair coat,' Pierson continued.

'That was Abbot?' Henri asked him.

Pierson nodded. Bill leaned back in his chair again.

'I saw him too,' Bill replied, 'he just went into the next carriage. Are you sure that's Abbot?' but he realised that Pierson should have been able to recognise his former boss. Pierson raised his eyebrows at Bill, but answered anyway.

'I'm sure,' he said with almost dismissive arrogance.

Both Henri and Bill were too cool for Pierson's liking, so he decided to test their reaction. 'Selway was in the queue when I got aboard,' Pierson remarked as nonchalantly as possible, quickly glancing at Bill and then at Henri.

Bill didn't react. It now looked as though he already knew. Henri smiled as though he knew something else and that some sort of plan was working to schedule. The gambit didn't help Pierson at all. He needed something more dramatic.

Before Pierson could do anything else, an announcement came over the public address system from the guard, firstly in French. Henri's look immediately changed to one of grave concern and he turned straight away to face Francesca as though he was making some secret telepathic link with her.

Then after a short pause, the same announcement was made in English 'Ladies and gentlemen we are sorry to announce the delay of this 09:40 departure to Paris. There have been news reports of rioting asylum seekers at the French end of the tunnel, who have now penetrated the tunnel access and services. We have been asked to slow the train in order to avoid fatalities on the track. Once the situation has been resolved we will be given clearance to increase our speed again. Unfortunately we are limited now to travelling at ten kilometres per hour until further notice. If it becomes necessary we will bring the train to a halt. There is no cause for alarm and passengers should remain seated. Hostesses will come through the carriages soon with complementary drinks. For those of you attending business meetings in Paris, or with follow on connections, the franchise operator will make arrangements for you to get to your final destination. We apologise for any inconvenience.'

Most of the passengers groaned loudly and then the train began to slow down and within a minute had reverted to a crawl. Pierson studied Bill closely to see if he'd been surprised by the news, but he remained impassive although he checked his watch. It was Henri who was looking concerned though.

Pierson pulled out the pass that Francesca had doctored for him. He attached it to the lapel of the jacket. Bill leaned forward to read the name and spoke aloud, 'Roger Williams?' His face took on a look of horror and he began to stand. Pierson mirrored his movements.

'Where did you get that?' he asked Pierson, prodding him in the chest and looking as though he'd been caught out.

Pierson looked at Henri, who now still looking concerned, seemed to be in deep thought. The false pass meant nothing to him. Francesca took her pass and likewise placed it on her lapel.

The fury in Bill's eyes was unmistakeable.

'Anything you want to tell me Bill?' Pierson remarked almost spitting out each word. 'Something that maybe you've forgotten? Or that we don't know about?'

The other passengers nearby were beginning to notice the friction between the two men. Pierson moved to one side and gestured for Francesca to get out of her seat. Francesca led the way into the separation between the first and second carriages, Pierson was right behind her and then came Bill and Henri.

They stood looking at each other.

'Begin,' said Bill.

'What's more sinister?' Pierson asked him, 'the fact that I have Roger's pass, or that fact that he and I must have met, along with his friend Leslie?'

Bill didn't answer.

Henri looked at the other three and spoke. 'If there is a game here, then I don't know the rules,' Henri refrained from accusing Bill at this stage and Pierson assumed it was because he wanted to give nothing away about Sebastien having named Bill as the inside man.

The train suddenly lurched to a halt. Falling into each other, it was Pierson who kept his wits and began to run to the front of the first carriage. He just managed to brush past the hostesses much to their consternation, but they were busy trying to stand up, having fallen into the laps of passengers near where they'd been standing.

Opening the door at the end of the carriage, Pierson stepped over the gap to the engine section. There was a small platform and a door allowing them entry. He opened that door too and Pierson found himself in a kind of air lock for the entire engine compartment. There was only room enough for two people and within moments Francesca joined him.

The door of the first passenger carriage swung closed and then locked. As Pierson looked back, he could see first Henri, and then Bill struggling with the door trying to open it. But someone had locked it electronically—using Elektra no doubt.

Bill and Henri were joined by one of the hostesses and Bill showed her his treasury pass. After a few moments of spoken interaction, she nodded at him and let him continue, although he gave up in a short while.

A small terminal and keyboard was positioned to Pierson's left. The screen was displaying the AIX login prompt, obviously ready for genuine users such as the guards, hostesses, stewards or drivers. Pierson was surprised that he'd not seen a guard or steward, but he kept his mind on the task at hand.

'Elektra?' Francesca asked.

'Yes,' replied Pierson, 'now we'll see if we can use the system.'

'You have an account for it?' she asked him as he began typing. He nodded and showed her what he was typing in.

'There are two default accounts on the system called nobody and guest. When I was working on Elektra I changed the installation process to create two new accounts during the installation itself. One account is called somebody and the other is called host. I'm trying to get in with somebody now. Listen carefully the password is in2ition.' He spelled it for her making sure she heard it correctly including the third character being the digit 2.

They watched the screen for what seemed like an eternity.

'Why's it taking so long? Isn't it working?' she asked him.

'I don't know,' he replied uttering each word with slow precision, 'Unless they're running a lot of work, or a CPU eater.'

'What's a CPU eater?' she asked him.

'It's a program in a complex loop that will never end and just stops anyone else accessing the system using up central processing unit cycles.'

'What's wrong with that?' she asked him. 'Can't you just switch it off and reload.'

Pierson shook his head. 'Not on this system: it's supposed to stay on all the time, unless someone shuts down the grid to the Channel Tunnel. Remember it gets its power from outside the train. The train is powered by the tunnel's electricity and if that fails it has an uninterruptible power supply to run for at least sixty minutes.'

'Long enough to get out of the tunnel,' Francesca remarked, beginning to understand the set up.

'Precisely,' said Pierson now drumming his fingers on the small desk supporting the keyboard.

The system finally acknowledged his request. He entered a command to run the Elektra program and just typed in the word 'unlock' and then the door in front of them, leading to the full engine compartment, opened.

He pushed it back against the carriage wall and raced through.

Two gunshots were fired at the far end of the engine carriage, with a small pause between the first and second shot. Pierson and Francesca ran through the compartment and when they got to the front, they both slowed down slightly. As they neared the end, they were confronted with Selway. Francesca already had her gun out, aiming at him.

Selway's eyes narrowed as he looked at Pierson. On the floor were two bodies, one was the driver and the other appeared to be Abbot, but he was face down.

Selway made no reference about why Pierson was still alive. 'Dobrowiecki was aboard as the driver,' he remarked to Pierson, who was still trying to capture his thoughts. 'I was in hiding here,' he continued 'and then Abbot appeared. They argued over the software, it was clear that Dobrowiecki had no intention of buying it. It was all a scam.'

Pierson just looked at Selway as he spoke. Selway began to sweat. A single bead could be seen running down his temple and he was very red in the face. 'Dobrowiecki had a gun and forced Abbot to keep the train from starting again once he himself had brought it to a halt; and then he shot him. That's when I appeared and shot Dobrowiecki. From what Dobrowiecki said, it seems that he'd planned to steal the gold somehow. I've got agents aboard but I want to find out what's happened back there,' he said, pointing to the back of the train. 'With the riots in the asylum centre in France I'm taking no chances.'

Selway stopped and moved towards the outer door and opened it so that it was unclipped. Then at the terminal that Abbot had been operating, he entered another command and the door on the other side of the train locked.

'You stay here,' he said, 'I might need you later to get it all going again.'

'Where are you going?' Pierson asked him.

'Back to the merchandise,' Selway replied.

'We'll help,' Pierson answered.

'Not if you're dead,' said Selway, 'you stay here where I need you most.'

'One more thing,' Pierson stopped Selway in his tracks, 'where did you get the picture of Madeleine? You know the one where she was at the supermarket?'

Again Selway's eyes narrowed slightly. Holding every muscle in his face still, he then answered.

'Bill gave it to me.'

Jumping out of the train, he slammed the door behind him, and it locked automatically as a result of the command he'd typed in moments earlier.

'That was unexpected,' Pierson remarked emphasising the word 'was'.

'Which particular part?' Francesca replied as she scanned to see if anyone else was there.

'Take your pick,' said Pierson.

THE FACE OF GREED

Pierson surveyed the cabin and scrutinised the two bodies. Crouching down, he turned Abbot's body over. He'd been shot once in the head. The reddish purple pool of blood was still expanding on the floor next to where he'd fallen.

'Idiot,' Pierson muttered under his breath. He turned to look at the other man. 'All this just for money,' he remarked as he glanced up at Francesca.

'We need to find a way out of the train,' she said to him.

'No,' Pierson replied, 'actually we need to get the train out of the tunnel. Check to see if you can find operating instructions or something that might help to tell us how to drive it.'

'Are you joking?' she remonstrated.

He shook his head as his eyes flared briefly, but he held his impatience in check. Something inside him was at breaking point. He slowly stood again, looking in disgust at the carcasses of the two dead men.

'If we can get the train moving, then if someone is trying to offload the gold we will have made it extremely difficult for them.'

She nodded as she realised what he said made sense.

'Every time we seem to get close they're one step ahead of us,' he growled, clearly angry and irritated at getting so close, only to find himself shut off again. But his frustration was now fuelling his anger, and it was beginning to tell in his voice.

Francesca was taken aback; and for a few moments she actually found herself slightly flustered. She'd not seen him this way before and although she hadn't thought of him as a man of action up to that point, she was now beginning to realise that she'd underestimated his strength of feeling—and what he might be capable of.

She could see that he was in no mood to be messed about, even armed and with all her training, she was beginning to feel uneasy in his presence. Something was beginning to manifest itself in Pierson that was new. She didn't like it initially, but the passing moments found her experiencing a thrill at the prospect of this new facet of his personality. His single-minded and newfound passion aroused something in her that she simply hadn't expected, and her concentration was split by the ongoing distraction that it caused her.

Pierson dragged the bodies out of his way, one at a time. Then standing by the system console he started typing furiously, trying to get computer access. Francesca meanwhile searched through the lockers and shelves adjacent to the driver's seat. She found two useful items; one was a manual of instructions detailing from start to finish how to drive the train; the other was a series of checklists to be carried out when starting and stopping the engines, along with precise instructions for emergency procedures.

Pierson thumped the desk on which the keyboard was sitting. 'Come on!' he shouted, 'Interrupt!'

Only turning around briefly as a result of his outburst, and then returning to the documents, Francesca read the start and stop checklists and tried the train's controls, but they didn't respond.

As time swiftly moved on, strange noises and erratic flashes of light from the tunnel were the only things that interrupted his concentration as Pierson desperately struggled with the computer console. In the background the movement of heavy metal plating and machinery was itself interspersed with military like instructions being barked by more than one disembodied voice; and it was only the sound insulation within the carriage that kept the noise suppressed to the point that only someone with excellent hearing could have followed the conversations.

Concerned by the sheer amount of time they'd wasted, Pierson's eyes frequently glanced to the face of his watch as the computer continued to grind through it's predefined processing, but he'd made no significant progress with the system access.

After slamming closed the final instruction manual triumphantly, Francesca interrupted his thoughts.

'Mike,' she said in an uncharacteristically faltering voice, clearing her throat before he turned to face her. 'I know how to drive the train.'

He looked unimpressed and this served only to increase her mild anxiety. So she continued.

'I don't know about signals and what to do when I see them. But I know how to move it.'

After another pause—this time to consider whether it would help—he finally responded.

'Good enough.'

She waited as he concluded his mental deliberations, signalled by him taking a long and deep breath.

'Don't worry about the signals. They're the least of our problems now. If necessary we'll drive straight through; nothing will be on this track coming at us.' He turned back and faced the screen again.

'What's happening there?' she asked him cautiously.

'I'll tell you for sure soon, if I can login,' he replied, 'this thing's on a countdown timer,' he continued, 'it's performing a tight CPU loop and I can get in, but it's taking five minutes or more for each of my commands to work.'

'Countdown to what?' she asked.

He didn't answer, but continued to wrestle with his own anger. Realising that he was in danger of losing control, and also perhaps letting his perspective slip from his grasp, he raised his head towards the ceiling, closed his eyes with his fists clenched tight and resting either side of the keyboard, and took a deep breath. Then after a few seconds of silence he began to feel a little more in control as evidenced by a more serious but less aggressive tone.

'I haven't got time for this,' he muttered referring to the well-planned delay built in to the computer. 'The gold is probably being stolen right under our noses.' He stopped as another array of flashes illuminated the tunnel outside. The light was so intense and almost continuous they both independently realised that it must have been caused either by arc welding or oxyacetylene cutting.'

'What have you managed to do so far?' Francesca asked him.

'My first login is useless,' he said, 'but the second seems good.'

'You mean host?' she remarked.

'Yes,' he replied, 'look,' he continued shaking his head slowly with his eyes closed again, as if to get a new perspective. 'I'm sorry, but I feel powerless. The password is Mad4you, M a d 4 y o u,' he said. 'If anything happens to me then you can login and use it.'

'But what do I do next?' she asked him.

'Type in a command at the prompt, it's a shell script that's part of Elektra. Just type in Brady press enter, then type the word reset,' he replied.

'What will that do?' she asked.

'It'll do a soft IPL, that is, it'll do a soft boot and re-initialise Elektra, if it's all still there,' he answered.

'How will that help though?' she looked at him and saw that his mind was still not completely tuned in to her yet.

'It'll stop whatever's running now, and the engines can then be engaged for propulsion allowing you to drive the train, wait five minutes after the reset command and that'll give it time to work. You'll know it's ready when the screen shows you a prompt like this,' Pierson pointed to the prompt symbol on the display, and then looked at her to see if she was taking it in.

'Can you unlock the doors?' she asked him.

'Oh yes,' he replied, 'I'm going to do that now.'

'But how? The computer's not taking any commands,' she replied pointing at the screen and sounding confused.

'One thing that Abbot always accused me of was being a creative thinker,' said Pierson as he turned away from the console and looked at her.

'Give me your gun,' he said, extending his hand.

She raised one eyebrow at him and shook her head. 'No,' she replied firmly.

'Fine, in that case, stand back.' He picked up the gun Dobrowiecki had used. Moving Francesca behind himself, he aimed at the door lock on the right hand side of the train, pumping in a single bullet. The noise was deafening and the recoil surprised him, even though he had held the gun with both hands. He pumped another bullet into the door glass and it shattered. Walking to the door he punched the glass out and felt for the handle outside, but he couldn't reach. Then, taking aim at the windscreen he fired three more bullets into the glass and with the second shot it shattered and the third made it partially blow out.

He'd had the gun clamped in his hands under such great pressure that blood was being squeezed out of his taught knuckles, from where he'd apparently cut himself on the door glass moments earlier.

He threw the gun back on the floor near the dead men; then, sitting himself on the driver's seat, he raised his legs together and kicked the windscreen, time and time again, making a hole large enough to climb through. 'Are you coming?' he asked her, holding out his arm and looking back. She needed no second invitation, holstering her gun she reached out to take his hand. She noticed that it was hot, but it grasped her firmly.

Once outside they both slid down onto the floor, jumping the final few feet. From his new viewpoint, Pierson noticed that the train was a lot taller than he'd realised and he'd need a different way back in.

They crouched slightly, as the two of them walked stealthily along the side of the carriages. Passengers were banging the doors and windows trying to get out. They were being calmed and asked to sit down by the hostesses and stewards. Pierson now spotted a guard too, helping to keep things as peaceful as possible.

'What's happened?' Francesca asked.

'It looks like they've cut the air flow, those people in there are going to die, unless we can get them out or more air in.'

'We can just shoot out a window and let the air in,' she said.

'Yes and let the passengers break out causing mayhem on the lines,' Pierson replied.

'They'll die if we don't,' she continued.

'They might die if we do,' Pierson added, 'we don't know what's going on out here yet, besides which, it may be part of Bob Selway's plan to keep the passengers safe.'

'By suffocating them?'

'He might not know about that part, but we've still got time to go back and help if necessary. I'm sure the stewards will know if and when it'll become necessary to break the glass. We've got other things to think about.'

'So what are we going to do?'

'We're going to find out exactly what's going on first,' Pierson replied, 'and then we're going to make it down to the other engine carriage at the far end of the train.'

'Why?' she said, this time pulling him back.

He stopped to face her, 'for two reasons; first because it's a separate system and if we can get that one going it will negotiate with the engine of the lead engine carriage and let us start driving this thing out.'

He started to walk again still crouching. She stopped him again. Her hair was now ruffled and falling into her eyes. 'What's the other reason?' she asked him brushing her hair aside.

He held her stare. 'Why do you use a countdown?'

'To allow time to pass before something happens,' she replied.

'Such as?' he asked her.

'I don't know?' she exclaimed losing her patience, but not wishing to shout, her anger increasing.

'For a bomb,' he said, 'to blow this whole thing up!' he added, pointing at the train and tunnel.

'Why?' she replied. 'Why would anyone do that?' the frustration now coming through in her voice more dominantly.

'Because it leaves no trace,' he answered through clenched teeth as though he was trying to control his own temper.

He faced her properly and he grabbed her upper arms and held her firmly.

'There are five tankers on this train marked Constantinou Pharmaceuticals. They contain powdered potassium. Do you know what happens when potassium hits water? How many tons of the stuff are on those lorries do you think?'

'Oh no,' she said looking at him aghast with her mouth dropped slightly open. Clearly the audacity of the plan had exceeded even her imagination.

'How many people are aboard this train?' he asked her.

'I don't know,' she said.

'I do,' he replied, 'there are one hundred and twenty seats per carriage, and that doesn't include guards, stewards or the like; that's almost five hundred people in anyone's money.'

He turned back to the matter in hand and began moving towards the back of the train again.

They soon drew level with the car shuttle. Nobody appeared to be in the cars any longer. Climbing aboard one of them and looking inside, he could see clothes strewn around. The same was true in the other cars.

As they looked towards the end of the shuttle, he noticed light: a lot of it, and he could hear noise too. The sounds of voices and the machinery were much louder now they were both outside the cocoon of the sound insulated carriage. In fact Pierson noticed how much the sound seemed to bounce around as though they were inside a cathedral.

The two of them gradually made their way towards the source of the activity and peered through the gaps in the shuttle's structure. Finally they got to a much better vantage point.

Work was being carried out in the access tunnel between the two main tunnels—something was being constructed.

Pierson noticed that the train's lorry shuttles were positioned right next to one of the crossover chambers hence the acoustics. He could see a man with a blowtorch. He was using it to weld some circular plating the same size as the access tunnel, as though he were sealing it.

Then Pierson and Francesca heard another voice. It was closer to them and clearer than the others they'd been listening to and it was on their side of the train.

'Hey you there! What are you doing?' the man shouted as he walked briskly towards them exercising some caution, but even so he still quickened his step as he kept his eyes on the spot where they'd been watching. It looked as though he couldn't quite pick them out from the darkness properly, giving them some slight but nonetheless measurable advantage. As he drew closer, they could see that he was dressed in a wet suit and was wielding a machine gun.

He let out two short bursts from the weapon and Pierson and Francesca dived under the rolling stock. Being dark on their side of the train they used the cover of the shadows to shuffle along the track: Francesca taking the lead.

Pierson lay there as Francesca moved further towards the back of the train and closer to the gunman.

The man stopped next to her and pointing his gun in her direction, he had obviously spotted her because he gestured for her to get out.

Pierson was out of his view briefly, so taking his chances he rolled over and out from under the train and carried on rolling completely to the outer wall of the tunnel. The gunman, now with one eye on Francesca, walked along looking under the train for him.

Keeping Francesca just to his left he trained his machine gun at her, holding it in such a way that with just a slight change of angle he could point it under the carriage quickly if he needed to.

He drew close to Pierson.

Pierson's heart began racing. His mouth and throat became dry. He could hear his own heartbeat and the pulsating sound of the blood coursing through his head.

He lay motionless, convinced the gunman could hear the erratic thumping from his chest.

The gunman stopped. Trying to focus under the train.

Pierson stopped breathing.

The gunman moved closer again, now only about six feet away and walking quietly. Even now he remained tantalisingly out of Pierson's reach.

Time stood still as the gunman moved only his head, scanning the floor. He inched forward.

Pierson's lungs were bursting as he gently allowed himself to breathe through his partially open mouth.

Then as if he sensed he was being watched, the gunman suddenly wrenched his head around and faced Pierson directly.

One thought flashed through Pierson's mind 'was he close enough?' Pierson had no time to answer his own question and with all his strength he unleashed an almighty kick as he swung his foot into the shin of the man. The force of the impact gave his victim an immediate, excruciating and sickening pain, dropping him to his knees, his hands sprawled out in front of him as he knelt there, drooling from not being able to control the agony. The machine gun had been thrown half on and half off the track by the force of his fall. Francesca wasted no time and delivered a precisely aimed kick to the man's head instantly rendering him unconscious.

Pierson stood and looked down at the spread-eagled body before him as he bent over to pick up the man's machine gun before handing it to Francesca, while she brushed the hair out of her eyes.

Looking down at the man, Pierson apologised to him 'I'm sorry about this,' he said, and then jumped on the man's lower leg. The splintering of the bones was all too obvious from the noise it made. Pierson then rolled his limp body onto the track and out of view.

Moving along again, the two of them could see a great deal of activity taking place on the five lorry shuttles, but they couldn't afford to get too close for fear of being seen, so they backed up and waited by the car shuttle.

'What are we doing here?' Francesca asked Pierson.

'Waiting until all that activity stops, so that we can get to the other end of the train,' he replied pointing across to the movement and noise.

'Why wait, why not just go through?'

'There's too many of them and from what we've just seen, at least some of them are heavily armed. Walking right by the lorry shuttles while they're aboard is too stupid to even think about. Remember, these shuttles are really just big open frames, they don't have solid sides so we'll be spotted before we get as far as the end of the first one.'

'What about the passengers though—we're probably their only hope,'

'I know, but they'll have no chance at all if we get caught. Especially as I suspect they won't be taking prisoners. If we take that chance and we're wrong then it's all over. And judging by this,' Pierson touched the machine gun, 'they're taking it very seriously.'

Francesca nodded. 'What about the other track though, couldn't we get across and try going down there?'

'They seem to be working in the service tunnel doing something; and if I'm right we'd be seen immediately—there's no train in the other tunnel for us to hide behind, we'd have no cover. Our best chance is to wait.'

Francesca checked her watch in the available light and then waited quietly with Pierson as they observed the activity modify and then gradually move location until it seemed to slow down considerably.

They both lost track of time but they were beginning to get very restless from standing in the one spot for so long; and then finally the activity on the lorry shuttles ceased, although there was still noise and movement between the two tracks in the crossover section.

Pierson moved along nearer the first lorry shuttle and looked through towards the crossover. He could see four men clearing up tools and equipment; and at the same time he could see two others, standing nearby: on guard and both of them armed with automatic weapons. All of the men were dressed in wet suits and had the fronts unzipped.

'What do you think they're doing?' Francesca asked.

Pierson looked closer and saw the men disappearing into the service tunnel, closing a heavy circular metallic door behind them. The door gave a resounding clang as it shut and Pierson and Francesca watched as a wheel style handle turned through a complete revolution, locking it in place.

The two of them climbed onto the lorry shuttle and looked at the crossover area. It was strewn with items including an oxyacetylene torch, a forklift truck and various crow bars and tools.

Pierson climbed up to the cab of the first tanker. Inside he could see the driver laid down, tied and gagged and apparently knocked out.

He climbed down and looked at the refrigerated lorry behind. The doors were locked.

'Stand back,' Francesca declared, taking aim at the locking mechanism. She fired a single bullet and the lock broke.

Swinging the huge doors open, they looked inside, but it was empty.

They looked at each other as though to say the words 'it's gone,' but neither of them felt the need to state the obvious.

Francesca pointed to the metallic door on the service tunnel.

'In there?' she said curiously not really believing it.

Pierson nodded. 'Where else?' he said, 'we could check the other trucks for the gold, but we've got to move quickly. If we're right, then the next thing you'll hear is an explosion as they break through the service tunnel from the seabed above. I still don't know what the countdown timer is doing though or what it's for.'

Francesca now weighed up the options and quickly considered the best tactics.

'What happened to Selway?'

'Who knows?' Pierson replied, 'Perhaps he's the inside man. Let's get to the other engine and see if we can get this thing moving again.'

Climbing off the train and keeping it between them and the service tunnel to retain the best cover, they ran alongside toward the engine at the rear.

With some difficulty they climbed up to the doorway of the engine compartment, released the catch to stand inside and typed the account name and password. The inner door clicked open.

They raced to the other end and stopped suddenly as soon as they got there. Sitting in the driver's seat, facing them was Selway: bound and gagged.

Without hesitation Pierson quickly released the cloth straining at his mouth and then began to free the ropes.

Selway retched slightly as he contorted his face, using his tongue to slowly but forcibly disgorge a dirty looking rag from his mouth, finally uttering with a gasp, 'thank you,' meeting Pierson's gaze as he spoke.

'I misjudged you,' Pierson declared as Selway massaged his now freed wrists—which were suffering from severe rope marks from where he'd been bound.

Selway's glasses were on the floor and one of the lenses was cracked. 'We haven't got much time,' he said with controlled urgency in his voice, bending over and picking them up. 'They've rigged the train to blow up. Can you drive it?'

Francesca nodded and was staggered that he'd even asked. 'I think so,' she said; but Selway had been expecting Pierson to answer. He looked astonished that it was Francesca who'd replied, as though he needed to work something out.

'Good,' he continued, 'then get to the front and get it moving.'

'We can't,' Pierson insisted 'they've rigged the computer on a countdown timer for something and it won't release control.'

'Well it's not the explosive,' said Selway, 'that's separate.'

'Explosive?' quizzed Pierson.

'Yes,' replied Selway as though Pierson had missed something, 'they've been setting it on every carriage along the side of the train,' he raised his eyebrows at Pierson as though he should have known it.

Remembering why they'd entered that engine compartment Pierson continued. 'I need to interrupt the other computer and I can only do it from here.'

He logged in to the terminal and sent a command to the computer at the front of the train to try and reset it.

'Is it working?' Francesca asked with some urgency in her voice.

'It will work, but it will take five minutes to complete. The only problem with that is it automatically unlocks all the doors as part of the failsafe system,' he replied. 'When the computer stops, passengers cannot be locked in. It was part of the original design.'

'You've got to keep them inside,' said Selway now looking concerned. 'Leave the explosives to me, but don't let anyone off the train. Whatever happens to me, don't let Bill out of your sight. I'm afraid he may be the one behind all this.'

Pierson and Francesca looked at each other with some relief and nodded. As Pierson was about to open the cab door Selway continued, 'give me a gun.' Francesca looked at Pierson and then at Selway. Pierson said nothing, so Francesca handed Selway the machine gun that Pierson had given her earlier.

Selway took it from her and jumped out with them.

Pierson wasn't convinced that giving Selway a gun was such a good idea—he still had some doubts about him. But looking down at the side of the train he could see that sticks of dynamite had been taped to the train at points above the wheels. Each cluster of explosive was more than could be held in one hand, comprising at least a dozen sticks and beside each bundle was a red rimmed, glass-faced clock. As he looked along the length of the train he counted one bundle of explosive above each set of wheels, thirteen in all.

'Move!' Selway demanded as he crouched to start disassembling the first explosive.

Pierson and Francesca began running toward the front of the train, wary that there might be a lurking gunman.

As they approached the passenger cars, so the doors unlocked in unison to the screams of delight from the passengers and they spilled out of the carriages. Like a prison break-out, it was pandemonium: a human stampede.

'Do something!' Pierson shouted at Francesca.

'What?' she screamed.

Amongst the first people off the train were the stewards and hostesses. In the ensuing chaos with hundreds of passengers trying to climb over each other to get off, Pierson fought through the crowd and grabbed the arm of one of the hostesses. He showed her one of the explosives strapped to the side of the train. 'Get everyone back aboard. The entire tunnel is going to be blown up. When you've done it, close all the doors. We've only got minutes left to get the bombs off the train and to get the train moving!'

The hostess found one of her colleagues and then other stewards who managed to begin herding the passengers back onto the train.

Pierson looked back down the track and saw Selway working to defuse the bombs and take them off the rolling stock.

He and Francesca raced to the front engine, only slowing as they suddenly spotted Henri and Bill who had climbed out. 'Up front with us now!' Pierson shouted at them and grabbed Bill's arm.

'I can't,' Bill replied, 'I've got to check something.'

Francesca looked at him and without giving a second thought she raised her arms holding her gun and pointing directly at his head. 'You're coming with us,' she said to him, fixing him coldly with her stare and for the first time a strong Italian accent coming through.

Henri placed his hand on top of her gun and pushed her arms down just shaking his head to and fro once in each direction and looking sternly at her. Putting his arm around Bill he spoke to him. 'My friend let's do as they say.' Henri pointed at the explosives further down the train. Pierson meanwhile had been taking the taped dynamite and placing it on the floor next to the track.

'What are they going to do with that?' Bill asked him, turning around as Henri led him to the front of the train.

'Take it off the train,' came the answer.

'But you can't just leave it here!' he said emphatically.

'Our man at the back is trying to defuse it for us,' Pierson replied as he pulled the last of them off.

'Bob!' Pierson shouted, hurry up.

The last of the passengers were being gently pushed in just as Selway had worked his way to the car shuttle.

'You get aboard I'll get on once you've got it moving. Now go!' Selway shouted pointing at the front of the train, vigorously waving his arm forward and pointing in their direction.

Pierson watched him for a second before obeying.

Francesca, Bill and Henri had already climbed aboard. They could see the two dead bodies of Dobrowiecki and Abbot lying on the floor.

Pierson leapt in the cabin and surveyed the mess. The windscreen was almost completely gone and so was the glass in the door on the right hand side.

He looked at the computer console.

'Good,' he declared. 'It's IPL'd okay.'

He tried to login to the system, conscious of the time. He typed furiously, hammering on the keyboard with each deliberate finger stroke.

Within moments he had access and he started executing the Elektra software turning to Francesca the moment it was operational. Behind them they heard the engines start. Then there was an explosion from the back of the train.

Pierson opened the cab door and looked out. All he could see was smoke and dust, but he couldn't see Selway any more.

'Bob!' he shouted.

'Get in! Close the door!' Henri demanded pulling at him. 'The tunnel could blow up at any moment.'

Pierson slammed the door closed and then he watched as Francesca held down a lever with her left hand as she pushed another smaller one forwards with her right hand.

The train lurched forward.

'Where exactly are we?' Henri asked.

Pierson checked on the console by typing in a two commands.

'According to this,' he said, stopping momentarily, 'we're about seven kilometres from Calais, five sixths of the way through.'

Henri was puzzled by the look on Pierson's face. 'Is there something else?' he asked him.

'Yes,' said Pierson, pointing upwards, 'this is the closest point to the sea above.'

'And your point?' Henri continued.

'They've taken the gold into the service tunnel. Francesca and I saw them seal it off. They were all wearing wet suits.'

'Gold?' said Bill, 'you know about the gold?'

Henri nodded at him. 'We had a communiqué yesterday. So I told them,' he said.

'I had a memo telling me in London,' Bill replied.

'I'm sorry Bill,' Pierson remarked, 'you had your chance. You could have told us that on the train, or at any time since you found out.'

'No I couldn't,' he replied. 'It was top secret: eyes only. I was forbidden from telling you.'

'Is there anything else you'd like to share with us?' Pierson asked him.

Bill looked uncertain as he spoke, 'I think Selway is the leak.'

'Too late,' Pierson replied, 'Selway may be dead, but we found him tied up at the other end of the train. We released him and he defused the bombs. He said you gave him the photograph of Madeleine.'

Henri looked surprised.

Pierson continued. 'He also told us to watch you closely.'

'Well he would, wouldn't he?' Bill replied cautiously, almost with a sneer.

'But as well as that, Sebastien told us about you,' Pierson continued, leaning on the desk for the console.

Bill said nothing but just squinted at Pierson.

Francesca had managed to get the train to accelerate to thirty kilometres per hour, and air was rushing in through the hole in the windscreen, but there wasn't much build-up of pressure, because it was escaping through the hole where the glass had been, in the side door of the cabin.

'There's something else too,' Pierson added.

'Roger Williams and Leslie Garrett were aboard last night's ferry looking for me. They came to my cabin armed and ready to kill me. At first I thought Henri sent them, because they only tried to kill me and not Francesca. But Henri has no link with them. You gave the order.'

Henri looked on and listened as these revelations poured out. Not really believing the man he thought of as his friend could have done all of this.

'What happened to Williams and Garrett?' Bill asked, 'did you kill them?'

Pierson wondered whether he should answer the question, remembering what Henri had said about never giving away information. Before he had time to answer, Francesca did it for him.

'We made them swim ashore, naked and shackled together. You might want to check with the English police to see if they were roaming the beaches near Dover this morning.'

Nothing further was said for a few moments as they stared out of the front of the train.

'What happened here?' Henri asked, pointing at the corpse of Abbot and Dobrowiecki.

Pierson looked back at them. 'Dobrowiecki never planned to pay Abbot—according to Selway—who said he'd been lying in wait for the transaction to take place. Dobrowiecki then ordered Abbot to stop the train from being moved again once he'd halted it, and as soon as that happened he shot him, then Selway shot and killed Dobrowiecki.'

Henri nodded and looking as though he'd been given inspiration he squinted slightly at Pierson before taking a look around. He began to search the cabin. Opening one of the bigger lockers near Francesca's feet he pulled out a large tartan suitcase.

He unzipped it and inside was a vast amount of currency all in used notes. Henri spent a minute or so calculating how much was there, picking up the bundles and seeing how deeply they had been stacked. 'Fifteen million Euros, or so,' he said zipping closed the case again and dragging it to one side.

'Why would Dobrowiecki bring the money and then not use it?' Henri asked stroking his moustache as he began thinking about his own question.

'Because Selway lied,' Bill suggested, 'it didn't happen the way he said it did.'

'Or maybe Dobrowiecki got creative,' said Pierson, 'seeing that he was armed, he could have the software without paying for it. Not that he necessarily wanted it. He got Abbot to stop the train so the gold could be stolen and then kept the fifteen million Euros for himself.'

'Then why bother getting on the train at all?' Henri asked.

'For the gold,' Pierson replied, 'the fifteen million Euros would be like pocket money or just a windfall. Or maybe he had to return it.'

Pierson walked over to Dobrowiecki's lifeless body, crouching down by it he looked closely at the man. 'The face of greed,' he muttered under his breath as he studied the corpse.

He stood up once again and looked through the broken windscreen glass. In the distance he could see daylight ahead of them. Francesca slowed the train and then only a minute or so later it emerged from the tunnel, now just slightly faster than walking pace.

Gendarmes were guarding the exit as a result of the riots that morning and when the train stopped, Henri was the first to disembark. Briskly walking up to one of them he spoke animatedly to the man, gesturing with wild arm movements.

The gendarme picked up his handset from the lapel of his jacket and began speaking into it. Within a minute, an entire group of gendarmes had appeared by the train to help secure the crime scene, being given orders they had been paired up; some to stand guard and others to run towards the rear of the train to check and control operations from that end.

Pierson had made his way into the second carriage and got his and Francesca's bags and picked up his camera, which during the commotion had been thrown onto his seat. But it was still operational, having had a soft landing.

Henri returned to the engine carriage and collected Bill. 'I can drop you at your car near the ferry car park,' he said to Francesca. 'You and Mike can go separately from Bill and I. We'll talk in the morning to gather together the pieces of this mess.'

'Okay uncle,' she replied.

They stood waiting for a short while. Before long, a police car drew up, allowing them to get in and go the short distance to Henri's car. He'd gone across the channel by train both ways, so he'd parked nearby.

After emerging from the police vehicle and transferring to his own, Henri drove the other three to the ferry car park. Francesca and Pierson got into her car and with Pierson sitting next to her, looking dazed and tired she drove them back to the apartment in Paris.

MANIFESTLY OBVIOUS

Henri was in good spirits the following morning when Pierson arrived. Laughing to himself at the headlines in the newspaper and then at the information on the piece of paper in his hands.

Francesca was standing next to him reading the details.

'Thanks for your hospitality,' Pierson announced as he walked in, 'but I'm certain that it must be time for me to go home to England.' He smiled feebly as he made the declaration.

Francesca looked up in surprise.

Pierson dumped his rucksack on the desk he'd been using.

'Why?' Henri asked him, his face sporting a more serious expression.

'My job's done. The secret I had is out, I got the Elektra software up and running and the gold has been stolen. I'm not a policeman, it's not my job anymore and I'm just taking up valuable space. I'll have to go back sometime and it may as well be now.'

Pierson walked forward to shake Henri's hand. 'Thank you,' Pierson said and turned to Francesca, 'thank you for everything. Both of you.'

There was silence for a few moments. As Francesca who was stunned by the unexpected announcement reached for his hand and looked with her disbelieving eyes into his, saying nothing verbally, yet saying it all with her body language.

Pierson picked up his bag and began to walk towards the door.

'What about the inside man? The snake in the grass? Aren't you at all worried that he's still out there, and that he'll kill you just for revenge.' Henri suggested almost as a throwaway line.

'Revenge for what?' Pierson asked, 'they've won. Bill and his friends have got what they want. I'm not a threat any more.'

'Revenge for costing them four hundred million dollars,' came the reply, 'if we get the gold back too, then they'll be even more out of pocket,' Henri looked at the paper in his hand and chuckled to himself again.

'What do you mean?' Pierson asked, turning and walking back slowly.

Henri showed him the morning's headlines. He'd managed to get a copy of the Times especially for Pierson.

'Largest gold bullion theft in history,' the headlines stated and underneath was subtitled. 'Euro goes into meltdown and loses fifty percent of its value.'

'And that was just yesterday afternoon, guess what might happen today?' Henri challenged him poking him in the stomach with the end of the newspaper.

'But we knew this would happen,' Pierson replied, 'it's not my fault.'

'No,' replied 'Henri, but I told Bill after you left on Monday, that you'd modified the computer programs on the criminal's system to buy Euros and then sell them when the price slumped. So their two hundred million dollars is now worth half that amount. Later today at it's lowest price we'll instruct the brokers via computer to sell the almost worthless Euros and buy gold, which is very unstable at the moment due to the large amounts of it floating around,' Henri winked.

'Go back to England if you wish, but if Bill is the inside man, then he knows just who cost them this money. Of course, they may not find out until the end of the month, when the brokers have to be paid.'

Pierson sighed slightly as he dropped his bag, but he was secretly pleased at delaying his return—after all there really was nothing in England for him except a bleak reminder of everything he'd lost. 'What have you got in mind?' he asked with no hint of emotion in his voice.

'Help us solve this thing. It would be nice to find the gold and show the British, just who has the best police force in the world; and anyway how about causing these criminals, some grief too. Wouldn't that be good?'

This appealed to Pierson, and as it was a definite task to clear up the loose ends, the thought of causing the criminals some grief was too delicious to turn down. He smiled and then chuckled too, 'If you put it like that, how could I refuse?'

Henri placed his arm around Pierson's shoulders and squeezed him like a father would, nodding at him with a satisfied look on his face.

'Where do we begin?' Pierson asked, 'interrogating Bill? This I have to see.'

'I don't think so,' said Henri 'But we will have to keep him here, until we can prove he's innocent of course.'

'You're still convinced he's innocent then?' Pierson asked.

Henri nodded and his look underlined his certainty. There was clearly no doubt in his mind.

'How do you know?' Pierson continued.

'I just know,' Henri replied slowly giving a Gallic shrug.

Having listened to Henri and Pierson, Francesca interrupted, 'but Sebastien said Bill set this whole thing up. He's an eyewitness. What you're saying is that he's been lying to us.'

Something struck Pierson. He looked puzzled.

'What?' said Francesca as she noticed his look.

'I have an idea,' said Pierson as he reached for the cameras in his bag. 'It may be nothing, but why would he lie?'

Nobody could answer, although Henri definitely gave the impression that he was trying harder than the others to think of a good reason.

'Let me upload the shots from these,' said Pierson as he got the laptop out and switched it on.

'Henri. Can you get us a room with a projector for this thing, in say thirty minutes? I'd like to show Sebastien something.'

Henri nodded and picked up the nearest phone and speaking in French, he made the arrangements.

'Any chance of a coffee while were waiting?' Pierson asked without looking away from the screen as he connected the first camera. Francesca obliged by pouring him a fresh cup from the waiting urn.

Within moments the first digital films began uploading, Pierson glanced up to see Henri who just seemed to be sitting opposite him staring at the Englishman, but without saying a word.

'Something wrong Henri?' Pierson asked after a few moments.

'Yes,' came the reply, 'you.'

'What?' said Pierson before taking a quick mouthful of coffee.

'You seem very different from the man who walked in here a few minutes ago wanting to leave our beautiful country.'

Pierson looked into his coffee cup that he was now holding in both hands. Before he could say anything further, Henri continued.

'Why go back? There's nothing there for you. Stay here, work for us. Work for me.'

Pierson said nothing, he wanted to get back to England but he couldn't think why. It was like instinct, but it even made no sense to him; and France was indeed a beautiful place.

'We have a good legal system here,' Henri argued, 'Our judges are not corrupt,' implying that British justice was rotten to the core, a thought that Pierson was beginning to nurture anyway.

Pierson smiled and nodded. 'Let me think about it,' he said and looked at Francesca. She was busy reading and trying to take no notice.

'What's being done about the gold?' he asked.

'We're looking for it,' Henri replied, 'but remember, there's no evidence it was ever on the train, so the British government is in rather a delicate situation. They would like to claim it was stolen in France, but maybe it was never on the lorries in the first place. Our Minister of the interior voiced his concerns at the lack of security. Until someone proves to us that it was on the train, then there is no requirement for us to look for it. At least that's our official line. Unofficially we're pulling out all the stops to find it, and we hope perhaps to embarrass our friends in your country's government: just a little.'

Pierson finished his drink and within a few more minutes the digital video camera had finished uploading its final sequences.

He powered off the laptop and closed the lid. Placing it back in the case, he checked his watch.

'Shall we go?'

'If you're ready,' said Henri. 'By the time we get there, everything should be set up.'

Henri took Pierson and Francesca down to the interview suite. They stopped en route and waited while the on duty observer unleashed Sebastien—whose beard was now quite thick looking—and then their captive walked with them unaided to another office, where a technician was making the final set up arrangements for the projector.

Pierson connected the projector to the laptop and switched on the power.

Henri invited Sebastien to sit at one of the seats around a large, centrally placed oval table, big enough to seat twenty people.

The projector and laptop were positioned near the end of the table furthest from the door.

Pierson sat to one side and projected the first image.

'Can you see the picture okay?' he asked Sebastien.

Sebastien looked at each of them in turn with great suspicion and then just flatly said, 'yes,' with only a hint of his voice cracking from fear.

'We'd like you to tell us if you recognise anyone in this picture,' Pierson said.

'Yes. Her,' Sebastien blurted out the answer and pointed at Francesca.

'Other than people in this room,' Pierson added.

Pierson displayed each picture, one at a time, some for longer than others, but he made a point of stopping on shots that showed a lot of people.

'I can zoom in if you wish,' Pierson offered.

'No it's okay,' Sebastien replied, looking vaguely more interested than before. One after another, the photographs were projected and then came the shot of the passengers queueing for the train. The next shot on the screen caught the attention of Henri, Francesca and Pierson. Sebastien was silent.

Pierson looked at him, 'I expect you to volunteer information if you have it and not make me drag it out of you.' It was a picture of one of the train's passengers.

Sebastien began to look worried and was visibly uneasy. 'I don't want to be in here,' Sebastien remarked, 'but believe me, I'll tell you when I recognise someone, honest.'

'Who is this man?' Pierson asked him directly pointing at the screen.

'I don't know. I've never seen him before.' Sebastien replied.

Pierson looked at Henri and Francesca. 'Back to square one,' he said to them.

He turned to Sebastien once again 'This man's name is...' he stopped himself as he looked at the screen to confirm it, to make sure he wasn't going mad, 'Norman King,' he continued 'known as Bill to his friends.'

'No it isn't,' said Sebastien with a puzzled indignant look, checking the screen and then looking back at Pierson and the others. 'I mean he might call himself that, but that's not the man I know as Norman King. You know. Bill.'

Pierson suddenly felt a sense of relief. But they were left with a problem, specifically who was the man that had set Sebastien up? Henri shook his head as though he realised something that he should have thought of earlier.

'This man that set you up; the man you call Norman King,' Henri waved his hand to one side trying to phrase his English better, 'your contact: Bill.'

Sebastien was hanging on his every word. 'Describe him to us,' Henri asked.

'Six feet one may be six two, gold hair going grey, late forties, early fifties, thin, speaks well, nice accent and, oh yes he wears glasses with thin silver rims and he has a beard.'

Pierson and Francesca looked at each other briefly and Pierson gave a wry smile.

He displayed the previous photograph on the laptop. There on the screen was the picture of the passengers waiting to get on the train the previous day.

'Can you see him in this picture?' Pierson asked Sebastien.

'Yes: over on the right, there, in the queue. That's him. I swear it, the one with the tartan suitcase,' he replied.

Pierson zoomed in on the man.

'No mistake,' Sebastien nodded confidently crossing his arms. 'He's the one that set me up. Norman King.' He almost spat out the words.

Henri smiled again, 'thank you,' he remarked to Sebastien. 'His name is Bob Selway.'

There was silence for a few moments. 'But this doesn't work does it?' Francesca said. 'What about the fact that he was tied up on the train and helping us take the explosives off and escaping.'

'Look what he's carrying,' Pierson remarked slowly, as though he'd seen a ghost.

Henri nodded as he recognised the suitcase as being identical to the one containing the money found in the locker in the engine carriage.

'We'll discuss this later,' Henri said in a commanding voice. 'First I have an idea for our friend here. I think letting him languish in some jail for the rest of his life may be a waste. What would you say if I offered you an employment opportunity?'

'Depends on the deal.'

'You have very little to bargain with,' Henri replied, 'but we would want you for a minimum of a year, maybe two, you'd be paid and you wouldn't have a sentence hanging over you: we'd wipe the slate clean—even though it's a British slate.'

Sebastien needed no second chance. 'Where do I sign?'

'Get yourself cleaned up and I'll arrange for you to meet us in an hour.'

Henri reached for the phone on the table and tapping in four digits he spoke almost immediately, in French, and then carefully placed the receiver back in the cradle. Pierson had no idea what was said, although he picked out the words Monsieur King.

'Okay,' said Sebastien, 'then if I'm working for you there's something else you might want to know.'

Pierson looked at him. Sebastien then continued 'That photograph you're showing there, can you zoom back out again?'

Pierson obliged.

'Yeah I think it's him, zoom in on the silver haired man two people in front of Selway,' Sebastien was pointing and leaning forward slightly, squinting too.

Pierson did as he was asked.

'Yeah. He was there, the crafty old so and so,' he said with an increasing realisation.

'Who is it?' said Pierson.

Bill was escorted into the room. The escort left and Bill squinted at the screen as he walked slowly towards it.

'Sir Henry Young,' said Bill.

'Yes, the judge.' Sebastien added.

'Welcome back,' Pierson commented to Bill. 'I'm sorry I misjudged you,' he added, standing to shake Bill's hand again.

'You did the right thing,' said Bill magnanimously. 'I can understand why you mistrusted me and I hope you understand why I couldn't mention the gold.'

'Not entirely,' Pierson replied, 'remember you already killed me once…and dead men don't talk.'

Francesca scrutinised the man in the photograph. 'He was sitting next to Abbot,' she declared. 'I'm sure of it. It looked like they knew each other too.'

'What makes you say that?' quizzed Pierson.

'I don't know. It was just something that happened,' she replied, thinking back to the previous day. 'I was walking towards them, talking to Mike in Italian and that man did something that made me think he knew Abbot. What was it though?'

She paused momentarily and then talked it through. 'He was looking out of the window and then he looked at his watch.' She paused again for a few moments before her face almost lit up. 'I know what it was!' she declared.

The others sat there waiting for her to speak.

'As we got near, so he took Abbot's left arm and lifted it so he could see the time on his watch. Abbot didn't even turn towards him. He just let him do it.'

'So it may be that it was a pre-arranged time for Abbot to go to the engine car,' Pierson noted, 'and it wasn't necessarily us walking by that triggered it.'

Henri raised his eyebrows wondering what new revelations were going to be made so he interrupted the discussion to take it elsewhere. 'We have work to do ladies and gentlemen. There is the small matter of finding some gold.'

Within a few minutes they were back in Henri's office and studying the contents of his large whiteboard.

Henri began reading the accumulated faxes that had arrived whilst they'd been in the interview suite and paraphrased the contents for Pierson, Bill and Francesca.

'The bullets that killed Dobrowiecki and Abbot came from different guns. Abbot was shot with the gun in Dobrowiecki's hand.'

'So Selway told us the truth,' Pierson said 'Dobrowiecki shot Abbot and then Selway shot him.'

'No,' said Henri, there's one small flaw, 'according to this,' he waved the paper at them. 'The forensic report shows that Abbot had blood group O and Dobrowiecki had blood group A. There were splatters of blood group O on the back of Dobrowiecki's driver's uniform.'

Sitting in silence, each of them began thinking about and realising the sequence of events that must have caused this. Pierson spoke first. 'So Abbot was shot first and Dobrowiecki was standing behind him with his back to Abbot, then turning around Dobrowiecki was shot. That's why there was a delay between the shots. Selway swapped guns, but killed them both.'

'But why?' Francesca asked.

'Because they'd both outlived their usefulness,' Pierson replied, 'it was never about the software, it was always about the gold.'

'So where is the gold?' Bill asked, 'have you found it yet?'

Henri shook his head, 'the French Navy has been searching the channel since they got there early this morning, but they haven't found the breach yet.'

'They won't,' Pierson replied

'How do you know that?' Bill asked him.

'Because the judge was on the train,' Pierson replied. Nobody spoke for a few moments waiting for Pierson to continue. 'That means the explosives on the train were never going to blow up. They were fake or never set.' Pierson started to see a more complete picture developing in his mind.

'But Selway was tied up and he helped us when we set him free. Who tied him up?' Francesca asked.

'His own people.' answered Pierson. 'Remember there were a lot of them there—and all in wet suits—when he saw us on the train, in the cab, he knew we'd get the train moving for him, he was going to do it himself, but we screwed up his plans.'

'So why didn't he just kill us?' said Francesca.

'Because you had a gun and he couldn't risk trying to shoot you and missing or letting you kill him.'

'What about the ferry though,' said Henri, 'how did he manage to track you down there?'

'I don't know about that yet,' Pierson replied, 'but it fits that Selway sent Williams and Garrett, because they both knew that I was still alive and they probably knew my new identity too,' he looked at Bill as he finished speaking for confirmation. Bill nodded.

'It also explains why they didn't try and kill me,' Francesca remarked.

'They wouldn't have known about you,' Bill commented, 'so it does fit.'

'Take me back to the train,' Henri asked them, 'are you saying they wanted you to see them in wet suits?'

'Perhaps,' Pierson replied, 'we can't know for sure yet. But what we do know is that the train had to come out of the tunnel intact, Selway wanted it. There was no way that the judge was going to be blown up.'

'So what was the countdown timer that stopped you accessing the computer at the front of the train?' Francesca interrupted them with her question.

'I can only guess,' Pierson replied, 'but my guess is that it was a program in a tight loop that was counting down to unlock the train doors. They correctly guessed that everyone would be gasping for breath and would rush out causing chaos. This would let the robbers finish off their work.'

'Finish off what?' Bill asked.

'Finish off letting the passengers see the men in wet suits,' Pierson replied.

'But they might not have seen any,' Bill answered, 'so that was a gamble.'

'No it wasn't,' said Pierson. 'They would have the cast iron word of a high court judge who would have sworn to that afterwards, regardless of what he saw. The fact that no other passengers would have seen anything wouldn't have aroused anyone's suspicions that he was lying, they would just have assumed that he was extremely observant and acted with a cool head.'

'Imaginative,' Henri declared, 'very clever indeed and this man Selway, he's very good.'

'He's also very alive,' replied Pierson, 'and I can't believe that the judge was aboard just to provide witness evidence. Doesn't he have cases to handle?'

'No,' Bill replied, 'it's August and they're on summer recess until about October.'

Bill looked at Henri and moved the topic back to the gold. 'You think the gold really did get taken out through to the sea bed?'

'I don't even know whether the gold got on the train,' he replied, 'but the Navy is checking that possibility.'

'It got on the train alright, I checked it personally and I saw it with my own eyes,' Bill replied.

'Then I'm afraid we should be looking in earnest,' Henri remarked.

'How big is the submarine that you thought they used?' Pierson asked Henri.

'I don't know how to answer your question,' said Henri.

'How many cubic metres of water does it displace and how heavy is it?'

'Why do you want to know?' Henri asked, 'what good will the information do?'

'We can work out whether it was possible to move the gold that way,' replied Pierson, 'and if it wasn't possible then it can't have been stolen through the sea bed.'

'Of course,' Bill remarked slowly, 'one hundred and fifty tons of gold would take a long time to get to the surface. They'd have to do more than one trip.'

'And probably to a waiting ship,' Pierson added.

Henri made a telephone call and within minutes a fax came through with the information, the others sat quietly as they waited.

'It displaces one hundred and fifty metric tonnes and had a weight of twenty metric tonnes' Henri said reading from the fax.

'It could be done in two trips then, in theory,' Pierson replied. Henri nodded.

'It doesn't feel right though,' Pierson added.

'If the French Navy are handling that part, then let's work on a different assumption. Let's assume it didn't go out of the tunnel that way,' Bill suggested 'Where might it be?'

'Only two places,' Pierson replied, 'in the tunnel or outside.'

'That's not very helpful,' Bill remarked.

'Think about it,' said Pierson, 'has the tunnel been checked?'

'There are one hundred and twenty kilometres of tunnel to search, not including access tunnels between the service tunnel and the other two,' Henri replied, 'it's a long job, but the gendarmerie have found the substitute doors in the access tunnel by the crossover point where the train stopped yesterday.'

'Have they opened them yet?' Pierson asked.

'No,' Henri replied.

'What doors are these?' said Bill.

'Francesca and I saw them building and installing circular metallic plate doors in the access tunnel, each with a hinged central door, like the ones you find on submarines, to withstand the pressure of a lot of water,' Pierson answered.

'Hence the wet suits,' Bill remarked.

Pierson nodded and then continued, 'So, Henri, what will the gendarmerie do to open the doors?'

Henri shuffled through a pile of reports on his desk and picked out one particular one. 'They're going to get the Navy to create two more doors either side of the two put in yesterday. Then when they've secured them they'll send a team in from one end and seal the door they've installed and open the inner one.'

'Isn't that dangerous?' Pierson asked.

'No,' Henri replied, 'according to this they'll have special pressure suits. The pressure of water coming in from the sea above will crush them otherwise.' Everyone sat there aghast except Henri. 'What?' he said, 'what have I said?'

'Aren't wet suits good enough?' Francesca asked.

Henri looked at the paper again, 'not according to this,' he replied, 'they'd be crushed or get the bens. They need special pressurized suits almost like astronauts wear.'

Henri still hadn't realized what he'd said.

'So it was a scam?' said Pierson, 'the gold didn't go out through the sea.'

'How do you know?' Henri asked, now becoming agitated that he hadn't seen what they all seemed to know.

'Because there's no point in wearing a wet suit if you're going to get crushed,' Bill replied. 'As the criminals were wearing wet suits, then it was all for show.'

Henri read the paper again. 'Voila,' he declared quietly with depressing realisation.

'What about Selway being tied up?' Francesca asked.

'That proves it really,' said Pierson

'How?' Bill exclaimed.

'If we hadn't got to him, he would have been released by one of the other members of his team, who was clearly aboard the train,' Pierson replied. 'They've played us for mugs all the way through,' he added.

'But what was the point of him being tied up?' Henri asked.

'Because,' Pierson replied, 'if we'd found him free and the gold gone it would have looked less convincing. We might have easily concluded he was one of the bad guys. As it was, we thought he was on our side because he was tied up, and there's no way he could have got himself free without help. In this case he banked on getting our help, and if we hadn't got there he would have had help from one of his own team. And that explosion too, right at the end, just as the train started, it must have been deliberate, so that Selway and the rest got aboard, behind the cover of the smoke.'

'Going back to your point Mike, what did you mean about the gold being either inside the tunnel or outside?' Francesca asked.

'Well, if it's not in the tunnel and it didn't go into the sea, then it was still on the train,' Pierson replied.

'Where though?' Bill asked. 'The lorries were empty,'

'They had an oxyacetylene torch with them,' Pierson replied, thinking about what he'd seen.

'Are you saying they melted it down?' Bill asked disbelievingly.

'No,' Pierson replied. 'There must be an easy way to sort this out, it'll come to me. In the mean time, Henri, can you get me the passenger manifest for the train I'd like a complete list of all the people there.' Henri nodded. 'And is there any way we can find out who came off the train?' Pierson continued.

'The gendarmerie will know that,' said Henri 'I'll get the information from them.'

'What about the cars?' Francesca asked, 'can we find out who owned them? That's where we saw men changing into wet suits just before the train stopped.'

'Yes we did,' Pierson agreed, remembering the walk they took to the back of the train.

With that, Sebastien was escorted in.

'Here is our latest recruit,' said Henri extending his arm and gesturing towards Sebastien. The others turned around.

Sebastien was standing there somewhat tidier than when they'd last seen him and clean-shaven now as well. He looked at the whiteboard and saw his name there. He frowned but said nothing.

Antoine then burst in panting. He stood there diligently waiting for Henri to give him the cue to speak. Henri raised his eyebrows and tilted his head like a dog that had heard a strange noise. 'Bien?' he said.

'They've lost three hundred million dollars. We've just sold Euros to gold and that's how far down they are, so they'll owe a lot of money soon.'

Henri smiled and looked at Bill. 'It seems that the judge was trying to make some extra money on the side, but that's not going to happen now. They've lost their original two hundred million dollars and another three hundred million now too. I think Monsieur Selway may have just become a target himself.'

'Can I login and see what you've been doing to my system,' Sebastien asked, 'there might be some e-mails for me.'

'Ah Oui,' said Henri, 'please be my guest.'

'When you're done,' said Pierson, 'can you set me up an account of my own please?'

'Yeah, fine,' said Sebastien. Pierson walked outside with him and sat at the laptop and watched as Sebastien sat at the terminal next to him that was connected to the criminal's system.

'Oh no!' Pierson declared and he then slumped over the keyboard of the laptop.

Francesca, Bill and Henri had by now come out of Henri's inner office.

'Mike!' Francesca exclaimed. 'What's wrong?'

'I don't believe it. How can I have been so stupid?' he said with resignation.

'Why?' asked Henri 'What's happened?'

'It was staring us in the face all the time,' Pierson replied.

'Every time I logged in to this system I used account TN and password TAUQMUC' he said pointing at the terminal in front of Sebastien.

'So?' Francesca asked looking at Henri and then back at Pierson. Pierson continued. 'On AIX once the mail server is set up, every user gets mail.'

He paused and looked at them for a few seconds. Sebastien nodded and sat back in his chair.

'And your point?' Henri prompted him.

'What do the initials SHY stand for?' Pierson asked them.

'Sir Henry Young,' replied Henri.

'And GB?' Pierson asked again.

'George Bannister,' Francesca replied looking puzzled, but remembering the name from Henri's whiteboard.

Sebastien looked surprised that they knew this, as even he didn't know what GB stood for, but it made sense to him.

'And TN?' he asked them, 'the name of the account I've been using. Given to us by this man here,' he added pointing at Sebastien.

Henri's face changed as he realised what Pierson was saying, 'it stands for Trevor Norris,' Henri said to Pierson. 'Aha,' he continued, jabbing his finger towards Pierson in the air, realising there was some impact of the statement, but not quite sure what.

'So what?' said Francesca.

'Well he doesn't need two accounts on the system, he already had an account named TN, he didn't need an account called RS as well.' Pierson added.

Henri gently pulled his moustache again.

'You'll have to help us here,' he said, raising his eyebrows at Pierson. 'I thought I could see where this was leading, but now I'm not sure,' Henri pulled up a chair and sat down.

'In England the name Bob is short for Robert. The initials RS stand for Robert Selway, or as we know him Bob Selway. That's why Sebastien wasn't missed on the train. He wasn't supposed to be there. The person called RS who was going to be there, was in fact aboard and his name is Bob Selway.'

Francesca and Henri smiled at each other and at Pierson's insight.

'Brilliant,' said Henri looking very pleased.

Bill smiled too.

Sebastien just looked at them. 'Why didn't you just ask me?'

'Why would we?' Pierson replied, 'you kept saying your name was...' Pierson paused '...is Rene Sebastien'.

'But your account name has the initials for Trevor Norris,' Pierson continued.

Sebastien nodded. 'I still think of myself with that name. Now what account name would you like?' he asked Pierson.

Pierson just asked for a simple name the same as his new initials.

Henri walked back into his inner office and then emerged again moments later.

'What were you doing with the steward before the train pulled off,' Pierson asked Bill.

'I wanted them to load the lorries carrying the gold next to each other, but the steward told me he had specific instructions from his superiors not to do that, but to mix them with the chemical tankers.' Bill replied.

'Did he say precisely who he got the orders from?' said Pierson.

'No. His English suddenly deteriorated at that point and he just ignored me,' Bill answered.

'Look at this,' Henri interrupted them. He had the manifest for the train before and after the journey.

Pierson checked it and saw the judge allocated the seat next to Abbot just as Francesca had said.

'It seems that Francesca was right,' he commented. As Pierson thumbed through the pages, he saw the details for the cars and lorries.

'Nothing special about the cars,' he noted, 'not that shows up here anyway.' He carried on reading. 'The lorries had two people aboard on the chemical tankers and on the gold lorries.'

'That's right,' said Bill 'I saw them as they all shuffled around.'

'Yet we only saw one man tied up in that chemical tanker,' Pierson said looking at Francesca. She frowned and agreed with him.

'So what happened to the other person in the cab?' Pierson asked muttering to himself.

'And of course,' he continued, 'they weren't going to blow up the train with all that potassium aboard. I wonder if the tankers were even full? In fact did they have anything aboard them?'

He thumbed through again to find the vehicle weights for the lorries and tankers. 'The gold lorries weighed thirty seven tonnes each, so that's seven tonnes unladen weight I assume.'

Bill nodded, 'That would be about right.'

Pierson then read down the list and saw the entry for the chemical tankers 'They weighed ten tons before the journey!'

'So they were empty,' said Francesca 'They wouldn't have caused a problem.'

'So why ship empty lorries?' Bill asked.

'Don't get excited,' Pierson replied. 'They probably just offloaded their merchandise and were returning home. But let's check any way.'

Pierson shuffled the paperwork until he found the last page and there he found the entries he sought. 'They weighed forty tons when they left the marshalling yards at Frethun this morning. Every one of them.'

'So the gold's on board those lorries?' Henri asked.

'If not,' said Pierson, 'they've each got thirty tonnes of something! Now where could they have got that from?'

Again this was a moment for thought.

'Can we stop them?' Pierson asked. 'And search them.'

'Our powers of stop and search are more limited than in your country Mike,' Henri replied. 'We need to know where they're going.'

'Maybe we can work it out,' Pierson replied.

Francesca, Bill, Henri and Sebastien all looked at him curiously.

'Be my guest,' said Bill, now interested in Pierson's analysis.

'They won't make for any port. In the open sea they can be attacked and boarded by the French Navy. Or any Navy in the EC.'

Henri raised his eyebrows and curling down the corners of his mouth he nodded in agreement.

'They'll want to get out of France though; and better still out of the EC to escape from EC authorities,' Pierson added.

'That leaves one place,' Henri observed, 'La Suisse.'

They each looked at one another and gradually as none of them could think of anything better, one by one they agreed.

'After all they may be going to Greece with a name like Constantinou on the tankers,' Pierson continued.

'But if you're right then they'll be in the Alps some time tomorrow, possibly later today if they've travelled non stop and how do we stop them?' Henri asked.

'With the gendarmerie of course,' Sebastien replied.

'We can't,' said Henri. 'I already told you we don't have the same powers of stop and search as you have in England.'

'So, you want to stop them without touching them and make sure they can't move again is that right?' Pierson asked Henri.

'Oui,' said Henri, 'but it is impossible. If they make it to one of the tunnels through the mountains, we won't be able to touch them.'

'We won't have to touch them,' Pierson said.

'We can't block the tunnels or the roads either,' Henri added.

'That's okay,' said Pierson, 'we won't need to do that either.'

'We can't shoot them or fire anything at them, or bomb them. If you can follow those rules then you can do whatever it is you have in mind,' Henri added almost triumphantly as though there was no solution.

'You give me your word that those are the only conditions?' Pierson added.

'Mais oui,' said Henri, 'but of course,' he added.

'Fine,' Pierson added.

He looked at Bill.

'What?' said Bill.

'Chinooks,' said Pierson, remembering the day he was taken to France.

'Chinooks,' said Bill slowly, nodding at the same time.

'What is this Chinooks?' said Henri.

'They are helicopters,' said Francesca, 'and if you're looking for a pilot…'

'Oh no,' said Henri wagging his finger and interrupting her, 'absolutely not. I forbid it, you're not going to pilot anything with me on board.'

CHINOOKS

Henri had his way. Francesca settled for being a passenger. Her uncle made arrangements for two Chinooks to be available, although it was going to take two hours to prep them and get them to Orly airport—the nearest place they could land.

Henri, Pierson, Francesca and Bill continued to review the other peripheral matters in the mean time. It wasn't long before Henri was able to confirm what they had surmised, that the gold wasn't in the Channel Tunnel and the tunnel had not been breached at all and was still intact. More than this though, the Nouveau as they had referred to it—the French submarine—had been found abandoned at the shore near Calais.

There was however one disturbing report that Henri had been given, and addressing the others he began to impart the details.

'Even though we found no gold in the tunnel,' he said 'we did have a gruesome discovery.'

Pierson leaned back in his chair and saw Henri's demeanour, written clearly across his craggy face and deeply furrowed brow. Before Henri could continue however, Pierson gave him the answer. 'They found a badly injured man in a wetsuit, with a broken leg.'

Henri nodded at Pierson. 'Do you know what else was there?'

Pierson thought for a few moments as the others looked at him. 'The dead bodies of ten treasury employees,' he replied.

Henri looked at Pierson with stunned curiosity. 'How did you know?'

'Something Francesca and I saw on the train when we were in the tunnel.'

'And that was?' asked Bill.

'Too few drivers for the lorries,' Pierson replied. 'I only worked it out just now as Henri brought this news. The first piece of evidence was on the film I shot yesterday morning with the digital camera.' He pointed at a still shot on his laptop screen. 'I didn't really register it at the time. I didn't need to. But later, after we got out of the tunnel it came back to me briefly. When Francesca and I looked into the tanker cab there was a man bound and gagged. Yet on this film, with the angle I shot it, and being such a bright day, you can see two men in the tanker cab.'

Pierson turned the screen around to show the others. 'So I was wondering why there was only one person later. But I couldn't figure it out. So I then wondered why there were two of them in the first place and suddenly it dawned on me. If they were travelling a long way then they might need two drivers, especially if they were going to be travelling non-stop, or at least with no overnight stops.'

'So what happened to the second person on the tanker in the tunnel?' Bill asked.

'He was in the treasury lorry on that same shuttle,' Pierson replied, 'and no doubt there were originally two drivers on those lorries. Later in this film,' he pointed at the laptop again, 'you'll see one of those lorries being loaded onto the shuttle and in the cab will be two men.'

'So why kill them?' Bill asked.

'Because it was quicker than knocking them out and it guaranteed they didn't see where the gold really went,' replied Pierson. 'That's why there was one lorry and one tanker on each shuttle, whoever arranged for them to be loaded arranged for that too. That's also why they were reversed back to back.'

'Selway?' Bill asked.

'Who else?' Pierson replied. 'Probably arranged in advance at diplomatic or senior government levels.'

'But tankers don't open up at the back,' Henri remarked. 'They fill from the top.'

'Usually,' replied Pierson, 'that's why they didn't look suspicious. Normally I'd agree with you, but I'll bet if we can stop those things, then we'll find the answer. Besides, we know they're thirty tons heavier coming off the train than going on.'

'The thing that still bothers me is the riot at Sangatte,' Bill commented, 'was it deliberate or accidental?' Bill didn't really expect anyone to answer, but Pierson did anyway. 'Deliberate. It was too good to be true for our gold thieves, it gave them the extra time they needed and I'd guess, that by the time the train had stopped, all the gold had been moved.'

'But we saw them changing into their wet suits when the train was still moving,' said Francesca.

'Yes we did,' replied Pierson, 'and I said at the time that it was stupid because in wet suits they'd just fry. It may be that only some of them were in wet suits, just enough to show us. Why else would they do that in the lead car of the shuttle in view of passengers? It was done for show.'

'They're on their way to Switzerland.' Sebastien declared confidently.

'How do you know for sure?' Henri asked, dubious about Sebastien's source of information.

'It's all here in the deleted e-mails. I've re-instated them from a couple of months ago. We've got so much disk space on this system that I got in to the habit of archiving old data to disk and I've just got it back now,' Sebastien replied.

'But why didn't you tell us that before?' Bill asked him. 'You were on the mailing list weren't you?'

'No I wasn't,' said Sebastien, 'not for Jury. Remember, account RS was on the mailing list and my account is TN.'

Bill nodded and Sebastien printed off details of the route for the Constantinou Pharmaceuticals tankers. The e-mails were also quite explicit, and showed that the tankers had temporary names on their sides that would be switched to a different identity, but the new identity wasn't shown.

'How about the licence plate numbers,' Pierson asked.

'Probably switched too,' Bill remarked.

'Well there's one thing for sure,' said Pierson, 'We know they're in five tankers.'

'They may change that and move the gold,' Bill replied.

'And spend more time in France? That's unlikely,' said Pierson, 'especially with the change of name on the tankers and probably the colours too.'

'So we're looking for five tankers in convoy,' Bill remarked.

'Yes,' Pierson replied, 'and my guess is they have five different names on the sides. In addition you're looking for at least one high powered escort vehicle, probably all terrain.'

'How do you know that?' Bill asked.

'In case any of the tanker drivers get creative and try to drive off with thirty tons of gold.' Pierson replied. 'Those drivers must know what they're carrying, can you imagine trusting them to deliver it to the right place unescorted? I don't think so.'

Bill just nodded in agreement.

Henri checked his watch 'If there's nothing else, then it's time to get underway.'

Henri drove Bill, Francesca and Pierson to Orly airport. The city was busy, as would have been expected on a weekday. The headlines on newspaper stands told the story of the gold theft, and Pierson was able to work that out, even with his minimal knowledge of French.

By the time they reached the airport, it was two in the afternoon. Henri drove around to a side entrance and it looked like the same one where Pierson had arrived almost two weeks earlier.

Henri and the others flashed their passes at the security man at the gate as he let them through.

The Chinooks were hidden from view initially, but driving behind one of the hangars, suddenly the huge machines loomed large.

Henri parked some distance from them, in a designated parking area. As the others were about to get out he spoke to Pierson again. 'Why Chinooks?' he asked.

'Because,' said Pierson turning back to Henri. 'They're fast, almost three hundred kilometres per hour.'

Henri stroked his chin. 'And?' he said, realising that other helicopters could match that speed.

'And they generate 25 tonnes of downdraft,' Pierson replied.

Henri smiled and began to realise the ingenuity in Pierson's plan.

Francesca flashed her pass to one of the Air Force personnel guarding the first Chinook and pointed to Bill and Pierson as she spoke to him. The serviceman nodded and waved her through, directing them at the large side opening.

Armed with the details of the route taken by the lorries, Francesca sat up front just behind the co-pilot. The pilot invited her to put on a helmet, and with its built in microphone she was able to communicate with him and the co-pilot.

Speaking to the control tower, the pilot requested clearance to take off.

Bill and Pierson were sat in seats slightly further back from Francesca, but had excellent views. There were two other men aboard, dressed in air force uniforms, also wearing helmets with built in headsets. One of them was seated near Francesca and the other slid closed the large side door and took his seat next to the door itself.

The pilot started the engines and that's when Pierson and the others began to feel the slow rhythmic pounding of the air. Pierson looked out at Henri. He could see him standing outside his car on the apron, trying to light his pipe, but he had to turn his back to the helicopters as their engines' power increased to maximum. The twin contra-rotating rotors lifted the heavy machines into the air.

Henri had by now given up lighting his pipe, and was struggling to get back in his car. Even though he was parked at a safe distance from the helicopters it took all his force to open the door and then close it again.

Strange though, it seemed to Pierson at first, the Chinooks were required to follow the runway for a while until they reached a minimum altitude, only then did they veer off to begin to track and follow the main motorway south.

As they turned so Pierson noticed for the first time that the second Chinook was filled with gendarmes. He frowned as he looked back at Francesca.

'Just in case we find them,' she shouted at him.

Being August, the traffic flow was heavy in both directions. There was a lot of motorway to cover and they had no idea where to begin.

It appeared that the last chance they would have of tracking down the lorries would be just as they were about to enter a tunnel at the edge of the Alps, between France and Switzerland.

Almost two hours passed with many sightings of various tankers, the Chinooks dropped down for a closer look from time to time, but not so low as to cause a problem with the traffic, and even then usually flying parallel to the vehicles over adjacent fields.

Eventually the traffic became sparse, as much of it had continued on the route down to the south of France, Spain and the Mediterranean. This gradually made the search easier.

They came within 30 kilometres of the tunnel in the Alps and were beginning to believe they'd got it wrong.

Francesca took off her helmet and walked back to Pierson and Bill. 'Six more minutes and we run out of motorway at this speed,' she told them.

Pierson shrugged his shoulders and sat back in resignation at their apparent approaching failure.

'They've done it again,' he said to Bill.

The six minutes came and went and the pilots banked for the Chinooks to turn back around.

They'd been travelling for about 15 minutes retracing their previous route, when Pierson saw a Range Rover on the motorway with three tankers behind it.

Then a hill obscured the traffic and the motorway from view as it meandered its way around. The Chinooks followed it and suddenly two more tankers followed by a second Range Rover emerged into view.

'That's them!' Bill yelled. 'Turn around!'

'How far to the tunnel?' Pierson called out to Francesca.

She checked with the pilots as she placed her helmet back on again. '75 kilometres,' she shouted back.

Pierson stood up, and with some difficulty walked towards the front of the Chinook, as the pilot banked the helicopter around.

'Take us down,' he shouted and pointed at the vehicle at the back. 'I want to see in that one.'

They swooped down to the fields and ran parallel to the trailing Range Rover.

Francesca handed Pierson binoculars. Holding them as steady as possible he looked over at the driver. 'It is them!' he declared, the adrenalin now beginning to surge through his body. His face muscles relaxed and his entire focus centred on the occupants of that one vehicle, as he watched the car, knowing that the people responsible for his wife's death were now tantalisingly within his grasp. Putting the binoculars back to his eyes, he noted the car registration ended with the characters '2 THJ', the same as the car that had sped away when he and Madeleine had had their picnic. Pierson thought this couldn't have been a coincidence.

There was a spare headset on a rack at the side. Francesca helped Pierson on with it. He spoke to the pilot. 'Get past that lead tanker and fly by its side.'

'If we get too close it'll flip over!' The pilot barked back, not taking his eyes off the tankers. Pierson was surprised at his remarkable grasp of English and then he remembered that English was the international language of aviation.

'That's the whole idea,' Pierson told him with deadly purpose in his voice.

The co-pilot turned to look at Pierson and then shrugged his shoulders at the pilot who nodded and overtook the tankers, flying past each one until it reached the first in the convoy. The five tankers had separated slightly but no other vehicles were in between. They were in fact all marked with names of different petroleum companies, making it look as though they had explosive materials aboard.

Drawing level with the lead tanker and matching it's speed, the pilot held the Chinook steady as Pierson looked across at the driver now only 50 metres or so away. These tankers were right hand drive and were driving on the right so he had a direct view.

The Chinook swooped low across the fields; trees almost bowing down as it flew overhead.

'Move it in,' Pierson said to the pilot gesturing at the same time. The pilot didn't look back at Pierson though as his concentration was completely on his flying. He gradually eased the Chinook closer.

At a distance of 40 metres from the tanker, the tanker driver's arms stiffened to hold the wheel steady against the increasing crosswind.

From only 30 metres he began to fight with the weight of the tanker as it started to snake, looking out of the window and fixing his stare on the first Chinook wondering what it was doing there.

At 20 metres the tanker began swerving wildly across two lanes of the motorway.

At 10 metres, the Chinook took a close overhead pass in front of the lead tanker and it began to jack knife, the driver now fighting a losing battle and the fear was apparent in his eyes and clearly uppermost in his mind, as he almost stood up out of his seat to wrestle with the steering wheel applying his bodyweight to the brakes and his upper body's strength to the steering wheel.

Within seconds of the pass of the first Chinook in front of the tanker driver the change in down draft flipped the tanker once and then a second time as it was hurtled along the motorway, sparks flying from the friction of the steel side as it gouged through the surface of the motorway.

The following tankers had already begun to hit the brakes and were skidding uncontrollably towards the first one whilst the second Chinook circled towards the front of the carnage now developing below.

With Pierson's Chinook now flying over the field on the opposite side of the motorway, after cutting across the lead tanker, Pierson looked back just as the tanker burst into a fireball.

The remaining four tankers came to a standstill, their drivers and passengers leaping from the cabs and running in all directions leaving the doors open in their haste, fuelled by abject terror as they left their huge vehicles strewn across all three lanes of the motorway.

'Find that Range Rover at the back!' Pierson shouted to the pilot, desperate to catch its occupants.

'Why the one at the back?' Francesca asked him.

'That's the one Selway's in and I want him.' Pierson shouted back at her.

The winds coming down from the mountains began spreading the smoke across both carriageways and obscured the view.

Bill, Pierson and Francesca all began scrutinising the scene.

'It looks like war zone down there!' Bill shouted.

Pierson just nodded with a half satisfied look.

'I want him,' Pierson declared defiantly. 'Where is he?' he continued in frustration.

They carried on looking for about thirty seconds and then Francesca began pointing and shouting, 'over in the fields!'

The co-pilot spotted it and pointed it out to the pilot as they turned to give chase.

They swooped down low but the Range Rover had taken a path through trees, so the helicopter couldn't get low enough. Every now and again it appeared through the gaps.

'Have you got a winch?' Pierson asked.

'Yes. Two, but you can't drop on the car,' the pilot exclaimed. 'You'll be killed.'

'My choice.' Pierson replied through gritted teeth.

Bill looked at him and shook his head. 'It's not worth it!'

'It is for me,' Pierson continued.

Bill saw the look in Pierson's eyes. There was an unstoppable build up of rage. Pierson didn't even waste time arguing. He simply turned away stepped across to Francesca and spoke as quietly as he could to her so that she could hear. Pierson was pointing and gesturing down towards the car and then when he stopped speaking he stood back and looked at her. She said nothing so Pierson moved towards the door to slide it back.

'Wait!' she shouted at him waving at him to stop. 'I'll tell them,' she conceded.

Bill frowned at Francesca, but he could only watch as she shouted in French at the co-pilot who in turn relayed the instructions to another member of the crew to come over to Pierson and fit him with a harness.

'What's the breaking strain of the cable?' Pierson said tugging at the large hook on the other winch mechanism. The man shrugged his shoulders. Unlike the pilot and co-pilot, he couldn't speak English well enough to reply. Francesca translated for them and spoke to each of them in their native tongues.

'Five tons on that one,' she said pointing at one.

Pierson smiled. There were two winches. Pierson was attached to one and on the other was a hook that must have weighed about thirty kilos.

'Lower this with me,' he shouted at the crewman, pointing as Francesca translated again.

'Okay,' she replied.

The crewman slid back the side door of the Chinook, exposing the occupants to the power of the air tearing past. The noise inside had now increased dramatically as the crewman secured Pierson to the winch. Carefully Pierson let himself out of the helicopter, his single-minded focus on stopping the car below. He held on to the huge hook from the second winch mechanism as both winches were set in action and extended downwards at the same rate.

Francesca stood at the doorway gripping the overhead bar and watched him being lowered, occasionally glancing up and checking the unravelling wires on both mechanisms. The Range Rover was only managing to travel at about 50 miles an hour at most. But the wind was tremendous. With the helicopter now about 30 metres up and Pierson slowly being winched down, he found himself dangling in mid air with only the trees for company.

The Chinook pilot managed to position him in front of the Range Rover and only a matter of a few metres above it.

Pierson's body was being buffeted by the wind and he tried to swing himself into more space as he moved dangerously close to the tree branches hitting his head on one twig as he swept past.

Then as he was lowered more, so Selway saw him in front of the car and couldn't believe his eyes. Neither could Pierson, because in the passenger seat was the judge.

Selway wrenched the steering, and it was clear that the judge was panicking as he leaned over to grab the wheel. Pierson found himself flying along to one side of the car once it had turned, so the pilot managed to lift him slightly and then drop him on the roof.

Pierson was thrown off almost immediately as the car turned again. He'd damaged his arm in the tumble but nothing serious and fortunately he'd missed the ground.

Francesca was furiously shouting instructions to the pilot as she and Bill clung on to the side of the Chinook, watching as best they could through the occasional and fleeting gaps in the trees below, the wind blowing them back as they looked down on the foray.

Pierson mustered all his strength as the pilot aimed again to lower him on the roof of the Range Rover. This time Pierson grabbed the large hook with both hands and as he was about to land, he smashed it with all his might from above through the windscreen, and with enough force that it came back through to the sunroof.

On seeing this, Francesca shouted at the pilot and he lifted the Chinook. Selway had jumped back from the steering wheel when the hook smashed through the windscreen. Without thinking he opened his door, fumbled with his seat belt and fell out of the car into the trees nearby.

The Range Rover however was being lifted into the air, it's roof being distorted as it did so. All four wheels spinning furiously from the drive mechanism that now had no ground resistance.

As though he had a death wish, Pierson tried to climb into the driving seat and was swung off the car twice before he managed it, knocking into the car and bruising himself in the face to add to his earlier injury. The judge was screaming and clinging on desperately.

Finally, Pierson made it into the car and he switched the engine off, the wheels then gradually ceased revolving.

The car itself was now more than a hundred metres in the air and the pilot was flying it back to the crash scene on the motorway where the other helicopter had already landed and it's passengers of gendarmes were beginning to secure the devastation. The response had been so quick that within a matter of minutes two fire engines could be seen hurtling towards them from the north.

Pierson's Chinook lowered the Range Rover into the field next to the crash site. It landed with a final bump that only added to the judge's terror. Pierson though, still pumped high with adrenalin fought with the hook to disengage it from the car. He then untangled himself from his own winch and the helicopter crewman reeled in both lines as it landed some two hundred metres away.

Pierson ran around to the passenger door of the Range Rover, opened it and beckoned immediately for the judge to get out. His hands were white from clinging on to the side of the car and dashboard. At first he couldn't move because of his seat belt and his eyes still showed nothing but the terror that was temporarily paralysing him.

Francesca came running across from the now landed Chinook, taking off her helmet as she ran. Bill was close behind, stepping out and walking crisply, his hands in his coat pockets.

From the other side a gendarme entered the scene. Francesca, now having dropped to a brisk walk, approached the gendarme and spoke to him, showing him her identity pass and then pointing at the Range Rover. The gendarme nodded and walking over to the car he spoke into his handset. Within moments one of his colleagues arrived. They released the judge from his seat and bodily marched him off to the second helicopter.

'You need your head read,' Bill declared as he got close to Pierson. Pierson took off his helmet and looked at the carnage on the motorway, but didn't pass any comment. Even the protection of the helmet hadn't stopped his face from being cut and bruised, and consequently blood was now running down his cheek from one of his injuries.

'I hope it was the right tankers,' he remarked feeling the wet patch on his face and checking the red stain on his fingers.

They got closer to the scene and saw the evidence that proved Pierson had been right. The last tanker had jack-knifed and fallen on its side; and having crashed into one of the others, the back had split open spilling gold bars in all directions.

'What about Selway?' Bill asked Pierson.

'He jumped out of the car once it began lifting,' Pierson replied. 'He's back there in the woods.'

'He'll turn up sooner or later,' Bill commented as he looked around. 'This was a good piece of work.' he added, 'we've cost them a lot today.'

'It makes you wonder where they got their financing in the first place,' Pierson remarked.

'Yes, but that's another matter,' said Bill 'the important thing is that we have the gold back.'

Francesca had been talking to the gendarmes and the matter was now under control. She walked back to Pierson and Bill. 'They'll handle the rest,' she told them pointing at the uniformed officers.

Pierson looked along the motorway and saw traffic already building up. 'How did they get the gold into the tankers?'

'Come with me,' Francesca replied.

'They looked at the last tanker and with its guts laid bare it became obvious. The end of the tanker was like a large plug or shield that just clipped on. It had been covered with huge sheets of sticky backed plastic material, with the company name on and just looked like a standard tanker.

Inside was a pair of rails and a loading mechanism that allowed the gold to be moved in large amounts on crates, rather than one bar at a time.

'That's why the lorries and the tankers were back to back on the shuttle, and that was probably where they stored the forklift truck and other equipment—in pieces—before the raid.' Pierson commented slowly as he looked around.

They walked back to their helicopter and once aboard Pierson took a final look at it but Selway's escape gnawed at him.

Francesca patched up Pierson's injuries on the flight back with the on board first aid kit as they took a more relaxing run, returning to Orly where Henri had arranged for a car to pick the three of them up.

The following day at the ministry once again, Pierson now wondered what was going to happen next.

The judge was in custody and Henri was already in the interview suite awaiting the others. Bill, Francesca and Pierson made their way to the observation room and when they arrived, they could see the judge pacing around, occasionally checking his watch, clearly both concerned and agitated.

Finally he sat down and Henri entered.

'Good morning,' Henri said to him. 'That was an ingenious plan, a plan of daring and novelty.'

'What plan?' the judge replied arrogantly.

Henri laughed. 'The plan to steal the gold and then take it to Switzerland.'

The judge merely shook his head and shrugged his shoulders. Henri remained silent and then the judge spoke briefly. 'If that was their plan.'

'Are you trying to say you weren't involved?' Henri asked him sitting back in the chair.

'How can I have been involved?' the judge replied, 'I was locked in the passenger compartment of the train when the gold was being stolen and I've got five hundred witnesses who were there too. Including yourself.'

Henri wasn't very happy with the answer, but he wasn't going to tell the man about Rene Sebastien now working for him, so he changed his approach.

'You were with Selway in the car when we picked you up,' said Henri.

'And your point?' the judge replied.

'You were following the gold and we have enough evidence on Selway to prosecute him for the theft and murder.'

'So take it up with this man Selway,' the judge replied. 'I've never heard of him.'

'He was your driver in the car,' Henri replied partly outraged at his opponent's arrogance.

'I didn't know the man's name,' the judge answered. 'I was hitching a lift to Switzerland. It's part of my vacation. The driver jumped out of the car when that maniac hooked it up to the helicopter.'

Pierson was watching these events with interest in the observation room and stood up. Francesca looked at him and waved her hand as if to say no.

'Now unless there's anything further,' the judge continued, 'unless you wish to charge me with hitchhiking or being a passenger on a train, then release me.'

'What's your relationship with Vicky Kennedy?' Henri asked him ignoring the man's comments.

He sat there and said nothing, but Henri could see he had this man's attention now.

'Yes my friend. We know that you knew her,' Henri continued.

'It's not a name I recall,' said the judge reluctantly and not very convincingly.

Henri said nothing but pulled out a piece of paper from his pocket. On it were written the details of the travel arrangements for both the judge and Abbot made by Vicky Kennedy. He slid the paper across the desk to a now more cautious man.

The judge now realised that he couldn't ask for a lawyer as he had proclaimed his innocence and asking for one would only make him look guilty. He wondered what differences the French legal process had with the English process—which he was intimately familiar with.

He now felt less confident and began to look it. But, as the only connection between him and Vicky Kennedy was shown on the travel documents, he weighed up his options and decided it was safe enough to answer.

'She used to work for me. She's a high class escort.'

Henri said and did nothing but remained fixed on him.

'Where did you get this from?' the judge asked, referring to the paper.

Henri uncharacteristically answered, and told him. 'Abbot's brief case.'

'I knew I should have picked it up,' the judge replied.

'That would have been theft. Even a stupid Frenchman knows that,' Henri remarked.

'No one would have known,' the judge replied.

'Abbot would have known,' Henri suggested.

'Not from beyond the grave,' the judge retorted realising instantly his stupid mistake and that his cleverness had caught him out.

'Really?' remarked Henri. 'Who told you he was dead?'

The judge's face dropped as he tried to limit the damage.

'Not only do you seem to be declaring that he's dead now, but also that he was dead by when? By the time you left the train? Earlier than that perhaps?' Henri said to him.

The judge said nothing.

'I know Selway murdered Abbot. I also know you had nothing to do with that. You claim that you don't know Selway, yet you knew he had killed Abbot before you left the train, so you must have known his plans even if you didn't know the man.'

The judge felt cornered.

Henri remained silent as he looked into the judge's eyes pressing home his advantage of confidence.

'But you're right, we cannot charge you for hitchhiking or being a passenger, so clear up one more matter for me and I will authorise your immediate release.'

Henri paused again. 'Why was Dobrowiecki killed?'

The judge's initial reaction was curious as though he thought it was a trick question. 'I spoke to him this morning,' he replied slowly and deliberately, as though he was waiting to be caught out by some new revelation.

'So who was killed with Abbot?' Henri asked again.

The judge paused, wondering if he was placing himself in a trap. 'It was supposed to be the driver,' he replied.

Henri wasn't sure whether to believe him, so he stood and walking to the door he swiped his pass down the lock mechanism. The door clicked unlocked and he walked out. He entered the observation room again, and the four of them looked at the judge.

'So that's it?' said Pierson, 'he's got away with it?'

'The fact he knew the plans doesn't make him guilty in this country,' Henri remarked. 'But remember my friend, he's got away with nothing,' Henri replied. 'We have the gold, the software and although he doesn't know it yet, his cartel colleagues in the so called 'Jury' will be getting a large bill from their brokers. Soon he will be more than a little annoyed with the person who cost him so much.'

Henri remembered that the personal cost to Pierson had been very high too. He placed his hand on Pierson's shoulder, as if to comfort him and then he turned and walked out with the others in tow.

Back in his office, Henri picked up his phone, dialled a short extension number and in French ordered the release of the judge.

'What now?' Pierson asked.

Henri passed a fax to Bill, before replying. 'Go take the rest of the day off we'll meet tonight in your apartment and discuss the future. Perhaps we can dine together?'

Bill read the fax and then informed the others. 'It seems that Leslie Garrett and Roger Williams were picked up naked and shackled,' he paused, as he read on and laughed. 'Wednesday morning. They'd been given instructions—they claimed were from me—to track a particular cell phone and eliminate the person wearing it.'

Pierson looked at his watch. 'This thing?' he said incredulously.

Bill nodded. 'It's switched on all the time, it's run by a rechargeable battery that itself is charged by kinetic energy every time you move your arm.'

'So you're saying they tracked me through this thing?' Pierson asked him hardly believing it.

Bill nodded again. 'Famous murder cases have been solved by tracking the location of someone's cell phone; and that one works anywhere in Europe.'

'Who gave the order to track and kill me?' Pierson asked. 'Selway?'

'Probably,' Bill replied, 'who else could it have been?'

Thinking for a moment, Bill looked at Henri. 'May I use your phone?'.

'Be my guest,' Henri replied.

Bill made his call, but didn't let on whom he had spoken to, or what about.

Pierson did as Henri suggested and made his way to the apartment and started to organise his things that were there, but he realised that none of it actually seemed to be his.

That evening, Francesca had been in the apartment for some time talking to Pierson when Henri and Bill arrived within minutes of each other.

'I've been trying to fight this man for you,' Henri said with a large smile. 'I told him that you wouldn't want to go back to that ugly, damp, cold country of yours.'

Pierson largely ignored the comments, smiling only briefly and then returning to a more serious look as he walked around the lounge, pacing back and forth.

'That money, that suitcase that Selway had. I've been trying to work out what was going on. If Dobrowiecki is still alive, then who was the driver on the train; the man that Selway shot?'

'Exactly that,' Henri replied, 'he was the driver, nothing special there.'

Bill interrupted, 'I've checked with my department and the driver was specially picked to be the driver of that gold train and he and Selway knew each other. Selway was in the cab with him for security reasons.'

'So why did Selway take the money aboard with him?' Pierson asked.

'Insurance,' Bill replied. 'I can only guess, but once the train was moving and in the tunnel, at a pre-defined time Abbot was sent forward by the judge to enter the correct commands to prevent the train from moving after it had been stopped; and to set the countdown program to unlock the doors later. Selway took the money aboard to pay the driver to stop the train, that's probably why it was in the driver's locker. Then when the driver had done his work, Selway shot him dead moments after killing Abbot.'

'To keep the money himself?' Pierson asked.

'No,' Bill replied. 'We're taught to make sure we have a backup plan, wherever possible. You've been my backup plan and it worked. What I'm saying is that Selway had no absolute guarantee he could get the train stopped and keep it that way for an hour, or whatever it needed. So he had three ways of doing it; paying the driver; getting Abbot to disengage the drive and lock the doors of the carriages; and finally pay certain people at or near Sangatte to riot and storm the tunnel.'

'But he didn't need all three,' Pierson remarked.

'For one point two billion dollars of gold, it was insurance well planned. You're right. He didn't need all three in hindsight. But what if Abbot had been late and missed the train? Abbot didn't know it absolutely had to be that train. What if the driver had been sick and a late replacement came in? There was too much riding on this. So I expect the money was for the key rioters and Selway never for one moment intended paying the driver, although he probably showed him the money.

The beauty of the whole deception is that when we caught up with the events, we assumed it was money from Dobrowiecki to

Abbot and that Dobrowiecki had reneged. The whole thing just adds to Selway's credibility, apart from that one photograph at the terminal where he was recognised by Sebastien and seen by us carrying the suitcase with the money.'

Pierson looked at Henri. 'There's a direct connection between the judge and the cell phones now that you confronted him with that paper for the travel arrangements. Sebastien already said the judge arranged for the phones and Vicky Kennedy gave mine to me. So originally they came from the judge. I expected them to have come from Selway.'

'What about the phone bills though?' Francesca asked. 'Wouldn't the company have been curious why four employees had phones that they weren't paying for?'

'No,' said Pierson. 'Another sweet part of the set up was that the phones were issued by Vicky Kennedy, Abbot's mistress; and the four users and Abbot were supposed to be dead within a month. Even if someone had mentioned it to Abbot, she could have merely said they were sent on a trial basis—and that would have given enough time for us all to have been killed.'

Francesca looked at Pierson as he sat down with the others. She leaned forward in her chair and behind her in the dark of the night Pierson caught a brief glimpse of a small flash of light.

'What was that?' he said, standing up and looking towards the apartment opposite.

Francesca stood and turned, and in an instant the window shattered as a bullet burst through. She had no time to escape its path, but it went past her and into the wall at the back of the apartment. Henri, Bill and Francesca hit the floor. Pierson just looked, as though nothing had happened and raced to the window to see the gunman standing there. A second shot rang out and missed Pierson again, but this time as the man turned, so Pierson could see his face.

'It's Selway!' he exclaimed.

Francesca was now kneeling up and looking out over the window sill. She already had her gun in her hands and began to discharge round after round into the apartment on the other side of the road.

All through this, Pierson remained standing.

'Let's get him!' he shouted running to the door, but Bill grabbed him and threw him into one of the chairs. 'Haven't you heard about keeping your head down?'

Francesca remained watching and saw Selway leave the building and get into a car outside, which he drove at speed into the night.

Pierson got out of the chair and standing up he looked at his watch. 'This thing again?' he said.

Bill looked. 'Yes. He's still tracking you.'

'So all the time I'm here, wearing this thing, then everyone around me is in danger?'

Bill nodded.

Pierson began to undo the strap.

'He knows this address now and that can't be good. Taking off the watch won't solve the problem permanently. There's a better way.' said Bill.

'And that would be?' Pierson asked him.

'Let him track you to England,' Bill replied. 'I've got an idea.'

Pierson secured the watch on his wrist again and looked at Francesca. She remained impassive; and then, her voice breaking slightly, she walked over to him and spoke. 'Come back soon Mike…alive.'

He just looked at her and said nothing as he picked up his rucksack containing a few items he'd sorted out earlier.

She stood back and her eyes never left him as he bid farewell to Henri and walked out with Bill.

They made their way to Orly and had to stay overnight at the airport before catching a plane the following morning. Bill stopped at his hotel first and the two of them got a taxi across Paris. When they arrived at Orly, Bill paid the driver and took out his luggage comprising two bags.

FLOWERS FOR TWO GRAVES

Pierson stared out of the small window of the airbus as it passed fleetingly through the clouds, momentarily affording and then taking away views of the ground below. This was where it had all begun, he thought to himself: on an aircraft.

His eyes held an empty look, drained of emotion. His thoughts drifted through the scenes of the recent events. He could hardly take in all the details. Even the bigger points were too bleak for his mind to accept. But accept them he would have to at some stage.

The news about his dead colleagues began this roller coaster ride. He'd lost his job, his car and his home. None of these things mattered, they were unpleasant, but in the scheme of life they were unimportant and they didn't really cause him any anguish. They were inconveniences.

Beyond these losses though, having had a new identity thrust on him he'd then lost himself. Even that didn't really bother him.

But the one thing that he couldn't get over was Madeleine's death. He didn't know whether to bury his love for her and push it down deep inside so that he couldn't find it again, or to try and take it apart, somehow dismantling it, if that was possible. As his anger subsided from the bullion robbery and the adrenalin dissipated, so his thoughts turned more and more to Madeleine. Whatever he tried just didn't work; and with England approaching, the weight of his morbid thoughts was beginning to crush him. Since he'd received the news of

Madeleine's death his soul felt numb and the flame inside him had been extinguished leaving a hole too big to fill.

He could think about all the other events, but the pain of Madeleine's murder was something he couldn't reflect on. It hurt too much; and so his thoughts kept revolving around everything else that had taken place, in a desperate attempt to stay off her. But he kept coming back to that one thought as her image invaded his consciousness and wouldn't leave.

Merely to stay alive he had to track down Selway and get him arrested. But in reality he was the bait for Selway, which under the circumstances suited him well.

He now realised that he had a death wish. He was tired. His face showed cuts and bruising from his skydiving antics the day before, but even without those injuries he looked empty and he was more than ready for the entire matter to finish. He wanted it all to stop. But he wasn't sure what would happen afterwards. He'd given it no thought. He simply hadn't considered a future. Tomorrow didn't exist for him—only yesterday, and the fleetingness of now: that moment. When each moment passed as empty as the previous one, he just knew that he didn't want too many more of them. Life was now an endurance. He hoped he could last long enough to see Selway's death, but that was as much as the picture of his short future afforded him.

There was no doubt in Pierson's mind that both Selway and the judge were extremely dangerous men, and he realised that his chances of survival lay solely in Bill's hands. He smiled to himself as he thought of the irony of his own future being the responsibility of the man who was supposed to have kept his wife alive.

'Drink sir?'

Pierson's thoughts were broken by the question from the airhostess. He looked into her pleasant cheerful face and found himself helplessly smiling back at her.

Instantly yet only momentarily captivated with her, he responded and ordered a drink. Serving it to Pierson, she handed him a small plate on which were two crackers and a slice of Gruyere. She then turned to Bill and, smiling, she offered him a drink too.

Pierson unwrapped the Gruyere and taking a small bite from it, he could soon sense its distinctive flavour. He took a swig of his drink, and unwittingly never really turned away from looking at the hostess. He noticed her name badge and on it he saw the name Madeleine. His heart missed a beat briefly and he moved his eyes away, having had his thoughts thrust back to his own dead wife.

The airhostess noticed the change in his demeanour, even though she was by now preparing Bill's drink, but she said nothing and continued to serve Bill efficiently, before moving the trolley onwards down the aisle, kicking it slightly to take off the brake.

'What's on your mind?' Bill said turning to face Pierson.

Pierson looked at Bill and shrugged his shoulders, 'I can't believe that we can't nail the judge.'

'It's not over yet,' came the reply. 'We now have a level playing field and even though we're not ahead yet, we've pretty well caught up.'

'What's going to happen when we get to England? Have you got something planned?' Pierson asked, but his tone gave away the fact that he wasn't really interested.

Bill smiled and looked into his drink. Then he turned and faced the younger man. 'Think about it: Selway was probably going to retire; now he can't be sure of even returning to work. Everyone in my department knows what's happened, some may be loyal to him, but he'll be arrested the moment he sets foot in the place.'

'Why can't he be sure of returning to work? He doesn't know we've got anything on him.'

'He saw you in the Range Rover coming down from a helicopter. He knows he can't just walk back into the fold.' Bill answered, not looking at Pierson.

'But he could go underground, you know, go into hiding,' said Pierson.

'And in so doing prove his guilt to those who may have been in doubt,' Bill replied.

'What are you saying?' Pierson asked. 'What do you think he's going to do?'

'He's got nothing to lose now, the gold has gone, even the fifteen million Euros has gone, he had to leave that in the train,' Bill replied.

'I still don't see your point,' Pierson continued.

'You were right. It must have cost them a fortune to set up this operation. The murders were a gamble, even though they were ingenious, you don't commit murder lightly. What I'm saying is that his only way out is to blame me; and to do that, he has to find me and kill me,' Bill finished off by looking at Pierson with a wicked smile. 'Of course if it goes wrong, you'll probably be dead too,' Bill continued nonchalantly as he finished his drink.

Pierson thought on this as he caught sight of the airhostess again and focussed on her name badge once more. 'I've got nothing to lose,' he declared glancing out of the window.

'How are you going to let Selway find us?' Pierson asked turning back to face Bill.

'I've made it known that I'm taking you to your wife's…' Bill stopped talking and looked at his glass before continuing in a softer tone, 'Madeleine's grave.'

Pierson took on a distant and somewhat anguished look. 'If I'm going to die then that's as good a place as any,' he remarked, bitterness engulfing his voice.

'Trust me. I have no intention of letting you die that easily,' Bill added. 'Besides which I'm not ready to sign out for the last time.'

'Well, if I do manage to live, then I'd better find some accommodation,' Pierson remarked, in a more practical, but almost sarcastic tone.

'As an interim measure I've organized somewhere for you to stay.'

'In London?' Pierson asked disdainfully.

Bill laughed. 'I thought about that and I knew you wouldn't like it there, or at least I knew you wouldn't like to only have a place in London, so I've arranged for a place in the west country for you; close to where you used to live, but by the coast.'

Pierson looked surprised, but as he gazed out of the window again he could see a break in the clouds. They were circling now and below them were both bridges that traversed the Severn.

The airliner crossed the M5 motorway from the west just south of Bristol and Pierson glanced over to the city, as they came in on their final approach.

Flying down low over the woods, on the west end of the runway, the jet touched down, quickly giving that familiar squeal of the aircraft's tyres. As it continued to hurtle along the tarmac, Pierson looked out of the window and saw the reflection of the airport in the wall of glass on the terminal.

This place held many memories for him, and now for the first time there was going to be nobody there for him: either at the airport or home—wherever that would be. This was the loneliest place on Earth he thought to himself; full of people, yet all of them strangers.

After disembarking they walked across the apron to the terminal and in a matter of ten minutes they were picking up their luggage.

Proceeding to the outside it was as though Pierson was still in a dream. It was midday and there was a throng of holidaymakers busily arriving in their cars and taxis, oblivious to these two men.

As they crossed the road outside of the building, Pierson had his bag in his hand and he turned to look at the crystal structure as though to confirm where he was.

Bristol's airport hadn't long been upgraded, in an attempt to place it more firmly on the international map. Still provincial in many respects, yet with every modern airport convenience, apart from those annoying travelators as Pierson called them.

Walking down the tarmac pathway, Bill had trouble controlling his trolley but he managed in time to swerve it enough to point at the car rental building, with its cleverly designed doors, that forced you to walk backwards through them when driving a luggage trolley. Naturally, as he did so, someone was walking out, oblivious to his incoming struggle.

Approaching the desk, Bill leant over and spoke quietly—almost in whispered tones—to the pretty blonde receptionist. She rose from her stool and disappeared into a back office, returning momentarily with a set of keys and a cardboard envelope and handed them to Bill with a ready smile.

Bill in turn smiled at the woman and thanked her, confirming his thanks by waving the envelope in a semi salute as he strode back towards the door, leaning his body weight strategically to encourage his baggage trolley to move in the direction of the exit.

Once more, Bill had to negotiate through the narrow gap whilst other ex passengers made their way in. On this occasion though, he was struggling to read the car registration on the key, when he almost swept the incoming elderly couple of their feet. After some looks of horror from them and hurried and sincere apologies from Bill, finally he and Pierson found themselves outside.

It was a beautiful day, although dark clouds in the distance heralded less settled weather.

They walked speechless until Bill arrived at one particular car. Pierson looked puzzled as Bill checked the registration on the key fob. They matched and pressing the fob twice Bill unlocked the car and it's boot.

It was a Mercedes. Bill seemed to have a particular liking for these vehicles. Its majestic beauty was enough to distract Pierson and he walked around it, nodding vague approval. Unnoticed by him, Bill lifted the boot lid and placed the large suitcase inside. Had Pierson been watching he would have noticed that it looked very light, and hadn't justified a luggage trolley at all. Bill managed to lift the second bag from the trolley and placed it on top.

After some moments of admiring the car's lines, Pierson slung his bag—all be it carefully—into the rear.

Having opened the driver's door and slid into the front seat, Bill started the engine. Pierson was standing by the open passenger door still admiring the bodywork as was evidenced by his cool appraising stare.

'Are you just going to look, or are you going to get in?' Bill asked in mock impatience, gesturing for some bodily movement from his younger friend.

Pierson merely raised his eyebrows and slid in to the passenger seat. It was lower than he expected and was strange to get into a right hand drive vehicle again. 'I didn't know they rented these,' he said almost under his breath as Bill made the wheels spin to reverse out of the slot, nearly colliding with the vehicle behind.

Over accelerating, Bill then took the Mercedes on the standard route out of the car park, which by any means was a mystery tour—a unique speciality of Bristol airport. By the time they reached the exit, a full five minutes had passed, having had to wait for other drivers to reverse into and out of their spots and then getting stuck behind a courtesy bus. But finally, they hit the open road and headed south, away from the city.

As they drove, so Pierson lowered the passenger window. He could smell the country air coming in. The trees began to shield the sky and the light from the sun danced through the small but numerous gaps. When the cover broke again, Pierson could see the closing storm clouds and the first of these was passing by quickly, casting its rapidly moving shadow across the field adjacent to them. These images thrust his thoughts back to the picnic with Madeleine when they'd chased each other.

For Bill, timing of another sensitive matter was again critical and he interrupted Pierson's dreamy thoughts.

'So that you'll know where it is, I'm going to take you there myself.' Bill began.

'Take me where?' came the reply as Pierson turned to face him. But Bill didn't answer him directly, trying to coax his way around the issue.

'Someone has to show you, so that you can visit whenever you wish.' Bill continued.

'What?' quizzed Pierson 'What must I be shown?'

Bill said nothing hoping that Pierson would work it out for himself. But keeping his eyes on the road and remaining impassive, he carried on detailing what to him was obvious.

'Have you thought about buying some flowers?'

'Flowers? For whom?'

Again there was silence. The road straightened out for a while and Bill took the opportunity to look Pierson in the eye. 'For Madeleine,' he added directly.

Confused, Pierson shook his head and his eyes took on a far away look.

'We don't have to of course, but if you see...' Bill stopped, again trying to phrase it in the best way he could without stamping all over Pierson's feelings to get there; in the end he submitted to the practicality of the direct approach.

'...Madeleine's grave,' he added. But no sooner had the words left his lips, than his demeanour saddened in anticipation of Pierson's pain.

Moments slipped away but it seemed more like minutes. The answer finally came, all be it slowly and with a heavy heart. Pierson spoke in a quiet voice trying to keep a rein on his emotions, trying hard for his voice not to crack.

'Yes.'

Pierson paused for a few moments more before continuing.

'I hadn't ever thought of her having a grave. I know you said about it on the plane. But it's different now we're on the ground.'

Not wishing to interrupt, Bill just let him speak.

'To me she's just not around any more.' Bill turned again to face Pierson, but Pierson had a far away look in his eyes again as he carried on with his intermittent sentences.

'A grave is too incongruous for me to accept in any reality. I know it sounds stupid but I don't understand it. I can't comprehend the sudden finality of it.'

Again there was no further talk, just the sound of the car's engine, the blustery wind and the noise of the wheels on the road. Pierson picked up once more, now talking to himself really, almost thinking aloud.

'I can't conceive that any place exists in our universe where Madeleine could be and that I could get so close to her without holding her and touching her again and speaking to her...' his voice tailed off.

As they drove on, so Bill turned off the main road and into a single-track lane. After a short distance he turned the car through a large gateway that was the entrance for a garden centre. Above the doorway was the sign with its name—the Flower Barn. It looked familiar to Pierson but his mind was too clouded and foggy to remember why.

'What are we doing here?' Pierson asked.

The single word reply came from Bill as if requesting confirmation and jogging Pierson's clouded memory. 'Flowers?'

Pierson gave no acknowledgement, but he got out of the car once it had pulled up and they each walked into the large greenhouse building before them.

There were books and cooking utensils, garden furniture; and towards the rear were hosepipes, fertilizer and other affiliated products, beyond which was a sign pointing to the plants and shrubs.

As they meandered to the correct point, there was a florist in the middle of the shrub area, selling potted plants, bouquets and various real and imitation flower arrangements.

'Can I help you sir?' The assistant spoke in her soft west-country drawl to Pierson. He failed to answer at first and then he smiled in a curious way and looked as though he'd just solved some problem that had been bugging him. Catching sight of the assistant's badge, he saw that her name was 'Trina'. He checked her left hand out of habit more than anything else and he noticed that there was no wedding ring present, but there was a bejewelled engagement ring, sparkling gently as she moved her hand. Pierson finally responded to her question.

'I'd like ten dendrobium sulawesiense please,' he said quietly, as though he expected to have to give a long explanation, or an English name in addition to a description of the flowers too, but in reality he didn't expect the garden centre to stock this variety.

Bill turned to him looking surprised and impressed. Trina replied quickly. 'Orchids. You mean?'

'Yes,' confirmed Pierson, smiling at her knowledge of what he had asked for 'Pink orchids in fact.'

'We don't have any right here sir, but there is someone who may be able to help you. She's not been here long. I can't remember her name, but she can make anything grow,' Trina paused, placing her right forefinger to her lips as though to ask for silence while she thought on this further. She continued more slowly and almost as though she was speaking to herself. 'Orchids are her speciality,' she smiled finally, as she uttered the words.

Pierson's heart missed a beat. His inner voice told him it couldn't be true, that it couldn't be Madeleine—she was dead. But he hoped he was wrong. How many people were as gifted as she was with growing these plants, he thought to himself? But he took as little notice as possible of his own answer, because that was an answer he didn't want to consider. His entire body had now become tense and this showed, especially in his face, which now had a look of anxious and disbelieving expectation.

'Gaby!' Trina called out to another assistant, filling the shelves nearby. 'That new girl. You know, the one who does the orchids. What's her name?'

Gaby stood up.

Like a film flashing before his eyes in slow motion, Pierson recognised Gaby and the building he was in. This was the place that Madeleine had taken him to on that Friday. He turned to Trina and saw the garden centre's name on her blouse—the Flower Barn—he suddenly realised it was the same place.

Could the new girl have been Madeleine? Was she still alive?

After a few moments Gaby shrugged her shoulders and shaking her head she replied. 'I'm not sure. Hilary, I think, isn't it? But I haven't seen her in today. I think it's her day off.'

Anxiety turned briefly to desperation for Pierson and then to despair as the vicious circle took him on that awful and still too familiar spiral of emotions once more.

Gaby smiled at Pierson. 'I think I can help you though sir,' she gestured for him to follow and as he did so, Trina watched closely seeing the now sad and slightly haunted look that had fallen on this new customer.

Tracking down the orchids was an easy process, and Gaby continued to talk to Pierson with him smiling awkwardly every now and again, nodding and responding when necessary.

She finally handed the flowers over to him; and Bill took out his wallet to pay for them, ordering some of his own too.

The two men walked out of the buildings and returned to the Mercedes. The clouds were gathering more quickly now and in greater numbers. Once he'd unlocked the doors, Bill then climbed in and awkwardly reached around to place his flowers on the rear seat. Pierson got in too. Closing the door, he put on his seat belt as Bill started the engine and began reversing out of the spot.

The orchids were beautiful but they brought back more memories. Pierson wasn't sure whether to endure them to lessen the pain, or to ignore them and put them out of his mind.

He turned and placed the flowers in the back, next to those Bill had already lain there.

Only minutes later the route Bill had taken led them to a village with houses nestled in the hill sides, just off the road, built from Cotswold stone that had been weathered across the centuries. Pierson could make out a signpost for the place and as if he were reading Pierson's thoughts, Bill dropped the speed of the car to something near the jogging speed of sheep.

Bearing right on the road, Bill then turned the car left into a gravel laid drive, bordered at its entrance by a short, but well maintained dry stone wall. As Pierson looked up, he could see they were in the grounds of a church. His heart raced again.

The long outer boundary wall followed the curve of the road, and the church itself was bordered by trees around the sides and back, with the front having open lawns. There was another entrance across from where Bill had parked the Mercedes. It too was at the front of the church, but on the other side of the main entrance. A Jaguar was parked there with a single occupant in the driver's seat of the small car park that allowed for twenty or so cars.

Stepping out of the Mercedes, Pierson thought he could feel the first spots of rain. Bill walked with him down one side of the church to a densely populated area of gravestones.

Another car began to pull into the other car park; it was a Ford of some description. It parked on the left of the Jaguar and was partly obscured from view because of that. A woman got out and Pierson stopped briefly to look, but she was too far away to be seen clearly enough to be recognised even if he had known her. She opened the rear door and pulled out some flowers. Dressed in a light coloured raincoat she had high heels, a scarf around her neck and dark glasses. She could have been a film star in disguise, but she was young, in her twenties or thirties at most Pierson thought.

From the driver's seat, a man stepped out of the Ford, dressed in a dark raincoat he stood by the car as the woman walked around the back of the church.

There was something strange about the woman. Pierson couldn't say what it was, but it gently gnawed at his subconscious.

As she disappeared out of view, Pierson stood looking at Bill, who had now stopped in front of a particular grave. He was standing to the far side of it with his back to the graves behind him and he gestured to the head stone for Pierson to read.

Walking slowly towards it, Pierson felt a shiver engulf his body; and now finally, he was able to see the truth that he had denied himself for the last week or so.

On the headstone were engraved the words 'Madeleine Brady 14th March 1983—12th August 2008'. Underneath was written—

'When you leave this world I want to leave with you so that we will never be apart, not even in death. Loving husband Tom.'

Pierson stooped, almost falling; and placed the flowers down. He stared at the headstone. His vision blurred with tears. He couldn't read the words any longer, they'd gone out of focus.

Bill placed a hand on his shoulder. 'Let's go,' he said softly.

The wind had picked up and although there was rain, there were pockets of bright sunshine too, shafts of brilliant light piercing the bleakness of the gloomy weather. Clouds were chasing their shadows across the front lawn of the church. Pierson stood up and felt inside his jacket. He pulled out a pair of sunglasses and put them on his bruised and scarred face.

Bill had slowly begun to walk back to the Mercedes. The rain began to get harder, but nevertheless Bill used the speed dial on his cell phone. Unnoticed by Pierson, the driver of the Ford on the far side of the church who had remained by the car answered a call on his phone.

The mysterious woman had by now walked around the back of the church and was approaching Pierson. He had already begun to step away from the grave, but he bent down to rearrange the flowers one more time before walking off.

Bill had made it to the Mercedes by this time and it was only moments later before Pierson too had almost returned there. The woman stopped at the grave next to, but behind Madeleine's and placed flowers on it. She crouched briefly as she arranged the flowers and then looking to her right, at Madeleine's grave, she made a slight rearrangement of the flowers Pierson had placed there and stood up.

Pierson wondered who she could be and took his glasses off in bewilderment. He started walking towards her. The rain was now getting heavier and as he walked faster, the woman began walking away, the rain now in a storm and his hair and head were drenched. Torrents of water were running down his face as he struggled to see who she was. Looking back briefly, she saw Pierson walking towards her, his face now becoming obscured in the rain, then she gasped as a man who had been standing in the cover of the trees stepped out.

Pierson saw him instantly. He was slightly in front of the woman and to her left. Pierson recognised him immediately. It was Selway.

Clasping a gun with both hands, Selway raised his arms and parted his legs for balance and stability, squeezing the trigger. The whole process was so well choreographed that it was clearly a manoeuvre he'd practised many hundreds of times before. Pierson raced towards him and the woman.

From behind Bill shouted out. 'Get down!'

Pierson ran to try and save the woman, but then he realised that Selway wasn't aiming the gun at her, and that the woman was merely incidental. He leapt behind one of the headstones as a shot rang out. But it wasn't the sound made by a handgun. It was the sound of a bullet from a rifle. The distinctive ringing after the initial explosion gave away its identity.

Looking up, Pierson saw Selway running past him and around the front of the church and across the lawn to the waiting Jaguar in the car park. The driver lunged over to open the passenger door. Pierson got up and chased him to the car slowing only when he was within ten metres.

Bill followed by racing around the back of the church and as Pierson got close he could see the driver. It was the judge. Pierson's mood changed. Having seen his dead wife's grave, it was all over. Now he was finally ready to die: welcoming it in fact. He had no thoughts beyond the next few moments.

Pierson kept on closing in, giving Selway the best possible chance not to miss.

Selway raised his hands with the gun aimed at Pierson, then on seeing Bill closing from the other direction, he turned his whole body alternating the gun from pointing at one to the other.

'Do you think I can get both of you before your rifleman gets me?' Selway declared.

Pierson fixed Selway with his stare, 'you might, but then you'd have trouble explaining how you told Trevor Norris to hide five hundred million dollars in a Swiss bank and rip off Jury. Your passenger might be interested in that at the end of the month.'

Selway laughed nervously. Pierson had enough information to make it sound authentic, but Pierson didn't care whether Selway believed him or not.

Bill looked at Pierson as though he'd said far too much. Selway observed Bill's reaction and as the two men knew each other well, this was the one thing that convinced him that Pierson was telling him the truth, much to Selway's alarm.

'So you're the clever so and so then.' Selway replied spitting out the words, keeping the gun on Bill but looking at Pierson.

'Make your proposal,' he added. 'If you have one.'

Pierson paused as he just stared at Selway, wondering if there could have been an earlier point in their various encounters where Madeleine could have been saved. He had no desire to give Selway anything, but to just let him shoot. He couldn't understand why, it certainly wasn't through fear for his own life, but his mouth began speaking—almost on autopilot—controlled by the subconscious part of his mind.

'You drive away from here, and I'll text you the account number and bank name, when you're over by the beach car park,' Pierson pointed into the distance.

'No phone I'm afraid,' Selway said almost shrugging.

'Not a problem,' replied Pierson. 'May I?' he added, gesturing to reach into his pocket.

Selway just shot his eyes at Pierson briefly, and gave an almost imperceptible nod of his head. Selway still looked worried now though, because for the first time he didn't feel in complete control, having to think on his feet and realising that a five hundred million dollar loss made him the next target, regardless of Pierson's fate.

Selway adjusted his hands on the gun slightly, keeping Bill firmly in his sights.

Pierson took out the Nokia and switched it on, making sure the judge had no chance to see it. But as the judge was still in the driving seat, with rain obscuring his view he wouldn't have been able to see much anyway.

Pierson walked close to the Jaguar and leaning across the roof he slid the phone to Selway. Selway glanced at it briefly and noted that it was switched on before he placed it in his inside jacket pocket. Then looking at the two men he spoke.

'Okay back off,' he snarled. Looking at Pierson, he added, 'this had better work.'

'Your threats mean very little me,' Pierson assured him calmly, 'after all you're only giving me a head start. You plan on killing me anyway.'

Selway smiled wryly, giving Pierson a look of vague admiration.

'Just one thing though,' Pierson added.

Appearing slightly more relaxed, Selway gave a gesture of superior magnanimity, inviting the question.

'Pareto?' quizzed Pierson. 'What was that all about?'

Selway gave an ironic laugh as he shook his head in some disbelief.

'You mean you haven't worked it out?' he replied almost incredulously.

Pierson gave no answer but waited for Selway to continue.

'You're Pareto: or at least proof of it.'

Pierson remained motionless.

'Only five people in the world could have had a back door into Elektra. Only five people on the planet could have got that train going again against our wishes: your three colleagues, Abbot and of course Tom Brady. We figured that according to Pareto one of you would be difficult to silence, but we had no idea it was going to be you. It started as a kind of joke—a goal we'd set ourselves. Pareto's principle is the 80/20 rule—you must already know that.'

Pierson nodded as he let Selway continue.

'You spend 20 per cent of your effort achieving 80 per cent of the result. Killing four of you was easy, but the last 20 per cent—you—we spent more than 80 per cent of our resources trying to nail you. Even Abbot warned us about you. He said you were bright. He liked you—strangely enough—but even he didn't trust you…said something about you being too honest and that made him uneasy. Frankly we thought he was rambling. It seems he was right. But now it's personal. Every time you survived we just used the codeword Pareto to indicate that you were still alive and that we'd failed yet again. It was like some annoying and tedious joke.'

Bill began to back off but Pierson remained fixed to the spot, wearing a look of uncaring defiance.

With Selway in the car, the judge reversed the Jaguar and looked briefly at Pierson as Pierson looked right back at him, keeping his eyes on the judge and turning his body to follow the car as it left them. Then moving at high speed, the Jaguar exited the car park.

Pierson looked at his watch as Bill walked over to him, looking surprised and slightly angry. 'You've probably blown our best chance with those two. But what's that about the Swiss bank account?'

'What Swiss bank account?' said Pierson dispassionately as he raised his arm to look at his watch. He pressed the buttons for memory and one and then he pressed send.

Bill was clearly puzzled.

Selway said nothing as the judge drove the car along towards the beach road. Wondering now whether it had been a bluff he glanced back at the church.

'Well?' said the judge.

Selway remained silent. Embarrassed by his own uncertainty; his anger and fear barely under control. Suddenly the sound of Mozart's fortieth symphony broke the silence. The judge recognised it immediately and it dawned on him what was about to happen. He took his eyes off the road, looking in horror at Selway. 'Shut it off!' he screamed. 'Just shut it off!'

'They're telling us where the money is!' Selway shouted back. 'I can't switch it off.'

The judge ignored him, 'Switch it off!' he shrieked grabbing Selway by the lapels and trying to shake him. Shocked by the judge's sudden outburst and seeing the bend in the road looming up on them, Selway reached across and grabbed the wheel trying to turn it.

The judge by now was violently struggling, trying to get at the phone, all reason lost in his terror, as his foot thrust the accelerator to the floor in uncontrolled panic.

'Get the damned phone!' the judge shouted, as the car smashed up over the kerb, flying off into the dunes, wheels spinning and the powerful engine now racing uncontrollably.

The Jaguar crashed down onto the first dune thumping its occupants into the roof. Both men shielded their faces but Selway smashed into the windscreen itself and slumped back with a bloodied head. The judge was severely dazed as the car careered towards the water. He couldn't see properly as he desperately lunged across to reach Selway's pockets for the phone.

'Noooo!' he shrieked. 'Not this! Where is it?' tearing at Selway. The seconds ticked by until finally he had it in his shaky grasp. He pulled it out, but the bump to his head meant that he couldn't focus to read the buttons.

Still the Jaguar pressed forwards onto the beach, water now slewing out from its tyres as it reached the wet sand. The judge held the phone and now in mortal fear of his life, scared of pressing the wrong button, but knowing he had only moments left, he began pressing every button he could feel.

With slightly blurred vision, Selway snatched the phone and pressed a single button.

Pierson's watch phone displayed the connect signal and he lifted it to his mouth to speak. 'Pareto,' he said.

He flicked up his eyes to see the Jaguar light up from the first explosion, briefly before the sound reached him, and then watching as the second explosion from the fuel tank turned it into a fireball, with panels and debris shooting off in all directions.

Both he and Bill had a direct view of the carnage through the gaps in the dunes. Bill watched open-mouthed. Pierson threw Bill a final look as he turned towards him and pressed the end button on his watch phone. Neither of them spoke, but Pierson began walking back towards Bill's car and then towards the graves.

Bill—stunned by what he'd seen—didn't move for some time and in a half daze he eventually turned away.

Strangely, no one had gathered around and no one had come running on hearing the earlier gun shot. The mysterious woman was now standing towards the back of the graveyard, only a matter of feet away from Pierson as he came back into view. The rifleman was still holding her, although he only had one arm around her, and in his other arm the rifle was slung low dangling from his hand.

Pierson looked down at the grave that the woman had attended moments earlier.

On the headstone were engraved the words 'Tom Brady 3rd April 1980—9th August 2008'. Underneath was written—

'When you leave this world I want to leave with you so that we will never be apart, not even in death. Loving wife Madeleine.'

Pierson immediately looked at the woman. The rain had subsided and a beam of light burst through the clouds silhouetting both her and the rifleman. With her back still to Pierson she took off her headscarf. Her blonde locks tumbled down; and in that instant between falling and the scarf coming off, Pierson saw it again.

He saw what he thought he wouldn't ever see again. At the back of her right ear was a birthmark, like Madeleine had had.

She stepped slowly backwards from her protector, as he released his hold. Turning towards Pierson, she gasped slightly and raising her hand she covered her mouth.

Pierson looked at her closely. She was still wearing the dark glasses. He began to walk towards her; looking worried, his thoughts were in turmoil.

For those few moments, time stood still.

As soon as he was within reach, he raised his hands to take off her glasses. She didn't resist. Lowering them, he almost had to dare himself to meet her eyes. But he did. The glasses fell from his hands as she fell into his arms. It was Madeleine. She was still alive.

They held each other and kissed, neither one believing what was happening.

Pulling back, Pierson looked at her. Tears obscured their vision. 'How?' Pierson said shaking his head slowly.

'I gave you my word she would be safe.' Bill said, stepping forward.

He looked at her silent guardian. 'Carswell: you have some clearing up to do. I'll take them from here.'

Pierson took Madeleine's hand and squeezed as if to confirm she was real. She responded and they started to walk back to Bill's car, hardly taking their eyes of each other. They stopped by the graves.

Reading the epitaphs again, Pierson realised that only he and Madeleine knew the words written on the headstones and as he hadn't told anyone else, she must have written them. He picked up one bunch of flowers, and from the other grave she picked up the second bunch. As they walked towards the front of the church they could see that the vicar had now stepped outside and was looking at the burning wreckage of the Jaguar; the swell of the sea now gently extending around it, although the car was still only sat in a half inch of water.

'Oh my goodness!' the vicar declared as Pierson and Madeleine came into view. 'What's all this?' he continued. Pierson looked at Madeleine holding the flowers and he gave his bunch to the vicar, nodding for her to do likewise.

'Flowers for two graves,' Pierson remarked. The vicar smiled politely.

Then, turning, Pierson placed his arm around Madeleine's shoulder as they walked back to Bill's Mercedes. They got in the rear, first Madeleine, sliding across, followed by Pierson.

Bill sat in and as they pulled out of the church grounds, Pierson looked back to see Carswell making his way to the fireball that had now subsided to another black cloud of smoke.

It took Bill only a short time before he turned off the main road and into a track that led to trees sheltering a secluded cottage. Pulling up outside, he parked next to a car that Pierson recognised as Madeleine's.

Bill stopped the engine, got out of the Mercedes and opened the back door.

'Ours?' Pierson asked looking at the cottage.

'Yes,' said Bill in unison with Madeleine. She was still holding on to his arm with both of hers, and still squeezing as she looked up at him.

Walking around to the boot, Bill opened it and inside was the tartan suitcase that Selway had used for the money on the train. Bill unzipped it, but it was empty except for one small slip of paper.

'Courtesy of Henri and myself,' he said handing it to Pierson.

It was a bank statement for Michael and Hilary Pierson. The balance showed a deposit of fifteen million Euros made the previous day in Paris.

'We couldn't do anything with the money,' Bill smirked, handing Pierson the paper, 'so we thought a bank was the best place for it.' Pierson read the statement and looking at Madeleine he spoke. 'You're Hilary.'

She just nodded.

'The Flower Barn,' he said slowly. 'You're the lady that Gaby mentioned.'

Madeleine smiled and nodded again; still unable to speak.

'What happened with you?' Pierson asked her.

Trying her utmost to overcome her emotions, she managed to answer, although her voice broke occasionally.

'Bill came to me after you 'died' and set me up here,' she said. 'He faked my death.'

'Mine too,' Pierson replied.

Pierson turned back to Bill. 'Why didn't you tell me?'

Bill stood hands clasped together in front of him and he smiled as he answered.

'It was too much of a risk. I needed everyone in the department to believe she was dead. I didn't know where the leak was, and if I hadn't told you the same thing then you might have let slip that Madeleine was still alive, making her a target herself. Carswell is ex SAS and only I knew he worked for us. He doesn't appear on our payroll.'

Pierson slowly nodded. 'In the circumstances the word thanks seems woefully inadequate, but thanks anyway,' he said quietly and he turned to look at Madeleine again, not wishing to take his eyes off her.

'What about Jury?' he mentioned as a half thought.

Bill smiled as he began to walk off. 'Another time: I'll be in touch.'

He opened the door of the Mercedes and got back in; then after starting the engine he drove away.

THE END

Would you like to see your manuscript become a book?

If you are interested in becoming a PublishAmerica author, please submit your manuscript for possible publication to us at:

acquisitions@publishamerica.com

You may also mail in your manuscript to:

**PublishAmerica
PO Box 151
Frederick, MD 21705**

We also offer free graphics for Children's Picture Books!

---

www.publishamerica.com

Lightning Source UK Ltd.
Milton Keynes UK
UKOW051401230412

191306UK00002B/21/P